DARK NEST II
THE
UNSEEN QUEEN

By Troy Denning

WATERDEEP
DRAGONWALL
THE PARCHED SEA
THE VERDANT PASSAGE
THE CRIMSON LEGION
THE AMBER ENCHANTRESS
THE OBSIDIAN ORACLE
THE CERULEAN STORM
THE OGRE'S PACT
THE GIANT AMONG US
THE TITAN OF TWILIGHT
THE VEILED DRAGON
PAGES OF PAIN
CRUCIBLE: THE TRIAL OF CYRIC THE MAD
THE OATH OF STONEKEEP
FACES OF DECEPTION
BEYOND THE HIGH ROAD
DEATH OF THE DRAGON (with Ed Greenwood)
THE SUMMONING
THE SIEGE
THE SORCERER

STAR WARS: THE NEW JEDI ORDER: STAR BY STAR
STAR WARS: TATOOINE GHOST
STAR WARS: DARK NEST I: THE JOINER KING
STAR WARS: DARK NEST II: THE UNSEEN QUEEN
STAR WARS: DARK NEST III: THE SWARM WAR—
   Dec. 2005

STAR WARS™

DARK NEST II
THE
UNSEEN QUEEN

TROY DENNING

arrow books

Published by Arrow Books in 2005

1 3 5 7 9 10 8 6 4 2

Arrow Books Limited
The Random House Group Limited
20 Vauxhall Bridge Road, London, SW1V 2SA

Random House Australia (Pty) Limited
20 Alfred Street, Milsons Point, Sydney,
New South Wales 2061, Australia

Random House New Zealand Limited
18 Poland Road, Glenfield
Auckland 10, New Zealand

Random House (Pty) Limited
Isle of Houghton, Corner Boundary Road & Carse O'Gowrie,
Houghton, 2198, South Africa

The Random House Group Limited Reg. No. 954009

www.randomhouse.co.uk
www.starwars.com
www.starwarskids.com

A CIP catalogue record for this book
is available from the British Library

Papers used by Random House are
natural, recyclable products made from wood grown in
sustainable forests. The manufacturing processes conform to
the environmental regulations of the country of origin

ISBN 0 09 949106 0

Printed and bound in Great Britain by
Bookmarque Ltd, Croydon, Surrey

**For Doug Niles
A Treasured Friend**

ACKNOWLEDGMENTS

Many people contributed to this book in ways large and small. Thanks are especially due to: Andria Hayday for advice, encouragement, critiques, and much more; James Luceno for brainstorming and ideas; Enrique Guerrero for his many fine suggestions; Shelly Shapiro and all the people at Del Rey who make writing so much fun, particularly Keith Clayton, Colleen Lindsay, and Colette Russen; Sue Rostoni and the wonderful people at Lucasfilm, particularly Howard Roffman, Amy Gary, Leland Chee, and Pablo Hidalgo. And, of course, to George Lucas for Episodes I through III.

THE STAR WARS NOVELS TIMELINE

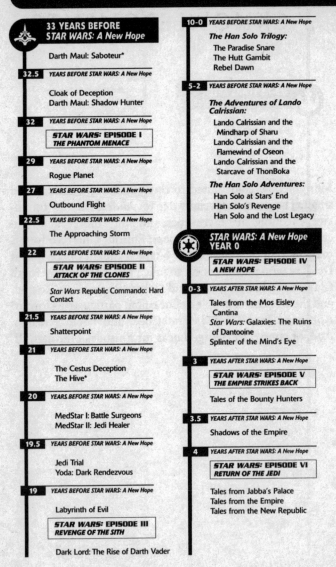

33 YEARS BEFORE STAR WARS: A New Hope

Darth Maul: Saboteur*

32.5 YEARS BEFORE STAR WARS: A New Hope

Cloak of Deception
Darth Maul: Shadow Hunter

32 YEARS BEFORE STAR WARS: A New Hope

STAR WARS: EPISODE I THE PHANTOM MENACE

29 YEARS BEFORE STAR WARS: A New Hope

Rogue Planet

27 YEARS BEFORE STAR WARS: A New Hope

Outbound Flight

22.5 YEARS BEFORE STAR WARS: A New Hope

The Approaching Storm

22 YEARS BEFORE STAR WARS: A New Hope

STAR WARS: EPISODE II ATTACK OF THE CLONES

Star Wars Republic Commando: Hard Contact

21.5 YEARS BEFORE STAR WARS: A New Hope

Shatterpoint

21 YEARS BEFORE STAR WARS: A New Hope

The Cestus Deception
The Hive*

20 YEARS BEFORE STAR WARS: A New Hope

MedStar I: Battle Surgeons
MedStar II: Jedi Healer

19.5 YEARS BEFORE STAR WARS: A New Hope

Jedi Trial
Yoda: Dark Rendezvous

19 YEARS BEFORE STAR WARS: A New Hope

Labyrinth of Evil

STAR WARS: EPISODE III REVENGE OF THE SITH

Dark Lord: The Rise of Darth Vader

10-0 YEARS BEFORE STAR WARS: A New Hope

The Han Solo Trilogy:
The Paradise Snare
The Hutt Gambit
Rebel Dawn

5-2 YEARS BEFORE STAR WARS: A New Hope

The Adventures of Lando Calrissian:
Lando Calrissian and the Mindharp of Sharu
Lando Calrissian and the Flamewind of Oseon
Lando Calrissian and the Starcave of ThonBoka

The Han Solo Adventures:
Han Solo at Stars' End
Han Solo's Revenge
Han Solo and the Lost Legacy

STAR WARS: A New Hope YEAR 0

STAR WARS: EPISODE IV A NEW HOPE

0-3 YEARS AFTER STAR WARS: A New Hope

Tales from the Mos Eisley Cantina
Star Wars: Galaxies: The Ruins of Dantooine
Splinter of the Mind's Eye

3 YEARS AFTER STAR WARS: A New Hope

STAR WARS: EPISODE V THE EMPIRE STRIKES BACK

Tales of the Bounty Hunters

3.5 YEARS AFTER STAR WARS: A New Hope

Shadows of the Empire

4 YEARS AFTER STAR WARS: A New Hope

STAR WARS: EPISODE VI RETURN OF THE JEDI

Tales from Jabba's Palace
Tales from the Empire
Tales from the New Republic

The Bounty Hunter Wars:
The Mandalorian Armor
Slave Ship
Hard Merchandise

The Truce at Bakura

6.5-7.5 YEARS AFTER *STAR WARS: A New Hope*

X-Wing:
Rogue Squadron
Wedge's Gamble
The Krytos Trap
The Bacta War
Wraith Squadron
Iron Fist
Solo Command

8 YEARS AFTER STAR WARS: A New Hope

The Courtship of Princess Leia
A Forest Apart*
Tatooine Ghost

9 YEARS AFTER STAR WARS: A New Hope

The Thrawn Trilogy:
Heir to the Empire
Dark Force Rising
The Last Command

X-Wing: Isard's Revenge

11 YEARS AFTER STAR WARS: A New Hope

I, Jedi

The Jedi Academy Trilogy:
Jedi Search
Dark Apprentice
Champions of the Force

12-13 YEARS AFTER STAR WARS: A New Hope

Children of the Jedi
Darksaber
Planet of Twilight
X-Wing: Starfighters of Adumar

14 YEARS AFTER STAR WARS: A New Hope

The Crystal Star

16-17 YEARS AFTER STAR WARS: A New Hope

The Black Fleet Crisis Trilogy:
Before the Storm
Shield of Lies

Tyrant's Test

17 YEARS AFTER STAR WARS: A New Hope
The New Rebellion

18 YEARS AFTER STAR WARS: A New Hope

The Corellian Trilogy:
Ambush at Corellia
Assault at Selonia
Showdown at Centerpoint

19 YEARS AFTER STAR WARS: A New Hope

The Hand of Thrawn Duology:
Specter of the Past
Vision of the Future

22 YEARS AFTER STAR WARS: A New Hope

Fool's Bargain*
Survivor's Quest

25-30 YEARS AFTER *STAR WARS: A New Hope*

The New Jedi Order:
Vector Prime
Dark Tide I: Onslaught
Dark Tide II: Ruin
Agents of Chaos I: Hero's Trial
Agents of Chaos II: Jedi Eclipse
Balance Point
Recovery*
Edge of Victory I: Conquest
Edge of Victory II: Rebirth
Star by Star
Dark Journey
Enemy Lines I: Rebel Dream
Enemy Lines II: Rebel Stand
Traitor
Destiny's Way
Ylesia*
Force Heretic I: Remnant
Force Heretic II: Refugee
Force Heretic III: Reunion
The Final Prophecy
The Unifying Force

35 YEARS AFTER STAR WARS: A New Hope

The Dark Nest Trilogy:
The Joiner King
The Unseen Queen
The Swarm War

*An ebook novella

DRAMATIS PERSONAE

Alema Rar; Joiner (female Twi'lek)

Ben Skywalker; child (male human)

C-3PO; protocol droid

Cal Omas; Galactic Alliance Chief of State (male human)

Corran Horn; Jedi Master (male human)

Gorog; mastermind (Killik)

Han Solo; captain, *Millennium Falcon* (male human)

Jacen Solo; Jedi Knight (male human)

Jae Juun; captain, *DR919a* (male Sullustan)

Jaina Solo; Jedi Knight (female human)

Kyp Durron; Jedi Master (male human)

Leia Organa Solo; copilot, *Millennium Falcon* (female human)

Lowbacca; Jedi Knight (male Wookiee)

Luke Skywalker; Jedi Master (male human)

Mara Jade Skywalker; Jedi Master (female human)

Nek Bwua'tu; admiral (male Bothan)

R2-D2; astromech droid

Raynar Thul; crash survivor (male human)

Saras; entrepreneur (Killik)

Saba Sebatyne; Jedi Master (female Barabel)

Tahiri Veila; Jedi Knight (female human)

Tarfang; copilot, *DR919a* (male Ewok)
Tenel Ka; Queen Mother (female human)
Tesar Sebatyne; Jedi Knight (male Barabel)
Unu; the Will (Killik)
Zekk; Jedi Knight (male human)

PROLOGUE

Like thieves all across the galaxy, Tibanna tappers worked best in darkness. They slipped and stole through the lowest levels of Bespin's Life Zone, down where daylight faded to dusk and shapes softened to silhouettes, down where black curtains of mist swept across purple, boiling skies. Their targets were the lonely platforms where honest beings worked through the endless night de-icing frozen intake fans and belly-crawling into clogged transfer pipes, where the precious gas was gathered atom by atom. In the last month alone, the tanks at a dozen stations had been mysteriously drained, and two Jedi Knights had been sent to bring the thieves to justice.

Emerging into a pocket of clear air, Jaina and Zekk saw BesGas Three ahead. The station was a saucer-shaped extraction platform, so overloaded with processing equipment that it seemed a wonder it stayed afloat. The primary storage deck was limned in blue warning strobes, and in the flashing light behind one of those strobes, Jaina and Zekk saw an oblong shadow tucked back between two holding tanks.

Jaina swung the nose of their borrowed cloud car toward the tanks and accelerated, rushing to have a look before the processing facility vanished behind another curtain of mist. The shadow was probably just a shadow, but down here at the bottom of the Life Zone, heat and pressure and darkness all conspired against human vision, and every possibility had to be investigated up close.

Spin-sealed Tibanna gas had a lot of uses, but the most important was to increase the yield of starship weapons. So if somebody was stealing Tibanna gas, especially as much as had been disappearing from Bespin in recent weeks, the Jedi needed to find out who they were—and what they were doing with it.

As Jaina and Zekk continued to approach, the shadow began to acquire a tablet-like shape. Zekk readied the mini tractor beam, and Jaina armed the twin ion guns. There was no need to remark that the shadow was starting to look like a siphoning balloon, or to complain that the strobe lights were blinding them, or even to discuss what tactics they should use. Thanks to their stay with the Killiks, their minds were so closely connected that they scarcely knew where one began and the other ended. Even after a year away from the Colony, ideas and perceptions and emotions flowed between them without effort. Often, they could not even tell in whose mind a thought had formed—and it did not matter. They simply shared it.

A blue glow flared among the holding tanks, then a small tapper tug shot into view, its conical silhouette wavering against the pressure-blurred lights of the station's habitation decks. An instant later three siphoning balloons—the one Jaina and Zekk had spotted and two others—rose behind it, chased by long plumes of Tibanna gas still escaping from siphoning holes in the holding tanks.

Jaina opened fire with the ion guns, narrowly missing the tug, but spraying the station's central hub. Ion beams were safer to use around Tibanna gas than blaster bolts, since all they did was disable electronic circuitry, so the barrage did not cause any structural damage. But it did plunge two levels of habitation deck into a sudden blackout.

Zekk swung the tractor beam around and caught hold of a siphoning balloon. The tappers released it, and the balloon came flying straight at the cloud car. Zekk deactivated the beam immediately, but Jaina still had to swing wide to avoid being taken out by the huge, tumbling bag of supercooled gas.

Jaina let out a tense breath. "Too—"

"—close!" Zekk finished.

By the time she brought the cloud car back around, the last two balloons were following the tug up into a dark, churning cloud. Jaina raised their nose and sent another burst of ionized energy streaming after the tappers, but Zekk did not reactivate the beam.

They agreed—the capture attempt had looked realistic enough. Now the quarry needed room to run. Jaina backed off the throttles, and they began a slow spiral up after the thieves.

A moment later, a fuzzy pinpoint of yellow appeared deep inside the cloud, rapidly swelling into a hazy tongue of flame that came shooting out into clear air almost before Jaina could bring the ion guns around. She pressed both triggers and began to sweep the barrels back and forth. She was not trying to hit the missile—that would have been impossible, even for a Jedi. Instead, she was simply laying a blanket of ionized energy in its path.

Zekk reached out and found the missile in the Force, then gently guided it into one of Jaina's ion beams. Its electrical systems erupted into a tempest of discharge lightning and overload sparks, then failed altogether. Once the tempest died down, Zekk used a Force shove to deflect it from the extraction platform. The dead missile plunged past, barely a dozen meters from the edge of the storage deck, then vanished into the seething darkness of the Squeeze Zone.

Jaina frowned. "Now, that was—"

"—entirely uncalled for," Zekk finished.

With all that supercooled Tibanna pouring out onto the storage deck, even a small detonation would have been enough to blow the entire platform out of the sky. But that had probably been the idea, Jaina and Zekk realized: payback for calling in Jedi—and a warning to other stations not to do the same.

"Need to get these guys," Zekk said aloud.

Jaina nodded. "Just as soon as we know who they're working for."

Judging they had allowed the thieves a large enough lead to feel comfortable, Jaina and Zekk stretched out into the Force in an effort to locate them. It was not easy. Even at these depths, Bespin was surprisingly rich in life, from huge gasbag beldons to their mighty velker predators, from vast purple expanses of "glower" algae to the raawks and floaters that scavenged a living from extraction platforms like BesGas Three.

Finally, Jaina and Zekk found what they were searching for, a trio of presences exuding relief and excitement and more than a little anger. The three thieves felt insect-like, somehow more in harmony with the universe than most other beings. But they remained three distinct individuals, each with a unique presence. They were not Killiks.

And that made Jaina and Zekk a little sad. They would never have changed the decision that had gotten them banished from the Colony. It had prevented the outbreak of a savage war, and they did not regret it. But being apart from Taat—the nest they had joined at Qoribu—was like being shut off from themselves, like being cast aside by one's sweetheart and friends and family without the possibility of return. It was a little bit like becoming a ghost, dying but not departing, floating around on the edges of the living never quite able to make contact. So they *did* feel a little sorry for themselves sometimes. Even Jedi were allowed that much.

"Need to get these guys," Jaina said, reiterating a call to action that she felt sure was more Zekk than her. He had never had much use for regrets. "Ready?"

Silly question. Jaina accelerated after the tappers, climbing up into a storm so violent and lightning-filled that she and Zekk felt as if they were back in the war again, fighting a pitched battle against the Yuuzhan Vong. After a standard hour, they gave up trying to maintain a steady altitude and resigned themselves to having their stomachs alternately up in their throats and down in their guts. After three hours, they gave up trying to stay right-side up and concentrated on just making forward progress. After five hours, they emerged from the storm into a bottomless canyon of clear, still air—only to glimpse the tappers entering a wall of crimson vortexes where two bands of wind brushed against each other in opposite directions. Amazingly, the tug still had both siphoning balloons in tow.

Jaina and Zekk wondered whether the tappers knew they were being followed, but that seemed impossible. This far down in the atmosphere, Bespin's magnetic field and powerful storms prevented even rudimentary sensor equipment from working. Navigation was strictly by compass, gyroscope, and calculation. If the tug was going through that wind wall, it was because it was on its way to deliver its stolen Tibanna.

Jaina and Zekk waited until the tappers had vanished, then crossed the cloud canyon and carefully accelerated into the same vortex. The wind grabbed them immediately, and it felt as if they'd been fired out of a turbolaser. Their heads slammed back against their seats, the cloud car began to groan and tremble, and the world beyond their canopy became a blur of crimson vapor and stabbing lightning. Jaina let go of the control stick, lest she forget herself and tear the wings of their craft by attempting to steer.

An hour later, Jaina and Zekk sensed the tappers' presences drifting past to one side and realized they had made it across the Change Zone. Still keeping her hand off the stick, Jaina pushed the throttles to full. The cloud car shot forward screaming and bucking; then the vapor outside faded from crimson to rosy, and the ride grew suddenly smooth.

Jaina eased off the throttles until the cloud car's repulsor drive finally fell silent, then began to circle through the rosy fog at minimum speed.

"Well, that was—"

"—fun," Zekk agreed. "Let's never do it again."

Once their stomachs had settled, Jaina brought the cloud car around and they crept back through the pink fog, unable to see a hundred meters beyond their noses, still using the presences of the tappers to guide them. It felt like they had overshot the thieves by a considerable distance, but it was impossible to say whether that distance was a hundred kilometers or a thousand. The Force did not have a scale.

After a quarter hour, they began to suffer the illusion that they were simply floating in the cloud, that they were not moving at all. But the instruments still showed their velocity at more than a hundred kilometers per standard hour, and it felt as if they were closing rapidly on their quarry.

Jaina wondered where they were.

Zekk said, "The gyrocomputer calculates our position as three-seven-point-eight-three north, two-seven-seven-point-eight-eight-six longitude, one-six-nine deep."

"Is that in—"

"Yes," Zekk answered. They were about a thousand kilometers into the Dead Eye, a vast region of still air and dense fog that had existed in Bespin's atmosphere at least since the planet's discovery.

"Great. Only nineteen thousand kilometers to the other side," Jaina complained. "Do the charts show—"

"Nothing," Zekk said. "Not even a marker buoy."

"Blast!" This, they said together.

Still, it felt like they were catching up to the tappers quickly. There had to be *something* out there.

"Maybe they've just stopped to—"

"No," Jaina said. "That gas was already—"

"Right," Zekk agreed. "They've got to—"

"And soon."

The stolen Tibanna gas had already been spin-sealed, so the tappers had to get it into carbonite quickly or see it lose most of its commercial value. And charts or no charts, that meant there was a facility somewhere in the Dead Eye. Jaina eased back on the throttles some more. It felt as if they were right on top of the thieves, and in this fog—

The corroded tower-tanks of an ancient refinery emerged from the pink haze ahead, and Jaina barely had time to flip the cloud car up on edge and bank away. Zekk, who was just as surprised but a lot less busy, had a moment to glance down through the open roof of a ruined habitation deck. The rest of the station remained hidden in the fog beneath, showing just enough ghostly corners and curves to suggest the lower decks had not fallen off . . . yet.

Focusing on the presences of the three Tibanna tappers, Jaina carefully spiraled down around the central tower complex while Zekk looked for ambushes. Much of the outer skin had long since rusted away, exposing a metal substructure caked and pitted with corrosion. Finally, the ruins of the loading deck came into view. Crooked arms of pink fog reached up through missing sections of flooring, and the docking berths were so primitive that they were serviced by loading ramps instead of lift pads.

A berth close to a missing section of floor held the conical tug Jaina and Zekk had been chasing. The vehicle was standing on three struts, with the boarding ramp lowered. The two siphoning balloons lay on the deck behind the tug, empty and flattened. There was no sign of the crew.

Jaina and Zekk circled once, then landed near the empty siphoning balloons. At once, they felt a rhythmic quiver—the station's repulsorlift generator was straining.

The hair rose on the back of Jaina's neck. "We need to make this fast."

Zekk had already popped the canopy and was leaping out onto the deck. Jaina unbuckled her crash webbing and followed him over to the tug, her lightsaber held at the ready but not ignited. The repulsorlift generator was in even worse condition than she had thought. The quiver was cycling up to a periodic shudder, and the shudder lasted a little longer and grew a little stronger every time it came.

Jaina and Zekk did not like the sound of that. It seemed odd that it should fail now, after so many centuries of keeping this station afloat. But perhaps power was being diverted to the carbonite freezing system—since that was clearly what the tappers were using this place for.

When they reached the tug, it grew apparent they would need to rethink that theory. They could feel the tappers inside the vessel, listless, far too content, almost unconscious. While Jaina stayed outside, Zekk ascended the ramp to investigate, and she received through their shared mind a complete perception of what he was finding.

The ramp opened onto an engineering deck, which—judging by the debris and nesting rags strewn about the floor—also doubled as crew quarters. It felt like the tappers themselves were on the flight deck, one level above. The air was filled with a cloying odor that Jaina and Zekk both recognized all too well, and the floor was piled high with waxy balls containing a dark, muddy liquid filled with stringy clots.

"Black membrosia?" Zekk asked.

There was only one way to be certain, but Zekk had no intention of tasting the stuff. After a brush with the dark side as a teenager, he held himself to a strict standard of restraint, and he never engaged in anything that even hinted of corruption or immorality.

So, after a last check to make sure nothing was creeping up on them out of the fog, Jaina ascended the boarding ramp. She picked up one of the balls and plunged her thumb through the wax, then withdrew it and licked the black syrup. It was much more cloying than the light membrosia of their own nest, with a rancid aftertaste that made her want to scrape her tongue . . . at least until her vision blurred and she was overcome by a feeling of chemical euphoria.

"Whoa. Definitely membrosia." Jaina had to brace herself against a wall, and she and Zekk were filled with a longing to rejoin their nest in the Colony. "Strong stuff."

Jaina could feel how much Zekk wanted to experience another taste—even through *her* mind—but the dark membrosia was almost narcotic in its potency, and now was hardly the time to have her senses dulled. She pinched the thumb hole shut and set the ball aside, intending to retrieve it on the way out.

"Bad idea."

Zekk used the Force to return the ball to the pile with the others. He could be such a zealot sometimes.

The image of a vast chamber filled with waxes of stringy

black membrosia came to Jaina's mind, and she recalled where black membrosia came from.

The Dark Nest had survived.

"And we need to know—"

"Right." Jaina led the way up the ladder to the flight deck. "What Dark Nest membrosia is doing *here*."

"Yes—"

"And what it has to do with Tibanna tapping."

Zekk sighed. Sometimes he missed finishing his own sentences.

On the flight deck, Jaina and Zekk found three Verpine slumped at their flight stations in a membrosia-induced stupor. The floor surrounding all three tappers was littered with empty waxes, and their long necks were flopped on their thoraxes or over their shoulders at angles unnatural even for insects. The long fingers and limbs of all three were fitfully jerking, as though in a dream, and when the pilot managed to turn his head to look toward them, tiny sparkles of gold light appeared deep inside his bulbous eyes.

"Won't get any answers here for a while," Jaina said.

"Right," Zekk said. "But they didn't unload those siphoning balloons themselves."

Jaina and Zekk left the tug and returned to the siphoning balloons, then followed a new transfer hose over to a section of missing deck. The line descended through the hole and disappeared into the fog, angling down toward the top of the unipod—where the carbonite freezing facilities were usually located.

Jaina and Zekk looked at each other, silently debating whether it would be better to slide along the hose or work their way down through the central hub of the station . . . and that was when the repulsorlift generator finally stopped shuddering.

They felt their stomachs rise and hoped that they were just reacting to the sudden stillness—that the sudden silence was not the bad sign they feared.

Then the blue glow of a large repulsor drive flared to life below.

"Rodders!" Jaina cursed.

The blue glow of the departing vessel swung around, briefly silhouetting the hazy lance of the station's unipod, then quickly receded into the fog.

"They shut the generator down!" Zekk said.

Jaina and Zekk turned to race to their cloud car, then remembered the tappers and started for the tug instead.

Their knees buckled as the deck suddenly lurched upward beneath them; then a strut collapsed beneath the tug, and it tumbled across the platform. Jaina and Zekk were too confused to react—until they noticed that they were also starting to slide.

The station was tipping.

Jaina spun back toward their cloud car and found it sliding across the deck, rocking up on its struts and about to tumble over. She thrust an arm out, holding Zekk with her other hand, and used the Force to pluck the vehicle up and bring it over. She caught hold of the cockpit and started to pull herself inside, then realized Zekk was still a deadweight in her other hand.

He was staring toward a missing section of deck, holding his arm out. But his Force grasp was empty, and Jaina could feel how angry he was with himself for missing the tug.

"Get over it!" She pulled herself into the cloud car's cockpit, dragging him after her. "They're Tibanna toppers. They're not worth dying for!"

ONE

Woteba.

The last time Han Solo had been here, the planet had had no name. The air had been thick and boggy, and there had been a ribbon of muddy water purling through the marsh grass, bending lazily toward the dark wall of a nearby conifer forest. A jagged mountain had loomed in the distance, its pale summit gleaming against the wispy red veil of a nebular sky.

Now the air was filled with the aroma of sweet membrosia and slow-roasted nerf ribs, and the only water in sight was rippling down the face of an artificial waterfall. The conifer forest had been cut, stripped, and driven into the marsh to serve as log pilings beneath the iridescent tunnel-houses of the Saras nest. Even the mountain looked different, seeming to float above the city on a cushion of kiln steam, its icy peak almost scraping the pale-veined belly of the Utegetu Nebula.

"Interesting, what the bugs have done to the place," Han said. He was standing in the door of the glimmering hangar where they had berthed the *Falcon*, looking out on the nest along with Leia, Saba Sebatyne, the Skywalkers, and C-3PO and R2-D2. "Not so creepy after all."

"Don't call them bugs, Han," Leia reminded him. "Insulting your hosts is never a good way to start a visit."

"Right, we wouldn't want to insult 'em," Han said. "Not for a little thing like harboring pirates and running black membrosia."

He crossed a spinglass bridge and stopped at the edge of a meandering ribbon of street. The silver lane was packed with chest-high Killiks hauling rough lumber, quarried moire-stone, casks of bluewater. Here and there, bleary-eyed spacers—human and otherwise—were staggering back to their ships at the sore end of a membrosia binge. On the balconies overhanging the tunnel-house entrances, glittered-up Joiners—beings who had spent too much time among Killiks and been absorbed into the nest's collective mind—were smiling and dancing to the soft trill of spinning wind horns. The only incongruous sight was in the marshy, two-meter gap that served as the gutter between the hangar and the street. A lone insect lay facedown in the muck, its orange thorax and white-striped abdomen half covered in some sort of dull gray froth.

"Raynar must know we've arrived," Luke said. He was still on the bridge behind Han. "Any sign of a guide?"

The bug in the gutter lifted itself on its arms and began to drum its thorax.

"I don't know," Han answered, eyeing the bug uncertainly. When it began to drag itself toward the bridge, he said, "Make that a maybe."

The Killik stopped and stared up at them with a pair of bulbous green eyes. *"Bur r rruubb, ubur ruur."*

"Sorry—don't understand a throb." Han knelt on the street's glimmering surface and extended a hand. "But come on up. Our protocol droid knows over six million—"

The insect spread its mandibles and backed away, pointing at the blaster on Han's hip.

"Hey, take it easy," Han said, still holding out his hand. "That's just for show. I'm not here to shoot anybody."

"*Brubr.*" The Killik raised a pincer-hand, then tapped itself between the eyes. "*Urrubb uu.*"

"Oh, dear," C-3PO said from the back of the bridge. "She seems to be *asking* you to blast her."

The bug nodded enthusiastically, then averted its eyes.

"Don't get crazy," Han said. "You're not that late."

"I think it's in pain, Han." Mara knelt on the street beside Han and motioned the insect to come closer. "Come here. We'll try to help."

The Killik shook its head and tapped itself between the eyes again. "*Buurubuur, ubu ru.*"

"She says *nothing* can help," C-3PO said. "She has the Fizz."

"The Fizz?" Han echoed.

The Killik thrummed a long explanation.

"She says it is very painful," C-3PO said. "And she would appreciate it if you would end her misery as soon as possible. UnuThul is waiting in the Garden Hall."

"Sorry," Han said. "I'm not blasting anyone this trip."

The Killik rumbled something that sounded like *rodder,* then started to drag itself away.

"Wait!" Luke extended his hand, and the Killik rose out of the mud. "Maybe we can rig an isolation ward—"

The rest of the offer was drowned out as Saras porters turned to point at their nest-fellow's frothy legs, drumming their chests and knocking the loads out of one another's arms. The Joiner dancers vanished from their balconies, and startled spacers staggered toward the gutter, squinting and reaching for their blasters.

Luke began to float the Killik back toward the bridge. It clacked its mandibles in protest and thrashed its arms, but its legs—hidden beneath a thick layer of froth—dangled motionlessly beneath its thorax. A steady drizzle of what looked like dirt specks fell from its feet into the gutter.

Han frowned. "Luke, maybe we'd better leave—"

A blaster bolt whined out from down the street, taking the Killik in midthorax and spraying a fist-sized circle of chitin and froth onto the hangar's milky exterior. The insect died instantly, but another uproar erupted on the street as angry spacers began to berate a wobbly Quarren holding a powerful Merr-Sonn Flash 4 blaster pistol.

"Ish not my fault!" The Quarren waved the weapon vaguely in Luke's direction. "Them Jedi wash the ones flyin' a Fizzer 'round."

The accusation diverted the angry looks toward Luke, but no one in the group was membrosia-smeared enough to harangue a party that included four beings dressed in Jedi robes. Instead the spacers staggered toward the hangar's other entrances as fast as their unsteady legs could carry them, leaving Han and the Jedi to stare at the dead Killik in astonished silence. Normally, they would have at least taken the killer into custody to await local law enforcement, but these were hardly normal circumstances. Luke just sighed and lowered the victim back into the gutter.

Leia seemed unable to take her eyes off it. "From the way those spacers reacted, this is fairly common. Did Raynar's message say anything about an epidemic?"

"Not a word," Mara said, standing. "Just that Unu had discovered why the Dark Nest attacked me last year, and we needed to discuss it in person."

"I don't like it," Han said. "Sounds more convenient all the time."

"We know—and thanks again for coming," Mara said. "We appreciate the backup."

"Yeah, well, don't mention it." Han returned to his feet. "We've got a personal interest in this."

Strictly speaking, the pirate harboring and membrosia running in which the Killiks were engaged was not Han and Leia's concern. But Chief of State Omas was using the trouble as a pretext to avoid keeping his side of a complicated bargain with the Solos, saying that until the nests of the Utegetu Nebula stopped causing so much trouble for the Galactic Alliance, he could not muster the votes he needed to give the Ithorians a new homeworld.

Han would have liked to believe the claim was just a big bantha patty, but someone had leaked the terms of the deal to the holopress. Now both the Solo name and the Ithorian homeworld had become linked in the public mind with the pirate raids and "tarhoney" dens that were blighting the frontier from Adumar to Reecee.

Once the street traffic had returned to normal, Luke said, "We seem to be out a guide. We'll have to find Raynar ourselves."

Han started to send C-3PO into the street to ask directions from a Killik, but Luke and the other Masters simply turned to Leia with an expectant look. She closed her eyes for a moment, then turned down the street and confidently began to lead the way deeper into the shimmering nest. Fairly certain that she knew exactly where she was going, Han fell in beside C-3PO and R2-D2 and followed the others in silence. Sometimes hanging out with Jedi was almost enough to make him feel inadequate.

For a quarter of a standard hour, the nature of Saras nest did not change. They continued to meet long lines of Killik porters coming in the opposite direction, to crave the roasted nerf they smelled in the air, to marvel at the iridescent sheen of the sinuous tunnel-houses—and to gasp at the purling beauty of the endless string of fountains, sprays, and cascades they passed.

Most of the Killik nests Han had visited had left him feeling creepy and a little sick to his stomach. But this one made him feel oddly buoyant and relaxed, perhaps even rejuvenated, as though the most pleasant thing in the galaxy would be sitting on a tunnel-house balcony, sipping golden membrosia, and watching the Joiners dance.

It made Han wonder what the bugs were up to *now*.

Gradually, the streets grew less crowded, and the group began to notice more froth-covered bodies in the gutter. Most were already dead and half disintegrated, but a few remained intact enough to raise their heads and beg for a merciful end. Han found himself torn between the desire to stop their suffering and a reluctance to do something so drastic without understanding the situation. Fortunately, Luke was able to take the middle road, using the Force to render each victim unconscious.

Finally, Leia stopped about ten meters from an open expanse of marsh. The street continued, snaking through a brightly mottled sweep of bog flowers, but the road surface turned dull and frothy ahead, and the ends of the nearby tunnel-houses were being eaten by gray foam. In the center of the field stood a massive spinglass palace, its base a shapeless mass of ash-colored bubbles and its crown a braided tangle of iridescent turrets swimming with snakes of color.

"Tell me that's not where Raynar was waiting," Han groaned. "Because there's no way we're going—"

"Raynar Thul could not be waiting there," a gravelly voice said from a nearby tunnel-house. "You should know that by now, Captain Solo. Raynar Thul has been gone a long time."

Han turned around and found the imposing figure of Raynar Thul standing in the tunnel-house entrance. A tall man with regal bearing, he had a raw, melted face with no ears, hair, or nose, and all of his visible skin had the shiny, stiff quality of a burn scar. He wore purple trousers and a cape of scarlet silk over a breastplate of gold chitin.

"Guess I'm a slow learner that way," Han said, smiling. "Good to see you again, uh, UnuThul."

Raynar came into the street. As always, he was followed by the Unu, a motley swarm of Killiks of many different shapes and sizes. Gathered from hundreds of different nests, they accompanied Raynar wherever he went and acted as a sort of collective Will for the Colony.

"We are surprised to see you and Princess Leia here." Raynar made no move to take the hand that Han extended. "We did not summon you."

Han frowned, but continued to hold out his hand. "Yeah, what's the deal with that? Our feelings were kind of hurt, seeing how we're the ones who gave you this world."

Raynar's eyes remained cold. "We have not forgotten." Instead of shaking hands, he reached past Han's wrist and rubbed forearms in a buggish greeting. "You may be sure of that."

"Uh, great." Han tried to hide the cold shudder that ran up his spine. "Glad to hear it."

Raynar continued to rub arms, his keloid lip rising into a faint sneer. "There is no need to be afraid, Captain Solo. Touching us will not make you a Joiner."

"Never thought it would." Han yanked his arm away. "You're just enjoying it way too much."

Raynar's sneer changed to a small, taut smile. "That is what we have always admired most about you, Captain Solo," he said. "Your fearlessness."

Before Han could respond—or ask about the gray foam eating the Saras nest—Raynar stepped away, and Han found himself being stared down by one of the Unu, this one a two-meter insect with a red-spotted head and five blue eyes.

"What are *you* looking at?" Han demanded.

The insect snapped its mandibles closed a centimeter

from Han's nose, then drummed something sharp with its thorax.

"The Colony certainly seems impressed with your courage, Captain Solo!" C-3PO reported cheerily. "She says she is either looking at the bravest human in the galaxy—or the dumbest."

Han frowned at the bug. "What's that supposed to mean?"

The Killik looked away and walked past him, leading the rest of the Unu to join Raynar and the Skywalkers. Han motioned C-3PO and R2-D2 to his side, then shouldered his way through the softly droning mass to stand with Saba and Leia.

"I'm not liking the buzz around here," he whispered to Leia. "It's beginning to feel like a setup."

Leia nodded, but kept her attention fixed on the center of the gathering, where Raynar was already exchanging greetings with the Skywalkers.

". . . apologize for receiving you in the street," he was saying to Luke. "But the Garden Hall we built to welcome you was . . ." He glanced toward the marsh. ". . . destroyed."

"No apologies are necessary," Luke answered. "We're happy to see you anywhere."

"Good." Raynar motioned them up the street, toward a small courtyard only a couple of meters from the marsh. "We will talk in the Circle of Rest."

Alarm warnings began to knell inside Han's head. "Shouldn't we go someplace safer?" he asked. "Farther away from that froth?"

Raynar turned to Han and narrowed his eyes. "Why would we do that, Captain Solo?"

"Are you kidding me?" Han asked. "Why *wouldn't* we? I've seen what that foam does."

"Have you?" Raynar asked. Han's vision began to blur

around the edges, and soon all that remained visible of Raynar's face were the cold, blue depths of his eyes. "Tell us about it."

Han scowled. "What do you think you're doing? Don't you try that Force stuff . . ." A dark weight began to gather inside his chest, and words began to spill out of Han of their own accord. "There was a bug outside our hangar covered in gray froth. It was disintegrating before our eyes, and now we get here and see the same thing happening to your—"

"Wait a minute!" Leia's voice came from in front of Han. "You think *we* know something about this 'Fizz'?"

"You and Captain Solo *are* the ones who gave us this world," Raynar said. "And now we know why."

"I don't think I like what you're saying." Han could still see only Raynar's eyes. "We pull your feet out of . . . the fire at . . . Qoribu, and . . ." The weight inside his chest grew heavier, and he found himself returning to the original subject. "Look, this is the first time we ever saw the stuff. It's probably some bug disease you guys brought baaarrggh—"

The weight became crushing, and Han dropped to his knees, his sentence ending in an unintelligible groan.

"Stop it!" Leia said. "This is no way to win our help."

"We are not *interested* in your help, Princess Leia," Raynar said. "We have seen what comes of your 'help.' "

"You must want something from us," Luke said. It sounded to Han as though Luke had also stepped in front of him. "You went to a lot of trouble to lure us here."

"We did not *lure* you, Master Skywalker." Raynar's blue eyes slid away. The weight vanished from inside Han's chest, and his vision slowly returned to normal. "Unu *did* discover why Gorog is trying to kill Mara."

"*Is* trying to?" Luke's tone was one of clarification rather than surprise. Gorog was a furtive nest of Killiks—

called the Dark Nest by Jedi—that acted as a sort of evil Unconscious for the Colony's collective mind. The Jedi had attempted to destroy it last year, after it had precipitated the Qoribu crisis by secretly persuading Raynar to establish several nests on the Chiss frontier, but they had realized they had failed as soon as the Dark Nest's black membrosia began appearing on Alliance worlds. "We're listening."

"In good time," Raynar said. "We will tell you about the plot against Mara *after* you tell us about the Fizz."

He turned and started toward the Circle of Rest.

Han rose and stomped after him. "I told you, we don't know anything about that—and if you ever try that heavy-chest thing on me again—"

Leia took Han's arm. "Han—"

"—I'm going to buy myself a spaceliner," Han continued. "Then I'm going to start booking culinary tours—"

Leia's fingers bit into Han's triceps hard enough to stop him from uttering the fateful *from Kubindi,* and he turned toward her, scowling and rubbing his arm.

"Ouch," he said. She had spent the last year training under Saba, and even without the Force, her grasp could be crushing. "What'd you do that for?"

"Maybe we *do* know something," she said.

Han's frown deepened. "How do you figure?"

"Because we have Cilghal—and a state-of-the-art astro-biology lab," Leia said. "Even if we've never seen this stuff before, we can probably figure it out."

Raynar stopped at the Circle of Rest and turned to glare at them. "We want to know *now.*" His entourage began to clack and thrum thoraxes. "We will not stand for your stalling, Princess."

"I don't care for the way you're speaking to us, UnuThul." Leia met Raynar's gaze from where she was standing, about three meters down the street. "We've done nothing to deserve that tone."

"You cheated us," Raynar insisted. "You tricked us into leaving Qoribu and coming here."

"*Cheated* you?" Han exploded. "Now just a blasted—"

"I'm sorry," Leia interrupted. "But if that's the way the Colony feels, we have nothing to discuss."

She turned away and started back up the street toward the *Falcon*. Luke and the other Jedi instantly followed Leia's lead, and Han did likewise. This trip had become, he sensed, something of a test of Leia's progress toward becoming a full Jedi, and he was not going to mess it up for her—no matter how much he was aching to put that ungrateful bughugger in his place.

An indignant rumble sounded from the Unu entourage, and Raynar called, "Stop!"

Leia continued to walk, and so did Han and everyone else.

"Wait." This time, Raynar managed to sound as if he was asking instead of ordering. "Please."

Leia stopped and spoke over her shoulder. "These discussions can proceed only in an atmosphere of trust, UnuThul." She slowly turned to face him. "Do you think that's possible?"

Raynar's eyes flashed, but he said, "Of course." He motioned them back toward the Circle of Rest. "You may trust us."

Leia appeared to consider this for a moment, but Han knew she was only posturing. She and Han wanted these discussions as badly as Raynar did, and there was no way Luke was going to leave the planet without learning more about the Dark Nest's vendetta against Mara. No matter how crazy and paranoid Raynar sounded, they had to deal with him.

Leia finally nodded. "Very well."

She led the way back up the street, and Raynar waved them into the courtyard with the Unu. Basically a walk-in fountain, the Circle of Rest consisted of four egg-shaped monoliths arrayed in a semicircle, the open side facing the Garden Hall. All four had sheets of water rippling down the sides, and looking out from inside each monolith was the hologram of a blinking, smiling Joiner child or pucker-mouthed Killik larva. Han found the place oddly soothing—in a cold, creepy sort of way.

They joined Raynar in the center of the semicircle, where C-3PO immediately began to complain about the fine mist spraying them from all sides. Han silenced him with a quiet threat, then tried not to complain himself as the insects of the Unu began to crowd around.

"Perhaps I should begin by explaining why Han and I are here," Leia said. She looked from Raynar to his entourage. "If that's agreeable to you and Unu."

The insects clacked their approval, and Raynar said, "We approve."

Leia's smile was polite, but forced. "As you may know, after Han and I discovered these worlds inside the Utegetu Nebula, our first intention was to give them to refugees who are still looking for new homeworlds after the war with the Yuuzhan Vong."

"We have heard this," Raynar allowed.

"Instead, Chief of State Omas encouraged us to give them to the Colony, to avoid a war between you and the Chiss," Leia continued. "In return, he promised to secure a new homeworld for one of the refugee species we had hoped to settle here, the Ithorians."

Raynar's gaze drifted out across the marsh, to where the gray foam was steadily creeping higher up the Garden Hall. "We fail to see what that has to do with us."

"The arrangement has become common knowledge in the Galactic Alliance," Leia explained. "And people are blaming us and the Ithorians for the trouble your nests in the Utegetu Nebula are causing."

Raynar's eyes snapped back toward Leia. "What trouble?"

"Don't play dumb with us," Han said, unable to restrain his anger any longer. "Those pirates you're harboring are raiding Alliance ships, and that black membrosia you're running is eating the souls of whole species of Alliance insect-citizens."

Raynar lowered his fused brow. "The Colony kills pirates, not harbors them," he said. "And you must be aware, Captain Solo, that membrosia is gold, not black. You certainly drank enough on Jwlio to be certain of that."

"The Dark Nest's membrosia was dark," Luke pointed out. "And Alliance Intelligence has captured dozens of pirates who confirm that their vessels are operating out of the Utegetu Nebula."

An ominous rumble rose from the thoraxes of the Unu, and Raynar turned on Luke with blue eyes burning. "Pirates lie, Master Skywalker. And you destroyed the Dark Nest on Kr."

"Then why did you say *is*?" Saba demanded. "If it'z still hunting Mara, then it hasn't been destroyed."

"Forgive our exaggeration." Raynar returned his attention to Luke. "You destroyed *most* of the nest on Kr. What remains couldn't supply a starliner with black membrosia—and certainly not whole worlds."

"Then where is it all coming from?" Leia asked.

"You tell us," Raynar replied. "The Galactic Alliance is filled with biochemists clever enough to synthesize black membrosia. We suggest you start with *them*."

"Synthetic membrosia?" Han echoed.

He was beginning to feel as if they had had this conversation before. The Colony's concept of truth was fluid, to say the least, and its peculiar leader was incredibly stubborn. Last year, Raynar had literally had to be hit in the face by a Gorog corpse before he would believe that the Dark Nest even existed. It had been just as hard to convince him that the mysterious nest had been founded by the same Dark Jedi who had abducted him from *Baanu Raas* during the war with the Yuuzhan Vong. Now Han had the sinking feeling it would prove even harder to convince Raynar that the Utegetu nests were misbehaving.

Han turned to Luke. "Now *that*'s something we hadn't thought of—synthetic membrosia. We'll have to check it out."

"Uh, sure." Luke's nod could have been a little more convincing. "As soon as we get back."

"Good." Han turned back to Raynar. "And since you're so sure that the Utegetu nests *aren't* doing anything wrong, you shouldn't have a problem sharing a log of your legitimate traffic with the Galactic Alliance. It would really help them out with the pirate problem."

Raynar's eyes grew bright and hot. "We are telling the truth, Captain Solo—the *real* truth."

"The *Jedi* understand that," Mara said. "But the Galactic Alliance needs to be convinced."

"And Chief Omas is willing to make it worth your while," Leia added. "Once he's convinced that the Utegetu nests aren't supporting these activities, he'll be willing to offer the Colony a trade agreement. It would mean larger markets for your exports, and lower costs for your imports."

"It would mean regulations and restrictions," Raynar said. "And the Colony would be responsible for enforcing them."

"Only the ones you agreed to in the first place," Leia said. "It would go a long way toward bringing the Colony—"

"The Colony is not interested in Alliance regulations." Raynar signaled an end to the subject by stepping closer to Luke and Mara and presenting his back to Han and Leia. "We invited the Masters Skywalker here to discuss what Unu has learned about the Dark Nest's vendetta."

Leia refused to take the hint. "Strange, how you can remember the vendetta," she said to Raynar's back, "and still not know what's really happening here inside the nebula."

Raynar spoke over his shoulder. "What are you saying?"

"You know what she's saying," Han said. "The Dark Nest fooled you once—"

The air grew acrid with Killik aggression pheromones, and Raynar whirled on Han. "*We* are not the ones being fooled!" He glanced in Leia's direction, then added, "And we will prove it."

"Please do."

Leia's wry tone suggested she believed the same thing Han did—that it could not be done, because Raynar and the Unu *were* the ones being fooled.

Raynar smirked their doubts aside, then turned to Mara. "When you were the Emperor's Hand, did you ever meet someone named Daxar Ies?"

"Where . . ." Mara's voice cracked, and she paused to swallow. "Where did you hear that name?"

"His wife and daughter came home early." Raynar's tone grew accusatory. "They found you searching his office."

Mara narrowed her eyes and managed to put on a good impression of collecting herself. "Only three people could know that."

"And two of them became Joiners."

Luke reached out to steady Mara, and Han knew she had *really* been shaken.

"All right," Han said. "What's going on?"

"Daxar Ies was a . . ." Mara's hand slipped free of Luke's, and she forced herself to meet Han's and Leia's gazes. "He was a target."

"One of *Palpatine's* targets?" Leia asked.

Mara nodded grimly. Recalling her days as one of Palpatine's special "assistants" was not something she enjoyed. "The only job I ever botched, as a matter of fact."

"We would not call it *botched*," Raynar said. "You eliminated the target."

"That was only part of the objective." Mara was looking at Raynar now, *glaring* at him. "I didn't recover the list . . . and I left witnesses."

"You let Beda Ies and her daughter live," Raynar said. "You told them to vanish forever."

"That's right," Mara said. "As far as I know, they were never harmed."

"They were well protected," Raynar said. "Gorog saw to that."

"Wait a minute," Han said. "You're saying these Ies women joined the Dark Nest?"

"No," Raynar said. "I am saying they *created* it."

Han winced, and Leia's eyes flashed with alarm.

"I thought we already knew how the Dark Nest was created," Leia said. "The Gorog were corrupted when they absorbed too many Chiss Joiners."

"We were mistaken," Raynar said.

Han's wince became a genuine sinking feeling. To broker a peace between the Colony and the Chiss, Leia had been forced to bend the truth and contrive an origination tale for the Dark Nest that would make the Killiks want to stay far away from the Chiss. The Colony had readily embraced the new story, since it was less painful than believing one of its own nests could be responsible for the terrible things they had found in the Gorog nest. If Raynar and the Unu were trying to develop a new version now, it could only be because they wanted to renew their expansion toward Chiss territory.

"Look," Han said, "we've been through all that."

"We have new information," Raynar insisted. He looked back to Mara. "Mara Jade told Beda Ies and her daughter to vanish and never to be found. They fled into the Unknown Regions and took refuge with Gorog—before it was the Dark Nest."

"Sorry, but this story won't work for us," Han said. "You should have brought the Ies women up last year."

"We did not know about them last year," Raynar said.

"Too bad," Han said. "You can't just make up a new—"

"Han, I don't think they're making this up," Mara interrupted. "They know too much about what happened—at least the part about the Ies women."

"So what if the Ies girls did become Joiners?" Han asked. He was beginning to wonder whose side Mara was on. "That doesn't mean *they* created the Dark Nest. They could have joined some other nest, and the Colony would still know enough about them to put together a good story."

"The story we have put together is the truth," Raynar said. "When Beda and Eremay became Joiners, the Gorog absorbed their fear. The entire nest went into hiding. It became the Dark Nest."

Han started to object, but Leia took his arm.

"Han, it could be the truth," she said. "I mean, the *real* truth. We need to hear this."

"Yes," Saba agreed. "For Mara'z sake."

Han let his chin drop. "Blast it."

"You should not feel bad, Captain Solo," Raynar consoled. "We have believed the new truth for some time. Nothing you could say would make us change our mind."

"Thanks loads," Han grumbled. "That's a real comfort."

A flash of humor danced through Raynar's eyes, and he turned back to Mara. "We are sure you have figured out the rest," he said. "Gorog recognized you at the Crash last year—"

"And assumed I had come to find the list," Mara finished. "So they attacked first."

Raynar shook his head. "We wish it were that simple. Gorog wanted revenge. Gorog *still* wants revenge—against you."

"Of course." Mara did not even blink. "I killed Beda's husband and Eremay's father, and condemned *them* to a life in exile. Naturally they want me dead."

"They want you to suffer," Raynar corrected. "*Then* they want you dead."

"And you had to bring Mara and Luke all the way out here to tell them that?" Han asked. He could tell by their expressions that the Jedi—well, at least the *human* Jedi—were all convinced that Raynar was telling the truth. But something here smelled rotten to Han, and he had noticed the stench as soon as they arrived on the planet. "You couldn't have sent a message?"

"We could have." Raynar stared at Luke a moment, then turned and looked across the bog toward the froth-covered walls of the Garden Palace. "But we wanted be certain that Master Skywalker understood the urgency of our situation."

"I see." Luke followed Raynar's gaze out across the bog, and his face slowly began to cloud with the same anger that was welling up inside Han. "And Unu's Will isn't strong enough to change what Gorog feels?"

"We are sorry, Master Skywalker, but not yet." Raynar tore his gaze off the Garden Hall and faced Luke coolly. "Perhaps later, after we have stopped the Fizz and are less concerned with our own problems."

TWO

The interior of the hangar smelled of hamogoni wood and containment fluid, and the air was filled with the clatter and drone of Killik workers—mostly cargo handlers and maintenance crews—scurrying from one task to another. The *Falcon* sat a hundred meters down the way, looking deceptively clean in the opaline light, but berthed directly beneath one of the gray blemishes that were beginning to mar the hangar's milky interior.

Luke took the lead and used the Force to gently nudge a path through the frenetic activity. The companions were hardly fleeing, but they did want to launch the *Falcon* before Raynar had time to reconsider the agreement Leia had negotiated after his veiled threat against Mara—and before the blemishes on the ceiling turned into the same gray froth spreading over the exterior of the hangar.

"Looks like we're not the only ones eager to clear this bug hive," Han said, moving up beside Luke. "That Fizz must be even faster than it looks."

"This one does not think so," Saba said. In her hands, she was holding a sealed stasis jar containing a thumb-sized sample of gray froth. "If it workz so fast, why would they stay to load their shipz?"

"I see you haven't spent much time around smugglers," Luke said. "They *never* leave without their cargo."

The boarding ramp descended, and Leia's longtime Noghri bodyguards, Meewalh and Cakhmaim, appeared at the top armed with T-21 repeating blasters.

"What a relief!" C-3PO clinked ahead and started up the ramp. "I can't wait to step into the sterilizer booth. My circuits itch just holding a record of that Fizz."

"Sorry, Threepio. Han and I need you and Artoo with us, to translate and look for patterns in the froth attacks." Luke stopped at the foot of the ramp and turned to Han and Leia. "If that's all right with you."

"No problem," Han said. He stepped closer and spoke in a whisper so low that Luke barely heard it. "We'll just wait until the boarding ramp starts to go up, then jump on. Leia can cold-start the repulsor drives, and we'll—"

"Han, we gave Raynar our word."

"Yeah, I remember." Han continued to whisper. "But we can do this. We'll be out of here before—"

"We're staying." Luke spoke loudly enough so that the eavesdroppers he sensed watching them would have no trouble overhearing. "A Jedi Master's promise should mean something."

Han glanced at the Saras cargo handlers loading moirestone into the next ship over, and a glimmer of understanding came to his eyes. Each nest of Killiks shared a collective mind, so as long as there was a single Saras within sight of them, all of the Saras Killiks would know exactly what they were doing. And since the Unu included a delegate from the Saras nest, that meant *Raynar* would always know exactly what they were doing.

"I see your point," Han said. "We wouldn't want to double-cross *UnuThul*."

Luke rolled his eyes. "Han, you *don't* see."

The ease with which Alema Rar had fallen under the sway of the Dark Nest during the Qoribu crisis had prompted Luke to do a lot of soul searching, and he had come to the conclusion that the Jedi had been injured by the war with the Yuuzhan Vong in ways even more serious than the deaths they had suffered. They had embraced a ruthless, anything-goes philosophy that left young Jedi Knights with no clear concept of who they were and what they stood for, that blurred the difference between right and wrong and made them far too susceptible to sinister influences. And so Luke had decided to rebuild a sense of principle in the Jedi order, to demonstrate to his followers that a Jedi Knight *was* a force for good in the galaxy.

"If we leave now, it will make solving other problems with the Colony more difficult," Luke continued. He hated having to drag Han into his quest to revitalize the Jedi, but Raynar had agreed to allow Mara, Leia, and the others to leave peacefully only if Luke *and* Han remained on Woteba until the Jedi found a remedy for the Fizz. "We have to build some trust, or we'll only have *more* pirates and black membrosia coming out of these nests."

Han scowled. "Luke, you just don't understand bugs," he said. "Trust isn't that big in their way of seeing things."

"Captain Solo is quite correct." C-3PO remained halfway up the ramp. "I haven't been able to identify a word for 'trust' or 'honor' in any of their native languages. It really would be wiser to flee."

"Nice try, Threepio," Mara said, stepping to Luke's side. "But you may as well come back down here. We're staying."

As the droid clanked reluctantly down the ramp, Luke turned to Mara. He knew she could sense his unspoken plan as clearly as *he* sensed her anxiety, but this was one time he would truly be better off without her at his side.

"Mara, I think—"

"I'm not leaving here without you, Luke."

Leia touched Mara's elbow. "Mara, the Dark Nest wants you *dead*. Staying on Woteba will only make Luke and Han targets along with you."

Mara's eyes grew narrow and angry, but she dropped her chin and sighed. "I hate this," she said. "It makes me feel like a coward."

"Coward? Mara Jade Skywalker?" Saba snorted. "That is just rockheaded. Leaving is the best thing you can do for Master Skywalker and Han."

"Yeah, but before you go, I want to know who this Daxar Ies was," Han said. "I've never heard of him."

"You wouldn't have. He was one of Palpatine's private accountants," Mara answered. "He embezzled two billion credits from the Emperor's personal funds and stashed it in accounts all over the galaxy."

Han whistled. "Brave guy."

"Foolish guy," Saba corrected. "He believed he could deceive the Emperor?"

Mara shrugged. "You'd be surprised how many people believed that," she said. "And Daxar Ies was a strange man. All that money, and I found him living in a shabby twilight-level apartment on Coruscant. He never left the planet."

"Maybe he lost the list of accounts, or couldn't get to it," Leia suggested. "That would explain why you couldn't find it."

"Maybe," Mara said. "But the Emperor didn't think so. Ies knew where one of the accounts was. He made a withdrawal, and that's how I tracked him down."

Though Mara showed no outward sign of her feelings, Luke could sense how much she disliked talking about that part of her life, how angry she grew when she thought of how the Emperor had manipulated her trust—and how sad it made her to recall her victims. He took her in his arms, silently reminding her that that part of her life was long over, and kissed her.

"Go back to the academy," Luke said. "Cilghal will need you on Ossus, to tell her everything you can remember about the Fizz. Han and I will be fine."

Mara pulled herself back and forced a smile. "You'd better be telling the truth, Skywalker."

"This one will make sure of it." Saba passed the stasis jar to Mara. "She is also staying."

"No way," Han said. "You'll make the bugs think we're up to something. Raynar picked me to stay with Luke because he figured one Jedi Master would be more than enough to watch."

"And because he knowz you are disturbed by insectz," Saba said. "This one does not like the way this feelz, Han. Raynar is showing a cruel streak."

"So it seems," Luke said. He reached out with the Force, urging the Barabel to board the *Falcon* with the others. "But Han's right—we don't want to make the Killiks suspicious of us."

"If you wish, Master Skywalker," Saba said. "You are the longfang here."

Saba took the stasis jar back from Mara, then turned and ascended the ramp with no further comment. In any other species, the abruptness might have indicated anger or hurt feelings. In a Barabel, it just meant she was ready to go.

Luke kissed Mara again and watched her start up the ramp.

Han hugged and kissed Leia, then stepped back with an overly casual air. "Be careful with my ship," he said to Leia. "I've finally got that hyperdrive adjusted just right."

Leia rolled her eyes. "Sure you do." She gave him a wistful smile, then said good-bye to Luke and started up the ramp. "I'll send Cakhmaim out with your bags."

"And please don't forget my cleaning kit," C-3PO called after her. "This planet is unsanitary. I feel contaminated already."

"Who doesn't?" Han asked.

Being careful to do nothing that would make the Killiks think they intended to flee, Luke and Han waited at the foot of the ramp until Cakhmaim returned with their bags and C-3PO's cleaning kit. Though Luke had not yet had a chance to outline his plan, he was fairly certain that Han had guessed it. He was going to search out the Dark Nest, determine how big a threat it posed to Mara and the Galactic Alliance, and find a way to destroy it for good.

Once Cakhmaim had passed them their bags, Leia raised the ramp and sounded the departure alarm. Luke, Han, and the droids backed away to a safe distance, then watched in silence as the *Falcon* lifted off without them and glided over the bustling floor. When it reached the hangar mouth, it paused briefly and flashed its landing lights in a complicated sequence of flashes and blinks.

R2-D2 let out an astonished whistle.

"I don't know why that should surprise you," C-3PO said. "Of course they're concerned about us."

"What did they say?" Luke asked.

"Be careful," C-3PO translated. "And don't let anything drip on the droids."

"Drip on the . . . ?" Han looked up. "Uh, maybe we'd better get out of here."

Luke followed Han's gaze and found the gray blemish on the ceiling beginning to blister. There was no froth yet, but a long shadow down the center suggested the surface would soon start bubbling.

Luke was about to turn toward the exit when his danger

sense made the hairs on his neck stand upright. He did not sense anything unusual from the eavesdroppers who had been watching them—no hardening of resolve, no cresting wave of anger or gathering lump of fear. He remained where he was, pretending to study the blemish on the ceiling as he opened himself more fully to the Force.

But instead of expanding his awareness as he would normally do when searching for an unseen threat, Luke waited quietly, patiently, without motion. He was trying to feel not the threat itself, but the ripples it created in the Force around it. The technique was one he had developed—with his nephew, Jacen—to search for beings who could hide their presences in the Force.

"Uh, Luke?" Han had already taken a dozen steps toward the exit and was standing in the middle of a long column of Saras porters. The insects were swinging their line around him, rushing a load of five-meter hamogoni logs into the hold of a boxy Damorian SpaceBantha freighter. "You coming?"

"Not yet," Luke said. "Why don't you go on ahead and ask about a place to stay? I'll join you in a few minutes."

Han frowned, then shrugged. "Whatever you say."

"Perhaps Artoo and I should go with Captain Solo." C-3PO was two steps ahead of Han. "He's sure to need a translator."

But R2-D2 remained behind. Luke had been forced to remove a motivation module to preserve a secret memory cache that had surfaced last year, and now the little droid refused to leave his side.

As Han departed, Luke worked to quiet his mind, to shut out the booming and banging and whirring of the busy hangar, the swirling mad efficiency of the Killiks and filmy hot weight of the dank air, to sense nothing but the Force itself, holding him in its liquid grasp, lapping at him from all sides, and soon he felt one set of ripples that seemed to come out of nowhere, from an emptiness where he sensed only a vague uneasiness in the Force, where he felt nothing except a cold, empty hole.

Luke turned toward the emptiness and found himself looking under an old Gallofree Star Barge that was listing toward a collapsed strut. The shadows beneath its belly were so thick and gray that it took a moment to find the source of the ripples he'd felt, but finally he noticed a pair of almond-shaped eyes watching him from near the stern. They had green irises surrounded by yellow sclera, and they were set in a slender blue face with high cheeks and a thin straight nose. The thick tendrils of a pair of lekku curled back from the top of the forehead, arching over the shoulders and vanishing behind a lithe female body.

"Alema Rar." Luke let his hand drop to the hilt of his lightsaber. "I'm glad to see you survived the trouble at Kr."

" 'Trouble,' Master Skywalker?" The Twi'lek scuttled forward into the light. "That's a pretty word for it."

Alema was dressed in a Killik-silk bodysuit, the color of midnight and as close fitting as a coat of paint. The cloth was semitransparent, save for an opaque triangle that covered the sagging, misshaped shoulder above a dangling arm. Luke's danger sense had formed an icy ball between his shoulder blades, but both of the Twi'lek's hands were visible and empty, and the only weapon she carried was the new lightsaber hanging from the belt angled across her hips.

Luke began to quiet his mind again, searching for another set of unexplained Force ripples.

"Worried, Master Skywalker?" Alema stopped a dozen paces away and stared at him, her eyes as steady and unblinking as those of an insect. "There's no need. We're not interested in hurting you."

"You'll understand if I don't believe you."

Though Luke had noticed no other suspicious Force ripples, he pivoted in both directions, scanning the shadows beneath nearby ships, the churning Killik swarms, the hexagonal storage cells along the walls, and anywhere else an attacker might be lurking. He found nothing and turned back to Alema.

"I don't suppose you're here to ask the Jedi to take you back?"

"What an interesting idea." The smile Alema flashed would have been coy once, but now seemed merely hard and base. "But no."

Fairly confident now that Alema was not going to attack—at least physically—Luke moved his hand away from his lightsaber and advanced to within a few steps of the Twi'lek.

"Well, what are you doing here?" Knowing it would upset her and throw her off balance, Luke purposely allowed his gaze to linger on Alema's disfigured shoulder. "Just stopping by to let us know you and Lomi Plo are still alive?"

Alema gave a low throat-click, then said, "Lomi Plo died in the Crash."

"With Welk, I suppose."

"Exactly," Alema said.

Luke sighed in frustration. "So we're back to that, are we?" He had slain Welk during the fight at Qoribu, only a few minutes after he had cut Alema's shoulder half off, and he had good reason to believe that the apparition that had nearly killed *him*—and Mara—was what remained of Lomi Plo. "Alema, you were at Kr. You saw Welk before I killed him, and it had to be Lomi Plo who pulled you out of the nest at the end."

"You killed BedaGorog," Alema said. "She was the Night Herald before us."

"The person I killed was male." Luke suspected he was arguing a lost cause. The Dark Nest remained determined to hide the survival of Lomi Plo behind a veil of lies and false memories, and—as a sort of collective Unconscious for the entire Colony—it was adept at manipulating the beliefs of Joiners and Killiks alike. "He had a lightsaber, and he knew how to use it."

"BedaGorog was Force-sensitive." A lewd smile came to Alema's lips. "And as we recall, you did not take the time to check inside her pants before you killed her."

Luke let his chin drop. "Alema, you disappoint me."

"The feeling is mutual, Master Skywalker," Alema said. "We have not forgotten the slaughter at Kr."

"There wouldn't have been a slaughter if you had done your duty as a Jedi." Luke sensed a familiar presence creeping toward him, skulking its way under the stern of the old Star Barge, and realized that Han had returned to the hangar without C-3PO. "But you let your anger make you weak, and the Dark Nest took advantage."

Alema's unblinking eyes turned the color of chlorine. "Don't blame us for what—"

"I'll lay the blame where it belongs. As a Master of the Jedi council, that is *my* duty—and my privilege!" Hoping to keep Alema's attention too riveted on him to notice Han sneaking up behind her, Luke moved to within lightsaber range of the Twi'lek. "Now I ask you one last time to return to Ossus. I know it will be hard to face those you betrayed, but—"

"We are not interested in 'redemption' . . . or anything else you have to offer, Master Skywalker. We are here with—"

Alema stopped in midsentence and cocked her head, then reached for her lightsaber.

Luke had already extended his arm and was summoning the weapon to himself, literally ripping Alema's belt off her waist and leaving the Twi'lek with an empty hand as Han hit her in the flank with a stun bolt.

Alema dropped to her knees, but did not fall, so Han fired again. This time, the Twi'lek collapsed onto her face and lay on the hangar floor twitching and drooling. Han leveled the weapon to fire again.

"That's enough," Luke said. "Are you trying to kill her?"

"As a matter of fact, yeah." Han scowled at the setting switch on the barrel of his blaster, then thumbed it to the opposite position. "I could have sworn I had it set on full power."

Luke shook his head in dismay, then used the Force to turn the weapon's barrel away from Alema. "Sometimes I wonder if I still know you, Han. She's defenseless."

"She's a Jedi," Han said. "She's *never* defenseless."

Still, he flicked the selector switch back to stun, then stood behind the Twi'lek and pointed the barrel at her head. Luke removed her lightsaber from her belt, then squatted on the floor in front of her and waited until she started to come around—which was incredibly quickly, even for a Jedi.

"Sorry about that," Luke said. "Han's still a little sore about what you did to the *Falcon*."

Alema opened one eye. "He always did carry a grudge." She struggled to bring Luke into focus, then said, "But perhaps you should make something clear to him. We are not at *your* mercy."

A tremendous clamor rumbled through the hangar as

nearby insects began to drop their loads and scurry toward the Star Barge.

"You are at *ours*."

Luke began to slap Alema's lightsaber against his palm, allowing his frustration to pass, trying to remind himself that the Twi'lek was not in control of herself, that it was impossible for her to separate her own thoughts from those of the Dark Nest. But Jaina and Zekk had found themselves in a similar situation, and they had not turned their backs on the Jedi. The difference was, they had *tried* to resist.

Finally, Luke tucked Alema's lightsaber into his belt and stood. "You could have fought this," he said. "Maybe you still can. Jaina and Zekk became Joiners, and yet they remained true to their duty."

"You place too much faith in others, Master Skywalker." Alema braced her good arm on the floor and pushed off, then brought her feet up beneath her. "That has always been your weakness—and soon it will be your downfall."

A cold shiver of danger sense raced up Luke's spine, and he resisted the temptation to ask Alema's meaning. This *was* the reason she had come to the hangar, he felt certain. She was trying to trap him, to draw him into some dark and twisted maze where he would become as lost as she was.

Unfortunately, Han did not have Jedi danger sense. "Too much faith? What's *that* supposed to mean? If something's going on with Jaina—"

Alema glanced over her shoulder at Han, pouting at the blaster still pointed at her back, then said, "We didn't mean to alarm you, Han. Jaina and Zekk are fine, as far as we know." She looked back to Luke. "We were talking about Mara. She has been dishonest with Master Skywalker."

"I doubt that very much." Luke saw what the Dark Nest

was attempting, and he could not believe they would be foolish enough to try such a thing. Nobody was going to drive a wedge between him and Mara. "And even if I didn't, I would hardly take the Dark Nest's word over that of a Jedi Master."

"We have proof," Alema said.

"And I doubt *that*." Han glanced at her skintight body-suit. "You don't have a place to put it."

"We're glad you're not too old to notice," Alema said. "Thank you."

"It wasn't a compliment."

The smile Alema flashed Han was both knowing and genuine. "Sure it was." She turned back to Luke, then glanced at R2-D2. "But we should have said *you* have proof."

Luke shook his head. "I really don't think so. If that's all you have to say—"

"Daxar Ies wasn't the Emperor's *accountant*," she interrupted. "He was an Imperial droid-brain designer." She glanced again at R2-D2. "He designed the Intellex Four, as a matter of fact."

Luke's mind raced back to the year before, to his discovery of the sequestered sector in R2-D2's deep-reserve memory, trying to remember just how much Alema might have learned about those events before fleeing the academy.

"Nice try." Han had clearly noticed her glance toward the droid as well. "But we're not buying it. Just because you heard someone say that Luke was looking for information on the Intellex Four designer—"

"Han, she couldn't have overheard that," Luke said. "She was already gone. We were in flight control when Ghent told us about his disappearance, remember?"

"That doesn't mean she didn't leave bugs all over the place," Han pointed out.

"We didn't—as we are sure your eavesdropping sweeps have already revealed." Alema continued to stare at Luke. "Do you want to find out more about your mother, or not?"

Luke and Leia had long ago guessed the woman in the records R2-D2 had sequestered—Padmé—might be their mother, but hearing someone else say it sent a jolt of elation through him . . . even if he *did* feel certain that the Dark Nest was counting on exactly that reaction.

Han was more cynical. "So Anakin Skywalker was making holorecordings of his girlfriend—I know a lot of guys who used to do the same thing. It doesn't mean she's Luke's mother."

"But it means she *could* be—and we can help Master Skywalker learn the truth." Alema shot Luke a sardonic smile. "Unless you prefer ignorance to knowing that Mara has been deceiving you. Daxar Ies was no accountant. He was the one being who could have helped you unlock the secret of your mother's past."

"Nice story," Han said. "Hangs together real well—until you get to the part where Daxar Ies is the Intellex Four designer. Why would the Emperor have his best droid-brain designer *killed*?"

Alema's face grew enigmatic and empty. "Who knows? Revenge, perhaps, or merely to keep him from defecting to the Rebels, too. That is not as important as the reason Mara lied to you about who he is."

"I'm listening." Even saying the words made Luke feel hollow and sick inside, as though he were betraying Mara by hearing the Twi'lek out. "For now."

Alema wagged her finger. "First, what *we* want."

"That does it," Han said. He thumbed the selector switch on his blaster to full power. "I'm tired of being played. I'm just going to blast her now."

Alema's gaze went automatically to Luke.

Luke shrugged and stepped out of the line of fire. "Okay, if you have to."

"Please . . . ," Alema said sarcastically. She flicked a finger, and the selector switch on Han's blaster flipped itself back to stun. "If you were really going to blast me, you wouldn't stand here discussing it."

"You're right." Han flicked the selector switch back to full power. "We're done dis—"

"Perhaps you will be more inclined to hear us out after we have proved that we can access the records," Alema said to Luke. She gestured at R2-D2. "May we?"

Luke motioned Han to wait. "May you what?"

"Display one of the holos, of course," Alema said. When Luke did not automatically grant permission, she glanced up and added, "If we wished to harm him, Master Skywalker, we would already have sprinkled him with froth."

Luke looked up at growing blister on the ceiling, then let out a breath. Alema was telling the truth about that much, at least—it would have been a simple matter to use the Force to pull some of the gray froth down on them. He nodded and stepped aside.

As the Twi'lek approached, R2-D2 let out a fearful squeal and began to retreat as fast as his wheels would carry him. Alema simply reached out with the Force and floated him back over to her.

"Artoo, please show . . ." She paused and turned to Luke. "What would you like to see?"

Luke's heart began to pound. He was half afraid that Alema's claims would prove hollow—and half afraid they would not. While he was extremely eager to find some way to retrieve the data that did not involve reprogramming R2-D2's personality, Luke was also keenly aware that the

Dark Nest was trying to manipulate him to ends he did not yet understand.

"You choose."

Alema let out a series of throat-clicks. "Hmmm . . . what would *we* want to know if we had been raised without our mother?" She turned back to the beeping, blinking droid she was holding in the air before her. "We have an idea. Let's look for something that confirms the identity of Master Skywalker's parents, Artoo."

R2-D2 whistled a refusal so familiar that Luke did not even need a translation to know he was claiming to have no such data.

"You mustn't be that way, Artoo," Alema said. "We have your file security override code: Ray-Ray-zero-zero-seven-zero-five-five-five-Trill-Jenth-seven."

"Hey," Han said, "that sounds like an—"

"Account number, yes," Alema said. "Eremay was rather special—she barely knew her own name, but she never forgot a list of numbers or letters."

Artoo let out a defeated trill; then his holoprojector activated. *The image of a beautiful brown-haired, brown-eyed woman—Padmé—appeared before the droid, walking through the air in front of what looked like an apartment wall. After a moment, a young man's back came into the image. He seemed to be sitting on a couch, hunched over some kind of work that was not visible in the hologram.*

Without looking up, the young man said, "I sense someone familiar." The voice was that of Luke's father, Anakin Skywalker. "Obi-Wan's been here, hasn't he?"

Padmé stopped and spoke to Anakin's back. "He came by this morning."

"What did he want?"

Anakin set his work aside and turned around. He appeared tense, perhaps even angry.

Padmé studied him for a moment, then said, "He's worried about you."

"You told him about us, didn't you?"

Anakin stood, and Padmé started walking again. "He's your best friend, Anakin." She passed through a doorway, and the corner of a bed appeared in front of her. "He says you're under a lot of stress."

"And he's not?"

"You have *been moody lately," Padmé said.*

"I'm not moody."

Padmé turned around and faced him. "Anakin . . . don't do this again."

Her beseeching tone seemed to melt Anakin. He turned away, shaking his head, and vanished. "I don't know," he said from outside the image. "I feel . . . lost."

"Lost?" Padmé started after him. "You're always so sure of yourself. I don't understand."

When Anakin returned to the image, he was looking away, his whole body rigid with tension.

"Obi-Wan and the Council don't trust me," he said.

"They trust you with their lives!" Padmé took his arm and pressed it to her side. "Obi-Wan loves you as a son."

Anakin shook his head. "Something's happening." He still would not look at her. "I'm not the Jedi I should be. I'm one of the most powerful Jedi, but I'm not satisfied. I want more, but I know I shouldn't."

"You're only human, Anakin," Padmé said. "No one expects any more."

Anakin was silent for a moment, then his mood seemed to lighten as quickly as it had darkened a moment before, and he turned and placed a hand on her belly.

"I have found a way to save you."

Padmé frowned in confusion. "Save me?"

"From my nightmares," Anakin said.

"Is that what's bothering you?" Padmé's voice was relieved.

Anakin nodded. "I won't lose you, Padmé."

"I'm not going to die in childbirth, Anakin." She smiled, and her voice turned light. "I promise you."

Anakin remained grave. "No, I promise you," he said. "I'm becoming so powerful with my new knowledge of the Force that I'll be able to keep you from dying."

Padmé's voice turned as grave as Anakin's, and she locked eyes with him. "You don't need more power, Anakin. I believe you can protect me from anything . . . just as you are."

This won a smile from Anakin—but it was a small, hard smile filled with secrets and fear, and when they kissed, it seemed to Luke that his father's arms were not embracing so much as claiming.

The hologram ended. R2-D2 deactivated his holoprojector and let out a long, descending whistle.

"No need to apologize, Artoo." Alema's eyes remained fixed on Luke. "The file you chose was excellent—wasn't it, Master Skywalker?"

"It served to illustrate your point," Luke allowed.

"Come now," Alema said. "It confirmed the identity of your mother—just as we promised it would. We're sure you would like to learn what became of her."

"Now that you mention it, yeah," Han said. "One file doesn't prove a thing."

"Nice try." Alema shot Han an irritated scowl. "But one sample is all you get. And we advise you not to try opening any files yourself. The access code changes with each use, and the file will be destroyed. When three files have been lost, the entire chip will self-destruct."

"That would be unfortunate, but not disastrous," Luke said. Though he had little doubt now that the woman in the holos was indeed his mother, his father's brooding nature had left him feeling uneasy inside—and a bit frightened for the woman. "Leia and I have learned a great deal from Old Republic records already. We're fairly certain that the woman in the holos is Padmé Amidala, a former Queen and later Senator of Naboo."

"Will those old records tell you what she looked like when she smiled? How she sounded when she laughed? Why she abandoned you and your sister?" Alema pushed her lip into a pout. "Come, Master Skywalker. We are only asking that you leave Gorog alone. Do that, and each week we will feed you one of the access codes you need to truly know your mother."

Luke paused, insulted that Alema could believe such a ploy would work on him, wondering if there had ever been a time when he could have seemed so unprincipled and self-serving to her.

"You surprise me, Alema," Luke said. "I would never place personal interests above those of the Jedi and the Force. You must know that—even if Gorog doesn't."

"Yeah, but that doesn't mean we're looking for trouble, either," Han added hastily. "We're just here to help with the Fizz. As long as the Dark Nest isn't bothering us, we won't bother it."

"Good." Alema trailed her fingertips across Han's shoulders, smirking as though she had won her concession. "That's all we can ask."

Han shuddered free of her. "Do you mind? I don't want to catch anything."

Alema cocked her brow, more surprised than hurt, then held her hand out to Luke. "If you'll return our lightsaber, we'll let you be on your way." She glanced at the ceiling, which was already starting to froth, then added, "We wouldn't want anything to happen to Artoo."

Luke took the weapon from his belt, but instead of returning it to Alema, he opened the hilt and removed the Adegan focusing crystal from inside.

"It pains me to say this, Alema." He began to squeeze, calling on the Force to bolster his strength, and felt the crystal shatter. "But you are no longer fit to carry a lightsaber."

Alema's eyes flashed with rage. "That means nothing!" Her lekku began to writhe and twitch, but she managed to retain control of herself and turned toward the door. "We'll just build another."

"I know." Luke turned his hand sideways and let the crystal dust fall to the floor. "And I'll take that one away, too."

THREE

The mourners wore gaily patterned tabards brighter than anything Cal Omas had ever imagined a Sullustan owning, but they approached the vault in somber silence, each masc setting a single transpariblock into the seamweld the crypt master had spread for him, each fem taking the weld-rake in her left hand and carefully smoothing the joints.

This being Sullust, and Sullustans being Sullustans, the tomb-walling ceremony followed a rigid protocol, with the crypt master inviting mourners forward according to both their social status and their relationship to the deceased. Admiral Sovv's younglings and seven current wives had placed the first blocks, followed by his grown children and the other husbands of his warren-clan, then by his blood relatives, his closest friends, the two Jedi Masters in attendance—Kenth Hamner and Kyp Durron—and the entire executive branch of Sullust's governing corporation, SoroSuub. Now, with only one gap remaining in the wall, the crypt master summoned Cal Omas forward.

Omas's protocol droid had warned him that before placing the last block, the person called upon at this point was expected to deliver a brief comment of exactly as many words as the deceased's age in standard years. This was not to be a eulogy—recounting the departed's life would have been considered an affront to those present, implying as it did that the other mourners had not known the dead person as well as they thought. Instead, it was to be a simple address from the heart.

Omas took his place in front of the vault and accepted the transpariblock. The thing was far heavier than it looked, but he pulled it close to his body and did his best not to grimace as he turned to face the assembly.

The gathering was huge, filling the entire Catacomb of Eminents and spilling out the doors into the Gallery of Ancestors. The throng contained more than a hundred Alliance dignitaries, but they went almost unnoticed in the sea of Sullustan faces. As the Supreme Commander of the force that had defeated the Yuuzhan Vong, Sien Sovv had been a hero of mythical proportions on Sullust, an administrator and organizer who rivaled the stature of even Luke Skywalker and Han and Leia Solo in other parts of the galaxy.

Omas took a deep breath, then spoke. "I speak for everyone in the Galactic Alliance when I say that we share Sullust's shock and sorrow over the collision that took the lives of Admiral Sovv and so many others. Sien was my good friend, as well as the esteemed commander of the Galactic Alliance military, and I promise you that we *will* bring those who are truly responsible for this tragedy to justice . . . no matter what nebula they try to hide within."

The Sullustans remained silent, their dark eyes blinking up at Omas enigmatically. Whether he had shocked the mourners with his suggestion of foul play or committed some grievous error of protocol, Omas could not say. He knew only that he had spoken from the heart, that he had reached the limits of his patience with the problems the Killiks were causing, and that he intended to act—with or without the Jedi's support.

After a moment, an approving murmur rose from the

back of the crowd and began to rustle forward, growing in volume as it approached. Kenth Hamner and Kyp Durron scowled and peered over their shoulders at the assembly, but if the Sullustan mourners noticed the censure, they paid it no attention. There had already been rumblings about Master Skywalker's conspicuous absence from the funeral, so no one in the crowd was inclined to pay much attention to the opinions of a pair of bug-loving Jedi.

Once the murmur reached the front of the crowd, the crypt master silenced the chamber with a gesture. He had Omas hoist the heavy transpariblock into place, then invited the mourners to retire to the Gallery of Ancestors, where SoroSuub Corporation was sponsoring a funerary feast truly unrivaled in the history of the planet.

As Omas and the other dignitaries waited for the catacombs to clear, he went over to the two Jedi Masters. Kenth Hamner, a handsome man with a long aristocratic face, served as the Jedi order's liaison to the Galactic Alliance military. He was dressed in his formal liaison's uniform, looking as immaculate and polished as only a former officer could. Kyp Durron had at least shaved and sonismoothed his robe, but his boots were scuffed and his hair remained just unruly enough for the Sullustans to find fault on such a formal occasion.

"I'm happy to see the Jedi were able to send *someone*," Omas said to the pair. "But I'm afraid the Sullustans may read something untoward into Master Skywalker's absence. It's unfortunate he couldn't be here."

Rather than explain Luke's absence, Kenth remained silent and merely looked uncomfortable.

Kyp went on the attack. "You didn't help matters by suggesting that the Killiks were responsible for the accident."

"They were," Omas answered. "The Vratix piloting that

freighter were so drunk on black membrosia, it's doubtful they ever *knew* they had collided with Admiral Sovv's transport."

"That's true, Chief Omas," Kenth said. "But it doesn't mean that the Killiks are responsible for the accident."

"It certainly does, Master Hamner," Omas said. "How many times has the Alliance demanded that the Colony stop sending that poison to our insect worlds? How many times must I warn them that we'll take action?"

Kyp frowned. "You know that the Dark Nest—"

"I *know* that I've been attending funerals all week, Master Hamner," Omas fumed. "I *know* that the Supreme Commander of the Alliance military and more than two hundred members of his staff are dead. I *know* who is responsible—ultimately, utterly, and undeniably responsible—and I know the Jedi have been shielding them ever since Qoribu."

"The Killik situation is complicated." Kenth spoke in a calming voice that immediately began to quell Omas's anger. "And inflaming matters with hasty accusations—"

"Don't you *dare* use the Force on me." Omas stepped close to Kenth and spoke in a low, icy tone. "Sien Sovv and most of his staff-beings are dead, Master Hamner. I will *not* be calmed."

"My apologies, Chief Omas," Kenth said. "But this sort of talk will only make matters difficult."

"Matters are already difficult." Omas lowered his voice to an angry whisper. "You told me yourself that Master Horn suspected this was more than an accident."

"I did," Kenth admitted. "But he hasn't found any evidence to suggest that the Killiks were the ones behind it."

"Has he found any evidence to suggest that someone else was?" Omas demanded.

Kenth shook his head.

"Maybe that's because it *was* only an accident," Kyp

suggested. "Until Master Horn finds some proof, his suspicions are just that—suspicions."

"Taken with what we already know, Master Horn's suspicions are quite enough for *me*," Omas said. "The Killiks must be dealt with—and it's time that you Jedi understood that."

"Hear, hear!" a gurgly Rodian voice called.

Omas glanced over and found Moog Ulur—the Senator from Rodia—eavesdropping with several of his colleagues from barely an arm's length away. To be polite, the Sullustan dignitaries had moved off to a distance of a dozen meters or so—but, of course, Sullustans had better hearing.

Omas straightened his robes. "Gentlemen, I think it's time I made my way to the feast." He turned toward Ulur and the other Senators, then spoke over his shoulder to the two Masters. "Have Master Skywalker contact me at his earliest convenience."

FOUR

DARK NEST II: THE UNSEEN QUEEN

The Queen's Drawing Room smelled of emptiness and dis-
use, with the odor of polishing agents and window cleanser
hanging so thickly in the air that Jacen wondered if the
housekeeping droid needed its dispensing program adjusted.
An octagonal game table rested in the center of the opulent
chamber, directly beneath a Kamarian-crystal chandelier
and surrounded by eight flow-cushion chairs that looked as
though they had never been sat upon. The Force held no
hint of any living presence, but the silence in the chamber
was charged with a sense of danger and foreboding that
made Jacen cold between his shoulder blades.

Jacen's nine-year-old cousin, Ben Skywalker, stepped
closer to his side. "It's creepy in here."

"You noticed. Good." Jacen glanced down at his cousin.
With red hair, freckles, and fiery blue eyes, Ben appeared
typical of many boys his age, more interested in hologames
and shock ball than in studies and training. Yet he had more
innate control over the Force at his age than any person
Jacen had ever known—enough to shut himself off from it
whenever he wished, enough to prevent even Jacen from
sensing just how strong in the Force he really might be.
"What else do you feel?"

"Two people." Ben pointed through a door in the back
of the room. "I think one's a kid."

"Because one has a smaller presence in the Force?" Jacen asked. "That's not always a guide. Sometimes, children have—"

"Not that," Ben interrupted. "I think one's holding the other, and she feels all . . . mushy."

"Fair enough." Jacen would have chuckled, save that he had already sensed through the Force that Ben was right, and he could not understand what Tenel Ka was doing alone in her chambers with a child. It had been nearly a year since their last meeting, but they had spoken several times since—whenever they could arrange a secure HoloNet connection—and Jacen felt certain that she would have told *him* if she had decided to take a husband. "But we shouldn't make assumptions. They can be misleading."

"Right." Ben rolled his eyes. "Shouldn't we get out of here? If a security droid catches us in here, this place is gonna be dust."

"It's all right," Jacen said. "The Queen Mother invited us."

"Then how come you used your memory rub on the guards?" Ben asked. "And why do you keep Force-flashing the surveillance cams?"

"Her message asked me to come in secret," Jacen explained.

"Asked *you*?" Ben furrowed his brow for a moment. "Does she know *I'm* coming?"

"I'm sure she has sensed your presence by now," Jacen said. Spies were so pervasive in the Hapes Cluster that Tenel Ka had asked him not to acknowledge her message, so there had been no opportunity to warn her that he would have to bring Ben along. They were supposed to be on a camping trip to Endor, and a sudden change in plans would have aroused suspicion. "But I know Tenel Ka will be happy to see you."

"Great." Ben cast a longing glance toward the security door behind them. "I'll be the one the security droid blasts."

A motherly voice spoke from the next room. "And why would I do that?"

A large droid with the cherubic face and padded, synthskin chest of a Tendrando Arms Defender Droid—similar to the one who guarded Ben when he was not with Jacen or his parents—stepped into the room. Her massive frame and systems-packed limbs were still close enough to the YVH war droids from which she had been adapted to give her an intimidating appearance.

"Have you been causing any trouble?"

"Not me." Ben glanced up at Jacen. "This was *his* idea."

"Good, then we'll get along just fine." The corners of the droid's mouth rose into a mechanical smile, then she turned her photoreceptors on Jacen. "Jedi Solo, welcome. I am DeDe One-one-A, a Tendrando Arms Defender—"

"Thank you, I'm familiar with your model," Jacen said. "What I don't understand is what Queen Tenel Ka needs with a child protection droid."

The smile vanished from DD-11A's synthskin face. "You don't?" She stepped aside and waved him forward. "Perhaps I should let the Queen Mother explain. She is expecting you in her dressing chamber."

The droid led them into an extravagant bedchamber dominated by a huge bed covered by a crown-shaped canopy. Around it were more couches, armchairs, and writing desks than ten queens could use. Again, the chamber smelled of cleanser and polish, and there was no indentation to suggest that the bed, pillows, or chairs had ever been used.

"Creepier and creepier," Ben said.

"Just be ready." Until Jacen knew what was causing the cold knot between his shoulder blades, he would have preferred to leave Ben somewhere safe—except he had no idea where 'safe' might be, or even if they were the ones in danger. That was the trouble with danger sense—it was just so blasted vague. "You remember that emergency escape I taught you?"

"The Force trick you said to keep really . . ." Ben fell silent and glanced at DD-11A, then his voice grew more subdued. "Yeah, I remember."

DD-11A stopped and swiveled her head around to stare down at Ben. "The Force trick that Jedi Solo said to keep really *what*, Ben?"

Ben's gaze slid away. "Nothing."

The corners of DD-11A's mouth drooped. "Are you keeping secrets, Ben?"

"I'm *trying* to," Ben admitted. "Jacen said—"

"No harm, Ben," Jacen interrupted. Defender Droids were programmed to be suspicious of children's secrets, and this particular Force trick was not one he cared to have investigated. He faced DD-11A. "The secrecy is a security precaution. The trick's effectiveness would be compromised if its nature was revealed."

DD-11A fixed her photoreceptors on Jacen for a moment, then extended a telescoping arm and took Ben by the shoulder. "Why don't you wait here with me, Ben? The Queen Mother wishes to see Jedi Solo alone first." The droid turned to Jacen, then pointed her other arm toward the far side of the chamber. "Through that door."

Jacen did not start toward the door. "I'd rather keep Ben with me."

"The Queen Mother wishes to speak to you alone first." DD-11A made a shooing motion with her hand. "Go on. We'll come along in few minutes."

When the cold knot between Jacen's shoulder blades did

not seem to grow any larger, he nodded reluctantly. "Leave the doors open between us," he said. "And Ben—"

"I know what to do," Ben said. "Go on."

"Okay," Jacen said. "But mind your manners. Remember, you're in a queen's private chambers."

Jacen went through the door into a third room, this one much smaller and less opulent than the first two. One end was filled with shelves and clothing racks, mostly empty, and furnished with full-length mirrors, unused vanities, and overstuffed dressing couches. The other end held a simple sleeping pallet, of the kind Tenel Ka had preferred since her days at the Jedi academy, and a night table containing a chrono and reading lamp.

The Queen Mother herself was through the *next* door, leaning over a small baby crib in what was plainly a nursery. Her red hair hung over one shoulder in a loose fall, and she was dressed in a simple green robe with nursing flaps over both sides of her chest. When she sensed Jacen studying her, she looked up and smiled.

"You cannot see anything from there, Jacen. Come in." Tenel Ka was as beautiful as ever—perhaps even more so. Her complexion was rosy and luminous, and her gray eyes were sparkling with joy. "I have someone to introduce you to."

"So I see." It was all Jacen could do to hide his disappointment. Though he had long known that Tenel Ka's position would require her to take a Hapan husband, this was hardly the way he had expected her to break the news. "Congratulations."

"Thank you." Tenel Ka motioned him over. "Come along, Jacen. She won't bite."

Jacen went to the crib, where a round-faced newborn lay cooing and blowing milk bubbles at Tenel Ka. With hair so thin and downy that it still lacked color and a face more wrinkled than an Ugnaught's, she did not really look like anyone. But when the infant turned to squint up at Jacen, Jacen experienced such a shock of connection that he forgot himself and reached down to touch the child on the chest.

"Go ahead and pick her up, Jacen." Tenel Ka's voice was nearly cracking with excitement. "You do know how to hold a newborn, don't you?"

Jacen was too stunned to answer. He could feel in the Force—and in his heart—that the girl was his, but he could not understand *how.* The child could be no more than a week old, but it had been more than a year since he had even *seen* Tenel Ka.

"Here, let me show you." Tenel Ka slipped her one arm under the baby, cradling the head in her hand, then smoothly scooped the infant up. "Just keep a firm hold, and always support her neck."

Finally, Jacen tore his gaze away from the baby. "How?" he asked. "It's been twelve months—"

"The Force, Jacen." Tenel Ka slipped the baby into Jacen's arms. She groaned a couple of times, then returned to cooing. "I slowed things down. Life will be dangerous enough for our daughter without my nobles knowing *you* are the father."

"*You're* a father?" Ben's voice came from the doorway behind Jacen. "Astral!"

Jacen turned around, his daughter cradled in his arms, and frowned at Ben. "I thought you were waiting in the Royal Bedchamber with DeDe."

"You told DeDe you wanted to keep me with you," Ben countered. "You *asked* if I knew what to do."

"I meant if there was trouble, Ben."

"Oh." Ben came closer. "I thought you meant trip her circuit breaker."

"No." Jacen sighed, then turned to Tenel Ka. "Allow me to present Ben Skywalker, Your Majesty."

Ben took his cue and bowed deeply. "Sorry about your droid. I'll turn her back on if you want."

"In a minute, Ben," Tenel Ka said. "But first, stand up and let me have a look at you. I haven't seen you since you were a baby yourself."

Ben straightened himself and stood there looking nervous while Tenel Ka nodded approvingly.

"I apologize for bringing him unannounced," Jacen said. "But your message said to come immediately, and we were supposed to be on a camping trip while Luke and Mara are in the Utegetu Nebula."

"Jacen's my Master," Ben said proudly.

Tenel Ka cocked her brow. "In my day, apprentices did not address their Masters by their first names."

"It's an informal arrangement," Jacen said. Now was not the time to explain the complicated dynamics of the situation—that while Mara disapproved of much of the Force-lore Jacen had gathered on his five-year journey of discovery, she was truly grateful to him for coaxing Ben out of his long withdrawal from the Force. "I'm working with Ben while he explores his relationship with the Force."

Tenel Ka's eyes flashed with curiosity, but she did not ask the question Jacen knew to be on her mind: why Ben was not exploring that relationship at the Jedi academy like other young Force-adepts.

"So far, I'm the only one Ben feels comfortable using the Force around," Jacen said, answering the unspoken question. He looked at Ben. "But I'm sure that will change once he realizes that the Force is our friend."

"Don't hold your breath," Ben replied. "I'm not interested in all that kid stuff."

"Perhaps one day." Tenel Ka smiled at Ben. "Until then, you're a very lucky young man. You could not ask for a better guide."

"Thanks," Ben said. "And congratulations on the baby. Wait until Uncle Han and Aunt Leia hear—they'll go nova!"

Tenel Ka furrowed her brow. "Ben, you mustn't tell anyone."

"I mustn't?" Ben looked confused. "Why not? Aren't you guys married?"

"No, but that isn't why. The situation is . . ." Tenel Ka looked to Jacen for help. ". . . complicated."

"We *are* in love," Jacen said. "We always have been."

"Fact," Tenel Ka said. "That is all that matters."

"But you're not married—and you had a baby!" Ben's eyes were wide and gleeful. "You guys are gonna be in *so* much trouble!"

Tenel Ka's voice grew stern. "Ben, you must keep this secret. The baby's life will depend on it."

Ben frowned, and the cold knot between Jacen's shoulder blades began to creep down his spine. Even Tenel Ka seemed to be growing pale.

"Ben can keep a secret," Jacen said. "But I think it's time to reactivate DeDe. Ben—"

"On my way." Ben turned and ran for the door.

"Bring her here," Tenel Ka called after him. "And tell her to arm all systems."

The baby began to mewl in Jacen's arms. He took a moment to forge a conscious link to Ben's Force presence, then slipped the child back to Tenel Ka.

"Is this why you asked me to come?" he asked.

"It is why I asked you to come *now*," Tenel Ka corrected. "This feeling has been growing worse for a week."

"And the baby is—"

"A week old."

Jacen's chest began to tighten with anger. "At least we know what they're after. Any idea who—"

"Jacen, I have kept myself in seclusion for months," Tenel Ka said. "And most of my nobles have guessed why. The list of suspects includes every family who has reason to believe the child does not carry their blood."

"Oh." Jacen had forgotten—if he had ever really understood—just how lonely and perilous Tenel Ka's life really was. "So that would include—"

"All of them," Tenel Ka finished.

"Well, at least it's simple," Jacen said. "And I suppose *who* really doesn't matter at the moment."

"Correct," Tenel Ka agreed. "First we defend."

Jacen sensed a sudden confusion in Ben's presence, then saw him coming through the queen's dressing room with DD-11A close on his heels. There was nothing chasing them, but a muffled scurrying sound was arising behind them.

"Insect infestation!" DD-11A reported. "My sensors show a large swarm in the ceiling, advancing toward the nursery."

The baby began to cry in earnest, and Jacen pulled his lightsaber off his utility belt.

"Jacen, it's okay!" Ben cried. "It's Gorog!"

"Gorog?" Jacen began to still himself inside, trying to calm his anger so he could focus on the ripples he felt in the Force. "Are you sure?"

Ben entered the nursery and stopped. "Yeah."

"Who is Gorog?" Tenel Ka asked. The scurrying sound was drawing closer. "And what is he doing in my vents?"

"They," Jacen corrected. He found a set of ripples that seemed to be coming from a cold void in the Force and knew Ben was right. "*Gorog* is the Killik name for the Dark Nest."

"The Dark Nest?" Tenel Ka used the Force to depress a wall button, then turned to Ben. "Why is it okay to have the Dark Nest in my air vents?"

"They're not *in* your vents." Ben's eyes were fixed on the ceiling above the closing door. "Your vents are shielded and lined with security lasers."

Jacen's heart sank. For Ben to know so much about the insects' entry route suggested that even after a year apart, he remained sensitive to Gorog's collective mind—and perilously close to becoming a Joiner.

"Very well." Tenel Ka began to rock the baby gently, and her crying faded back to mewling. "What is the Dark Nest doing in my *ceiling*?"

"They have a contract." Ben furrowed his brow for a moment, then turned to Jacen. "I don't understand. They want to—"

"I know, Ben," Jacen said. "We won't allow it."

The scurrying noise stopped outside the nursery door, still in the ceiling, then rapidly built to a gnawing sound. Ben stared up toward the sound, his face pinched into a mask of fear and conflict.

"You can't!" He seemed to be speaking to the insects. "She's only a little kid!"

The gnawing grew louder, and the indecision suddenly vanished from Ben's expression. "They're almost through." He rushed to the rear of the nursery, though there was no exit there that Jacen could see, and began to pull at the sides of a tall shelving cabinet. "We have to get her out, now!"

"Ben, calm down." Jacen began to study the floor, reaching into the Force to see if there was anyone in the room below them. "Losing your head—"

"Ben, how do you know about the escape tunnel?" Tenel Ka interrupted. "Did you find it through the Force?"

"No," Jacen said, answering for Ben. Joiners had trouble separating their own thoughts from those of the collective mind of the nest. He used the Force to pull Ben away from the cabinet, then said, "Gorog told him."

Ben scowled. "No way!" He tried to go back to the cabinet. "I just knew."

"*Gorog* knew," Jacen countered. He activated his lightsaber, then plunged it into the floor and began to cut a large circle. "And if *they* want you to open that door—"

"—*we* don't." Tenel Ka reached out with the Force and pulled Ben to her side. "Let us do this Jacen's way."

A loud metallic patter sounded inside the cabinet Ben had tried to open and quickly changed to a cacophony of scratching and scraping. Jacen continued to cut his circle in the floor, at the same time trying to puzzle out who had contracted the Dark Nest to attack Tenel Ka's child—and how. The Gorog were notoriously difficult to locate—the Jedi had not even been certain the nest had survived the battle at Qoribu until about three months ago—and experience suggested they were far too interested in their own agenda to accept an assassination contract for credits alone. So whoever had hired the nest possessed the resources to find it in the first place—and to provide whatever the Dark Nest had asked in return.

The gnawing above suddenly grew more distinct, and a section of ceiling dropped to the floor. Jacen lifted his free hand toward the hole, but DD-11A was already taking aim. As the first cloud of insects began to boil down into the room, her wrist folded down and discharged a crackling plume of fire.

Ben screamed and began to thrash about, trying to break free of Tenel Ka's Force grasp.

"Ben, stop it!" Tenel Ka ordered. The baby was wailing in her arm now. "We cannot let theeemmmargh—"

Tenel Ka's command ended in a startled cry as Ben whirled on her with an untrained but powerful Force shove. She slammed into the corner two meters above the floor, her head hitting with a sharp crack, her eyes rolling back and her shoulders slumping, but her arm never slackening beneath the crying baby.

Jacen used the Force to gently guide Tenel Ka to the floor, then turned to find Ben leaping toward DD-11A's up-raised arm. His eyes were bulging and he was screaming at the droid not to burn his friends, and Jacen was too un-nerved by his young cousin's anger—and the raw Force-strength he had displayed—to take the chance of being gentle. He extended his arm and used the Force to pull Ben into his grasp, grabbing him by the throat.

"Enough!" Jacen pinched down on the carotid arteries on the sides of the neck. "Sleep!"

Ben gurgled once; then his eyes rolled back in his head and he sank into a deep slumber that would not end until the Force command was lifted. There was a time, before Vergere and the war with the Yuuzhan Vong, when Jacen would have felt guilty for having to use such a powerful attack on a nine-year-old boy. But now all that mattered was protecting Tenel Ka and the baby, and Jacen felt nothing but relief as he laid his young cousin aside.

He cut through a few more centimeters of floor, and the ferrocrete substructure began to sag. He continued cutting until he judged that the droid's mass would be enough to fold the circle down like a trapdoor, then shut off his lightsaber and stepped to DD-11A's side.

The hole above the droid's head was rimmed with white foam from the palace's fire-suppression system, but the

Gorog were not foolish enough to peer out of the same hole DD-11A had just blasted with flame. Instead Jacen could hear the insects scurrying past overhead, spreading out across the ceiling and beginning to gnaw in several different places.

"What do you have that can generate a good-sized fireball?" Jacen asked DD-11A.

"Grenades." The droid pivoted around to the other side of the hole and sprayed a stream of fire at a line of scurrying, blue-black shadows. "Two each, thermal, concussion, and flash—"

"That'll do. Here's what I want you to do."

Jacen outlined his plan, then gathered Ben in his arms and retreated to the corner with Tenel Ka and the baby. The Gorogs in the secret tunnel had scratched their way into the cabinet, and the tips of hundreds of tiny blue-black pincers were beginning to protrude through the thin line between the doors.

Jacen laid Ben beside Tenel Ka, then pointed. "DeDe!"

The droid swiveled around and poured flame into the crack. A trio of fire-suppression nozzles popped down to coat the doors with suppressant, but by then black wisps of smoke were already seeping out the back of the cabinet.

Jacen pulled his cloak off and held it in front of them at chin height.

"Okay, go!"

DD-11A's photoreceptors lingered on the cloak. "Your camouflage is inadequate. I can't leave the child with you."

"It's . . . fine." Tenel Ka's voice was groggy, but firm. "Do as Jacen commands."

Jacen was already immersing himself in the Force, allowing it to flow through him as fast as his body would allow. Small pieces of plasrock began to rain from the ceiling. DD-11A raised her arm and began to spray flame into the holes, but openings were appearing faster than even a droid could target. Still, DD-11A did not move to obey.

"Now, Honeygirl!" Tenel Ka snapped.

DD-11A's head swiveled around. "Override command accepted."

The droid stepped into the sagging circle Jacen had cut in the floor. The flap gave way beneath her weight and folded down, and she crashed into the room below.

Jacen exhaled in relief, then glanced over his shoulder and touched the corner behind them, forming a complete sensory image of how the walls looked and smelled and felt, even of the nearly inaudible sounds coming from the pipes and ducts concealed inside, then looked forward again and quickly expanded the image into the Force.

The baby continued to cry.

Tenel Ka started to open one of her nursing flaps, hoping to silence the child by feeding her, but Jacen stopped her. He *needed* that crying.

Instead of *allowing* the Force to flow through his body, he began to use his fear and anger to consciously pull it through. His skin began to nettle and his head to ache, and still he continued to draw the Force, catching his daughter's wailing voice in the stillness of its depths, sending the sound streaming down through the floor after DD-11A, not allowing it to return to the surface until it had overtaken the metallic clank of the droid's receding footsteps.

He was almost too late. The fire retardant had barely started to drip from the holes DD-11A had left in the ceiling before clouds of tiny blue-black Killiks began to drop into the room on their droning wings. They were much smaller than the assassin bugs that had attacked Mara and Saba the year before, only a little larger than Jacen's thumb. But they had the same bristly antennae and black bulbous eyes, and they all had long, venom-dripping proboscises protruding between a pair of sharply curved mandibles.

Instead of dropping down through the hole, the Gorog simply seemed to swirl about the room, gathering in an ever-darkening swarm, ignoring the hole in the floor and the sound decoys Jacen had arranged. They began to land on the cabinet that concealed the escape tunnel and on the surrounding walls, on the door that closed off Tenel Ka's dressing chamber, on the empty crib in the center of the nursery.

A few even came and landed on the cloak that Jacen was using as the basis of his Force illusion, and when a pair of Gorog started to hover in the air above the top edge of the cloak, he feared his plan would fail. The illusions he had learned to craft from the Adepts of the White Current were powerful, but even they would not keep an insect crawling in midair. Jacen began to think that he had overreached in planning to take out the entire swarm at once; he should have settled for leaving DD-11A behind to slow the assassins while he and Tenel Ka fled with Ben and the baby.

Then suddenly Tenel Ka's palm was there for the insects to land on, and the illusion held.

Jacen looked over and saw the baby floating on a cushion of Force levitation, her head resting on the stump of Tenel Ka's amputated arm and her feet kicking the empty air.

A tense moment later, the cabinet doors clanged open. The insects on Tenel Ka's palm and Jacen's robe sprang into the air, joining the black fog of Killiks that came growling into the nursery, and the whole boiling mass swirled down through the floor in pursuit of DD-11A and the sound of the baby's crying voice.

Jacen maintained the illusion until the last insect had followed, then continued to maintain it for another hundred heartbeats. When no sound in the room remained except the pounding of their own hearts, he waited *another* hundred heartbeats, his eyes scanning every dark corner of the nursery, searching the shadows for any hint of blue carapace, examining the Force for ripples with no tangible source.

An uneasy feeling remained in the Force, but the ripple pattern was too diffuse and confused for Jacen to locate the observers Gorog had almost certainly left to watch the nursery. Still, the swarm would catch up to DD-11A any instant and discover it had been fooled.

Jacen dropped his illusion, then reached out in the Force and began to pull the folded circle of floor back into place. The ferrocrete substructure rose with a loud, grating shriek, and he felt the Force ripple as the swarm reversed course.

A handful of blue-black insects rose into the air from the dark corners of the nursery and came streaking toward the corner. Tenel Ka's lightsaber sizzled to life behind Jacen, and one of the bugs burst into a yellow spray as she Force-smashed it against the wall.

Jacen finished pulling the floor section back into place, then flung his cloak up in front of the approaching insects and used the Force to pin them against the wall. The tough molytex lining lasted about a second before the tips of their slashing mandibles started to work through.

Jacen sprang across the room, Force-leaping over the crib, and smashed the insects beneath the pommel of his lightsaber.

A loud bang sounded from the corner as Tenel Ka's lightsaber ignited the methane sac the assassin bugs carried inside their carapaces as a final surprise. He glanced over to see Tenel Ka trying to blink the spots from her eyes, her lightsaber weaving a defensive shield in front of her. The

baby lay crying in the corner behind her, and two more insects were flitting around her knees, trying to dodge past
her guard to attack.

Jacen stretched out in the Force and nudged them both
into the path of her turquoise blade. They detonated with a
brilliant flash that left stars dancing before his eyes and the
baby screeching louder than ever, but Jacen sensed no pain
in the infant, only fear and alarm.

Realizing he still had not heard the *carumpf* of DeDe's
first grenade, Jacen started to reach for his comlink—then
heard a muffled drone building behind him and spun around
to find the first Gorog crawling through the seam his blade
had left in the floor.

"*Now*, DeDe!" Jacen screamed at the floor. He jumped
into the center of the circle and began to drag his lightsaber
along the seam, igniting the insects before they could take
flight. "What's taking so—"

A sharp jolt struck Jacen in the pit of his stomach, then
suddenly he found himself kneeling in the middle of the circle, surrounded by a curtain of yellow flame, the air filled
with the naphthalene smell of a thermal grenade.

"About—"

He was jolted by another explosion, and this time he was
unsurprised enough to feel the floor buck as more flames
came shooting up through the seam.

"—time."

The floor bucked another time, then another, and suddenly white foam was showering down from the ceiling,
smothering the smoke and the fumes beneath the soapy
clean smell of flame retardant. A series of wet thuds sounded
on the surrounding floor as the foam weighed down the
handful of Gorog assassins that had escaped DD-11A's
grenades.

The insects immediately turned toward the corner and

began to scurry toward where Tenel Ka was kneeling with the baby and Ben. Jacen used the Force to sweep them all back toward him, then batted them into oblivion with a single stroke of his lightsaber. They exploded brilliantly, but Jacen did not allow himself to look away. He was too afraid of letting one of the creatures slip past his blade.

A moment later, with spots still dancing before his eyes, he turned toward the corner. "Are you okay?" he asked Tenel Ka. "Both of you?"

"We are fine," she answered. "It is Ben I worry about."

"Don't." Though Jacen knew Ben's behavior had not been the boy's fault, he could not quite keep the anger he felt out of his voice. "I don't think Gorog would hurt him. He's practically a Joiner."

"I am not worried about what Gorog did to him," Tenel Ka answered. "I am worried about those bruises on his throat."

Jacen stood, his vision clearing, and went to his young cousin's side. The impression of his thumb and forefinger were purple and deep, clearly made in anger, but Ben's breathing was regular and untroubled.

"There's no need to worry." Jacen placed his fingers over the bruises and touched Ben through the Force. "They'll fade in no time."

Tenel Ka frowned. "That is not the point, Jacen."

Jacen looked up. "Then what is?"

A globule of fire retardant dropped off the wall and splatted at Tenel Ka's feet. There were no insects inside, but she stomped on it anyway.

"Never mind. I will tell you later." She stepped past Jacen and started toward the door to her dressing room. "We need to leave here. If I know my grandmother, she already knows that her first attempt failed."

"Your grandmother?" Jacen lifted Ben in his arms and followed. "You think Ta'a Chume is behind this?"

"I *know* she is," Tenel Ka said. She stopped at the door and faced Jacen with narrowed eyes. "The only ones who know about the escape tunnel are the Queen Mother . . . and the *former* Queen Mother."

FIVE

The route to Cilghal's lab on Ossus was as meandering as any across the academy grounds, winding through a labyrinth of shrubbery and detouring past carefully planned vistas, following a path of tightly placed stepping-stones that deliberately forced walkers to slow down and contemplate the garden. Even so, Leia's gaze kept coming back to the stasis jar in her hands. The glob suspended inside was pulsating like a silvery heart, growing larger each time it expanded, trembling a little more noticeably each time it contracted. She shuddered to think what might happen if the mysterious froth exploded over the interior of the jar. Anything that throbbed inside a stasis field could probably eat its way through seven millimeters of nonreactive safety glass.

The path rounded a gentle bend, and a dozen meters ahead, the trapezoidal span of Clarity Gate framed a tranquil courtyard accented by a small fountain. Leia passed under the crosspieces without stopping, then turned toward an opening to one side of the fountain—and heard a disapproving hiss behind her.

"This one is shocked at the forgetfulnesz of her student," Saba rasped. "What must a Jedi do as she enterz the academy groundz?"

Leia rolled her eyes and turned to face the Barabel. "We don't have time to meditate right now, Master."

Saba blinked twice, then clasped her claws together and remained standing on the other side of the gateway.

"Really." Leia went back through the gate and tapped the side of the jar. "Look at this stuff."

Saba looked, then said, "That is no excuse for ignoring the rulez."

"We don't have *time* for rules," Leia said. "We need to get this jar to Cilghal."

"And the sooner you complete your meditationz, the sooner we will do that."

"Saba—"

A rumble sounded low in Saba's throat.

"*Master* Sebatyne," Leia corrected, "don't you think Luke would want us to hurry?"

The Barabel tipped her head and glared down at Leia out of one eye. "You are doing it again."

"Doing *what*?"

"*Reasoning*. That is a skill you have already mastered." Saba's tone grew stern. "What you have not yet learned is obedience."

"I'm sorry, Master." Leia was growing exasperated. "I promise to work on that later, but right now I'm more worried about this stuff getting loose inside the academy."

"It is when we are alarmed that meditation is most important." Saba reached for the stasis jar. "This one will hold the froth so you can concentrate."

Realizing that her determination was no match for a Barabel's stubbornness, Leia reluctantly yielded the stasis jar. She focused her attention on the fountain, watching its silver spray umbrella into the air, listening to it rain back into the pool, and began a Jedi breathing exercise. She grew aware of the crisp scent of anti-algal agents and the coolness of mist on her skin. But even that faded after a moment, and she was left with only her breathing to concentrate on . . . *in through the nose* . . . *out through the mouth* . . . and the knots inside her started to come undone.

Leia began to realize that she was not worried about the froth at all. She had seen on Woteba that it did not disintegrate anything instantly. Even if the glob were to explode inside the stasis jar, she would still have plenty of time to reach Cilghal's lab and contain it in something else.

What troubled her was Han—or, rather, Han's absence. She felt guilty about having to leave him on Woteba, especially to honor a promise *Luke* had made . . . and especially knowing how he felt about "bugs." Even more than that, everything just seemed wrong. It was the first time in years she had traveled more than a few hundred thousand kilometers without Han, and it felt as if a part of her was missing. It was as if an MD droid had removed the wisecracking part of her brain, or she had suddenly lost a third arm.

And Leia knew that her sister-in-law felt much the same about Luke. After landing on Ossus, the first thing Mara had done was head for the Skywalkers' apartment to see if Ben was back from his camping trip with Jacen. She had claimed she only wanted to be sure that the academy rumor mill did not alarm him with a tangled version of why Luke had not returned with the *Falcon,* but Leia had sensed the same hollow in her sister-in-law that she felt in herself. Mara had been trying to fill the uncomfortable void caused by leaving Luke behind, to reassure herself that her family's life would quickly return to normal . . . just as soon as Cilghal told them how to stop the froth.

Leia was about to end her meditation when it was ended for her by Corran Horn's throaty voice.

"Where's Master Skywalker?" Corran entered the small

courtyard via a path leading from the academy administration building. He was dressed in breeches, tunic, and vest, all in various shades of brown. "The hangar chief said he didn't disembark from the *Falcon*."

"Neither did Han," Leia said. Judging by the expression of shock that flashed across Corran's face, she had not quite managed to conceal the irritation she felt at being tracked down even before her legs had grown accustomed to Ossan gravity again. "They stayed on Woteba to guarantee our good intentions."

Corran lowered his thick brows. "Guarantee?"

"Woteba is having a Fizz problem." Saba lifted the stasis jar toward Corran's face.

He frowned at the silvery froth inside. "A Fizz problem?"

"It's corrosive . . . *very*." Leia told him what was happening to the Saras and their nest, then added, "The Colony believes the Jedi knew about the problem all along, *before* we convinced them to relocate their nests from Qoribu."

Corran's face fell, and alarm began to fill the Force around him. "So Master Skywalker stayed behind to convince them we *hadn't*?"

"Not exactly." Leia began to grow alarmed herself. "And Han stayed, too. What's wrong?"

"More than I thought." He took Leia's elbow and tried to guide her toward a bench near the fountain. "Maybe I should go get Mara. She'll need to hear this, too."

Leia pulled free and stopped. "Blast it, Corran, just tell me what's wrong!"

Saba rumbled low in her throat, a gentle reminder to follow the rules.

"Sorry." Leia kept her eyes fixed on Corran. "Okay, *Master* Horn—tell me what the chubba is going on!"

Saba nodded approvingly, and Corran nodded cautiously.

"Very well. Chief Omas has been trying to get Master Skywalker on the HoloNet all morning. The Chiss are furious—transports are landing Killiks on planets all along their frontier." Corran's tone grew worried. "It's beginning to look like the Killiks have this whole thing planned out."

"Or the Dark Nest does." Leia turned to Saba, then pointed at the froth inside the jar. "Can you think of a better way to destroy our relationship with the Colony?"

"Perhapz," she said. "But the Fizz is working well enough. It has already turned Raynar and Unu against us."

"And now the Colony has Han and Luke for hostages," Corran said. Signaling them to follow, he turned toward the path that led toward academy administration. "Chief of State Omas needs to hear about this as soon as possible."

"No, he doesn't." Leia started toward the opposite corner of the courtyard, toward the path that led to the academy science wing. "We should handle this ourselves."

"I have no doubt we will," Corran said, speaking to Leia across several meters of paving stone. "But our first duty is to report the situation to Chief Omas."

"So the Galactic Alliance can start blustering and making threats?" Leia shook her head. "That will only polarize things. What we need to do is get this stuff to Cilghal so she can tell us how the Dark Nest is producing it—and give us enough proof to convince Raynar and Unu."

Corran scowled, but reluctantly started toward Leia's side of the courtyard.

"No," Saba said. She placed a scaly hand on Leia's shoulder and pushed her toward Corran. "This one will see to the froth. You may help Master Horn with his report."

"Report?" Leia stopped and turned back toward the Barabel. "Did you hear what I just said?"

"Of course," Saba said. "But you did not hear what *this* one said. It is not your place to question Master Horn'z decision."

This shocked even Corran. "Uh, that's all right, Master Sebatyne. Princess Leia is a special case—"

"Indeed. She knowz how to give orderz already." Saba's gaze shifted to Leia. "Now she must learn to take them. She will help you with your report, if you still think that is best."

"I *know* how to take orders," Leia fumed. "I was an officer in the Rebellion."

"Good. Then this will not be a difficult lesson for you."

Saba started down the path toward Cilghal's lab, leaving Leia standing beside Corran with a stomach so knotted in anger, it felt like she had been punched. She knew what Saba was doing—teaching her how to fight from a position of weakness—but *now* was not the time for lessons. The lives of her husband and her brother would be placed at risk if she lost, and Corran Horn could teach even Barabels a thing or two about stubbornness.

Once Saba was beyond earshot, Corran leaned close to Leia. "Tough Master," he observed in a quiet voice. "Did you really pick her yourself?"

"I did," Leia admitted. "I wanted someone who would challenge me in new ways."

"Hmm." Corran considered the explanation a moment, then asked, "Well, is training with her what you expected?"

"More rules and less sparring." Leia fell silent a moment, then grew serious. "Corran—Master Horn—you don't actually intend to send that report to Chief Omas, do you?"

Corran studied her for a moment, then said, "I always

did." He started down the path toward academy administration. "Now that Saba's pulled rank for me, I guess there's no harm in admitting that I just didn't see any point in arguing with you about it."

Leia nodded. "Silence is not agreement." Feeling a little foolish for forgetting one of the first lessons she had learned as a Chief of State, she started to follow. "But you know what will happen when Chief Omas hears that Luke has been taken hostage by Killiks."

"He'll demand that they release him."

"And the Killiks will refuse. Then he'll threaten them, and they'll draw in on themselves, and we'll have no chance at all of convincing the Colony to withdraw from the Chiss frontier peacefully."

"If you were the Chief of State, you'd be free to handle it differently," Corran said. "But you're not. Cal Omas deserves to know what's happening."

"Even if it means sacrificing control of the Jedi order?"

Corran stopped. "What are you talking about?"

"I think you know," Leia said. "The Chief of State has been frustrated with the Jedi since the Qoribu crisis. He thinks we've put the good of the Killiks above the good of the Alliance. With Luke out of contact, you don't think Omas would jump at the chance to take control of the order and make sure our priorities are what he believes they should be?"

Corran frowned, but more in thought than alarm. "He could do that?"

"If the Jedi were divided, yes. I know how strongly you believe our mission is to serve the Alliance. But you *do* see how dangerous it would be for the order to fall under the Chief of State's direct control?"

"Of course. The will of the government is not always the will of the Force." Corran fell silent for a moment, then finally shook his head and started walking again. "You're worrying about nothing, Princess. Omas will never take direct control of the Jedi order."

Leia started after him. "You can't know that."

"I can," Corran insisted. "The Masters may disagree on a lot, but never that. It could lead to the Jedi becoming a political tool."

Leia followed him down a narrow promenade flanked by more cedrum trees, cursing Saba for insisting that they continue training even in the middle of a crisis. What did Saba expect her to do, hit Corran over the head with a rock? It would have been such a simple matter for the Barabel to pull rank on *him* instead of goading him into doing the same to her. After all, Corran was the newest Master, promoted on the basis of his actions during the war against the Yuuzhan Vong, the disruption of several pirate rings, and having trained an apprentice—a young Jedi named Raltharan whom Leia had never met. Saba, on the other hand, was a highly respected member of the Advisory Council who had produced more than a dozen highly skilled Jedi Knights before she had even *seen* Luke Skywalker.

The path descended to a shallow brook and continued across the water via a zigzag course of stepping-stones, but Leia stopped at the edge and simply stared at Corran's back. In sparring practice, Saba was always rasping at her to stop making things hard on herself; to save her own strength by using the attacker's against him.

Leia smiled, then called, "Master Horn?"

Corran stopped with his feet balanced precariously on two rocks. "There's no sense discussing this any further," he said, looking back over his shoulder. "My mind is made up."

"I know that." Leia looked to her side, where a winding stone-chip walkway snaked along the edge of the brook toward the academy residences. "But before you make your report, shouldn't you tell Mara? You owe that much to her, if you're determined to place her husband's life in danger."

"Danger?" Corran's face fell, his green eyes blazing with conflict as he realized that performing his duty to Chief Omas would mean betraying his personal loyalty to Luke. "Chief Omas wouldn't push things that far."

"I'm not the Master here," Leia said, shrugging. "You'll have to decide that for yourself."

Corran did not even need time to think. His chin simply dropped, then he swung a leg around and started back across the stepping-stones.

"You win," he said. "This isn't something I should decide on my own."

"Maybe not," Leia allowed.

Corran stepped off the last stone and gave Leia an exaggerated frown.

"No gloating at Masters," he said. "Hasn't Saba taught you anything?"

SIX

The big hoversled emerged from behind a massive hamogoni trunk and skimmed across the forest floor, crashing through the underbrush and weaving around bustling crews of insect loggers. Han slipped the landspeeder he was piloting behind a different trunk, this one at least twenty meters across, then stopped and took a moment to gawk around the grove of giants. Many of the trees were larger than Balmorran skyscrapers, with knee-roots the size of dewbacks and boughs that hung out horizontally like enormous green balconies. Unfortunately, most of those balconies were shuddering beneath the droning saws of Saras lumberjacks, and a steady cascade of branch trimmings was raining down from above.

"Okay, Han," Luke said. He was sitting in the passenger's seat beside Han, using a comlink and datapad to follow the tracking beacon they had planted on their quarry back in Saras nest. "The signal's getting scratchy."

Han cautiously moved the landspeeder out of its hiding place, then, when they saw no visible sign of their quarry, hurried after the hoversled. In mountainous terrain like this, a scratchy signal could quickly turn into no signal at all, so they needed to close the distance fast. He dodged past a crew trimming the sprigs off a log as big around as a bantha, then decelerated hard as something big and bark-covered fell across their path. A tremendous boom shook the landspeeder, rocking it back on its rear floater pads, and the route ahead was suddenly blocked by a wall of hamogoni log twelve meters high.

Han sat there, waiting for his heart to stop hammering, until a shower of boughs and sticks, knocked loose by the falling tree, began to hit the ground around them.

"Perhaps Master Luke should drive," C-3PO suggested from the backseat. "He has taken better care of himself over the years, and his reaction time is point-four-two second faster."

"Oh, yeah? If we'd been point-four-two seconds farther ahead, you'd be a foil smear right now." Han jammed the landspeeder into reverse and hit the power, then said to Luke, "Okay, I give up. How are these guys leading us to the Dark Nest?"

Luke shrugged. "I don't know yet." His eyes remained fixed on the datapad, as though he had not noticed how close they had just come to being crushed. "But the barrels they're carrying are filled with reactor fuel and hyperdrive coolant. Do you see anything out here that needs so much power?"

"I haven't seen anything on this whole planet that needs that much power." Han started the landspeeder forward again and began a hundred-meter detour around the fallen tree. "That doesn't mean our smugglers are headed for the Dark Nest."

"It's the best explanation I can think of," Luke said.

"Yeah? What would the Dark Nest do with hyperdrive coolant? And that much reactor fuel?"

"I don't know yet," Luke repeated. "That's what scares me."

Han rounded the crown of the fallen tree, drawing a cacophony of alarmed drumming as he nearly ran into a line

of Saras loggers scurrying toward the tree from the opposite side. A few of the insects carried modern laser cutters,
but most were equipped with primitive chain saws—or even
long, double-ended logging saws powered by hand. C-3PO
thrummed a polite apology; then the Killiks opened a hole
in their line, and Han took the landspeeder over to where
the hoversled had disappeared.

"Blast!" Luke said, still staring at his datapad. "We lost
the signal."

"Don't need it," Han said. He swung the landspeeder
onto a deep-cut track—it was not quite a road—that led in
the same direction the smugglers had gone. "I'll follow my
nose."

"Your nose?" Luke looked up, then said, "Oh."

They followed the track over a knoll, then found themselves looking into a valley of mud and giant tree stumps.
The smugglers, four Aqualish and a flat-faced Neimoidian,
were about three hundred meters down the slope, parked
outside the collapsed stone foundation of what had once
been a very large building. The Aqualish had hoisted one of
their fuel barrels onto a hamogoni stump that was two meters high and as big around as a Star Destroyer's thrust nozzle. The Neimoidian—presumably the leader—was standing
next to the barrel, talking to half a dozen Killiks. With
bristly antennae, barbed, hugely curved mandibles, and dark
blue chitin, they were clearly Gorog—the Dark Nest.

The Neimoidian held something up to the light, examining it between his thumb and forefinger, then nodded and
slipped the object into a pouch hanging beneath his robes.
The closest insect handed him something else, and he began
to examine that.

Han ducked behind a giant stump and brought the landspeeder to a halt. "Sometimes I hate it when you're right,"

he said to Luke. "But I'm not crawling down any bug holes with you. I'm through with that."

Luke grinned a little. "Sure you are."

"I'm serious," Han warned. "If you go there, you're on your own."

"Whatever you say, Han."

Luke pulled a pair of electrobinoculars from the landspeeder console, then slipped out of the passenger's seat and disappeared around the side of the tree stump. Han shut the vehicle down and told C-3PO to keep an eye on things, then joined Luke behind a lateral root so high that he had to stand on his toes to peer over the top.

"Interesting," Luke said. He passed the electrobinoculars to Han. "Have a look."

Han adjusted the lenses. The Neimoidian was examining a reddish brown mass about the size of a human thumb, shaped roughly like a tear and so transparent that Han could see a tiny silver light glimmering in its core. After studying the lump a moment, the Neimoidian placed it in his pouch and held out his hand. The closest Gorog placed in it another globule, this one so cloudy that the Neimoidian did not even bother raising it to his eye before he tossed it aside.

"Star amber?" Han asked, lowering the electrobinoculars.

Luke nodded. "At least now we know where it's . . ." He spun toward their landspeeder, his hand dropping toward his lightsaber, then finished his sentence in a whisper. ". . . been coming from."

"Why are you whispering?" Han whispered. He pulled his blaster from its holster. "I *hate* it when you whisper."

Luke raised his finger to his lips, then slipped over the root they had been hiding behind and started around the stump, moving *away* from their landspeeder. Han followed, holding the electrobinoculars in one hand and his blaster in the other. The route took them into full view of the smugglers and the insects down the slope. Luke flicked his fingers, and the entire group turned to look in the opposite direction. Han would have accused him of cheating, except that just then C-3PO's voice came over their comlinks.

"Be careful, Master Luke! They're trying to come—"

The warning ended in string of metallic thunks. A loud boom echoed across the valley, and black smoke billowed up behind the stump. Han scrambled over another lateral root and raced the rest of the way around the stump behind Luke.

They came up behind the fuming wreckage of their landspeeder, which sat on the ground surrounded by a pool of fuel and cooling fluid that had spread halfway up the tree stump. C-3PO was standing two meters in front of the vehicle, looking scorched and soot-covered and leaning forward at the waist to peer around the tree stump. R2-D2 had jetted himself onto the top of the stump and was wheeling along the edge, using his arm extension to hold out a mirror and spy on something moving along around the base.

Luke signaled Han to continue around the stump, then Force-jumped up with R2-D2. Han crept up behind C-3PO.

"Back here, Threepio," he whispered. "What have we got—"

C-3PO straightened and turned to face him. "What a relief!" he exclaimed. "I was afraid they were going to come on you from behind."

A familiar scurrying sound rose from down the slope, just out of sight around the stump, and Han suddenly felt sick to his stomach.

"Thanks for the warning," Han growled. He thrust the electrobinoculars at C-3PO and raced for cover next to the stump. "Get back, *now*."

Han barely managed to kneel partway inside a small hollow before six Gorog Killiks scuttled into view. It was about what he had been expecting, but being right only made him more queasy. He just couldn't handle bugs, not since those crazy Kamarians had tracked him down on Regulgo . . . but he couldn't think about that now, not if he wanted to keep control of himself.

"Okay, fellas, stop right there. Drop those . . ." Han hesitated when he realized that it was not blaster pistols the insects were holding. ". . . shatter guns and tell me why you shot up my landspeeder."

The Gorog began to thrum, raising their weapons as they turned.

"You *know* why," C-3PO translated. "The Night Herald told you to stay out of Gorog's business."

"Too bad." Han leveled his DL-44 at the closest bug's head. "Now hold it right there."

They did not, of course, and Han put a blaster bolt through the first one's head the instant its shatter gun swung toward him. He burned another hole through the thorax of the second bug as it extended its weapon arm, then Luke dropped down behind the group with his lightsaber blazing. The blade droned a couple of times and two more Gorog fell, then the stump around Han erupted into acrid-smelling bark shards as the surviving insects squeezed off their first shots. Han fired back, Luke's blade whined again, and the last two insects collapsed.

Han stood, holding his blaster in both hands, and Luke lowered his blade and spun in a slow circle, examining each of the corpses. He had almost finished when he suddenly staggered, then abruptly shut down his lightsaber.

"Blast!"

"What's wrong?" Han started forward. "I didn't hit you with a stray, did I?"

Luke turned with a scowl. "I'm a little better than that, Han." He lifted his gore-slimed boot and scraped the sole across a Gorog mandible, then said, "They're all dead. I was hoping to get some answers out of them."

R2-D2 chirped something from the tree stump, then began to rock back and forth on its treads.

"What is it, Artoo?" Luke asked.

"He says you might be able to ask one of the six who were talking to the smugglers," C-3PO translated helpfully. "They're on the way up now."

"Yeah, but I don't think they're coming to talk to *us*," Han said.

After a quick scan of the area to make sure there were no other Killik surprise parties, Han and Luke returned to their original hiding place. The six Gorog were clambering up the slope with their weapons drawn. The four Aqualish smugglers had broken out G-9 power blasters and were kneeling on their hoversled, hiding behind the barrels of reactor fuel and aiming up the slope to cover the insects. The Neimoidian was fleeing toward the far side of the old building foundation.

"I've got the smugglers." Luke started toward the low end of the root. "Take the Gorog—and remember, we need one alive. I want to find out what that reactor fuel is for."

Han caught him by the arm. "Those bugs have shatter guns," he said. "Maybe we should just run for it. You know how the Dark Nest is. Once we're back over the hill with the loggers, they won't want to show themselves."

"I'm not worried, Han," Luke said. "You're covering me."

"Look, kid, I don't have their range," Han said. "And your lightsaber isn't that good against those pellets."

"It's okay. You'll do fine."

Luke moved along the root's length until it covered him only from the chest down. The hillside erupted into a river of blaster bolts and magnetically accelerated projectiles.

Han cursed Luke's misplaced optimism and began to fire back. His bolts either flew wide or crackled into nothingness before they reached their targets, but they gave the bugs something to think about. Most of the shatter gun pellets thumped harmlessly into the mud below them, and the few that didn't crackled past far overhead.

The power blasters were another matter. Their bolts sizzled into the other side of the root with unnerving accuracy, filling the air with smoke and wood chips. Han sent a couple of bolts their way just to see if he could startle the Aqualish into putting their heads down. They didn't even flinch, and smoke began to drift through holes on Han and Luke's side of the root.

Then Luke extended a hand toward the stump behind the smugglers, and the barrel they had already off-loaded rose into the air and came crashing down into the middle of the hoversled. Several of the containers broke, spilling hundreds of gallons of coolant and dozens of meter-long gray rods. The Aqualish stopped firing and jumped off the sled, fleeing after the Neimoidian.

The Gorog glanced over their shoulders, then began to drum their thoraxes in anger. Han thought for a moment that they would charge, but four of them simply fanned out across the slope to take up holding positions. The other two rushed back toward the hoversled.

"Are they crazy?" Han gasped. "Ten minutes with those rods in the open like that, and they'll start glowing."

"Gorog doesn't care. It *wants* that fuel." Luke stepped

back into full cover behind the root. "If our tracking equipment still works—"

"Run for your lives!" C-3PO came around the tree stump at a full clank, waving the electrobinoculars Han had passed him earlier. "We're doomed!"

"Doomed?" Han stepped out to intercept the droid—then nearly lost his head as a shatter gun pellet came hissing past his ear. He stepped back into the shelter of the root, pulling C-3PO after him. "What are you talking about?"

C-3PO turned and pointed back toward the landspeeder. "The Fizz! It has the landspeeder!"

"The Fizz?" Han asked. "Out here?"

"Perhaps we brought it with us," C-3PO suggested.

An alarmed whistle sounded from above, then R2-D2 rolled off the edge of the stump and began to drop. He would have crashed on their heads had Luke not reached out with the Force and caught him.

Luke lowered R2-D2 to the ground, then leaned down. "What's wrong with you, Artoo? You could have hurt someone."

R2-D2 whistled a long reply.

"Artoo says it probably doesn't matter," C-3PO translated. "There's a seventy-three percent chance that we're disintegrating already."

"Come on." Though R2-D2 was not normally given to doomsaying, Han tried not to be shaken by his evaluation of the situation. Despite the temporary repairs Luke had done on the little droid's personality, he was still acting as strangely as a Defel in a tanning booth. "It can't be that bad. I was just up there, and I didn't see any froth."

R2-D2 chirped curtly.

"Artoo suggests you go see for yourself," C-3PO translated. "Though I don't think that's a very good idea. It's all over the ground."

"All over the ground?" Han frowned, thinking. "Under the landspeeder? Where all that fuel spilled?"

"Precisely," C-3PO said. "And spreading rapidly. Why, I wouldn't be surprised if the entire landspeeder was engulfed by now."

"Great." Luke turned and started back toward the landspeeder. "I left the tracking set in the front seat."

"Hold on." Han caught him by the back of his robe. "I don't think it's going to matter."

Luke stopped but didn't turn around. "It's not?"

"Not if what I'm thinking is right." Han holstered his blaster and extended his hand toward C-3PO. "Threepio, hand me the electrobinoculars."

The droid looked down as though astonished to discover he was still holding the viewing device, then extended his arm. "Of course, Captain Solo—though I really don't think they're a viable substitute for the tracking set. Once the hoversled passes out of your sight line, they'll be no good to you at all."

"I don't think that hoversled *will* pass out of my sight line."

Han peered over the edge of the root and found the Gorog rear guard still holding their positions. The other two had reached the hoversled and were using their bare pincers to throw the spilled fuel rods back into the cargo bed. Han flipped the electrobinoculars to full power, then lifted them to his eyes and began to study the ground beneath the hoversled.

Luke came to his side. "What are you looking for?"

"Tell you in a minute," Han said, "in case I'm wrong about this and need to make something up to keep from embarrassing myself."

A series of sharp bangs sounded as shatter gun pellets began to strike the root, jarring Han so hard that the eyepieces slammed against his cheekbones. He stopped bracing himself on the root and continued to peer through the electrobinoculars.

"Uh, Han, maybe we should find a better observation post," Luke said. "This is getting dangerous."

"I'm not worried, kid," Han said. "You can cover me."

"Very funny," Luke replied. "But my blaster's range isn't much better than yours."

"It's okay." Han continued to study the ground beneath the hoversled. "You'll do fine."

Luke sighed, but he pulled his blaster and began to return fire. He must have actually hit something, because the pellet impacts dwindled to almost nothing. Han's arms started to ache from holding the electrobinoculars up, so he braced his hands back on the root and continued to watch.

The Gorog had almost finished loading the hoversled when they suddenly dropped one of the fuel rods and leapt into the cargo bed. They carefully began to examine the others, and Han was confused for a moment, until they tossed another rod onto the ground. It landed almost perpendicular to him, so that he noted a silver sheen starting to glitter along one side of its dull gray surface.

Han smiled in satisfaction, then backed away from the root and passed the electrobinoculars to Luke. "Take a look."

They exchanged equipment, and Han began to trade fire with the sole member of the Gorog rear guard that Luke had not already killed. Somehow, Han's shots kept sizzling out about thirty meters shy of their target.

After a moment, Luke said, "So that's what you were talking about. The Fizz."

"Almost," Han said. "Look at what it's *not* on."

"You mean the rocks in that old foundation?" Luke asked.

"And the stumps," Han confirmed. "If it's in the ground around here, how come it's leaving all that stuff alone? How come it's only attacking our landspeeder, and that coolant, and those fuel rods spilled around their hoversled?"

Luke lowered the electrobinoculars and turned to Han. "Contamination?"

Han nodded. "It only attacks what attacks Woteba," he said. "It's an environmental defense system."

SEVEN

The steamy spa air smelled of mineral mud and pore cleanser, and the soothing notes of a classic feegharp sonata were wafting out of the sound system, not quite masking the gentle whirring and tinking of the Lovolan Beauty Artist installed in one corner of the room. Reclining on the droid's built-in comfort chair was a mud-masked, seaweed-wrapped mummy whom Jacen assumed to be Tenel Ka's grandmother, Ta'a Chume. Her scalp was being kneaded by an undulating massage hood, while each of her eyelids was hidden beneath the translucent star of what looked like some small, tentacled sea creature. There was even a beverage dispenser that automatically swung a draw nozzle out to her lips, since both hands were enveloped inside automatic manicure gloves.

When Jacen sensed no other living presences nearby, he entered the spa. He passed a series of sunken basins filled with bubbling mud, water, and something that looked like pink Hutt slime, then stopped beside the droid. Ta'a Chume showed no sign of sensing his presence, and for a moment he considered whether simply ending her life might not be the surest way to protect his daughter. Certainly, the old woman deserved it. She had been liquidating inconvenient people since before Jacen and Tenel Ka were born, and currently she was under house arrest for poisoning Tenel Ka's mother. At one time, Ta'a Chume had even attempted to have Jacen's own mother assassinated.

But Tenel Ka had asked him not to kill the old woman, saying she would deal with her grandmother's treachery in her own way. Jacen suspected that meant a long and very public trial, in which Ta'a Chume might well escape conviction due to a lack of verifiable evidence—and Jacen was, quite simply, not willing to run that risk with his daughter's life.

Jacen took his lightsaber off its belt hook, but did not activate the blade. "I see you're making the most of your house arrest, Ta'a Chume."

A hole appeared in the mud mask as Ta'a Chume's mouth fell open, then she pulled out of the massage hood and raised her head. The sea creatures left her eyelids and slid down her cheeks, leaving trails of exposed skin in their wakes.

"Jacen Solo," Ta'a Chume said. "I'd ask how you sneaked into my private chambers—but that's what Jedi *do*, isn't it?"

"Among other things." Noting that she had not taken her hands out of the manicure gloves, he said, "You can signal for help all you like—your bodyguards won't be coming—but please don't attempt to point that hold-out blaster at me. I promised Tenel Ka I wouldn't kill you, and I'll be very angry if you make me break my word."

Ta'a Chume's eyes faded to paler shade of green, but she cracked her mud mask by forcing a superior smile. "What a pity—when I saw you standing there with a lightsaber, I thought my granddaughter had finally grown a spine."

"Had Tenel Ka lacked courage, you would have died never knowing I was here," Jacen said. "Instead she's willing to risk keeping you alive for a public trial. Her security team will be arriving soon. I've made sure they won't need to kill anyone to reach you."

The tension left Ta'a Chume's shoulders. "How very considerate of you." A cunning light came to her eyes, then she slowly removed her hand from the manicure glove and dropped a small hold-out blaster to the floor. "Would you mind telling me why?"

"You know why," Jacen said. Ta'a Chume was playing a game with him—he could feel it in her presence as clearly as he heard it in her voice—but what he could not figure out was the reason. "You tried to kill her daughter."

Ta'a Chume poured anger into the Force, but her voice grew aggrieved. "The Queen Mother has a child?" She drew her second hand out of the manicure glove and pressed her fingers to her temples. "And she did not even trouble to tell her own grandmother?"

Jacen scowled. "Your act isn't fooling me. I sense your true emotions in the Force."

"Then you must sense how shocked I am—and worried." Ta'a Chume put her hands down and turned to look at him, but her gaze lingered on his chest, running up and down the lapels, pausing at every wrinkle. "Certainly, I resent being imprisoned on the orders of my own granddaughter, but I'd never wish her harm—much less have anything to do with it!"

Jacen finally understood. "There is no spycam, Ta'a Chume." He pulled his robe open to show her that he had no equipment hidden underneath. "I'm here looking for answers to my own questions—not gathering evidence for Tenel Ka."

"That never crossed my mind, Jedi Solo, but I do hope that when you see my granddaughter again, you'll be good enough to pass along my concern for her and her daughter." Ta'a Chume looked up and batted her eyes at him.

"By the by, you wouldn't happen to know who the father is, would you?"

The smirk in Ta'a Chume's voice was clear, as though she was taunting Jacen, telling him that he would never beat her at this particular game—and it made him angry.

"That would be me." Jacen stepped around behind the beauty droid and used the Force to pull Ta'a Chume back in the seat. "And I'm very determined to protect my daughter."

Ta'a Chume grew nervous. "What are you doing?"

"I'd like some answers, and we don't have long before the security team arrives."

Jacen pushed the scalp hood aside, then plunged his fingers into Ta'a Chume's red-dyed hair and began to massage her scalp.

"So we can do this the easy way . . ." He pressed his thumbs into the base of her skull, then sent a tiny charge of Force energy shooting through her brain. ". . . or we can do it the hard way."

Ta'a Chume gasped in pain, then said, "You're a Jedi! You can't do this."

"Sure I can," Jacen said. "The Jedi learned some new tricks during the war with the Yuuzhan Vong—or hadn't you heard?"

Jacen felt a warning jolt from Ben, whom he had left hidden with his skiff outside Ta'a Chume's estate, then heard the distant *crump* of the front gates being blown by Tenel Ka's security team.

Ta'a Chume's head twitched toward the sound, and Jacen knew that she believed her arresters would be her saviors—that if she could just hold out long enough, her secrets would remain safe. He sent another charge of Force energy into her mind.

This time he did not stop with a short surge. He continued to pour more Force energy into Ta'a Chume's head, pushing in behind it, expanding his own Force presence inside her mind. He was not as sure or strong with the technique as Raynar—in fact, he was not even sure it was the same technique—but he *was* good enough to overpower a surprised old woman who did not know how to use the Force.

A long cry escaped Ta'a Chume's lips; as it died away, Jacen felt her resistance crumble. Outside on the palace grounds, voices began to yell commands at Ta'a Chume's servants.

Jacen ignored the commotion and leaned close to Ta'a Chume's ear. "First, I want to know why."

Ta'a Chume tried to resist. "Why wha . . ." Jacen pushed harder, and she said, "You couldn't believe I would allow the child of two *Jedi* to claim the throne. Hapes will never be a Jedi kingdom!"

"I don't think that's Tenel Ka's intention."

"It is *your* intention that concerns me," Ta'a Chume said. "You've already persuaded Tenel Ka to involve a Hapan fleet in a matter of no concern to us. I won't allow you to make a Jedi tool of the Hapes Consortium."

"You see? That wasn't so hard. Now tell me about the Dark Nest."

"The Dark Nest?"

"The Gorog," Jacen clarified. It felt like she was genuinely confused. "The Killiks. How did you get them to go after the baby?"

Muffled crashing sounds started to rumble up through the palace itself, and Ta'a Chume began to hope again that she could hold out.

"I don't know . . ."

Jacen expanded his presence.

"They came to *me*!" she cried. "They were unhappy about Tenel Ka's interference at Qoribu, and they knew I had reason to want her dead."

The statement made sense. Hoping to expand its influence in the Colony—and to expand the Colony into Chiss territory—the Dark Nest had deliberately been trying to start a war with the Chiss Ascendancy. But he could feel Ta'a Chume fighting to hold back, struggling to leave something unsaid. He expanded further into her mind. She screamed, and something slipped, like a hand opening on a rope, but Jacen did not back off. He needed to know what the Dark Nest was doing.

"The Gorog . . . were wrong," Ta'a Chume said. "I don't want Tenel Ka dead . . . at least not . . . until I'm in a better position . . . to reclaim the throne."

"But your spies had told you about the baby," Jacen surmised. "And you wanted the baby dead . . ."

"So I told Gorog . . . that killing Tenel Ka's daughter would be even better." Ta'a Chume tried to stop there, but Jacen was pushing so hard that she barely had a hold on her own mind. "But they weren't doing it out of revenge. I had to strike a deal to save . . . to take the baby instead of Tenel Ka."

Male voices began to echo up through the building as Tenel Ka's security team started its ascent. Jacen had already made sure that they would encounter no resistance, so the climb would be a quick one, with each floor requiring only a cursory clearing before they climbed to the next.

"The deal terms?" Jacen asked.

Despite the apparent proximity of the security team, Ta'a Chume did not even try to resist. Her grasp on her mind was just too tenuous.

"They wanted . . . navicomputer technology," she said.

"Navicomputers?" Jacen could not imagine what the Dark Nest wanted with that particular technology. "To travel insystem?"

"No," Ta'a Chume said. "To go through hyperspace."

"Why?" Jacen asked. "Killiks don't build hyperspace-capable vessels. They hire transports."

"They didn't say, and I didn't ask," Ta'a Chume answered. "This was a political arrangement, not a marriage."

Jacen would have pressed harder, but he could feel that she was telling the truth, that she had not cared why the Gorog were interested in the technology—so long as Tenel Ka's baby was killed. He had to move his fingers away from Ta'a Chume's throat. They were beginning to squeeze.

A muted thump sounded from the outer door of Ta'a Chume's private wing, and a loudspeaker voice began yelling at her to deactivate the locks and lie down on the floor. Jacen's interview was coming to an end—and Ta'a Chume knew it. He could feel her starting to fight back, trying to claw her way back into control of her mind.

"Just one more question," Jacen said. "Will there be any more attacks on my daughter?"

"Not your daughter, no." Ta'a Chume was lying—Jacen could feel that she would never give up, and she hoped and expected that the Dark Nest never would, either—but he did not call her on it. There was more, something she was eager for him to know. "But your daughter should not be your only concern."

"I'm listening," Jacen said.

"I didn't rule Hapes for all those years by being a fool," Ta'a Chume said. "I knew you and Tenel Ka would figure out who attacked your daughter—and I knew you would come after me."

A loud bang sounded from the outer door of the wing.

"We're out of time," Jacen said. "Tell me why I shouldn't kill you now, or—"

"If I die, Tenel Ka is a target. If I am imprisoned, if I am disgraced . . . Tenel Ka is a target." Ta'a Chume eased her neck out of Jacen's hands, then twisted around to face him. "If you want your daughter to grow up with a mother, Jacen, you must spare me. That is the only way."

The anger that Jacen felt suddenly turned to something else—something cold and calculating.

"Not the only way," he said. "There is another."

He grabbed Ta'a Chume by the shoulder and pulled her back into the seat. Then, as the muted tramp of boots began to pound through the outer warrens of her living chambers, Jacen poured hot, crackling Force energy into her head, pushing hard with his own presence, violently, until they both blasted free of her brain and Ta'a Chume gave a last, falling shriek, plunging down into the depths of her mind, plummeting into the darkness of a soul that had never loved, that had cared only for power and wealth and control, leaving only a black fuming void ringed by torn neurons and seared dendrites and a shattered, broken brain.

And Jacen suddenly found himself outside Ta'a Chume, outside himself, a passive observer outside time itself, his presence filling the entire room, the entire palace, a witness to something he could not control. He saw the whole Hapes Cluster and the whole galaxy, and all of it was burning— not just the suns, but also the planets and the moons and the asteroids, burning, every speck of stone or dust solid enough to hold a sentient foot. And the fires were traveling from place to place on tiny flickering needles of ion efflux, being set by torches carried in the hands of men and Killiks and Chiss, and the inferno just kept growing brighter, until worlds blazed as brightly as suns and systems flared as brightly as novae, until sectors shined as brightly as the Core and the whole galaxy erupted into one huge eternal flame.

The flame vanished when a loud pounding began to echo through the spa door. "By the Queen Mother's order, unlock the door and lie down on the floor!"

Jacen stumbled away from the beauty droid feeling horrified and confused. He had experienced enough Force-visions to recognize what had happened, but he could not bring himself to accept what he had seen. Visions were symbolic, but the meaning of this one seemed clear enough to him. The galaxy was about to erupt into a war unlike anything it had ever seen before—a war that would never end, that would spread from world to world to world until it had consumed the entire galaxy.

And the Killiks were at the heart of it.

A sharp bang sounded from the spa entrance, sending the durasteel door flying into the opposite wall and filling the chamber with an impenetrable cloud of blue smoke. Jacen pushed the massage hood back down on Ta'a Chume's head and jumped into the sunken basin of mineral mud. He sank down to his chin and looked around him, taking careful note of the mud's surface, then carefully expanded that illusion into the Force—as he had learned from the Adepts of the White Current.

He was not quite finished when the eye-goggled, body-armored forms of a dozen Hapan security commandos charged into the room. They advanced in a bent-legged shuffle that seemed vaguely insect-like, then rushed over to the Beauty Artist, all twelve of them pointing their assault blasters at Ta'a Chume's unmoving form. When the old woman showed no sign of resistance, the squad leader reluctantly lowered his weapon and placed three fingers on her throat.

"She's alive." He handed his assault blaster to a subordinate, then leaned over Ta'a Chume and stared into her unmoving eyes. "But get Doc up here—I think she's had some sort of brain hemorrhage."

EIGHT

A two-story hologram of the planet Woteba hung in the projection pit a few meters beyond the command console, a nearly featureless reminder of just how valid Leia's fears really were. Han and her brother were trapped and alone on a half-known world, surrounded by insects answering to an enemy queen, and—judging by her sense of Luke's emotions in the Force—they did not even realize they were in trouble. That was what really worried Leia. Han and Luke could take care of themselves, but only if they knew there was a need.

"Maybe the Dark Nest isn't even *on* Woteba," Kyp Durron suggested. "What do we know about the other planets?"

"Only that they were all as deserted as Woteba before we helped the Killiks settle there." Leia swung her gaze toward the shaggy-haired Master. Along with Mara and Saba, they were in the Operations Planning Center in the Jedi Temple on Coruscant, conversing with several other Jedi via the HoloNet. "And fourteen were habitable."

"The Killiks weren't interested in detailed surveys," Mara explained. "All they wanted to know was which worlds were habitable. We have a basic planetary profile and not much else."

"Because they didn't *want* us to know too much." The

comment came from Corran Horn's hologram, arrayed with several others on a shelf curving along the back edge of the control console. "To me, it's beginning to sound like the Killiks never intended to keep the peace with the Chiss."

"Don't confuse the Killiks with the Gorog," Jaina warned. She and Zekk were sharing the hologram next to Corran's, their heads touching above the temples and their unblinking eyes fixed straight ahead. "It was only the Dark Nest that wanted the war, not the Colony."

"Whoever wanted it *then,* the entire Colony is clearly involved *now,*" Corran countered. "And they have Master Skywalker to guarantee that we don't interfere with their plans again."

"You don't understand how the Colony's mind works," Zekk objected.

"It may look like the entire Colony is involved," Jaina added, "but the Dark Nest is the one behind this."

"Remember last time?" Zekk asked. "UnuThul summoned us to *prevent* a war."

"That is called a false flag recruitment," Kenth Hamner said from the end of the array. With Corran, Kenth had argued forcefully that the Killiks should be left to their own devices during the Qoribu crisis. "A valuable asset—a team of young Jedi Knights, shall we say—is convinced to undertake a mission under false pretenses."

"That's not how it was," Jaina said.

"Unfortunately, we can no longer afford to give the Colony the benefit of the doubt," Kenth said. "Until Master Skywalker and Captain Solo are safe, we must consider the evidence: despite the *fifteen* worlds we gave them— worlds that the Galactic Alliance's own beings desperately need—the Killiks are harboring pirates and poisoning the minds and bodies of our own insect species with black membrosia."

Jaina and Zekk spoke simultaneously. "That's just the—"

"Let me finish." Kenth did not raise his voice, but, even coming from a holopad speaker, his tone was as hard as durasteel. "Raynar Thul lured Master Skywalker into a trap so the Colony could take him hostage, and now the Killiks are provoking a confrontation with the Chiss. We have no choice but to assume the worst."

"Because the *Dark Nest* has taken control!" Zekk blurted.

A tight smile came to Kenth's hologram. "Precisely."

Jaina rolled her eyes. "Master Hamner, if you hold the entire Colony responsible—"

"—you're creating a self-fulfilling prophecy," Zekk added.

"And the Killiks *will* turn on us," Jaina finished. "Why don't you get that?"

"What I 'get,' Jedi Solo, is that you and Jedi Zekk still have an emotional attachment to the Killiks." The hologram wavered as Kenth's gaze shifted, and now his image seemed to be looking Leia straight in the eye. "Frankly, I question the wisdom of allowing these particular Jedi Knights to participate in the discussion at all."

"No one is more familiar with the Killiks than Jaina and Zekk." Leia purposely allowed some of the resentment she felt to creep into her voice. After what Jaina and Zekk had sacrificed to prevent the Qoribu conflict from erupting into a galactic war, Kenth Hamner did not have the right to cast aspersions on their loyalty. "They're our best hope of figuring out where the Dark Nest might be located."

"I understand that." A purple tint came to Kenth's image, indicating that he had closed the channel to all other participants and was now conversing only with the Operations Planning Center. "But there's something you don't know—something that we can't trust with your daughter and Zekk—or with any of the Jedi Knights who spent too much time with the Killiks."

Leia's blood began to boil. "Master Hamner, Jaina and Zekk have already demonstrated their loyalty to the order—"

Mara cut Leia short by reaching past her and suspending transmission to everyone else. "What is it, Kenth?"

"I apologize if I offended you, Princess Leia," Kenth said. "But Chief Omas asked me not to tell *anyone* in the order what I'm about to reveal. I hope you'll understand. It has a bearing on our discussion."

"Of course." Leia understood when she was being told that she wasn't going to hear something without a promise of confidentiality. "I won't reveal it to anyone. I give you my word."

"Thank you."

Kenth's head turned as he consulted something off cam. Kyp, Corran, and Jaina and Zekk, aware by the sudden silence from the Operations Planning Center that they had been cut out of the conversation, fell quiet and tried not to look impatient.

A moment later, Kenth's gaze returned to his holocam. "Sorry for that, but I wanted to check the latest. The Fifth Fleet has put out for Utegetu."

"The whole fleet?" Leia was stunned. Moving the Fifth Fleet would shift the responsibility for patrolling the entire Hydian Way to local governments—and that was not something Chief Omas would do lightly. "To do what?"

Kenth shook his head. "Those orders are sealed, but we can be certain they're trying to appease the Chiss. What concerns me is that I only found out by accident. Someone had forgotten to remove my name from the routing list. Chief Omas called personally to ask me to keep the information to myself."

"They don't want us to know?" Leia gasped.

"Clearly," Mara said. "Omas didn't like how the Jedi handled the Killiks last time—and you must admit things aren't going well now."

"Do they know about Han and Luke?" Leia asked.

"Not from me," Kenth answered. "But I doubt it would make any difference. Chief Omas was very adamant that we need to support the Chiss this time."

"Then time is chewing our tailz," Saba said. Standing behind Leia with Mara, she was also party to their private discussion. "We must get a team to Woteba *now.* Yez?"

"Agreed," Kenth said. "But—"

"Then we will discusz *that,*" Saba said.

"I think we should," Kenth said. "But Jaina and Zekk—"

"—will not be told." Saba leaned over Leia's shoulder and reactivated the suspended channels. "Where do we look for the Dark Nest?"

Jaina and Zekk gave a simultaneous *cloq-cloq* of surprise, and the irritation they had shown at being left out of the conversation vanished from their faces. A blue dot appeared on Woteba's empty face, next to one of the few mapping symbols that the hologram already contained: Saras nest.

"You don't find Gorog," Jaina said.

"Gorog finds you," Zekk added. "But we know the nest will be watching Han and Master Skywalker."

"So we must watch them, too," Jaina finished.

Leia and Mara exchanged glances. They did not have time for "watching." The instant the Fifth Fleet entered the Utegetu Nebula, the Dark Nest would move against Han and Luke. The memory of the Kr nursery—where Luke and Mara had found thousands of Gorog larvae feeding on paralyzed Chiss prisoners—flashed through Leia's mind, and she firmly shook her head.

"Too risky," she said.

"They'll see us watching," Mara added. "And we can't let Lomi Plo escape this time."

"Isn't there a faster way we can find it?" Leia asked.

Jaina and Zekk considered this for several moments, then Jaina said, "Perhaps *we* could feel where their nest is—"

"—if we went to Utegetu."

"This one thought nobody could sense the Dark Nest in the Force," Saba rasped. "Especially Joinerz."

"Jaina and I might be different," Zekk said. "We were in the nest at Kr."

"So we know what Gorog feels like," Jaina added.

Leia frowned. "And what about that gang of Tibanna tappers you're supposed to be hunting?" She did not like the eagerness she heard in their voices, the desire to experience again the all-encompassing bond of a collective mind. "Cloud City's shipments are down ten percent."

"Lowie and Tesar can take over," Zekk said.

"They finally found out who was hijacking the Abaarian water shipments," Jaina added.

"Forget it," Mara said, issuing the command before Leia could—and adding to it the authority of a Master. "You two aren't getting within five parsecs of a Killik nest. Clear?"

Jaina and Zekk leaned away from each other, making clicking sounds in their throats and blinking in unison. "Clear," they said.

"We were only trying to help," Jaina added defensively.

"Sure you were," Leia said. "Anybody have any *real* ideas?"

"I don't think there is a way," Kyp said immediately. "We've tried to trace the black membrosia back to the source and never made it past the blind drops in the Rago

Run. And with a collective mind, the Dark Nest will know if we start sniffing around the Utegetu Nebula too hard."

"Then maybe Jaina and Zekk are right," Corran said. "Maybe the best thing to do is to watch Han and Master Skywalker and just be patient."

"I thought we had already ruled that out." Though Leia's outward voice remained calm, inside she wanted to give him a Barabel ear-slap. The one thing they did not have was time—though, of course, Corran had no way of knowing that. He had not been a part of the private conversation with Kenth. "We'll just have to recover Luke and Han first, and hope they were able to find the Dark Nest on their own."

"No good," Kyp said. "That tips our hand. If the Dark Nest is watching them—"

"We *can* be discreet," Mara said in a tone that would abide no argument. "We're Jedi, remember?"

The rebuke in her tone made Corran wince, Kyp cock his brow, and Jaina and Zekk tilt their heads. There was a long moment of silence in which those who had not been privy to Kenth's secret were clearly trying to figure out why everyone else was in such a hurry.

Then a knowing light came to Kyp's brown eyes. "You're worried about your husbands!" He flashed a reassuring smile that came off as more of a smirk in the hologram. "That's only natural, ladies. But Han and Master Skywalker can take care of themselves. I've been in worse places than this with both of them, lots of times."

Mara sighed. "No, Kyp, that's not it."

"What Master Skywalker means is that we need to act quickly," Kenth said. "With the Colony provoking the Chiss again, the situation is too unpredictable. The sooner we resolve this, the less likely it is to blow up in our faces worse than it already has."

Corran nodded sagely. "Our reputation has already taken a bad hit, especially in the Senate."

Kyp looked doubtful. "That's it? You're worried that things might get a little messy?"

"Yes, Kyp, that's it," Leia said. "Except that if things get messy, they're going to get *very* messy. We need to prove to the Chiss—and everyone else—that the Jedi can be counted on."

Kyp considered this for a moment, then shrugged. "Okay. But we need a backup plan, because we're never going to get to Han and Luke without the Dark Nest knowing. Those bugs are good."

"Good?" Saba sissed in amused disbelief. "You spent too much of your life in the spice minez, Kyp Durron. There is too much methane in them. They taste like a—"

"I think he meant they were skilled observers, Master Sebatyne," Leia said. "I'm sure that Master Durron has never actually eaten a Gorog."

"No?" Saba's tail thumped the floor. "Not even a little one?"

"Not even a taste." Kyp was quick to change the subject. "Now, about our backup plan. I have one."

"That was easy," Corran said. "Will it work?"

"Of course," Kyp said. "We just take out Raynar and the Unu."

"Kill them?" Corran's tone was shocked.

Kyp grew thoughtful. "That would work, too, and it would be a lot easier than bringing Raynar back here alive— at least if he's as powerful as everyone says."

"You can't!" Zekk objected. "It would destroy the Colony!"

"Actually, it would only return the Killiks to their natural state," Mara corrected. "There *was* no Colony until Raynar came along."

"That's like saying there was no Jedi order until Uncle Luke came along," Jaina countered.

"You can't destroy an interstellar civilization just because it didn't exist ten years ago," Zekk added.

"Probably not," Kenth replied. "But when that civilization refuses to honor its agreements and live in peace with its neighbors, we may find ourselves duty-bound to try."

"I might argue with that," Corran said. "War is one thing. But assassination . . . that's not something Jedi *do*."

"Especially when you have a better way to handle the problem," Jaina said.

"Jaina," Leia said, "if you're talking about you and Zekk going back to the Killiks, forget it."

"Why?" Zekk demanded. "Because you're afraid you'll lose us the way you lost Anakin?"

Coming from Zekk's mouth instead of Jaina's, the question felt just bizarre enough that the dagger of loss it drove into Leia's chest did not find her heart. She retained her composure and studied her daughter's image in silence, but Jaina was too tough to be stared down over the HoloNet. She simply accepted Leia's glare with the unblinking eyes of a Joiner, then spoke in an even voice.

"We're sorry, Mother. That was uncalled-for."

"But we're still Jedi," Zekk added. "You can't stop us from doing what Jedi do."

Mara leaned close to the holocam and spoke in a sharp voice. "She isn't trying to—and you know it." She waited until the pair gave a grudging nod, then asked, "But if you can do this in a better way, let's hear it."

Jaina's and Zekk's eyes bugged in surprise. "You'd send us back?"

"*If* that was the best way," Mara said. "Of course."

Leia stiffened and would have objected, save that Saba sensed what she was about to do and gave a warning hiss.

It had not been her place to tell Jaina and Zekk to forget returning to the Killiks, and now Mara had to waste valuable time correcting the mistake. After a lifetime of leadership in both politics and the military, Leia sometimes found it difficult to remember that in the Jedi order, she was technically just another Jedi Knight—and, as far as Saba was concerned, a fairly junior one at that.

After a few moments' silence from Jaina and Zekk, Mara prompted, "We're listening."

Jaina and Zekk furrowed their brows, then Jaina finally said, "We could talk to UnuThul."

"And say what?" Kyp demanded. "That he should make the Killiks stop harboring pirates and running black membrosia?"

"You said Gorog was controlling him," Zekk pointed out. "We could make him see that."

"Or watch him until Gorog shows herself," Jaina said. "Then follow her to her nest."

"Listen to yourselvez!" Saba said, leaning over Leia toward the holocam. "*That* is why you cannot go."

"I agree," Kenth said. "You're both outstanding Jedi. But when it comes to the Colony, it's clear that all you want is to return."

"You can't go back," Kyp agreed. "It would be bad for you and worse for us."

In the face of the Masters' opposition, Jaina and Zekk dropped their gazes. "Sorry," Jaina said.

"We'll go back to the Tibanna tappers."

As Zekk spoke, a hailing light activated on the command console.

"It's just that—"

"Hold on," Leia said, relieved to have an excuse to cut off Zekk's plea. "Someone's trying to contact us on this end."

She opened a sequestered holochannel, and the pink, high-domed head of a Mon Calamari appeared over an empty holopad.

"Cilghal!" Leia said. "I wasn't expecting to hear from you so soon."

"Analyzing that froth turned out to be easier than we had feared."

"That's good news," Leia said.

"Not really," Cilghal replied.

"Is this something the whole planning group will need to hear?" Mara asked.

Cilghal's short eyestalks sagged. "Probably so."

Leia patched the Mon Calamari's channel into the network. "Cilghal has made some progress on the Dark Nest's froth."

"Actually, I doubt the Dark Nest is responsible for the froth," Cilghal said. "From what we know of Killik society, they have no nanotechnology abilities at all."

"Nanotech?" Kyp echoed. "As in molecule machines?"

"As in *self-replicating* molecule machines," Cilghal corrected. "The sample that Master Sebatyne gave me appears to be a terraforming system. From what I can tell, it's designed to create and maintain an environmental balance optimal for its creators."

"Yes," Saba said. "But what does it *do*?"

"I'm not sure we'll ever understand completely." Cilghal steepled her webbed fingers beneath her chin tentacles. "It's very advanced, far beyond any nanotechnology capabilities here in the Galactic Alliance."

Saba rasped in impatience.

"Basically," Cilghal continued, "the system consists of many different kinds of tiny machines. Some of those machines monitor the soil, the air, the water. When they detect a notable imbalance in the environment, they join together and become machines that disassemble the contaminants, molecule by molecule, then use that raw material to build more machines. That's what is happening when you see the froth."

"And these contaminants," Corran said. "They are . . . ?"

"Whatever lies outside the system parameters," Cilghal said. "Toxic spills, spinglass buildings, droids, Killiks—in short, anything in sufficient amounts that wasn't on Woteba when Leia and Han found it."

Leia's heart sank. Moving the Killiks to Woteba had felt a little too convenient all along, and now she knew there was a reason.

"This is great news!" Jaina said.

"The Colony isn't lying to us after all!" Zekk added.

"Don't start your victory rolls yet," Kyp warned. "Maybe the Killiks didn't make this stuff, but the Dark Nest is still using it to turn the Colony against us."

"Only until UnuThul understands what happened," Zekk said.

"Once we disable the nanotech, he'll see that we weren't trying to trick him," Jaina added.

"I'm afraid he's going to have to take our word for it," Cilghal said.

Jaina and Zekk frowned. "Why?"

"Because the system is probably worldwide, and it is certainly very resilient." Cilghal interlaced her fingers, then her hands dropped out of the hologram. "If the supernova didn't destroy it—"

"Supernova?" Corran asked. "What supernova?"

"The one that created the Utegetu Nebula," Leia clarified. There were many different kinds of nebulae, and most of them did not result from supernova explosions. "The Utegetu is a shell nebula."

"I see," Corran said.

"The blast would have destroyed all life on every planet within a dozen parsecs," Cilghal continued. "But my assistant's calculations suggest that the nebula is only a thousand standard years old."

"And you think the nanotech survived to restore Woteba and the other worlds," Leia surmised.

"Yes. Otherwise, the planets would still be dead." Cilghal glanced at something out of view, then said, "We calculate that it would have taken only a year or two for the first pockets of soil to become fertile again, and there would have been plenty of seeds trapped where the blast radiation wouldn't destroy them."

"But the animals wouldn't have lasted," Mara said. "They would have starved within months."

Cilghal nodded. "And that is how you end up with a cluster of empty paradise worlds."

"I don't suppose there's any chance of Raynar believing all this?" Corran asked.

"We'll certainly do our best to persuade him," Leia said. "But I suspect the Dark Nest will convince him that we're lying."

"What do you two think?" Mara asked Jaina and Zekk. They were silent for a moment; then they reluctantly shook their heads.

"Unu has already put the Colony's plans in motion," Zekk said.

Jaina added, "It will be easier to believe the Dark Nest."

"Then we're back to where we started," Leia said. "Recover Han and Luke, then hope we can find the Dark Nest—and take it out this time."

When no one voiced an objection, Corran asked, "What about our backup plan? I just don't see assassinating Raynar as an option."

The discussion descended into an uncomfortable silence

as they all considered their own interpretation of what it meant to be a Jedi. Not so long ago, during the war against the Yuuzhan Vong, they would not have hesitated to do *whatever* was necessary to safeguard the order and the Galactic Alliance. But Luke had been growing increasingly uncomfortable with that attitude, and over the last year he had quietly been encouraging Jedi Knights and Masters alike to contemplate just where the balance lay between good intention and wrong action.

Corran Horn, as usual in matters of conscience, came to his answer more quickly than most. "War is one thing, but taking out Raynar is murder."

"Maybe it's just because my husband is out there, but it seems more like self-defense to me," Mara said. "It feels like the Dark Nest is coming after us."

"It is more than a feeling," Saba said. "First there are the piratez and the black membrosia, then they lure Master Skywalker to Woteba, and now they are establishing Coloniez along the Chisz border. Who knowz what is next? They have been hunting us for a long time, and we have been asleep under our rockz."

"We've certainly given them the initiative," Kenth agreed. "And we need to win it back now. If that means taking Raynar out, so be it. Clearly, he intends to use Han and Master Skywalker as hostages, and that makes him a legitimate target."

"Even if he's under the Dark Nest's control?" Corran countered. "We can't be sure that he's responsible for his own actions."

"It doesn't matter," Kyp said. "You guys are really overthinking this. It's simple: Raynar is a Jedi, and now he's becoming a threat to the galaxy. He's our responsibility, and we have to stop him. *How* we do that matters a lot less than whether we still can."

The uncomfortable silence returned to the participants, and the eyes in all of the holograms vanished from sight as the Jedi on the other end stared at their respective floors.

Finally, Jaina and Zekk clicked several times in the back of their throats, then looked up and nodded.

"Master Durron is right," Jaina said.

"Raynar *is* our responsibility," Zekk added. "The Jedi must do whatever it takes to stop him."

NINE

A gentle Woteban breeze was wafting across the bog, cool and damp and filled with acrid wisps of the peat smoke rising from the chimneys of the nearest Saras tunnel-house. Close by, the serpentine skeletons of ten more structures were beginning to take shape beneath the bustling anarchy of Killik construction crews. A kilometer beyond, at the far edge of the nest expansion, more insects were moving hamogoni pilings off a steady stream of lumber sleds.

"Oh, boy," Luke said, eyeing all the new construction. "This is bad."

"Only if there are contaminants," Han said. "If there aren't any, it might be okay."

Their Saras escort, a chest-high worker that had been waiting to meet the logging sled on which they had hitched a ride back to the nest, thrummed a short question.

"Saras wishes to know what might be okay," C-3PO informed them. "And why you are so worried about contaminants."

"*Bur ru ub br urrb,*" the insect added. "*Rrrrr uu uu bub.*"

"Oh, dear," C-3PO said. "Saras says the nest has a perfectly sound method of disposing of toxins—it pumps them into the bog!"

"Great," Han growled. He turned to Luke. "We gotta get off this sponge before we start glowing or something."

"Let's talk to Raynar," Luke said. "Maybe once the Killiks understand what's happening, he'll consider our promise kept."

"*Urru buur rbur.*" Their escort waited as an empty lumber sled glided past and disappeared down a winding boulevard into Saras nest proper, then started toward the completed building. "*Ubu ruru buub.*"

"Raynar Thul is dead," C-3PO translated. "But UnuThul is waiting for us in the replica factory."

"Sounds like he's already heard part of it," Han said. "I just hope he doesn't blast the messenger when he hears the rest."

Luke led the others after the escort, through a large iris membrane into the throat of a twining, hangar-sized tunnel-house so filled with smoke and manufacturing fumes that the iridescent walls were barely visible. Along one wall stood a long row of peat-fired furnaces, serviced by hundreds of bustling Killiks. The middle of the chamber was filled with steaming vats, also surrounded by hundreds of Killiks. Along the far wall ran a serpentine workbench, flanked on each side by a seemingly endless Killik production line.

Luke stopped a few paces inside the door. Han let out a complaining cough, then leaned close.

"Better make this fast," he whispered. "It's a wonder this place hasn't been Fizzed already."

Luke did not reply, for Raynar had emerged from the swarm along the workbench and was coming toward them with a pair of spinglass sculptures in his hands. As usual, he was followed by the teeming Unu entourage. He stopped five paces away and stared at them expectantly, as though he assumed they would cross the remaining distance to him.

When they did not, there was a moment of tense silence.

Finally, Han demanded, "What's so important you couldn't let us hit the refresher first?" He pulled at his dirty tunic. "We're kind of ripe."

Raynar's scarred face seemed to harden. "We were worried you might be difficult to find later—if, for instance, you decided to get off this sponge before you 'started glowing or something.' "

Luke dipped his head in acknowledgment. "You've been keeping tabs on us through our escort," he said. "We thought as much. So you must also know we have no intention of leaving until *you* consider our promise kept."

"I have heard." Raynar's rigid lips pressed into an awkward smirk; then he turned to Han. "We apologize if our summons seemed abrupt, but we wished to thank you and Master Skywalker for discovering the star amber cheats. Saras did not realize they were taking something so valuable."

Raynar closed the last of the distance separating them, and Luke saw that the sculptures in his hands were spinglass replicas of *Millennium Falcon* and a T-65 X-wing.

Raynar turned to Luke first and presented him with the X-wing. "Unu wanted you to be the first to have one of these. It is an exact copy of the fighter you were flying when you destroyed the original Death Star."

More than a little stunned by the gesture, Luke accepted the sculpture with genuine gratitude. The piece was so intricately executed that Luke could identify both R2-D2 and the loose stabilizers the droid had been struggling to repair as he began the final assault run.

"Thank you," he said. "I'll treasure it."

"It's the first of a limited run commissioned by one of

our business partners in the Galactic Alliance," Raynar said proudly. "Turn it over. It's numbered and signed by the artist."

Luke did as Raynar asked. Etched into the bottom was SARAS: 1/1,000,000,000. SECOND MISTAKE ENTERPRISES.

Luke nodded politely, then turned it back over. "I'm sure the line will be a great success."

"We think so, too," Raynar said. He turned to Han and gave him the replica of *Millennium Falcon*. "Also a first run."

"Thanks. Real nice." Han turned it over and inspected the artist's signature. "Second Mistake Enterprises?" He frowned, then looked back to Raynar. "Your partners wouldn't happen to be three Squibs named Sligh, Grees, and Emala?"

Raynar's eyes widened. "How did you know?"

"Leia and I had some dealings with them, back before you were born," Han said. Luke remembered something about a trio of Squibs being involved when *Killik Twilight* fell into Imperial hands during the war. "They've got a nose for fine artwork—supplied Thrawn for a while, as a matter of fact."

Raynar's voice grew suspicious. "Do not bother contacting them," he warned. "Our agreement is exclusive."

Han's brow rose. "Wouldn't dream of it." He nonchalantly passed the replica to C-3PO. "You guys were made for each other."

"Good." Raynar almost smiled. "They expect the value of the first pieces to grow exponentially. That's why Unu wanted you and Master Skywalker to have these two replicas, as a reward for helping Saras catch the star amber cheat."

"I appreciate it." Han furrowed his brow and cast a questioning glance in Luke's direction, then, when Luke nodded, he continued, "But the guy Saras caught wasn't exactly a cheat."

"It was something of an inside job," Luke added. "We'll tell you about it later, but first—"

"Tell us about it now," Raynar interrupted. "If you believe any of our transacting partners are not being honest with us, we wish to hear it."

"Actually, it isn't your partners," Luke said. "The Dark Nest has been the one taking the star ambers."

The Unu began to clack their mandibles, and Raynar lowered his melted brow. "The Neimoidian is a Joiner?"

"No," Luke said. "We think—"

"We *know*," Han corrected.

"It *looked* like the Neimoidian had a deal with Gorog," Luke compromised. "He was trading reactor fuel and hyperdrive coolant to them."

This drew a tumult of mandible clacking from Unu.

"Perhaps we were mistaken about the nature of the material," C-3PO suggested quietly. "Unu seems quite amused by the idea that the Colony owns a reactor."

"They wouldn't know," Han insisted. "Who can say what Gorog is hiding?"

"Of course we would know, Captain Solo! The Colony learns from its mistakes." Raynar fell silent for a moment, then spoke in a calmer voice. "But we will discuss your idea while I show you our production facilities, if that will make you feel better."

He extended a hand toward the furnaces.

Luke and Han exchanged glances. Luke said, "It might be better to do that—"

"Come!" Raynar insisted. "What are you afraid of? Killiks do not have accidents."

Luke exhaled in frustration, but reluctantly nodded and led the others after Raynar toward the furnaces.

Their first stop was a large, semicircular basin. Dozens of huge-headed Saras were standing around the curved end on all sixes, spitting out long streams of sticky white fiber and using their mandibles to feed it into the tub. On the other side of the basin, a steady procession of workers was gathering up large bundles of the dried fiber and carrying it off toward the furnaces.

"This is the materials pit," Raynar explained. He pointed at the spitting Killiks. "Saras's spinners produce the raw spin, and the workers take it to the furnaces to be melted down."

"Yeah, real interesting," Han said. "But about that reactor—have you actually *been* to Gorog's nest?"

Raynar's reply was curt. "Of course not. Gorog keeps its nest secret."

"Then you really can't know whether they have a reactor, can you?" Luke asked, picking up on Han's line of thought. "And it's probably a pretty big one, too, judging by how much fuel the Neimoidian had with him."

An uneasy murmur rolled through the Unu, then Raynar said, "If there was so much fuel, why didn't Saras find any when they captured the Neimoidian?"

"Because the fuel went the same place as our landspeeder and the 'Moid's guards," Han said. "The Fizz took it."

"And that's something we should discuss *now*." Luke's throat was aching from all the smoke and soot in the air; even without the Fizz, he would not have wanted to stay inside the building long enough for a complete tour. "The Fizz didn't just bubble up when those fuel rods happened to be there. It was *attacking* them."

Unu's drumming grew more agitated.

"Now they don't believe there ever was any fuel,"

C-3PO reported. "They're accusing us of making up the whole story."

Han rolled his eyes. "I knew this would happen." He turned to Raynar. "Look, it's been a long couple of days. If you don't want to listen—"

"Hold on, Han," Luke said. "We have evidence."

Han frowned. "We do?"

Luke nodded. "Probably." He turned to R2-D2. "Artoo, do you have a record of what happened in the forest?"

R2-D2 whistled a cheerful affirmative and began to project a hologram of the incident. The quality was not as good as what came out of a dedicated holopad, of course, but it was more than adequate to show the blue-black forms of several Gorog sneaking down a slope of hamogoni stumps. C-3PO's voice came from R2-D2's acoustic signaler, warning Luke and Han about the sneak attack. A pair of Gorog turned toward the holocam, and the scene grew confused as the battle played out.

A few moments later, it showed the Neimoidian smuggler fleeing his hoversled, while his Aqualish bodyguards remained behind, kneeling behind the barrels in the cargo bed and trading fire with Han and Luke. When one of the barrels suddenly rose and crashed back down, spilling its cargo, a murmur of surprise raced through the Unu entourage. R2-D2 added to the excitement by displaying a set of ionic-decay readings that left no doubt about the nature of the rods.

By the time the froth began to consume the rods a few minutes later, a stunned silence had fallen over Raynar and Unu. Luke waited until the Fizz had engulfed the hoversled, its cargo, and the Aqualish guards, then had R2-D2 shut down his holoprojector.

Raynar remained silent a long time, and even the cacophony inside the replica facility grew subdued. A stream of orange slag began to shoot out of one furnace and disappear down a waste tube through the floor, and Han groaned and made a winding motion with his finger.

Luke signaled him to be patient. The froth had appeared very quickly after the reactor rods were exposed in the forest, but slag was not nearly as toxic as reactor rods—or even hyperdrive coolant. It would take a lot more slag to trigger the Fizz. So Luke hoped, anyway.

Finally, Raynar raised his gaze. "We thank you for bringing this to our attention."

"Friends *should* be willing to tell each other difficult truths," Luke said, feeling encouraged by Raynar's reasonable tone. "It's only a theory at this point. But if we're right, the Fizz is going to keep attacking Saras."

The pronouncement sent a peal of nervous drumming through Unu. Raynar's eyes seemed to sink even deeper into their dark sockets, but he said, "Theory or not, we are listening."

"Good." Luke glanced down at R2-D2. "Start the holo where we left off."

The droid reactivated his holoprojector. Unu crowded closer, the insects in back climbing onto the shoulders of those in front, and within moments they were towering over Luke and his companions in a great, teeming mass. Luke squatted down beside the holo and shifted the X-wing replica to one hand.

"Look how the Fizz is attacking the hoversled and the fuel, but not the hamogoni trunk." He inserted his finger into the holo, pointing out the features as he named them, then moved to the stone foundation, where the Aqualish had collapsed. "The same here. It's attacking the bodyguards, but not the stones they're on."

A low, chattery rustle rose from Unu, and Raynar asked,

"Are you saying that the Fizz does not attack anything native to Woteba?"

"Not quite," Luke said. R2-D2 continued to run the holorecording, and the hoversled and Aqualish began to disintegrate beneath the Fizz. "I'm saying it only attacks things that harm Woteba."

"And you think that is why the Fizz attacks us?" Raynar clarified. "Because we harm Woteba?"

"I think it attacks you *when* you harm Woteba," Luke corrected. "As long as you aren't hurting the environment, it remains inert."

The last bits of the hoversled and the Aqualish vanished. The froth quickly subsided, leaving only piles of brown dirt behind, and the forest in the holorecording returned to stillness.

R2-D2 shut down his projector, and when Raynar and Unu *still* remained silent, Han couldn't take it anymore.

"Well, that's our theory, anyway," he said. "There might be others that are just as good."

This brought Raynar out of his silence. "It is not a bad theory," he said. "It fits with what we have seen ourselves."

Luke felt like an immense weight had been lifted off his shoulders. He allowed himself a moment of self-congratulation—then a soft shudder, so faint it was barely perceptible, ran through Unu.

"Sometimes, Master Skywalker, we forget how clever you are." Raynar raised his hand and shook the stump of a gloved index finger toward Luke. "But not today."

"I don't understand," Luke said. Alarmed by Raynar's sudden hostility, he quieted himself inside and began to concentrate on the Force itself, on its liquid grasp, on its ripples lapping him from all sides. "You saw Artoo-Detoo's holo."

"We will not let you say we brought this on ourselves," Raynar said. "We *know* who is responsible."

"Not the Jedi," Luke said. It wasn't easy to match all the different ripples in the Force to an individual source—not with Saras and Unu obscuring the picture with their own hazy presences. "I promise you that."

The Unu mass began to disassemble itself and drop to the floor.

"Uh, maybe we should just forget the tour." Han began to ease toward the exit. "Thanks for the ship models. Really."

But Luke was not ready to give up. A familiar prickling had begun to rise between his shoulder blades, and he knew the Dark Nest was watching from the shadows, quietly reaching out to Raynar, carefully distorting the facts to put the Jedi in a bad light. Luke did not fight back. Instead he accepted his growing feeling of unease, allowing it to build into a chill along his entire spine, until the feeling had grown strong enough for him to have some sense of its source.

When Luke did not follow Han toward the exit, Han took his arm and began to pull. Raynar's eyes barely narrowed, but the Unu immediately moved to cut off their escape, mandibles spread.

"Uh, Luke?" Han said. "If you're going into a trance or something, now isn't the time. Really."

"Don't worry. Everything's under control." Luke passed the X-wing replica to Han, then pulled free and turned toward the nearest furnace, where there was a bantha-sized mound of dried spin he did not remember seeing a few moments before. "Just keep Raynar busy a second."

"Sure," Han said. "I'll let him explode my brain or something."

Luke used the Force to open a path through the Unu and

started toward the heap. His entire back began to nettle with danger sense; then Han's voice rose behind him.

"You know what I don't get? The *pilot*. How do you get that kind of detail inside—"

"Out of my way!" Raynar roared.

But that was all the time Luke needed to pull his lightsaber off his belt. He gathered himself for a Force leap . . . and that was when Alema Rar emerged from behind the spin mound, dressed in a midnight-blue jumpsuit with a plunging neckline and side slits.

"We are very impressed, Master Skywalker." Her lip curled into a smile that came off as more of a sneer. "But you won't need your lightsaber. We are not here to harm you."

"Is that so?" Luke deactivated his lightsaber—and allowed himself a small smile of triumph. Given the revulsion Raynar had shown on Kr when he saw the Dark Nest's slave-eating larvae, Luke felt certain that exposing the Dark Nest's presence now would redirect Raynar's hostility to where it belonged. "Then why were you hiding?"

"How could we have been hiding? We only just arrived." Alema started forward. "It came to our attention that we needed to correct a misunderstanding about what you saw in the forest."

"No misunderstanding," Han said. "We know what we saw."

"Do you?"

Alema slipped past Han without a second glance and continued toward Raynar. Luke tried to follow, but it was slow going. The mass of Unu seemed to part to let the Twi'lek pass, then crowd in behind her to gather in Luke's way.

"The rods *were* fuel rods, nobody is arguing that." Alema kept her gaze fixed on Raynar. "But maybe it was the *Jedi* who brought them to Woteba. Maybe Gorog discovered what you were doing and was there to intercept the reactor fuel."

"What?" Han cried. "That's backward. And a lie!"

Unu erupted into a tumult of clacking mandibles and booming thoraxes, and C-3PO reported, "Now Unu is saying *we* must have brought the rods!"

"That's ridiculous." Luke spoke in a calm voice, addressing Raynar directly, confident that Raynar's revulsion toward the Dark Nest would soon show itself. "Why would the Jedi bring reactor fuel to Woteba?"

Alema stopped two meters from Raynar. "Perhaps because you know more about the Fizz than you're saying." Though her words were addressed to Luke, her gaze remained fixed on Raynar. "Perhaps the Jedi knew it would trigger the Fizz. Perhaps that is why they sent reactor fuel to *all* of the Utegetu worlds."

"Wait a minute!" Han gasped. "You're saying *all* the Utegetu worlds have problems with Fizz?"

"Yes." Raynar's tone was bitter. "All the worlds you traded to us are poisoned."

"I'm sorry to hear that," Luke said, finally coming up behind Alema. "But the Jedi didn't know—and we *didn't* send reactor fuel to any of the worlds. We have no reason to wish the Colony harm."

"You serve the Galactic Alliance, do you not?" Raynar asked. "And the Alliance feels threatened by our rise."

"How do you figure?" Han scoffed. "Because you're harboring a few pirates and running some black membrosia? That's O-class stuff. If you were inside Alliance territory, you'd barely be a crime syndicate."

Raynar's face began to twitch beneath its scars, and it grew clear that he was not going to turn on Alema—at least not without some nudging.

"UnuThul, Han is right," Luke said. "The Galactic Alliance would like the Colony to be a good neighbor, but it is *not* afraid of you. The Dark Nest has been using your own fear to deceive you."

Given the Killiks' fluid sense of truth and fact, Luke knew his argument would be a difficult one to make—but the alternative was to ignite his lightsaber and cut a path back to the spaceport.

"Perhaps you are the one who is being deceived, Master Skywalker," Alema said. She turned to look at him, her eyes now smoky and dark and as deep as black holes. "Perhaps Chief Omas and Commander Sovv haven't told you just how afraid of us they really are . . . and perhaps *they* are not the only ones deceiving you."

Luke tried to puzzle out the Twi'lek's implication, then gave up and frowned at her. "What's that supposed to mean?"

As soon as Luke asked the question, he began to feel smoky and raw inside, and a cloudiness came to the edges of his vision.

"Have you given any more thought to why Mara lied to you about Daxar Ies?" Alema asked.

"No," Luke said. "And I doubt Mara did lie."

But even as he said it, Luke began to see why Mara could have been reluctant to tell him. She knew how much learning more about his mother meant to him, and being the one who had deprived him of that opportunity would have weighed heavily on her conscience. She might even have found the prospect to be more than she could bear.

Alema stepped closer, then spoke in a coldly alluring voice. "Of course, we hope that you're right, Master Skywalker, but, for everyone's sake, it's important that you consider the possibility that you're wrong—that you're being deceived by those close to you."

"There *is* no possibility," Han growled.

"Then no harm will come of considering it." Alema kept her gaze fixed on Luke, and the cloudiness at the edges of his vision began to darken. "But Master Skywalker must make up his own mind. That is why we have decided to give him the next code."

R2-D2 gave a little squeal of protest, and Luke said, "I don't want it."

Alema's voice grew sultry and knowing. "Now who are you deceiving, Master Skywalker? It is not us." She turned to C-3PO. "Remember this sequence. Master Skywalker will want it later."

She started to rattle off a string of numbers and letters, but Han pushed in front of her.

"All right, that's enough," Han said. "He said he didn't—"

"It's okay." Luke pulled him away. "Alema's right."

Han turned to face him. "You're sure?"

Luke nodded. "A code sequence isn't going to hurt us."

He knew, of course, that the sequence *would* hurt him; the Gorog's Night Herald would not be giving it to him otherwise. But Luke wanted the code anyway, not because he believed anything he might learn from R2-D2's files could change his love for Mara, or even because the smoke inside him was growing darker and harsher and harder to ignore every moment. He wanted the code because it had frightened him—and if he allowed himself to be afraid of what he did not know, then the Dark Nest had already won.

After giving the rest of the code sequence to C-3PO, Alema turned to Luke.

"You are as brave as we recall, Master Skywalker." The Twi'lek sent a cold shiver through Luke by trailing a finger down his arm, then added, "We don't know what Mara is trying to hide from you, but we hope it has nothing to do with your mother's death. It would be very sad if Daxar Ies was not her only victim."

The suggestion rocked Luke as hard as she intended, leaving him stunned, his mind clouded by the acrid smoke that had been rising inside since he had given her that first opening.

Not so with Han.

"What?" he roared. In a move so fast that even Luke barely saw it, Han pulled his blaster and leveled it at the Twi'lek's head. "Now you've just gone too far."

Alema calmly turned to look down the barrel. "Come, Han." She flicked her finger in the air, using the Force to send the barrel of Han's blaster jerking toward the ceiling. "If you were going to pull the trigger, you wouldn't have wasted your one chance talking about it."

She turned her back on Han, then went over to Raynar, rose up on her toes, and kissed his scar-stiffened lips.

"We'll see you in our dreams." She remained there for a moment, then dropped back down and looked toward Luke and Han. "And keep a closer watch on these two. We can't have them stirring up any more Fizz with those reactor rods."

Raynar spent a moment studying Luke and Han over Alema's head, then nodded and released her hand without looking at her. She slipped past and moved off through the mass of Unu, and though Luke was careful never to take his eyes off her, he somehow missed the moment when she vanished from sight.

Once Alema was gone, Raynar said, "We have decided to keep a closer watch on you two. We cannot have you two stirring up any more Fizz with your reactor rods."

"You don't say?" Han's tone was sarcastic. "Does she

tell you when to sanibrush your teeth and use the refresher, too?"

"She?" Raynar lowered his brow. "She *who*?"

"Alema Rar," Luke prompted. "The Night Herald?"

Raynar frowned, and Unu drummed their thoraxes.

"The Killiks seem to have no idea who you're talking about," C-3PO informed them. "Unu claims it has never met Alema Rar."

"*Burrurruru ubburr,*" one of the insects added. "*Uuubu burru.*"

"And everyone knows the Night Herald is just a myth you tell the larvae," C-3PO translated, "to make them regurgitate."

Han scowled and pointed his blaster at the ground in front of Raynar. "That myth was just standing there kissing you."

"Had we *ever* kissed Alema Rar, we are sure we would remember," Raynar retorted. "And we certainly were not *just* kissing her. Alema Rar is dead."

"Don't tell me," Han said. "She died in the Crash."

"Of course not," Raynar said. "She died at Kr, with the rest of the Dark Nest."

"Just great." Han let his chin drop. "Here we go again."

"We do not understand why you persist in this fantasy, but you are not going anywhere. That is the point." Raynar extended his hand. "You will give us your weapons."

Han's knuckles whitened around his blaster grip. "When Hutts ride swoops!"

"We would rather have it now," Raynar said. Han's blaster twisted free of his grasp and floated over, then Raynar turned to Luke. "Master Skywalker?"

Luke hated to yield his weapon—especially with Alema Rar running around loose—but he would have an easier time recovering it later than fighting to keep it now. He removed the focusing crystal from the handle—the Jedi equivalent of unloading a weapon before surrendering it—and handed both the crystal and the lightsaber over.

"A wise choice," Raynar said. A swarm of large, orange-chested worker insects began to gather around Luke and Han. "Saras will see you to your new quarters. Please do not force us to harm you by attempting to leave before Princess Leia returns with a way to stop the Fizz."

TEN

In the middle of the Murgo Choke hung the white wedge of an *Imperial*-class Star Destroyer, its hull lit by the harlequin blaze of four different suns. To its left hung two of the suns, an orange and yellow binary system well matched in both size and color. To its right hung an odd couple, a blue giant orbited by a crimson dwarf so small and dim Leia could barely tell it was there. And directly behind the Star Destroyer, stretched between the two sets of binary stars like the web of some enormous spider, was the sapphire veil of the Utegetu Nebula.

"You see? This one did not miscalculate!" Saba was perched on the edge of the *Falcon*'s copilot's chair, squinting out at the Star Destroyer. "We were *pulled* out of hyperspace."

"Maybe," Leia said. Threading its way between the two pairs of binary stars, the Murgo Choke was the trickiest of the many complicated hyperspace transits connecting the Rago Run to the Utegetu Nebula. "But there are a hundred things in the Choke more likely to revert us than the mass of a single Star Destroyer."

Saba hissed in annoyance. "The Star Destroyer'z *masz* did not pull us out—itz artificial gravity generatorz did. That is the *Mon Mothma* ahead."

Leia frowned at her tactical display, but the electromagnetic blast of the four stars was overpowering all the *Falcon*'s sensor and comm systems. She saw only a cloud of static on the screen.

"You can't know that," Leia said.

"This one findz your lack of faith disturbing, Jedi Solo." Saba ruffled her neck scales in what Leia had come to recognize as disappointment. "You must learn not to doubt your Master."

"You keep telling me to doubt everything," Leia pointed out.

"And do you listen?" Saba held her hand out. "You are a terrible student. Give me your lightsaber."

Leia shook her head. "The last time I did that, you hit me on the head with it. I had a knot for a week."

Saba's voice grew harsh. "So you are disobeying?"

Leia frowned. Saba kept saying that she needed to learn to obey—but Leia was not about to make the same mistake twice. She held out her own hand.

"First, give me *your* lightsaber."

Saba's eyes widened, then she began to siss. "You are so funny, Jedi Solo." She lowered her hand. "But at least you have learned *something*."

"Thanks," Leia said. "Now, how sure are you that's the *Mon Mothma* up there?"

"How sure are you that it is *not*?"

"This is no time for games, Master. I need to know."

"*Life* is a game, Jedi Solo," Saba said. "If you need to know, find out."

Leia let out her breath in exasperation, then reached into the Force. She felt Mara and three more Jedi StealthX pilots hanging off the *Falcon*'s stern. Because of the close tolerances involved in transiting the Choke, all five craft had needed to make their own jump calculations, and the likelihood of the entire flight making a mistake that brought them out so close together was practically nil. They had definitely been pulled out of hyperspace by an artificial gravity well.

But that still did not explain how Saba knew it was the *Mon Mothma* ahead. The Galactic Alliance had two *Imperial*-class Star Destroyers equipped with hidden gravity-well generators. Leia stretched out to the ship in the Force and felt the expected throng of life, but the concentration was too dense for her to recognize the presence of anyone in particular.

"Okay, we were interdicted," Leia said. "But I still don't see how you can be sure it's the *Mothma* up there. It could be the *Elegos A'Kla*."

"It is the *Mon Mothma*," Saba insisted. "But what does it matter?"

"It doesn't, really," Leia said. "Nobody in the Defense Force is going to interfere with a Jedi mission, but the *Mothma*'s commander, Gavin Darklighter, is an old family friend. He won't waste too much of our time."

"It would not be wise to place your trust in friendship, Jedi Solo," Saba warned. "Chief Omas tried to keep the fleet'z departure from us, and now this. Commander Dark-lighter will have orderz."

"Probably," Leia said. "But you don't know Gavin Dark-lighter. He always finds a way to do the right thing."

She touched Mara and the other StealthX pilots in the Force, alerting them that she was about to get under way, then activated the *Falcon*'s sublight drives and started forward. The Star Destroyer quickly began to swell in the viewport, and the comm signals and sensor returns soon grew strong enough for the electronic scrubbers to clarify. Finally, the *Mon Mothma*'s transponder code appeared on the tactical display, surrounded by a large cloud of symbols denoting war-era XJ3 X-wings and Series 4 E-wings.

A comm officer's voice crackled over the cockpit speaker, so raw and scratchy that it was impossible to recognize the owner's species. "*Millennium Falcon,* be advised that the Utegetu Nebula is under blockade. Please reverse course."

"*Blockade?*" Leia made herself sound more surprised than she really was. "Under whose authority?"

"The Galactic Alliance's, obviously," the comm officer replied. "I ask again, please reverse course. All vessels attempting to enter or leave the nebula will be impounded."

Leia's blood started to boil. "*You* be advised that the *Falcon* is on a Jedi mission."

She began to angle ahead of the *Mothma*'s bow. The tactical display, still smudged with blank streaks and small patches of static, showed a squadron of XJ3s moving to intercept the *Falcon.*

Leia frowned, then said to the comm officer, "I trust you've been in the Defense Force long enough to understand the grief you'll face if you interfere with us."

"I know the consequences of ignoring my orders," the officer said. "This is your last warning. Continue to advance, and the *Falcon* will be impounded."

The Force grew electric with the outrage and surprise of Mara and the other StealthX pilots, but Saba was more contemplative. She flicked the air absentmindedly with her forked tongue, then activated her own microphone.

"We will consider your threat," she said. "Stand by."

"Stand by?" the officer echoed. "That is not—"

Saba closed the channel, then turned to Leia. "We should reverse course."

"And leave Han and Luke stranded on Woteba?" Leia asked. "Never!"

"Having no ship and being stranded are different thingz," Saba replied. "Master Skywalker is . . . he is *Mas-*

ter Skywalker. He can find a way off Woteba anytime he wishez."

"But he *won't*," Leia objected. "He's waiting for us to return with a cure for the Fizz—and in the meantime, the Colony is provoking the Chiss again. We need to get him and Han off Woteba before a war breaks out."

Mara began to pour impatience into the Force, urging Leia and Saba to start their run.

Leia looked over at Saba.

Saba shook her head. "Not through the Murgo Choke. We cannot take a Star Destroyer."

"Take it?" Leia asked. "You think we're going to *attack* the *Mon Mothma*?"

"You know another way through the Choke?" Saba asked.

"Sure," Leia said. "We call their bluff."

Leia reached out to initiate the Jedi battle-meld and discovered that Mara and the other pilots had already opened it. Clearly in agreement with Leia, Mara was radiating confidence, reassuring them that the StealthXs were ready to drop in behind the XJ3s. Saba let out a hiss of resignation, then began rerouting extra power to the shields.

Leia reopened the comm channel to the *Mon Mothma*.

Before she could speak, the comm officer's angry voice came over the cockpit speakers. "*Falcon*, we have finished warning you. Slow and stand by for escort."

"Negative," Leia said. "Let me speak to Commodore Darklighter."

"Commodore Darklighter is unavailable," the officer replied.

Saba made a hissing sound deep in her throat, and Leia saw on her display that the XJ3 squadron had moved into firing position behind the *Falcon*.

"Kill your drives and stand by," the comm officer ordered, "or we *will* open fire."

Leia rolled her eyes. "You're not going to fire on the *Millennium Falcon* without Commodore Darklighter looking over your shoulder. Put him on *now,* or stand down and let us proceed with our mission."

Lock-alarms chimed in the cockpit as the XJ3s designated the *Falcon* a target. Leia could not believe that this would actually come down to being fired upon, but she began to juke and jink like a fighter pilot. It never hurt to be careful.

"You are certain they are bluffing?" Saba asked quietly.

"Nearly certain." Leia silenced the lock-alarms, and they quickly reactivated. The XJ3-wing pilots were selecting and deselecting the *Falcon,* repeatedly triggering the alarms in an effort to wear on the crew's nerves. "Almost, even."

A sense of satisfaction came to the battle-meld; Mara and the other StealthX pilots had slipped in behind the XJ3s without being noticed.

Saba switched her microphone to the ship's intercom. "Cakhmaim, Meewalh, shut down those quad cannonz."

"Good idea," Leia said. "The last thing we want is a shooting match with the *Mon Mothma.* It would only make Chief Omas believe that the Jedi have gone completely over to the Colony's side."

Saba gave her a sideways glance. "That, too."

Leia sensed through the meld that the Barabel's concern had been more immediate: they were not going to be much use to Han and Luke if they got blasted to atoms here.

"I find your lack of faith disturbing, Master," Leia said. "You must learn to trust your pilot."

Saba made a rasping sound low in her throat. "The pilot, this one trustz. It is her arrogant student that worriez her."

Leia laughed, then activated the intercom again. "Cakhmaim and Meewalh, when you're done in the turrets, go to engineering and power up Han's repulsor beam."

Saba raised her brow. "We are going to *push* the *Mothma* out of the way?"

"Hardly," Leia said. The repulsor beam was a special anti-dartship device Han had developed the year before by rigging the *Falcon*'s tractor beam so the polarity could be reversed. "But we may need to swat a few flitnats off our tail."

Leia reset the lock-alarms for what must have been the tenth time, and they did not reactivate. The XJ3s had stopped flicking their target selectors.

The meld began to fill with reptilian battle lust. "If this is a bluff, they are raising the stakez," Saba said. "It feelz to this one like they are about to open—"

Before Saba could say *fire,* eight of the XJ3s—four two-ship combat teams—broke into evasive loops and spirals, and the *Falcon*'s military comm scanner came alive with the alarmed voices of XJ3 pilots.

"Targeted! Targeted! . . . breaking right . . . breaking left . . . where are they? . . . still on me . . . can't shake him . . . find 'em, *find them!*"

Then a deep female voice announced, "StealthXs! We have StealthXs out here!"

Leia pushed the throttles past their safety stops, still angling ahead of the *Mon Mothma*'s bow. The tactical display showed the remainder of the XJ3s—the four craft that had been guarding the squadron's flanks—sliding into firing position and slowly closing to range.

Leia told the Noghri to activate the repulsor beam and dust two of the remaining starfighters off their tail.

"Only two?" Saba asked. "Why?"

"Just sending a message," Leia said. "Besides, we may need those XJs later."

The cabin lights dimmed, and the status displays winked out as every spare erg of the *Falcon*'s power was diverted to the repulsor beam. But unlike the first time they had used the device, the shields did not go down. When Han had decided that the repulsor beam was too handy to dismantle, Leia had insisted that they install a supplemental fusion unit so they wouldn't be quite so vulnerable to counterattack.

The *Falcon* gave a little jolt as the Noghri triggered the repulsor beam. Two of the XJ3s suddenly went out of control and veered toward the edge of the tactical display, and the comm scanner erupted into startled curses and a tense request for permission to open fire.

Gavin Darklighter's voice came over the comm an instant later. "Captain Solo, will you *please* stop kriffing around? Chief Omas is serious about this blockade."

Leia continued to accelerate, still jinking and juking. "Is that why he didn't inform the Jedi about it?"

Darklighter hesitated, and the *Falcon*'s lock-alarms whined again. Leia checked the tactical display and saw that the last pair of XJ3s had reached firing range. The rest of the squadron was still rolling and looping, either trying to recover from the repulsor beam or shake the StealthXs still threatening them with target-locks. Thankfully, there was no shooting.

"I apologize for the language, Princess," Darklighter finally said. "I was addressing Captain Solo."

"Han is unavailable," Leia replied. "I'm in command of the *Falcon* for now."

The channel fell silent for a long time, and Leia began to wonder if Darklighter had deliberately manipulated the admission out of her. He was a shrewd commander, and he would be analyzing even the tiniest scrap of information for hints as to the true nature of their mission. Normally, it would not have troubled Leia to share such information with a high-ranking Defense Force officer. But right now, the last thing she wanted was for anyone subordinate to the Chief of State to realize there was a power vacuum at the top of the Jedi order.

They passed in front of the *Mon Mothma*'s bow. The last pair of XJ3s remained on their tail, but Darklighter sent none of the other squadrons to cut off the *Falcon*—and that made Leia nervous.

"Keep an eye on the *Mothma*'s tractor beams," she said to Saba. "Let me know the instant any of them start to power—"

Leia felt a surge of alarm from Saba and knew the Star Destroyer was activating its tractor beams. She accelerated into an open, erratic spiral that would make it almost impossible for the beam operators to lock on to the *Falcon*.

The red cones of four tractor beams appeared on the tactical display, stabbing out from the *Mon Mothma*'s designator symbol to circle the *Falcon*. Leia aimed for the trailing edges of the beams, rolling and diving from one to the next, alert for the telltale hesitation that Han claimed always gave the operators away when they figured out the strategy.

An instant after the tractor beams appeared, Darklighter said, "I didn't . . . any offense, Princess." With the comm antenna constantly struggling to adjust to the *Falcon*'s gyrations, the signal had grown a little patchy. "Chief Omas has been . . . to reach Master Skywalker for a week. When there was no response, he decided the Jedi must be . . . the Killiks' side again."

Saba hissed, and Leia felt the same frustration rising in Mara and the other StealthX pilots that was welling up in her. She started to make a sharp reply—then realized what Darklighter was trying to do and remained silent.

"He is trying to provoke you," Saba agreed. She closed

the channel, then set the comm unit to burst mode to prevent the *Mon Mothma*'s tractor beam operators from riding a comm wave back to the *Falcon*. "Do you still believe Commodore Darklighter is bluffing?"

"If he weren't, he'd be shooting by now," Leia said. She opened the channel to Darklighter again. "Nice try, Commodore. But if Chief Omas is claiming that the Jedi have betrayed the Galactic Alliance just because he can't reach Luke—"

"What's . . . supposed to assume?" Darklighter interrupted. "And now . . . only proving him right. Kill your drives or . . . open fire."

Leia hesitated. Darklighter was really raising the stakes this time. If she refused to obey, he would either have to make good on his threat, or admit that it was a bluff. She reached into the battle-meld, urging Mara and the others to keep their fingers away from their triggers, then took a deep breath and activated her microphone again.

"I guess you'll have to open fire, Gavin. This is too important."

A long silence followed in which even the comm crackles seemed to be growing sharper. Leia angled back toward the center of the Choke, placing the last pair of XJ3s between her and the *Mon Mothma,* and the Star Destroyer's tractor beams flickered off. She felt a flash of approval from Mara and the StealthX pilots, then Darklighter's voice came over the comm again.

"Blast it, Princess! I'm not bluffing."

"Neither am I," Leia returned. Now that she was past the *Mon Mothma* and heading straight toward the blue curtain of the Utegetu Nebula, she was happy to keep talking. Every second carried her farther down the narrow alley between the two sets of binaries, closer to making that final jump to Utegetu. "Gavin, you know Luke. He would never betray the Galactic—"

"Nice try, Princess," Darklighter said. As the *Falcon* drew away from the *Mon Mothma,* the comm antenna was able to stay focused in one direction, and the signal grew stable again. "I won't let you stall your way out of this. You have ten seconds to kill your drives."

Leia glanced over at Saba. The Barabel was already on the intercom, warning the Noghri to be ready with the repulsor beam again.

"This is about Luke and Han, isn't it?" Darklighter asked. "They're still on Woteba. That's why Chief Omas can't reach Master Skywalker."

Apprehension filled the battle-meld. Darklighter's conjecture had been made over an open fleet channel, so there could be no doubt that it would be on Chief Omas's desk by this time tomorrow. Returning Luke to Alliance space had just become a bureaucratic race against Chief Omas.

"Commodore Darklighter, can we go to secure channel?" Leia asked. "In private?"

"I'm sorry, no." Darklighter's tone was sincere. "This is a matter of record. You have five seconds to kill your drives, Princess."

"Thank you for the warning, Commodore," Leia said. "No hard feelings."

Darklighter's voice grew genuinely alarmed. "Leia! I can't protect—"

Leia closed the channel, then slipped the *Falcon* out of her spiral pattern and returned to jinking and juking. It was just as hard for starfighter cannons to target, and she would make a lot more forward progress.

"Jedi Solo?" Saba asked. "What did Commodore Darklighter mean when he said this was a matter of record?"

"Just that he can't help us, I think," Leia said. "Admiral Bwua'tu must be aboard."

"*Nek* Bwua'tu?" Saba growled. "The Bothan who beatz the Thrawn simulator?"

"He *is* in command of the Fifth Fleet," Leia said. "But it doesn't matter. They're bluffing."

"And if they are not?"

"They *are*," Leia said. "And, anyway, there's a big difference between simbattle and the real thing. Don't worry."

"This one is curiouz, not worried." Saba's tone was even, but her irritation was pouring into the battle-meld. "She is *never* worried."

"Right—sorry."

The lock-alarms chimed, and the shield display flared yellow as they took an aft-port laser cannon hit.

"Still bluffing?" Saba asked.

"Yes, Master," Leia said. "We're still in one piece, aren't we?"

An instant later the *Falcon* gave a little jolt as the Noghri activated the repulsor beam, and a string of curses came over the comm scanner as the last pair of XJ3s tumbled away out of control. The battle-meld grew still and electric; the relationship between the Jedi and the Galactic Alliance had just changed in a way no one could foresee.

Leia checked the tactical display. The *Mon Mothma* was bleeding more squadrons into the Choke, while those that had been onstation were moving into screening formations in front of the StealthXs' last-known position. No one was coming after Leia and Saba, but the combat controllers were being careful to leave a clear firing lane between the Star Destroyer and the *Falcon*.

Mara reached out through the battle-meld, urging Leia and Saba to run for it. The StealthXs would have to hang back and sneak through later. They would rendezvous at Woteba.

Leia wished her good luck, then the canopy's blast-tinting went black as the first turbolaser strike blossomed ahead. Her shoulders hit the crash webbing as the *Falcon* bucked through the shock wave, then space around them erupted into exploding clouds of color as the gunnery crews began to refine their targeting.

"Jedi So-o-lo!" Saba's voice jumped as each shock wave shook the *Falcon*. "Next time, you wi-ill listen to your Ma-aster!"

"Trust me!" Leia said. "They're just trying to make us believe they're serious."

"They are doing a good job," Saba said.

Leia swung the *Falcon* toward the blue giant. "We'll run for the big guy. The EM blast will interfere with their targeting sensors, and the gravity well will give us some acceleration."

Saba nodded her approval. "Go-od! You have done this before."

"Only forty or fi-if-ty times." Silently, Leia added, *Just never without Han.*

The ride smoothed out for a moment as the *Falcon* slipped out from under the Star Destroyer's firing pattern. The canopy tinting went black as the face of the giant sun slid across the forward viewport, and still its boiling mass shined through the transparisteel, warming their faces and stabbing at their eyes. Their sensors and comm units quickly fell victim to the star's electromagnetic blast, and even the ship's internal electronics began to flicker and wave.

Then the *Mon Mothma*'s gunnery crews found them again. A curtain of a turbolaser strikes erupted ahead, circles of red and orange so pale against the star's glare that they were barely visible. Leia pointed the *Falcon* at the closest blossom and surrendered her hands to the Force. The shields crackled with crimson energy as they passed through the dissipation turbulence, then the *Falcon* shuddered as they bounced through the shock waves.

The pilot's console lit up with damage indicators and critical warnings. There were broken seals, leaking ducts, misaligned gyros.

"Will you look at that?" Leia complained. "Han's going to kill me!"

Another blast bounced them sideways, and Saba said, "This one only hopez we last long enough to give him the chance."

Judging they had descended about as deep into the star's gravity well as they dared, Leia pulled up and started around the curve of its massive blue horizon. The *Mon Mothma* continued to pour turbolaser fire in their general direction, but the electromagnetic camouflage had finally confused their targeting sensors, and none of the strikes hit closer than within a kilometer or two of the *Falcon*.

The turbolaser strikes soon faded altogether, and Leia knew they had rounded the horizon and vanished from the *Mon Mothma*'s line of sight. She rolled the cockpit away from the blue giant and started to pull out of its gravity well.

The canopy grew clear enough that the red orb of the blue giant's tiny satellite star shined through the bottom of the forward viewport. The other binary set, the orange and yellow stars, were shining through top of the canopy, and the blue veil of the Utegetu Nebula was barely visible directly ahead.

Leia glanced down at her tactical display, silently urging the sensors to come online so they could plot their jump to Utegetu. There was no reason to be anxious—neither the *Mon Mothma* nor her fighters could catch the *Falcon* now—but something still felt wrong. She had a cold, queasy feeling in her stomach, and she could not escape the feeling that someone was watching.

"Saba, do you—"

"Yes," Saba said. "It feelz like we have raced into the shenbit'z den."

The nacelle temperatures were already 20 percent beyond specification, but Leia grabbed the throttles and began to push them even farther beyond the safety locks . . . and the *Falcon* decelerated as though it had hit a perma-crete wall.

"What the—"

The last of Leia's exclamation was drowned out by the sudden screeching of proximity alarms and system alerts. The nacelle temperature shot past 140 and started toward 150, and the *Falcon* continued to decelerate.

Leia pulled the throttles back, then activated the intercom. "Cakhmaim, Meewalh, get into the cannon turrets and see—"

"Star Destroyer," Cakhmaim rasped. The *Falcon* began to slide sideways toward a point between the blue giant and its smaller satellite. "One of the new pirate hunters."

Leia used the attitude thrusters to spin the *Falcon* around, and saw that they were being drawn toward the distant wedge of a new version of the venerable *Victory*-class Star Destroyer. Mounted on its upper hull, in a turret nearly as large as the bridge itself, was one of the huge asteroid-tug tractor beams that Lando Calrissian had started selling the Defense Force to combat pirates and smugglers.

"Simbattle or not," Saba rasped, "this one thinkz maybe Admiral Bwua'tu *is* as good as they say."

ELEVEN

Han sat in his new quarters holding the model of the *Millennium Falcon* in his lap, running his thumbs over its silky surface, peering into the dark holes of the cockpit canopy, hefting its substantial weight in his hands. Sure, the workmanship was good, and there was something hypnotic about rubbing your fingers over the spinglass. But he could not imagine where the Squibs were going to sell a billion of these things. The stuff was hardly art—and with the galaxy still struggling to recover from the war against the Yuuzhan Vong, there were only so many people with credits to throw away on kitsch.

Someone was definitely being played here. But was the Colony playing the Squibs, or the Squibs playing the Colony, or both of them playing someone else?

Luke entered from his quarters, his eyes closed and his hands pressed to the iridescent spinglass, using the Force to search for a stress point in the exterior wall of their two-room prison. He did the same thing every hour or so, stopping in a different place and having R2-D2 use his utility arm to scratch a small x in the hard surface.

A few minutes later, they always heard a crew of Killiks scurrying over the same spot, reinforcing the outside of the wall with more spinglass. The barrier had to be close to a meter thick in places, but Han did not suggest that the xs were a waste of time. If Luke wanted to mess with Saras's mind, that was his business.

They both knew that Luke could break them out of their prison anytime he wanted—and Han suspected that Raynar knew it, too. Escape would be the easy part. But it would do them no good until they thought of a way to find the Dark Nest, and so Han and Luke were being patient— being patient and thinking hard and doing their best to look very bored.

Han flipped the model of the *Falcon* over again. There was no shift of weight inside, but that didn't mean anything. He had known a smuggler once who had molded his entire cargo of contraband explosives into landspeeder dashboards and walked them through Imperial customs with all the proper documentation.

Without opening his eyes, Luke said, "She's all right, Han."

"I know she is." Han put his ear close to the model and shook it, but heard nothing. "I still worry about her. It's not easy for her to be away from me this long."

"Is that so?"

"Yeah," Han said. "She has trouble sleeping if my snoring's not there to drown out the banging in the climate control lines."

Luke smiled. "Thanks for clearing that up." He returned to running his hand over the wall. "I've been wondering what she sees in you."

Though Han had not been dwelling on how much he missed Leia, he saw now that he had been thinking of her without realizing it—that he was *always* thinking of her, half expecting her to be there every time he turned around, imagining her voice in the distance whenever the tunnel-house fell silent, reaching out to her when he rolled over at night. And Luke had *known* all of that was going on in the back of Han's mind—just as Han knew that something similar was going on the back of Luke's.

Han spun around on his stool. "Did you just use a Jedi mind-reading trick on me?"

Luke stopped and looked puzzled. "We can't really do that, Han." he said. "Well, *most* of us can't."

Without having to ask, Han knew that Luke had been thinking of Jacen when he added that last bit. "I was afraid of that."

"Afraid of—" Luke stopped, then shook his head. "I don't think we're reading each other's minds, Han. We haven't been here long enough to become Joiners."

"Yeah? Then how come *I* know what you want for lunch today?"

"I don't see how Master Skywalker can be hungry already," C-3PO said from his place in the corner. "He just had breakfast."

"Threepio's right," Luke said. "It's too early to think about—"

"A nerfburger and hubba crisps," Han interrupted. "With a lurol smoothie to wash it down."

Luke furrowed his brow. "You're right, that *does* sound good. But I wasn't thinking about it until you . . . or was I?"

"It wasn't me," Han growled. "I hate hubba crisps."

Luke's face fell. "Raynar is trying to make Joiners of us."

"You think so?"

Luke was so upset that he failed to notice the sarcasm in Han's voice. "The Dark Nest must think the Colony will be able to dominate me and take control the Jedi order."

"Dominate *you*, Master Skywalker? Why, that's a perfectly absurd idea!" C-3PO cocked his head at the look of alarm on Luke's face. "Isn't it?"

Instead of answering, Luke went back to searching for

stress points. "They've just been playing for time, Han. We've got to get out of here."

Han flipped the model over. "And do what?"

"You know what," Luke said. *Find the Dark Nest.*

Han remained on his stool. "How, exactly? The bugs know every move we make. The second we step outside our quarters, Saras is going to come running with about a thousand Killiks—and we don't have any weapons. We're better off just waiting until Leia and Mara get back."

Luke frowned. "Are you feeling all right, Han?"

"Fine," Han said. Actually, he was feeling great, now that he knew how they were going to find the Dark Nest, but he could not tell that to Luke. The walls had ears—well, *something* did. "Just in no mood to hear any ronto-brained escape plans."

He rose and went over to the door membrane. It was opaque and bonded shut by some gooey fiber the bugs had spun over the outside, but the spinglass surrounding it was so thin and translucent that Han could see the silhouette of their Saras guard standing watch outside.

He waved an arm to get the guard's attention. "Hey, open up! I need to talk to you."

The guard came over to the wall and pressed its orange thorax to the spinglass. A muffled thrum reverberated through the wall.

"Saras says she can hear you through the wall," C-3PO said, clunking over to translate. "And she is reluctant to open the door, since Master Skywalker was just talking about escaping."

Han shot an irritated look over his shoulder.

Luke shrugged. "It's not like they couldn't figure it out on their own."

"Yeah, okay." Han raised the *Falcon* model up. "Can you get in touch with the Squibs who are buying these?"

"*Mooroor oom.*" The bug's rumbling was so softened by the wall that the words seemed mumbled. "*Oomoor ooo.*"

"She seems to be saying that the Squibs aren't *purchasing* the line—they're handling it on consignment." C-3PO turned to Han. "I don't think that's wise. From what I recall, the Squibs we met on Tatooine weren't very trustworthy."

"*Ooorr?*" Saras demanded. "*Ooom?*"

"Don't worry," Han said, addressing the bug through the wall. "They won't pull anything on Raynar—"

"*OoomoMoom.*"

"Right, *UnuThul* has trading in his blood," Han said. "Besides, with the idea I've got, we're all going to make so much money the Squibs won't *want* to cheat you."

"I can't believe this, Han," Luke said, coming over to the door. "You're thinking about *money* at a time like this?"

"Yeah," Han said. When it came to money, Squibs could do the impossible. But he didn't say *that* aloud—he tried not to even think it.

Luke rolled his eyes, and Han scowled at him, hoping he would finally get the message. "Why don't you go input those code sequences Alema gave you or something?"

The anger that flashed in Luke's eyes suggested their minds were not all *that* connected. "That was low, Han, even for you."

"Sorry—didn't mean to rattle your cage," Han said. "Just let me make my deal. I'm trying to make the best of a bad situation here."

"Fine." Luke scowled at him, then stepped back shaking his head. "Don't let me stand in your way."

"When have I ever?" Han turned back to Saras. "Now, how long will it take you to get in touch with the Squibs?"

The bug drummed something short.

"She wants to know what your idea is," C-3PO said.

Han shook his head. "No way. I deal directly with the furbags on this."

"*Ooomoor.*"

The bug spread its four arms and began to back away from the wall.

"Okay, okay," Han said. "But if you steal the credit—"

"Han, will you just tell it?" There was a glint in Luke's eye that suggested he finally realized Han was up to something more useful than having R2-D2 scratch x's in the spinglass. "You're getting on my nerves."

Saras returned to the wall.

"All right—you're going to love this." Han held the model of the *Falcon* up close to the wall. "You're going to produce a billion of these, right?"

Saras nodded.

"What if I signed some of them?" Han asked. "They'd be worth five times as much, and the publicity would help launch the entire line."

The bug was silent for a moment, then it clacked its mandibles and pointed at Luke. "*Moomor?*"

"She's inquiring whether Master Skywalker would also sign his models," C-3PO informed them.

"When Sarlaccs fly!" Luke said. "I'm a Jedi Master, not some cheap HoloNet personality."

"Sure, he'll sign," Han said. "If the price is right."

The bug thrummed something else.

"Oh, dear," C-3PO said. "*This* may be a deal killer."

"Let me decide that," Han said. "What is it?"

"Saras says you'd have to sign one percent of the production run," C-3PO said.

"No problem," Han replied.

"Ten *million* units, Han?" Luke asked. "That would take you the rest of your life."

"I *said* it's no problem," Han answered. Even if he were

serious about the deal, he knew the Squibs were never going to *sell* ten million units. "Once we become Saras Joiners, anybody in the nest will be able to sign."

"Joiners?" Luke cried. "Han, that's not going—"

"Look, I'm as disgusted by the thought as you are," Han said. "But it's going to happen. We might as well take advantage of the situation."

"Moom!" the bug boomed.

It clacked its mandibles and began to back away from the wall, but Han shook his head and motioned it to the wall again.

"Not so fast, fella," he said. "I don't come cheap, you know."

"Could have fooled me," Luke muttered.

Saras stopped in the middle of the corridor that ran past their quarters. *"Oom morr?"*

Han shook his head. *"That,* I talk about with the Squibs." He backed away from the wall. "If they're interested, tell them to come see me."

The bug gave a noncommittal throb and retreated to the other side of the corridor.

Han returned to his stool, and Luke came and sat on the bunk next to him.

"You really think your autograph is worth that much?" Luke asked.

He held Han's eye a little longer than was necessary, and Han *thought* he could sense something more in the question.

"A million credits, at least," Han said. He passed the *Falcon* model to Luke, casually flipping it belly-up as he did so. "And *your* signature would go double that. Maybe triple."

"Triple?" Luke looked genuinely flattered. "Really?"

"At least," Han said. He had always been a little too repulsed to ask Jaina and Zekk much about how things had progressed when they started to become Joiners, but just in case Saras was starting to share his mind, too, he tried to keep his thoughts away from what he really intended to ask of the Squibs. "With all the 'Net the Jedi are getting regarding the Reconstruction, you're going to be as hot as a blue star right now."

"In that case, maybe I *should* consider it," Luke said. He casually flipped the model back over, and Han thought he felt a little jolt of surprise in the back of his mind—or maybe that was just wishful thinking. "But first, I think I'll take your other advice."

Han frowned. "My other advice?"

"About the code sequence Alema gave me," Luke said. "I think it's time I had a look."

Now Han *knew* Luke understood.

"You sure?" Han asked. He was fairly sure that Luke had not used the code sequence because he was afraid of what it might reveal about Mara—it might bolster Alema's suggestion that Mara was hiding something terrible from him. "I thought you didn't want to give her the satisfaction."

"I don't," Luke said. "That's why I have to do it now— *before* we become Joiners."

Han nodded. He knew what Luke was thinking because he was thinking it, too. It was almost a given that Gorog had spies watching them, and the last thing they wanted was for the Dark Nest to start thinking about what Han *really* wanted from the Squibs. So Luke was going to keep Gorog occupied by giving it something to gloat over.

Luke passed the model back to Han, then turned to R2-D2. "Artoo, come here."

R2-D2 gave a sad whistle and started for Luke's quarters.

"No, Artoo," Luke said. "Come over *here*."

R2-D2 disappeared through the door, quietly tweeting and beeping to himself.

"Artoo!" C-3PO called. "Are you *ignoring* Master Skywalker?"

R2-D2 gave a one-beep reply.

C-3PO recoiled as though he had been struck, then turned to Luke. "It appears that his compliance routines have failed completely. I'll go see if I can reset them."

"That's okay," Luke said. "I'll handle this myself."

He extended a hand toward his quarters, and an electronic squeal sounded from inside. A moment later, R2-D2 floated back into Han's quarters, his treads whirring and his utility arm scratching along the wall.

"Artoo-Detoo!" C-3PO said. "This is Master Skywalker's last request before he becomes a Joiner. The least you can do is honor it."

R2-D2 shot back a string of whistles and trills.

"Don't be ridiculous," C-3PO said. "Of course I'll recite the override sequence that Jedi Rar provided, if Master Skywalker asks me to. That's what a protocol droid does. He facilitates."

R2-D2 let out a long bleat as Luke lowered him the floor between the bunk and Han's stool.

"Well, *you're* certainly not doing him any favors by behaving this way," C-3PO replied. "And don't talk to me like that. I'll trip your primary circuit breaker myself."

"That's enough, Threepio," Luke said. "Just give him the sequence."

R2-D2 screeched in protest and swung his holoprojector away from Luke, and it seemed to Han that he felt the *Falcon* replica give a faint shudder of anticipation, so soft and brief that it could have been a flutter in his own pulse. He pretended not to notice and put the model aside, turning the cockpit so that it was only partially facing Luke, and C-3PO dutifully recited the code sequence.

R2-D2 emitted a long, descending whistle, and the hologram of a large, fountain-filled chamber appeared on the floor in front of Han. The viewing angle was from high in one corner, where a security cam might be mounted, and the only movement in the room was the water falling from the fountains.

"What nonsense is this, Artoo?" C-3PO demanded. "You didn't record this. You're not that tall."

R2-D2 tweedled a reply.

"A *stolen* file?" C-3PO cried. "Stolen on whose authority?"

R2-D2 answered with a short whistle.

"I don't believe you," C-3PO said. "Even Artoo units have restraints against that sort of thing."

"What sort of thing?" Luke asked.

"Artoo claims he downloaded this file on his own initiative," C-3PO said. "But now I know he's running us a corrupted feed. He claims this is from the internal security computer at the Jedi Temple, and we all know there is no room like this at the Jedi Temple."

R2-D2 whistled a correction.

"Oh," C-3PO said. "Now he claims it's from the *old* Jedi Temple."

"The Room of a Thousand Fountains," Luke said. "I've seen it mentioned in some of those records we recovered from the *Chu'unthor*."

R2-D2 began to trill a long, additional explanation.

"He adds that he had no choice," C-3PO translated. "It was during the Jedi Revolt, and his owner had stopped talking to him. They were about to leave on a mission to Mustafar, and he needed to update his friend-or-foe data."

The hologram continued to show the empty room, and

Han began to think that the little droid had found one more clever way to keep his secret. Given the effect that secret was likely to have on Luke, Han almost hoped the droid had.

But R2-D2's acoustic signaler began to emit the tinny *pew-pew* of recorded blasterfire. Stray dashes of blue began to streak through the hologram, blowing fountains apart, burning holes in the walls, vanishing into the heights of the vaulted ceiling.

Dozens of children, dressed in simple Jedi robes and wearing a single braid on the sides of their heads, began to retreat into the room. The youngest, those under six or seven, simply tried to run or find a place to hide. The older ones were attempting to fight, using the Force to hurl benches and pieces of broken fountain at their attackers. Some were firing captured blaster rifles, while a few were trying to use their newly constructed lightsabers to ricochet bolts at the unseen enemy. For the most part, they failed miserably but bravely, deflecting half a dozen or a dozen attacks before one sneaked through and knocked them off their feet.

The teenagers came next, backing into the room with their lightsabers whirling, weaving a wall of flashing energy before a column of advancing infantry. Dressed in what appeared to be early stormtrooper armor, the soldiers assaulted ruthlessly, cutting down fleeing four-year-olds with the same brutal efficiency with which they slaughtered the Padawans.

Han had been just a boy in Garris Shrike's band of vagabonds when the Separatists tried to break away from the Old Republic, but he had seen enough of the war to recognize the finned helmets and independent joint covers on the white armor the soldiers wore.

"Clone troopers!"

R2-D2 gave a confirming tweet.

A huge Jedi with stooped shoulders and a gnarled face backed into view, anchoring the line of teenage defenders, his lightsaber sending bolt after bolt back at the attackers, lashing out to cut down one trooper after another. A pair of Padawans stepped in to support his flanks, and the entire line stopped falling back, the lightsabers of the young Jedi weaving an impenetrable wall of energy that—for a few short moments—allowed nothing past, not a blaster bolt, nor a clone trooper, nor even, it seemed to Han, a stray glance.

A blue lightsaber appeared at the edge of the holo, beating down the defense of the first Padawan and slashing through his torso, then slipping past the guard of the other one and cutting him down as well. The back of a blond head and a pair of caped shoulders appeared behind the blue blade and began to carry the attack to the stoop-shouldered Jedi.

The two stood battling toe-to-toe for only an instant before the caped figure slipped a strike and brought his own blade down on the defender's stooped shoulder, cleaving him deep into the torso. The Jedi's gnarled face paled with shock, and he collapsed in too much pain to scream.

The Padawans continued to battle on valiantly, but without the burly Jedi to anchor their line, they were no match for the sheer numbers assaulting them. Their defense collapsed, and the caped figure stepped aside, standing in seeming indifference as the clone troopers poured past to continue the slaughter of the children.

Han felt sickened and angered by what he was watching, but he also felt a little bit relieved. Mara would have been only a baby—and perhaps not even that—when the Jedi were slaughtered. Whatever Alema hoped to reveal with the code sequence, the scene they were watching could have nothing to do with Mara.

Finally, the last of the children had fallen, and the clones stopped firing. The caped figure studied the room for a moment, then gave a barely perceptible nod and turned back toward the entrance. The face that stared into the cam was clouded with anger, the eyes sunken and dark, the mouth set in a grim slash, but there was no mistaking who it belonged to.

Anakin Skywalker.

"That's enough, Artoo," Luke said. His face remained a mask of composure, but he rose and turned toward his own quarters. "Thank you."

R2-D2 deactivated his holoprojector, then emitted a long descending whistle and started to follow Luke through the door.

Han quickly rose and blocked the little droid's path. "Better stay put for a while," he said. "I'll handle this."

R2-D2 spun his photoreceptor toward C-3PO and trilled a long string of notes.

"I don't know why you're blaming *me*," C-3PO said. "I was only following instructions."

Han went to the doorway connecting his quarters to Luke's and found Luke floating cross-legged in the air, the backs of his wrists resting on his knees.

Without opening his eyes, Luke said, "I just need to center myself, Han."

"Yeah, that's what I figured." As Han spoke, he saw that Luke wasn't the only thing floating in the room. So were the stool, the bunk, and the X-wing replica Raynar had presented to him. The replica seemed to be trembling with excitement. "That was kind of rough in there, even on me."

"I'll be okay, Han," Luke said. "I just need to center myself."

"I'll bet," Han said. "What I don't get is how Alema knew what that code sequence was going to access. Even if she's telling the truth about that Daxar Ies character, she didn't say anything about him working on Artoo. There's no way he should have known what's in that memory sector Artoo's hiding."

"Oh, I'm quite certain he didn't," C-3PO said from behind Han. "The code Alema gave me was undoubtedly a universal key. Most droid-brain designers bury them in the circuitry architecture, as a safeguard against data lockouts and irreversible shutdowns. They simply force a unit to convert its most secure file to an open access file. In Artoo's case, that file was one incriminating him in the worst sort of data theft. No wonder he didn't want to reveal it!"

"That's great." Luke's eyes were still closed, but he was sitting on the floor now—as were the bunk, the stool, and the replica. "But I really need—"

"You said the code was a *universal* key?" Han said, turning around to face C-3PO. "You mean it could unlock all of Artoo's files?"

Artoo issued a sharp tweet, but C-3PO ignored him. "If we knew the basis for the code progression, of course. But not even Artoo knows that. It has self-changing variables, so unless we know the original algorithm and variables—"

"Okay, I get it." Han glanced back into the room, where Luke had given up trying to meditate and was simply sitting on the floor looking up at the doorway. "It's probably just as well."

A furrow came to Luke's brow. "Han—"

"All right, already." Han turned and shooed C-3PO away from the door. "Will you give the man some room? He needs to center himself."

"Han—"

"I'm going already."

"Han, that's not it." Luke closed his eyes. "I think it's time to close your deal."

"Already?" Han turned toward the door membrane. "I thought the Squibs would play it a little cooler than that."

Luke frowned. "I don't think it's the Squibs . . . You go on." He glanced down at the replica of his X-wing, then motioned Han out his door. "I need a minute to finish my meditations, but I'll be there when you need me."

Han turned toward the interior wall of his quarters, where a group of silhouettes was just growing visible through the translucent spinglass. Most of the figures were obviously Killiks, with shadows in their hands that suggested electrobolt assault rifles and Verpine shatter guns. But the two silhouettes in the center had only two arms each and carried no visible weapons. They were about Squib height, but a little too stocky and flat-faced.

A Saras guard pressed its thorax to the wall and boomed an order.

"She's ordering us to step away from the door," C-3PO said.

Han looked around and held his arms out to his side. "Where do you expect us to go? We're already in the back of the room."

The guard drummed an acknowledgment, then it and several other bugs used their mandibles to snip and rip the outer seal away from the doorway. A moment later, the two silhouettes they were escorting pushed through the membrane into Han's quarters, bringing with them a sweet-smelling cloud of the bond-inducing pheromones that pervaded the jail.

The first figure was a jug-eared Sullustan in a tidy white flight suit resembling that worn by the captains of commercial starliners. The second was a furry little Ewok with a white stripe running diagonally across a body that was otherwise as black as carbon.

"*Tarfang?*" Han gasped. He shifted his glance back to the Sullustan. "*Juun?*"

The Ewok chuttered something sharp at Han, while the Sullustan merely braced his hands on his hips and looked around the cell shaking his head.

"Tarfang suggests that since you're an inmate and Captain Juun is the owner of a fine Damorian *Ronto*-class transport, you should address him as *Captain* Juun," C-3PO reported.

"A *Ronto*?" Han did not bother to hide the disdain in his voice. Rontos were among the slowest, ugliest, and least efficient of the light transports crisscrossing the galaxy. He frowned at *Captain* Juun. "What happened to that Mon Cal Sailfish I set you up with?"

"She was too expensive," Juun explained. "My weekly payments were customarily running a week and a half late."

Han frowned. "But you were making them, right?"

"Yes," Juun said. "With the appropriate interest, of course."

"And Lando took her back for *that*?"

Tarfang jabbered an explanation.

"Captain Juun was too clever to give him the chance," C-3PO translated. "He traded his equity for *DR-Nine-one-nine-a*—free and clear."

"*Someone* got a real bargain." Han did not bother to ask what the pair were doing on Woteba; *Ronto*-class transports were just too slow for the inventory-running contract he had talked Lando into giving Juun. "I don't suppose the Second Mistake Squibs are the ones who gave you this steal?"

Juun looked surprised. "How did you know?"

"Because I sent for them and *you* showed up," Han replied. "It doesn't take a genius to know you're in deep with them."

Juun nodded proudly. "They gave us a ten-standard-year freighting contract." In a softer voice, he added, "We're exclusive."

"No kidding," Han said. "Let me guess, expenses included?"

Tarfang twitched his nose, then leaned toward Han and gibbered something suspicious.

"Tarfang requests—"

The Ewok whirled on C-3PO and barked a single word.

"—er, he *warns* you against discussing this with them," the droid corrected. "It's the Squibs' own bad fortune if they agree to such a poor bargain."

Han raised his palms to the Ewok. "Hey, that's between you guys—and I don't see why I should clue them in to *anything*, if they're not interested in my deal."

"Hold on!" Juun's voice was alarmed. "What makes you think they're not interested?"

Han made a show of looking around his quarters. "I don't see them here."

"Only because they are important business beings," Juun explained, "and this is a detention center."

Tarfang chittered an addendum.

"And they mustn't let themselves be seen with a pair of . . . oh, my . . ." C-3PO paused, searching for a diplomatic interpretation, until the Ewok growled. "With a pair of *dustcrusts* like you and Master Skywalker."

"That's okay," Han said. "I understand."

"You do?" Juun's cheek folds rose in relief. "In that case, they've authorized me to make you a very generous offer—they'll pay you a millicredit for each replica you sign."

"A whole millicredit?" Han repeated. "That much?"

Juun nodded eagerly. "That's ten thousand credits in all," he said. "And they're even willing to pay a third in advance. Emala said to tell you they haven't forgotten what you did for them on Pavo Prime."

Han pretended to consider the offer. "I'm willing to talk about it—have a seat." He motioned them to his bunk, then retrieved the *Falcon* replica and sat across from them on the stool. "But first, I want to make sure I've got this straight. You guys are running replicas like this one back into the Galactic Alliance?"

"We've already made our first run," Juun said proudly, "a promotional delivery to the Fifth Fleet."

"To the Fifth Fleet?" Han's heart rose into his throat. What was the Dark Nest doing—going after the entire Galactic Alliance? "No kidding?"

Tarfang growled a few words.

"Tarfang warns you that their deal with Second Mistake is vac-sealed," C-3PO translated. "He advises you that even thinking about moving in on them is a waste of time."

Han turned to the Ewok. "Us moving in on you is the *one* thing you don't have to worry about right now."

Tarfang chortled a spiteful reply.

"That's right!" C-3PO translated. "You're stuck here in a rehab house getting—"

C-3PO broke off to shoot a question at Tarfang in Ewokese, then seemed to stiffen at the response.

"Oh, my—Tarfang says this is an acceleration facility! Saras brings criminals here to rehabilitate them quickly—by making them Joiners!"

The Ewok jumped up, standing on Han's bed and chuckling so hard he had to hold his belly.

"Keep it up, fuzzball," Han said. "This place is a

vacation moon compared to where the Defense Force is going to lock you two."

Tarfang stopped laughing, and Juun asked, "Why would they lock us up?"

Before he answered, Han hesitated and started to glance back toward Luke's quarters.

"Go ahead, Han," Luke said from the door. "Show them."

Without saying anything more, Han raised the replica of the *Falcon* over his head and hurled it to the floor. The spinglass did not shatter so much as explode into a droning cloud of blue-black bugs about the size of Han's thumb.

Juun and Tarfang yelled in surprise and pressed themselves against the wall. Even Han cried out and tumbled off the stool backward as the swarm boiled into the air before him—he had been expecting to find a single hand-sized Killik inside the replica, not dozens of smaller ones.

The cloud began to arc toward Han, tiny droplets of venom glistening on the proboscises between their curved mandibles. He grabbed the stool and started to swing it up to bat them away—then felt Luke's hand on his shoulder.

"Stay down."

Luke stretched his arm out, and the swarm went tumbling across the room and splattered against the wall, leaving the ivory spinglass flecked with palm-sized stars of gore. The room fell abruptly silent, and the air immediately grew sickening with the smell of insect methane.

Luke pointed to Han's bag, sitting under his bunk. "Get some undershirts and wipe the wall down. I can only hold the illusion for a few minutes."

"Why *my* shirts?" Han demanded.

"Because mine are in the other room," Luke said. "And the illusion is only in here."

"Yeah—I'll bet you planned it that way." Han pulled the

bag out from under the bunk, then pulled out two under-shirts—all he had—and passed them to Juun and Tarfang. "Get busy."

Juun immediately went over to the wall, but Tarfang simply looked at the cloth and sneered.

Before the Ewok could ask the question that was almost certainly coming, Han pointed at him and said, "Because if you don't, I'm not going to tell you two how to fix the mess you've made for yourselves."

Tarfang chittered a long reply, which C-3PO translated as, "What mess?"

"Like the one we're cleaning up here—only a whole lot worse." Han pulled a spare tunic from his bag and went over to the wall. "I don't think the Defense Force is going to be very happy with you two when they figure out you were the ones who delivered a whole Ronto-ful of Gorog assassin bugs to the Fifth Fleet."

Juun's eyes grew even larger. "Tarfang, get over here!" Once the Ewok had jumped off the bunk, he turned to Han. "You can tell us how to fix *that*?"

"Sure," Han said. "Easiest thing in the galaxy—all you have to do is help us find the Dark Nest."

TWELVE

Leia and Saba stood shoulder-to-shoulder at the top of the boarding ramp, listening to a muffled string of beeps and chirps as the boarding party's slicer droid tried to outsmart the *Falcon*'s espionage-grade security system. The external monitors showed that the ship was surrounded by a full company of soldiers in full blast armor. Something did not feel quite right in the Force, as though the troops were nervous or hesitant about their orders, and Leia wondered if the commander could really believe that Jedi would attack Galactic Alliance troops.

"They feel frightened." There was a note of disdain in Saba's voice, for Barabels tended to regard fear as something felt only by quarry. "You are sure we should not draw our lightsaberz? Frightened prey is unpredictable."

Leia shook her head. "You're the Master, but I really think we need to defuse things. Somebody's going to get hurt if we keep pushing."

Saba glared down at Leia out of one eye. "*We* are not the onez pushing thingz, Jedi Solo."

Finally, the slicer droid stopped beeping and chirping. The monitor showed him releasing his interface clips from the wires dangling from the *Falcon*'s exterior security pad; then he turned to an officer and gave a dejected whistle.

"What do you mean you can't open it?" The security

system speaker made the officer's voice sound a little tinny. "That's what you were designed for—to open ship hatches."

The droid beeped a short reply, which Leia knew would include an explanation of how the access code kept changing. The security system's first line of defense was an automatic reset anytime two incorrect codes were entered into the keypad. Its second line of defense was to never grant access from the outside when the keypad cover was removed.

"Well, try again," the officer ordered. "I'm not going to use a flash torch on the *Millennium Falcon*!"

The droid gave a weary whistle, then started to sort through the security wires again.

Leia turned to Saba. "I think we've made our point."

Saba nodded. "If you are sure about the lightsaberz."

"I am," Leia said. "They may be scared, but they wouldn't dare blast us."

Leia instructed Cakhmaim and Meewalh to stay out of sight, then released the safety-hold and palmed the toggle button on the wall. The seal broke with a hiss, and the ramp began to descend.

A surprised murmur arose out in the hangar. The captain barked an order, and when there was enough space to see, Leia and Saba found themselves surrounded by a semicircle of blaster barrels.

Once the ramp clanged into position against the durasteel floor, the officer stepped to the foot and looked up at them. He was young—no doubt straight from the academy—and so nervous he could barely bring himself to meet the gazes of Leia and Saba.

"You will p-place your hands on your heads." Despite his cracking voice, he was clearly being deliberately rude, ordering them about as though they were common pirates and neglecting to address them by any sort of title. "Descend the ramp slowly."

Leia heard Saba's scales rustle, then suddenly the Barabel's hand rose. "We are Jedi Knightz." The barrels of the blaster rifles began to swing away. "Poin: those somewhere else!"

Deciding it was better to follow her Master's lead than stand there looking confused, Leia raised her hand and used the Force to turn aside a trio of blaster rifles.

The officer paled and stepped away from the ramp. Behind him knelt two soldiers armed with bell-barreled Czerka HeadBangers—ultrapowerful riot guns designed to stun any target into submission.

"Oh, kr—"

That was as far as Leia made it before a blinding spark of silver lit the barrels of both weapons. Something like the head of a charging bantha hit her in the chest, then she felt herself go limp and start to fall, and the floor disappeared beneath her, sending her tumbling down into darkness.

The fall must have been a long one, judging by how Leia felt when she woke. The world was spinning. Her stomach was churning and her temples were pounding, and her body felt as if she'd run headlong into a dewback stampede. Her ears hurt . . . she could not even describe how her ears hurt, and some inconsiderate rodder was hammering words against her head.

"Princess Leia?"

The voice was familiar, but it was hard to place with all that lightning cracking through her head.

"Princess Leia?"

Hoping the Voice would give up and go away, she kept her eyes closed tight.

Instead, something popped in front of her face, and a

smell like burning hyperdrive coolant blistered her nostrils. She reacted with a blind Force shove and heard a body thud off the far wall. The Voice groaned and thumped to the floor.

Then a second voice gasped, "Commodore Darklighter?"

"Don't!" Darklighter gasped. "I'm okay . . . I think."

"Gavin?"

Leia opened her eyes to the stabbing light of a silver sun, then let out an involuntary groan of her own. She tried to push herself up and discovered her hands were cuffed behind her.

"Just how angry are you trying to make me?"

"Please settle down, Princess," Darklighter said. "Wurf'al isn't under my command, and he's just looking for an excuse to activate those stun cuffs."

"Avke Saz'ula is my mother's uncle's third wife's cousin," a gravelly voice said. "I owe you."

Leia glanced toward the gravelly voice and, as her vision began to clear, saw the long-snouted silhouette of a young Bothan naval officer standing in the doorway of what was obviously a detention cell.

"Who's Avke Saz'ula?" she asked.

The fur rose on the Bothan's cheeks. "You Jedi are lower than skalworms!"

Leia looked to Darklighter, who was standing just inside the door. The first streaks of gray were beginning to show in his brown hair and goatee, but otherwise his rugged face looked much the same as it had through the thirty years Leia had known him.

"Do I *care* who Saz'ula is?"

"Jedi rabble!" Wurf'al raised his arm, pointing a stun-cuff remote at Leia.

Darklighter's hand immediately pushed the arm down.

"How would Admiral Bwua'tu feel about using unnecessary force on a cooperative prisoner?"

"I doubt it would upset him—he *is* my mother's uncle." Nevertheless, Wurf'al pocketed the remote. "But he would be upset about the delay. He has been waiting long enough for these prisoners to awaken."

Leia breathed a silent sigh of relief. The remote was for a pair of LSS 401 Stun Cuffs—not as sophisticated as the LSS 1000 Automatics she and Han carried aboard the *Falcon*, but just as powerful and painful.

Wurf'al stepped out of the doorway, then Darklighter extended a hand toward Leia. She ignored it and rose on her own, trading a little unsteadiness on her feet for the opportunity to put Darklighter on the defensive. Saba was waiting in the corridor outside, guarded by a squad of detention personnel and also restrained in stun cuffs.

She lifted her pebbly lips, showing her fangs in something more than a scowl. " 'We don't need our lightsaberz,' you said," she quoted. " 'They wouldn't dare blast *us*.' "

They had not exactly been blasted, but Leia wasn't about to argue a fine point like that with a Barabel. Instead she shot a frown at Darklighter. "I didn't think they *would*."

Darklighter shrugged. "Wasn't my decision. Admiral Bwua'tu didn't even ask me to come over to the *Ackbar* until Saba was already starting to come around."

"You have only yourselves to blame for how you feel," Wurf'al said. "Admiral Bwua'tu anticipated that you would try to impress us with your Jedi sorcery and took appropriate measures."

The Bothan turned and started toward the front of the detention block.

Leia fell in beside Darklighter and quietly asked, "So who *is* Avke Saz'ula?"

"Gunnery officer aboard the *Avengeance*," he whispered.

"Wonderful." Leia grimaced. The crew of *Avengeance* was currently occupying its own wing of *Maxsec Eight*, after the Jedi caught them attempting to locate the sentient world Zonama Sekot. During the war, the Bothans had declared an ar'krai—a death crusade—against the Yuuzhan Vong, and many of them remained determined to follow the invaders into the Unknown Regions and finish what they started. "A Bothan with a grudge."

"I *gave* you a chance to turn around," Darklighter whispered. "Don't blame me."

They reached the front of the detention block and were admitted into the central processing area, where the bust of another Bothan in an admiral's tunic sat in a display niche across from the watch desk. It was made from a pale, iridescent material that resembled Saras spinglass.

"I see Admiral Bwua'tu likes to remind his prisoners who's holding them," Leia said.

"That is my doing," Wurf'al said proudly.

"But he hasn't made you take it down," Saba observed.

"Of course not," Wurf'al said. "Admiral Bwua'tu knows what an inspiration he is for the crew of the *Admiral Ackbar*. They feel privileged to serve under an admiral who has risen from the obscurity of a birth on Ruweln to become the finest fleet commander the Galactic Alliance has ever seen."

"The finest?" Leia echoed, taking offense on behalf of her dead friend Admiral Ackbar. "Really? I wasn't aware that Admiral Bwua'tu has actually seen fleet action as a commander."

"He hasn't," Wurf'al said, apparently not noticing the irony in his answer. "But he defeats the Thrawn simulator every time."

"I'm relieved to know the Fifth Fleet is in such capable hands," Leia said, struggling to keep the sarcasm out of her voice. "By the way, where did you come by the bust? The material is very distinctive."

"It was a gift, from a shipping line grateful for our protection along the Hydian Way," Wurf'al said. "Now, if you don't mind, my mother's uncle the admiral is waiting for us."

Wurf'al nodded to the watch sergeant, who keyed a code into his console. A security cam dropped down from the ceiling and scanned the face of each person in the group—Wurf'al and guards included. After it had finished, a green light came on above the outer doors, and they slid aside.

Wurf'al led the group out into the corridor and down to a lift station, where they were confronted by another bust of Admiral Bwua'tu—this one sitting on a small plasteel pedestal. Leia and Saba exchanged glances, and even Gavin quietly rolled his eyes. They ascended the lift with Leia and Saba encircled by guards, then Wurf'al led them through a maze of corridors on the operations deck. As they walked, Leia began to feel a faint tickle between her shoulder blades, the same uneasy feeling she had experienced in the capture bay just before she and Saba were stunned into unconsciousness. She reached out and could tell that the Barabel felt it, too, but even Saba did not seem able to identify its source.

Finally, they came to another lift, this one guarded by a pair of human sentries wearing the uniform of bridge security.

Wurf'al stopped and reached for his comlink, but one of the sentries waved him off. "Go on up. He's waiting for you."

The fur on Wurf'al's cheeks flattened noticeably. "He's *waiting*?"

"Five minutes now." The second sentry reached behind him and hit a slap-pad, and the lift doors opened to reveal a squad from bridge security already waiting inside. "Better hurry. He sounded like he was in a mood."

Wurf'al waved Saba and Leia into the lift. "Go on. He's waiting!"

Leaving the detention guards behind, they joined the security squad in the lift and ascended into the bridge. The squad escorted them into a small briefing room containing a large conference table, a service kitchen with its own droid, and, in one corner, another bust of the great admiral. The large chair at the far end of the table was turned away from the entrance, toward a full-wall viewing panel currently displaying a thin crescent of jewel-colored sun along each edge, with the crimson web of the Utegetu Nebula stretched between.

The security squad guided Leia and Saba to the near end of the table, then took up positions behind them. Wurf'al and Darklighter stood behind chairs on the opposite sides.

A gritty Bothan voice spoke from behind the chair. "Please forgive the stun cuffs, but with you Jedi, we must do what we can to make an escape attempt inconvenient."

The chair spun around, revealing a dignified-looking Bothan with a weather-creased snout and graying chin fur. He was dressed in an immaculate white uniform draped in medals and gold braid, and he held his shoulders square without appearing rigid or tense. He acknowledged Leia with a glance and a nod, then addressed himself to Saba.

"We can remove them, if you'll give me your word as Jedi that you won't attempt to escape. I'm sure Chief Omas will instruct me to release you shortly."

"You are very trusting," Saba rasped, "for a Bothan."

Bwua'tu flashed a canine-baring smile. "Not really. It would be far easier for us to rely on your honor than to attempt holding two Jedi against their wills." He glanced at Darklighter. "And Commodore Darklighter assures me that if you and Princess Leia give your words, you will honor them."

"That is so," Saba said. "But we will not give you our wordz."

Bwua'tu nodded. "I didn't think so." He looked to Wurf'al. "It seems you'll have to hole the *Millennium Falcon*'s drive nacelles."

"*What?*" Leia cried.

"We'll keep you locked in your cells in stun cuffs, of course." Bwua'tu's gaze shifted to Leia. "But we know better than to believe *that* will hold two Jedi. This is our best chance of preventing you from escaping."

"You can't do that!" Leia said.

"I'm quite certain we *can*," Bwua'tu replied. "I'm sure those Noghri we haven't been able to find will put up quite a fight, but I have no doubt we'll prevail in the end. If all else fails, we'll just use the capture bay battery on it."

"You would enjoy that, this one thinkz," Saba said. "Some revenge for your third wife'z cousin."

"Nonsense," Bwua'tu replied. "My clan relations have no more to do with this matter than the revulsion I feel for the Jedi's weakness in sparing the Yuuzhan Vong their just due. This is purely in the line of my duty as commander of the Fifth Fleet."

"I wonder if Gilad Pellaeon will see it that way?" Leia asked. With Sien Sovv dead, Pellaeon had agreed to come out of retirement until Chief Omas and the Senate appointed a new, permanent Supreme Commander. "You *know* how sticky Sullustans are about regulations."

"I do." Bwua'tu gestured at Darklighter. "That's why I had Commodore Darklighter consult with me on this. Holing the *Falcon*'s nacelles was *his* idea."

Leia's jaw dropped. "Gavin!"

"Sorry, Princess," he said. "But you *have* been trying to run a Galactic Alliance blockade."

Bwua'tu looked back to Wurf'al. "Why are you still here? You have your orders."

Wurf'al's fur flattened. "Sorry, sir." He passed the stun-cuff remotes to the leader of the security squad and turned toward the door. "On my way."

"All right," Leia said. "We give our words."

"*You* give your word," Bwua'tu said, looking to Saba. "What about Master Sebatyne?"

Wurf'al reached the door and left without waiting to be called back. Saba remained silent.

"Good," Bwua'tu said. "There is no regulation against enjoying my duty."

During her two decades of political service to the Rebellion and the New Republic, Leia had dealt with enough Bothans to know when one was bluffing. There was no tell-tale ruffling of the fur, no synthetic snarl. Bwua'tu was patiently waiting for Saba to make up her mind—and the gleam in his eye suggested that he hoped that she would remain silent.

"Saba, I don't think he's bluffing," Leia said.

"He is not," the Barabel said. "We will have to take one of the *Ackbar*'z message skiffz instead of the *Falcon*."

"I've no doubt you can," Bwua'tu replied. "But thank you for the warning."

Leia began, "Master Sebatyne—"

"If we give our word, we place Han and Master Skywalker at Chief Omas'z mercy," Saba interrupted. "That we cannot do."

"Master Sebatyne, I understand your concern."

As Leia spoke, she was reaching out to Saba in the Force, trying to make her see that Bwua'tu was not half as clever as he believed himself to be. He had asked for a very specific promise—that Leia and Saba not attempt to *escape*—so they could still make the rescue plan work, if they could find a way to get the supplies aboard the *Falcon* to Mara and the rest of the StealthX pilots without escaping.

"But you know how Cakhmaim and Meewalh are," Leia continued. "If something happens to the *Falcon,* they'll try to take out this whole Star Destroyer."

"There is no try." Saba flicked her tongue. "They *will.*"

Bwua'tu drummed his clawed fingers on the table and looked at the door.

"We can't let that happen," Leia pressed. "You must give Admiral Bwua'tu your word."

Saba let out a long, harsh croak that actually made Bwua'tu recoil. "Very well. This one promisez."

Bwua'tu's bushy brows fell. "Finally, you surprise me." He looked to the leader of the security squad. "Release the stun cuffs."

The leader punched a code into the remote, and the stun cuffs opened on both Leia and Saba.

"Please, sit." Bwua'tu gestured to the chairs at their end of the table. "Would you like something from the service kitchen?"

"No, thank you." Leia's throat was raw with thirst, but Saba had drilled into her time and again that it was as important to maintain the Jedi mystique as it was to master the Force. "I'm fine for now."

"This one will have a membrosia." Saba used the Force to pull out a chair, then perched on the edge, wrapping her tail onto her lap. "Gold, of course."

Bwua'tu eyes narrowed. "This is a military vessel," he said stiffly. "Spirits of any sort are not allowed aboard."

"None?" Saba let out a disappointed snort. "Then this one hopez it will not be *too* long before you hear from Chief Omaz."

"As do I." Bwua'tu asked the droid to bring him a tall glass of iced fizzwater, then said, "There is one other matter we must attend to before I have you escorted to your new cabins."

"Aren't you forgetting something?" Leia asked.

Bwua'tu frowned. "That's highly unlikely."

"I think she's worried about the *Falcon*, sir," Darklighter said.

"Is she?"

The admiral depressed a hidden button on the tabletop, and the door opened to reveal Wurf'al standing at attention on the other side. The younger Bothan smiled at Leia and stepped back into the cabin.

"You keep your promises," Bwua'tu said, "and I'll keep mine."

So much for the Jedi mystique, Leia thought.

"Good." Saba rose. "Then we are done here. This one is ready to go to her cabin."

"In a moment," Bwua'tu said. "First, I want you to call your fellow Jedi in. We've been trying to reach them for three days—"

"*Three days?*" Leia gasped.

"You've been unconscious for four," Darklighter said.

"I'm afraid I overestimated your Jedi resiliency," Bwua'tu added. "I ordered the boarding party to set their Head-Bangers to maximum. So you can see why we're growing concerned about your escort. They must be running out of air, water, and food by now."

"Maybe even power," Darklighter said. "I've heard that StealthXs draw down faster than the standard XJ series."

Leia glanced over to see how Saba wanted to play this— the Barabel *was* her Master—and received absolutely no hint, either in her expression or through the Force. Leia's choice.

Leia turned to Bwua'tu. "We *were* trying to run the blockade, you know." As she said this, Leia reached out to Mara in the Force and felt her somewhere nearby, deep in a Force-hibernation. "Has it occurred to you that our escort is already gone?"

"Frankly, no," Darklighter said. "I doubt they went to Woteba with no way to refuel before combat. No pilot would."

"By the way, we have removed your cargo to a safe location," Bwua'tu added. "I wouldn't want you to get any ideas about shooting a few fuel cells out to your friends without actually trying to *escape*."

Leia's heart sank, but she was careful to maintain a neutral face. Bwua'tu did not know as much about Jedi as he believed. Mara and the others could stay in their StealthXs for another week by remaining in their Force-hibernation.

The question was whether Luke and Han could last that long.

"Okay, they're still out there," Leia admitted. "But I won't call them in."

Bwua'tu's brow rose in surprise. "Why not?"

"You must!" Darklighter said. "They're going to start going under pretty soon, and we can't find those StealthXs. We won't be able to save them."

"They are safer out there than they would be in here," Saba said. "We will not call them into danger."

Bwua'tu's nostrils began to flare. "Whatever my feelings about Jedi meddling in the ar'krai, I assure you they will be in no danger aboard the *Ackbar*!"

"Not from *you*," Leia said. She had vague sense of where Saba was trying to go with this, but could not tell whether the Barabel had sensed some new menace or was simply trying to play Bwua'tu. "Something is wrong on this ship. Master Sebatyne and I have been sensing it since we came aboard."

Bwua'tu pushed back in his chair. "Please—you're talking to a Bothan! I see what you're trying to do."

"We are trying to *protect* you," Saba growled.

"From what?" Bwua'tu demanded.

Saba and Leia looked at each other, then Leia admitted, "The Force is not yet clear on the matter."

"Then please let me know when the Force *does* become clear on the matter." Bwua'tu's tone suggested that he did not think that would ever happen. "Until then, do not attempt frightening my crew again. I assure you, it will do nothing to speed your release."

Darklighter said, "Admiral, that isn't what's happening here. If Princess Leia says she feels something wrong, then it bears investigating."

Bwua'tu turned to glare at Darklighter. "Is that your opinion, Commodore, or is there some General Defense Force Directive that I'm unaware of?"

Darklighter drew himself up straight. "Sir, that is my opinion."

Bwua'tu fell silent, and Leia thought for a moment they had convinced him of the danger.

Then the admiral stood. "Do you know what I think, Commodore Darklighter? I think you have allowed your friendship with Princess Leia to affect your judgment." His gaze shifted to Leia and Saba. "And now you are dangerously close to supporting her in fomenting unrest among my crew."

Darklighter's face paled. "Sir, that's not my intention—"

"You are a dangerously naïve officer to be flying one of my Star Destroyers, Commodore Darklighter," Bwua'tu said. "I suggest you return to it while it is still yours to command."

"Sir."

Darklighter drew himself to attention and saluted, then cast one last glance in Leia's direction before he turned and left the room.

Bwua'tu turned to Wurf'al. "I fear Commodore Darklighter may have misjudged the value of a Jedi's promise. Place them back in their stun cuffs and return them to the detention center."

"This isn't a ploy, Admiral," Leia said. "You're making a mistake."

"Perhaps, but it is mine to make." Bwua'tu returned to his chair and spun around to stare at the sapphire web of the Utegetu Nebula. "Tell your guard when you wish to call your friends in, Princess. Chief Omas will not be happy if they suffocate in the Murgo Choke."

THIRTEEN

It was afternoon in Unity Green and a fierce storm was rolling across Liberation Lake, raising three-meter whitecaps and bombing the yammal-jells with fist-sized hail. In the flat light, the bluffs along the lake's far shore were barely visible, a mere band of darkness rising from the edge of the gray water. But the abandoned skytower project atop the cliffs was all too visible, a line of durasteel skeletons silhouetted against the flashing sky, twisted and bowing beneath the weight of the enormous yorik coral goiters hanging from their necks.

In many ways, Cal Omas viewed the skytower project—and the entire reconstruction of Coruscant—as emblematic of his service as Chief of State, a visionary undertaking being dragged down by the deadweight of selfish concerns and species rivalry. After the devastation wrought by the Yuuzhan Vong, rebuilding the galaxy would have been almost impossible under any circumstances. But doing it as the head of an alliance of semi-independent governments . . . he considered it a testament to his skill and hard work just to have kept the peace for six difficult years.

And now the Jedi were threatening even that one small accomplishment. They had been his most valuable asset for most of his tenure, able to eliminate criminal cabals with a single team of Jedi Knights, or to bring a pair of starving worlds back from the brink of war with the arbitration of a Master. Then the Killik problem had arisen in the Unknown Regions, and the Jedi order had become just one more problem, more deadweight threatening to bring the Galactic Alliance down around his ears.

Sometimes Omas truly did not know whether he was up to the job—whether *anyone* was.

A female voice spoke from the door to the council chamber. "Chief Omas, the Masters are here."

Omas turned away from the viewport. "Well, send them in, Salla. I *am* just a visitor in their Temple."

Salla, his personal assistant, twitched her whiskers in what someone unfamiliar with a Jenet might have mistaken for condescension, but which Omas knew was simply amusement.

"So you are." She stepped out of the door and waved the Masters inside. "I'm sure you heard Chief Omas."

"I'm sure he meant us to," replied the familiar voice of Kyp Durron. He marched into the chamber with the other Masters at his back, then stopped at the edge of the speaking pit. With a threadbare robe and unkempt hair, he was as raggedly groomed as always. "Thanks for letting us into our own council chamber, Chief."

Omas accepted the insolence with a smile. "Not at all, Master Durron. After all, the Reconstruction Authority gave the *entire* Temple to the Jedi."

Omas's irony might have been lost on Kyp, but not on Kenth Hamner. "And the Jedi are very grateful," he said. Though he usually dressed in a civilian tunic or his liaison's uniform, today he wore the same brown robes as the rest of the Masters. They obviously intended to present a united front. "We're all here as you requested, Chief Omas."

"And thank you for coming." Omas slipped into a comfortable flowform chair at one end of the speaking circle and motioned to the seats nearest him. "Please, sit. Can Salla get you anything from the service kitchen?"

The Masters all declined, of course. Omas had never seen a Jedi Master accept food or beverage when a confrontation was expected. It was part of their mystique, he thought—or perhaps they were simply more cautious than he realized.

"Very well."

Omas gestured again to the nearby seats, then waited in silence until the six Masters finally realized he was pulling rank on them and perched on the edges of the big flowform seats, their backs ramrod-straight and their hands resting on their thighs. Kyp took the seat nearest him. That was one of the things that had always troubled Omas about the rogue Jedi—he never backed down.

"We need to talk," Omas began. "Normally, I would bring a matter like this up with the six Masters who sit on the Advisory Council, but Masters Skywalker and Sebatyne seem to be unavailable. I've asked Masters Horn and Katarn to sit in their place."

"On whose authority?" Kyp demanded.

Omas raised his brow in feigned surprise. "No one's. I felt this discussion should include six Masters instead of four." He turned to Hamner. "Is that a problem?"

"Yes," Kyp blurted. "When you handpick—"

"It's fine," Hamner said, cutting Kyp off short. He shot the younger Master a warning glance, but the damage had been done. Corran furrowed his brow, and Katarn's brown eyes grew as hard as larmalstone. "We don't speak for the entire order, but we can certainly listen on its behalf."

Omas nodded. "That's all I ask." Knowing how easy it was for Jedi to read emotions, he tried not to gloat. He let his gaze drift toward Corran, then said, "First, I must start by saying how disappointed I am that you've been keeping

Master Skywalker's absence from me. It has led me to imagine some very disturbing scenarios, I'm afraid."

Corran's gaze shifted.

But Kyp said, "Master Skywalker's whereabouts aren't your concern."

"Actually, they *are* his concern," Kyle Katarn said. He was still a slim and fit-looking man; his beard and hair were just beginning to show the first shocks of gray. "I'm sorry you felt we were keeping secrets from you, Chief Omas. The truth is that Master Skywalker's absence took us by surprise, and we were afraid you would try to take advantage of the situation."

"Take advantage?" Omas kept his voice pleasant. Divide, *then* conquer. It was one of the lessons he had learned by watching Admiral Ackbar. "By trying to usurp his leadership?"

"We know how upset you have been over the Killiks," Tresina Lobi said. A golden-haired Chev woman, Lobi resembled a pale-skinned human with obsidian eyes, a heavy brow, and a sloping forehead. "So, yes, we are concerned about your intentions."

"My intentions are to protect the Galactic Alliance," Omas said simply. "What the Jedi are doing places our relationship with the Chiss at risk—"

"We prevented an interstellar war!" Kyp interrupted. "We saved billions of lives!"

"That is in the past," Omas said, raising a hand to stop Kyp's protest. "I'm talking about the present. The Jedi are the last ones who need to be reminded of the havoc black membrosia is wreaking on our insect worlds. Shipping losses to the Utegetu pirates are approaching wartime levels—and do I really need to remind you of the death of Sien Sovv?"

"The Jedi are well aware of the trouble the Killiks are

causing, Chief Omas," Katarn said. "That doesn't mean we are ready to surrender control of the order to you."

"The Jedi need leadership," Omas countered. "Surely, you all see that as clearly as I do. The situation just keeps growing worse. There's even a rumor that the Killiks tried to assassinate Queen Mother Tenel Ka!"

Though the Masters' expressions remained outwardly unreadable, their silence told Omas all he needed to know.

"Something else you have been keeping from me." He shook his head wearily, then looked out the viewport at the silhouettes of the distant skytowers, bowing and swaying in the wind. "My friends, we cannot go on like this. Too much depends on us."

"We all agree on that, Chief Omas," Corran said. "But we've discussed this, and we can't allow you to assume direct control of the Jedi order."

Omas nodded. "Of course. I'm not a Jedi."

"Actually, only Master Durron feels that has anything to do with it," Lobi said. "The problem lies in what you *are*—the Chief of State."

Omas frowned. "I don't understand."

"We can't allow the Jedi to become a tool of office," Hamner explained. "We are guardians as well as servants, and we cannot make ourselves beholden to the same authority we are pledged to watch."

"And, as the Chief of State, your concerns are too narrow," Kyp added. "You're only worried about the Galactic Alliance. The Jedi serve the whole galaxy—"

"The Force," Corran corrected.

"Right," Kyp said. "The point is, *we* have more to worry about. What's good for the Galactic Alliance isn't always what serves the Force."

"I see."

Omas grew thoughtful—though he was contemplating

not the wisdom of what the Masters were saying, but the care they had taken to meet him with a united front. Bringing the Jedi back into the Alliance fold was going to be more difficult than he had anticipated.

After a moment, he looked Kyp directly in the eye. "This may surprise you, but I agree."

For once, the Masters appeared stunned.

"You do?" Kyp asked.

"Who am I to question the wisdom of the Jedi?" Omas replied. "But that doesn't mean my concerns can be dismissed. The Jedi are floundering, which means the Galactic Alliance is floundering—and that is something I cannot allow. We must do something."

"We *are* doing something," Kyp said. "Han and Master Skywalker are looking for the Dark Nest, and then we're going to destroy it."

"Like you did last time?" Omas asked immediately. "I'm sure you'll understand my complete lack of confidence in that plan. Dark Nest membrosia has ruined the economy of the entire Roche asteroid field, and—as you know better than I—Dark Nest assassins have apparently attacked the queen of an Alliance member-state."

The Masters fell into silent contemplation. Omas allowed them to ponder his words for a few moments, then decided the time had come to drop his bomb.

"And there is something you may *not* realize. After the Jedi intervention at Qoribu, the Chiss seem to believe that it is your responsibility to persuade the Colony to withdraw from their frontier. They've given you ten days to stop further migration into the buffer zone, and a hundred days to persuade the Killiks to withdraw the Colonists who are already there."

For the first time he could recall, Omas had the pleasure of watching the jaws of several Jedi Masters drop.

"Those aren't unreasonable terms," Hamner said.

"And a remarkable expression of trust, considering that they're Chiss." Omas allowed himself one small smirk. "Though, considering the order's disarray without Master Skywalker available to guide it, I'm wondering if it wouldn't be more honest to let them know that they're on their own."

All of the Masters gave voice to their disapproval and dismay, but Kyp was loudest. "That's not your decision to make!"

Omas fixed the shaggy-haired Master with his iciest glare. "To the contrary, Master Durron, it is very much my decision. The Chiss chose to transmit their demand through me, so how I respond is entirely at my own discretion. If I feel that the Jedi order isn't up to the task, then it is not only my right to tell them so, it is my duty."

Kyp began to work his mouth in soundless anger. Omas sighed, then slumped back in his chair. Hamner, who had nearly as much experience on the bureaucratic battlefield as Omas himself, was the first to realize that the Chief was waiting for them to open negotiations.

"What are you looking for, Chief Omas?" he asked.

Omas allowed himself a moment of dramatic silence, then spoke without straightening himself. "A leader."

"A leader?" Katarn asked.

Omas nodded. "Someone to take charge of the Jedi and handle this mess until Master Skywalker returns."

Kyp frowned, clearly suspicious. "Who?"

"One of you." Omas leaned forward. "Starting today. Beyond that, I really don't care. How about you?"

Kyp was just as astonished the other Masters. "Me?"

"You seem to have a very clear idea of what the Jedi should be," Omas said. "I think you'd make a fine leader.

And, believe it or not, you and I want the same thing—a peaceful end to the Killik problem."

A distant light came to Kyp's eyes, and if he noticed the uncomfortable expressions on the faces of the other Masters, he did not show it.

"I suppose that's true," he said.

Hamner cleared his throat and sat forward. "No offense to Master Durron, but the Jedi order is led by a *council* of senior Masters. You know that, Chief Omas."

"Of course." As Omas replied, he was watching the light vanish from Kyp's eyes. "But we all know that Master Skywalker is first among the Masters. I'm merely suggesting that Kyp step up and take his place—just until Master Skywalker returns, of course."

"I see what you're doing—and it won't work," Kyp snarled. "Master Skywalker leads the Jedi."

"Not from Woteba, he doesn't," Omas replied. "And if you're counting on Princess Leia's rescue mission to bring him back soon, I'm afraid you're going to be waiting a very long time."

Omas had expected a feeling of alarm to fill the council room when he announced this, but the Masters disappointed him—as they were doing in so many ways, these days. They simply closed their eyes and fell silent for a moment.

Tresina Lobi was the first to open her eyes again and look at him. "Where is she?"

"I'm afraid Admiral Bwua'tu has impounded the *Falcon*." Omas forced an apologetic smile. "It seems Princess Leia and her friends were trying to run the Utegetu blockade."

"You interfered with their mission?" Katarn demanded. "You're putting Han and Luke in danger!"

"Not intentionally, I assure you," Omas said smoothly.

"But these things happen when we keep secrets from each other."

"We've already explained that," Katarn said.

Omas shrugged. "It doesn't change what happened." He turned to Hamner. "Forgive me, but when I couldn't get Master Skywalker to return my messages, I assumed the worst."

"That we were going to help the Killiks move the Utegetu nests to the Chiss frontier?" Hamner asked. "We would never—"

"How am I to know what the Jedi would or would not do?" Omas nodded toward Kyp. "As Master Durron says, your concerns go beyond the Galactic Alliance. Mine do not—and the Jedi have placed our interests second before."

"A peaceful galaxy is in everyone's best interest," Kyp countered.

"And when you can guarantee that, the Galactic Alliance will gladly support a Jedi government." Omas allowed his anger to show. "Until then, we will look out for our own interests—and if that means arresting Jedi when they attempt to run our blockades, so be it."

"You're holding Jedi hostage!" Kyp snarled.

"Not at all," Omas said. "Admiral Bwua'tu is merely providing accommodations until we come to an agreement."

"There won't be one." Kyp rose and started for the door. "Not while you're still Chief of State."

"Master Durron!" Hamner jumped up to go after him. "That kind of talk is—"

"Kenth . . . Kenth!" Omas had to yell before Hamner stopped and turned toward him. "Let him go. He's not wrong, you know. I *am* forcing your hand."

Hamner let out a breath of exasperation, then said, "It had not escaped our notice, believe me."

"And I'm sorry." Omas's apology was sincere. "But it's time we started to work together again, don't you think?"

"It appears we have no other choice," Lobi said. Her eyes flicked down the line of Masters beside her. "Who are we going to elect our temporary leader?"

"Not so fast," Katarn said. "Before we go on, maybe we should see if anyone else intends to join Master Durron."

"Of course," Omas said. "I wouldn't want to force anyone to be part of this."

"That's very considerate of you," Cilghal said.

To Omas's surprise, she rose and started for the door. He waited until she was gone, then turned to Katarn.

"And what is your decision, Master Katarn?"

"Oh, I'm staying." Kyle extended his legs and folded his arms across his chest. "I wouldn't want to make this too easy on you."

"Of course not." Omas smiled. Now that he had brought the Masters in line, he needed a temporary leader who was incapable of uniting the Jedi in support of the Killiks—and who would have no choice but to yield the position once Luke Skywalker was allowed to return. After all, Omas was not trying to *destroy* the Jedi, merely keep them out of the way while the Chiss dealt with the Killiks. "Perhaps you would care to be the one who nominates Master Horn as the temporary leader of the order?"

FOURTEEN

The barrier field at the mouth of the Jedi academy's main hangar was still up, despite the fact that Jaina and Zekk and the other pilots of the rescue squadron sat sweltering in their cockpits, itching inside their flight suits and choking on the stale, vapor-tinged air that accumulated within any starfighter in the long minutes before it launched. Their StealthXs were fully fueled and armed, their repulsorlift drives activated, their jump coordinates plotted all the way to the Murgo Choke . . . and *still* flight control held them in the hangar.

Kyp Durron's voice came over their cockpit speakers. "Flight control, this is Rescue One." He was speaking from the seat of his own starfighter, transmitting under the only circumstance in which StealthX protocols authorized use of the comm system. "Request deactivation of the hangar shield *again!*"

"Rescue One, please stand by," control responded.

"We *have* been standing by," Kyp retorted. "Deactivate this hangar shield now, or I'll do it for you!"

Kyp bolstered the threat by arming his laser cannons, then floating his StealthX around to target the generator housings at the top corner of the barrier field.

During the tense silence that followed, Jaina and Zekk felt Jacen's presence in the twin bond between him and

Jaina for the first time in weeks. He was reaching out to them—to Jaina, really, but it felt like *them*—urging them to wait.

Kyp's voice came over the comm unit again. "Control, you have five seconds. Five—"

"Rescue One, please stand by," control replied. "Someone is coming down to talk to you."

"I'm done talking," Kyp said. "Four."

Jaina opened a squadron-only channel. "Master Durron, we think it's Jacen."

"We felt him in the Force," Zekk added. "Urging us to wait."

"Don't tell me *he's* taking Horn's side!" Kyp said.

"You know better than that," Tahiri reproached. "The only side Jacen takes is the Force's."

"Toes is right," Tesar Sebatyne rasped, referring to Tahiri by her squadron call sign. "Jacen is above all this arguing."

Kyp sighed. "How long?"

Jaina and Zekk reached out to Jacen, sharing with him the impatience they were already feeling with the launching delay. A moment later, an image of the Jedi academy as seen from the air appeared on their mind. It was growing rapidly larger.

"Soon," Zekk said.

Kyp dropped his StealthX back onto its skids. "Okay. Everyone pop your tops and get some air." He switched back to the open channel. "Affirmative, control. We'll wait."

"You will?" Control sounded as surprised as she did relieved. Like most of the non-Jedi support staff caught up in the argument over Corran Horn's appointment as the temporary leader of Jedi order, she was just trying to carry on as usual . . . and failing miserably. "Thank you!"

The squadron popped their canopies and let out a collective sigh of relief as the relatively fresh air of the hangar flooded their cockpits.

Jaina and Zekk reached out to Jacen, trying to get some sense of what he was thinking. But he had drawn in on himself again, maintaining just enough presence in the twin bond to be sure the squadron was still waiting. That was typical Jacen. Since his return from his five-year journey to learn more about the Force, he seemed more determined to control his bond with Jaina and Zekk, more reluctant to share himself with them. It almost seemed as though he was trying to protect something from them.

Or protect *them* from something inside him.

That was probably the case, Jaina and Zekk decided. No one could suffer what Jacen had at the hands of the Yuuzhan Vong and remain completely whole. The torments Tahiri had suffered during her captivity had ultimately caused a personality split, and Jacen had been held prisoner far longer than she had—under even more brutal circumstances. What had shattered inside him was anyone's guess.

Jaina and Zekk would be patient. They would continue to hold the twin bond open, to share with him what he would not share with them. And when he finally came apart, they would be there to help him find the pieces. That was what nest-fellows did.

Jacen's presence was still somewhere far above the academy when the door to the main access corridor slid open. A moment later Corran Horn marched into the hangar with Kenth Hamner and several other Jedi following close behind. All were scowling, and all were heading straight for the rescue squadron.

Kyp twisted around to scowl at Jaina. "That's not Jacen."

"He's on his way," she said.

"He's too late." Kyp turned back around, then spoke over the squadron-only channel. "Button back up. We're leaving."

As the rest of the squadron started to lower their canopies, Kyp reactivated his repulsorlift drive.

"Put that craft back down!" Corran yelled.

He pointed at the hangar floor and yelled something else, but Jaina and Zekk's canopies were already down and they did not hear what he said.

Whatever it was, Kyp ignored it and turned the nose back toward the barrier field generator. "Control, this is my last warning."

Corran suddenly came bounding across the floor with an activated lightsaber. He landed beneath the nose of Kyp's StealthX, then reached up beneath the forward landing strut, slashed one of the hydraulic lines necessary to retract the gear, and leapt back just in time to avoid being hit with a spray of oily orange fluid.

"Nizzze move," Izal Waz commed over the squadron channel. "Didn't think Horn had that in him."

"Hold the chatter," Jaina commed. Izal Waz was one of the Wild Knights whom Saba Sebatyne had introduced to the Jedi order during the war with the Yuuzhan Vong, and he had a sharp tongue even by Arconan standards. "We don't need any zingers right now."

"Things are tense enough," Zekk added.

And getting tenser. Kyp had already returned his StealthX to the hangar floor and was climbing out of the cockpit. Jaina and Zekk and the rest of squadron reopened their canopies.

". . . wrong with you?" Kyp was yelling at Corran. "You could have gotten killed!"

"I ordered you to stop," Corran retorted.

"I heard you." Kyp dropped to the hangar floor and peered under the StealthX's nose. "And look what you did! That's going to set us back three hours."

"It doesn't matter," Corran said. "This mission isn't authorized."

Kyp looked up. "*I* authorized it."

He flicked his wrist, and Corran went sailing across the hangar back toward Kenth and the other Jedi. It was a particularly insulting dismissal, since Corran could not respond in kind, having never been able to master the skill of Force telekinesis.

The same was not true of Kenth Hamner. He extended his arm, and Kyp flew back against the hull of his StealthX and remained there, pinned.

"*You* were not appointed the leader of the Jedi order," Kenth said, leading Corran and the rest of the Jedi back toward Kyp. "Master Horn *was*."

"This is getting out of hand," Jaina commed over the squadron channel.

"Everybody out," Zekk added.

"But leave your lightsabers in your cockpits," Jaina finished.

"Leave our lightsabers?" Wonetun objected. Another Sebatyne-trained Jedi Knight, the powerfully built Brubb had a voice as raspy as his pitted hide. "They have *their* lightsabers."

"Doesn't matter," Jaina said.

"This *isn't* going to be a fight," Zekk added.

"*Yet*," Tesar Sebatyne finished.

Before Jaina could rebuke the Barabel for contributing to the general chaos, Tesar was dropping out of his cockpit and striding across the floor toward the rapidly growing showdown. Lowbacca caught up to him an instant later, and they took flanking positions behind Kyp's shoulders.

By the time Jaina and Zekk and the rest of the squadron reached the crowd, the argument was already in full roar.

". . . needs a leader," Kenth was saying. "And the Advisory Council confirmed Master Horn as the temporary leader of the Jedi order."

"The Advisory Council doesn't pick our leaders," Kyp retorted. "And even if it did, there were only two real Jedi representatives there!"

"Whose fault is that?" Tresina Lobi asked. "You and Cilghal left."

"Because it was a *bogus meeting*!" Kyp yelled. "Omas has just been waiting until Luke was out of the way to put somebody he could control in charge."

"No, my friend." Kenth spoke in a deliberately soft tone, at the same time pouring soothing emotions into the Force. "Chief Omas choose Master Horn deliberately, because he knew it would throw the order into convulsions."

"And he certainly succeeded," Corran said. "Look, I *know* I'm not the best person to lead the order—"

"At least we agree on something," Kyp interrupted.

"That's out of line, Master Durron," Kenth said evenly. "We need to be civil, or Omas has already succeeded."

An anticipatory lull fell over the argument.

After a moment, Kyp blew out his breath and said, "Fine. I apologize."

"Thank you, Master Durron," Corran said. "Now, as I was saying—"

"If I may," Kenth interrupted. "I believe I was speaking."

Corran raised his brow. "Sorry. Go ahead."

"Thank *you*." Kenth's politeness was exaggerated, but it was doing wonders to help calm the situation. He turned back to Kyp. "If you'll indulge me a moment, what I'm trying to point out is that Chief Omas is trying to neutralize the Jedi order so that he can take action against the Killiks."

"And keep the Chiss happy—we know," Kyp said. "So we ought to surprise him by sticking together."

"That's *two* points we agree on," Corran said.

"Great!" Kyp's enthusiasm was as exaggerated as Kenth's politeness. "We'll launch the rescue mission as soon as my StealthX is repaired." He eyed Corran. "Unless you're going to cut another hydraulic line."

"Only if I have to," Corran retorted. "Going off on a cockeyed rescue mission is exactly the *wrong* thing to do. We need to prove to Chief Omas that the Galactic Alliance has nothing to fear from us."

"By letting him hold Jedi hostage?" Tesar demanded. "Never!"

"Cooperation is both the fastest and the surest way to win their release," Tresina said. "We need to turn this situation around, and it arose in the first place because last time we chose the Colony over the Alliance."

"We chose peace over convenienzzze," Izal Waz said. "That is our duty."

"Our duty is to support the Alliance," Corran said, "even if we disagree with its leader."

"Our duty is to the Force," Kyp retorted. "Nothing else."

And they were off, voices rising and gestures growing sharp as they argued the same points they had been arguing since Kyp had called Jaina and Zekk and the rest of the rescue squadron back from their other missions. With a mother being "detained" by the Galactic Alliance and a father and an uncle trapped in the Utegetu Nebula, Jaina and Zekk's position was as firm as it was obvious. But they did not like seeing the order torn apart by the disagreement, either. They had spent literally their entire lives working to establish it, and the prospect of seeing it dissolve was only slightly less loathsome than the thought of letting Cal Omas control it.

They had to get Uncle Luke and Dad out of Utegetu.

After a few minutes, the debate grew so heated that when the hangar's barrier field went down, only Jaina and Zekk seemed to care. They turned and saw Jacen's sleek little Koensayr Starskiff gliding into the entrance.

The situation inside the hangar appeared even worse from the cockpit of Jacen's Starskiff than in the glimpses he had been stealing through his sister's eyes. Kyp's rescue squadron was more like a squadron and a half, including Tam Azur-Jamin, Kirana Ti, and half a dozen Barabel Jedi Knights from Saba's old Wild Knights squadron. Corran Horn's group was equally large, with two Council Masters, Tresina Lobi and Kenth Hamner, among them. The two sides were arguing fiercely, almost violently, and it was clear that no one was listening to anyone.

"What's all that about?" Ben asked from the copilot's seat. "It feels like they're ready to slug each other."

"They are," Jacen said. "It has something to do with a mission to rescue Master Sebatyne and my mother, and maybe your father and mine. It's a little unclear."

"To *rescue* them?" Ben cried. "What's wrong?"

"I don't know yet," Jacen said. "But don't worry about it."

"Why not?"

"Because *I'm* not." Jacen put the skiff down on the side of the StealthXs farthest from the argument. There was no use letting Ben actually *hear* what adult Jedi were capable of yelling at each other. "And I have two parents involved."

"That's a dumb reason," Ben said. "You never worry about anything."

"That's not true," Jacen said. At the moment, he was terribly worried about two people on the planet Hapes. "I just don't worry about things I can't control, and I fix things I *can* control."

"Can you fix what they're arguing about?"

"No one can fix what they're arguing about," Jacen said. "But everything is going to be okay. If your father or my parents needed help, I'd know about it."

"How?" Ben demanded.

Jacen looked over and said nothing.

"Oh, yeah," Ben said. "The Force."

By the time Jacen shut the craft down, Jaina and Zekk had left the argument and were picking their way through the StealthX squadron toward the Starskiff. Jacen grabbed Ben's travel bag, then lowered the boarding ramp.

Ben raced down the ramp and immediately confronted Jaina. "Where's Mom? What happened to Dad and Uncle Han and Aunt Leia?"

"Nothing—they're okay," Jaina said.

"Why do you think something has happened to them?" Zekk asked.

Ben pointed across the hangar. "Because you're arguing about whether to rescue them or not, aren't you?"

Jaina and Zekk raised their round eyes to Jacen.

"It's not my fault," Jacen said. "He could feel it in the Force. So can half the students in the academy, I'm sure."

They blinked—together—and looked back to Ben.

"It's not that kind of rescue mission," Jaina explained. "No one's in danger right now."

"The Killiks are sort of holding your father and Uncle Han," Zekk explained. "And we're, um, discussing whether we should allow that."

Ben considered this a moment, then frowned in suspicion. "Why aren't you talking about Mom and Aunt Leia?"

"Because they're in even less danger," Jaina said. "They're being held by the Galactic Alliance, on a Star Destroyer."

"So no one's in danger?" Ben asked.

"Not yet," Zekk said.

"Then what's everyone arguing about?" Ben shook his head in disappointment. "Dad wouldn't like that."

"There are a lot of things happening right now he wouldn't like," Zekk said. "That's why we're trying to get him back."

"But that's not something *you* should worry about," Jaina said. "Why don't you tell us about your trip?"

"Was it fun?" Zekk added.

"Uh, yeah." Ben hesitated for a moment, then frowned. "We went camping on the forest moon of Endor."

Jaina and Zekk gave simultaneous throat-clicks, then frowned and looked to Jacen.

"Ben, tell them about Moon Falls," Jacen prodded. He had given Ben two memory rubs already, but the boy was so strong in the Force that his mind kept resisting. "I don't think Jaina has ever seen them."

"It's awesome!" Ben said. "The upper lake drops over a ledge into the lower lake, and it's so far that the water turns to mist!"

"Tell them how wide the falls are," Jacen said. He casually began to ruffle Ben's red hair, using the Force to push the Endor trip deeper into the boy's mind, to block any lingering memory of their visit to Hapes. "And what happens when they face away from the planet."

"Right—the falls just stop!" Ben said. "I guess the planet pulls the lake back or something."

"And how wide are the falls?" Jaina asked.

"*Twenty* kilometers," Ben said. "You can't even see from one end to the other."

"Astral!" Zekk said.

"That's pretty big," Jaina said.

Though Jaina and Zekk were looking at Ben, Jacen sensed through his twin bond with Jaina that her attention—and Zekk's—was on him. He had hoped they would not notice what he was doing, but it hardly mattered. He could not endanger his daughter's life further by taking the chance that Ben would remember what had happened on Hapes, then let slip that Jacen was the father of the new heir to the Hapan throne.

Jaina and Zekk fell silent and simply stood waiting in the patient way of Joiners. Jacen was about to suggest that Ben tell them about their stay with the Ewoks when he sensed a familiar presence approaching the back of the hangar.

Relieved to have an excuse to get Ben away from his all-too-perceptive sister and her mindmate, he turned to Ben. "Can you tell me who's coming through that door?"

Ben furrowed his brow for a moment, then said, "It must be Nanna."

The door slid open, revealing the massive, systems-packed torso and cherubic face of Ben's Defender Droid, Nanna.

"Very good!" Zekk said.

"You can sense droids already?" Jaina asked.

"Naw!" Ben shook his head. "It had to be her—Jacen called her on the way in."

"Very resourceful!" Jaina laughed. "Using your mind is—"

"—even better than using the Force," Zekk finished.

"Go meet her." Jacen passed Ben's travel bag to him, then patted him on the back. "Tell her all about our trip to Endor."

"I will!" Ben piped. "See you, Jaina and Zekk!"

Jaina and Zekk said their good-byes, then, once Ben was out of earshot, turned to Jacen.

"Okay, what was *that* about?" Jaina demanded.

"What?" Jacen asked.

"The head rubbing," Zekk said. "We felt you using the Force."

"It was nothing." Jacen was not willing to tell even Jaina about his daughter—not when that meant he was also telling Zekk. "Ben saw something upsetting while we were away. I've been using a little Force trick I learned from the Adepts to block it."

"So you *didn't* go camping on Endor," Zekk surmised.

"We did—afterward." Jacen was telling the truth. He had needed *something* to take the place of Ben's Hapan memories. "I'll fill you in later. But first, what's that all about?"

He pointed at the argument.

"You *have* been out of touch," Jaina said. "Cal Omas appointed Corran Horn temporary leader of the Jedi order."

"Some of us don't like it," Zekk added.

Jacen continued to study the argument. "Does this have anything to do with the Colony?"

"Everything," Jaina said.

They told him the highlights, from Raynar blaming the Jedi for the Fizz attacks on the Utegetu nests to the Colony's return to the Chiss border. Then they summarized Cilghal's theory about the stuff being a self-replicating nanotech terra-forming system, and what they knew about Leia and Saba's detention by the Galactic Alliance. They finished by describing Chief Omas's attempt to take control of the Jedi order by appointing Corran Horn its temporary leader.

"And you can see how well *that's* working," Jaina said.

"Half the order thinks we need to mount rescue missions for Mom and Saba and Dad and Uncle Luke."

"And the other half thinks we need to support the blockade and intimidate the Colony into pulling out of the buffer zone," Zekk added. "Meanwhile, the Killiks are establishing nests all along the Chiss frontier."

Jacen felt the blood drain from his face, and he saw again the burning planets and the spaceships carrying flames from system to system, he saw the hands of humans and Chiss and Killiks setting those fires, saw the whole galaxy going up in one eternal blaze.

"Jacen?"

"What's wrong?" Jaina asked. "Jacen!"

"It's happening," Jacen gasped.

"*What's* happening?" Jaina demanded.

"Another war." Jacen was beginning to see what had to be done, why the vision had come to *him*. "An eternal one."

"All right, Jacen," Jaina said. "You're starting to scare us."

"Good," Jacen said. "Because *I'm* terrified."

He turned toward the argument still raging beyond the StealthXs, then touched Tesar in the Force and summoned him over.

The meaning of the vision was growing clearer to Jacen every moment. Ta'a Chume had attacked his infant daughter through the Dark Nest, just as the Dark Nest was attacking the Galactic Alliance through its black membrosia and its pirate harboring. The Force had shown him what was going to come of the Colony's actions—and it had shown him in the moment he was taking action to protect his daughter.

The Force wanted him to protect *its* child.

The Force wanted him to do to the Killiks what he had done to Ta'a Chume.

"Jacen?" Jaina asked. "Tesar said you—"

"Just a minute," Jacen said.

He summoned Lowbacca next, and then Tahiri, one at a time so their departure would go unnoticed by those in the argument.

Once they were all gathered around, he said, "I need your help. Now."

"Now?" Tesar asked. "Sorry. Master Durron needz us to rescue—"

"That isn't important."

"It's important to *us*," Tahiri said. "The Colony is holding Han and Master Skywalker hostage—"

"Free Uncle Luke or not, support Master Horn or oppose him, it makes no difference in the end." Jacen reached out to them all in the Force, trying to share with them the horror he had felt when he experienced that vision, offering them just a glimpse of the dark future he had foreseen. "I need you to do something that will make a difference."

Lowbacca groaned the opinion that Jacen should tell them what in space he was talking about.

"I had a vision."

The group grew quieter, and Tahiri whispered, "*That* can't be good."

"It isn't," Jacen said. "A war erupts between the Killiks and Chiss, and the Galactic Alliance is drawn into it."

"That is what we're trying to prevent," Tesar said. "That is why we must rescue Master Skywalker and put an end to the Galactic Alliance'z blockade."

Jacen met the Barabel's eye. "The war has already started—and the Killiks are the only ones who know it."

"The Killiks?" Jaina shook her head. "The Killiks are peaceful—"

"The Dark Nest *isn't*," Jacen said. He could see that the others were still too enamored of the Killiks to help him willingly, so he would have to explain things in terms they could accept. "The Dark Nest is leading the Colony astray again. The black membrosia, the Utegetu pirates, who knows what else—it's been working to destabilize the Galactic Alliance for months."

"Because they still want to expand into the Chiss frontier?" Tahiri asked.

"Because the Dark Nest still *wants a war* with the Chiss," Jacen corrected.

"This one is not so sure," Tesar said. "Why would the Dark Nest want a war with the Chisz?"

"The same reason they did last time," Tahiri said. "To conquer them."

"Remember how their larvae feed," Zekk said.

"It can't be easy to expand a nest when you need a constant supply of slaves to lay your eggs in," Jaina added. "A war is the ideal cover. When people disappear, they're casualties, not mysteries."

"Exactly," Jacen said. "Everything the Dark Nest has done has been designed to neutralize the things that prevented the war last time. The Galactic Alliance is so angry about the black membrosia and the pirates that it won't lift a finger to interfere with the Chiss."

Lowbacca nodded, then looked back toward the argument and growled that the Jedi had been neutralized as well.

Tahiri let out a breath, then asked, "So what do you want us to do, Jacen?"

"Stop the war." Jacen slowly drew a veneer of calm over his presence, projecting an aura of tranquillity into the Force that would prevent the others from sensing the lies he was about to tell. "In my vision, the war starts in earnest when the Chiss launch a surprise attack against the new Killik colonies."

"That makez no sense," Tesar objected. "Even Master Durron sayz the Chisz are waiting for the Jedi to make the Killikz withdraw."

Jacen used a smile to hide the grimace inside. This was something he had not heard about. "And how do we know this?"

Tesar remained silent and looked to Lowbacca and Tahiri, who merely shrugged.

"From the meeting where Master Horn was appointed our leader," Tahiri said.

"So we can assume that the information came from Chief Omas," Jacen said. "And he might or might not be telling the truth—as he knows it."

Lowbacca groaned a question.

"What I'm saying is that the information probably came from the Chiss themselves," Jacen said.

Jaina nodded. "And if they *were* planning a preemptive attack—"

"—they would want to keep the Galactic Alliance out of the way," Zekk finished.

"Exactly," Jacen said. "Chiss lie—visions don't."

Seeing the alarm in their faces—and sensing it in the Force even more clearly—Jacen fell quiet and allowed the others a few moments to contemplate what he was asking. With the Jedi essentially leaderless and in disarray, he had no doubts about their eventual decision. In times of turmoil, most people were eager to follow a being with a vision. Vergere had taught him that.

It was Tahiri, of course, who brought up the question that Jacen felt sure was nagging them all. "If the Dark Nest is *causing* all this trouble, why aren't we going after it?"

"Two reasons," Jacen said. "First, that's what Master

Durron and his squad will end up doing, after they get Dad and Uncle Luke back."

"And second?" Tesar asked.

"We're either going to be in the middle of the war with the Chiss or stopping it," Jacen said. "The Dark Nest will be coming to *us* soon enough."

Jaina and Zekk nodded at this, then the group fell silent and studied each other for a few moments.

Finally, Jaina asked, "When do we leave?"

Jacen thought for a moment, running through different ways to furtively deactivate the barrier field—which had been raised again after his skiff entered the hangar—then pointed at the six nearest StealthXs. "We'll take those."

FIFTEEN

The pearly light had drained from the outer walls of their prison three hours earlier, and still Luke sensed no hint of Juun and Tarfang's approach. Maybe the Ewok had convinced his Sullustan captain that Han was swindling them, or maybe the pair had decided they were in so much trouble they would be better off just running and hiding. Maybe Raynar had learned of their plans and imprisoned them, too. All Luke knew for sure was that *DR919a* should have signaled them more than two hours ago, and they were still waiting.

"You going to move that savrip or what, Skywalker?" Han asked.

"What's the hurry?" Luke asked, pretending to study the hologrammic dejarik board R2-D2 was projecting between their stools. "It's not like we're going anyplace."

Han's eyes finally left the game. "That's no excuse to bore me to death," he said. "Besides, the time will go faster if you keep your mind on the game. We'll be out of here before you know it."

It was clear to both Luke and Han that they were talking about their escape plans and not the game, but that was as close to *relax, they're coming,* as Han could say aloud. Luke had sent the X-wing replica—and the Gorog spies it contained—back to Raynar, and a Saras guard had immediately taken up residence inside their cells. Even now, it was hovering behind Luke, watching the dejarik game with great interest.

Luke spent a moment actually studying the game, then said to R2-D2, "Leave my savrip where it is. Have my closest grimtassh attack Han's ghhhk, then make a surprise-kill attack on his houjix."

"Oh, my—that is quite an unorthodox move," C-3PO said. "Are you sure you want to do it, Master Skywalker? If you defeat the ghhhk and take the surprise attack on Captain Solo's houjix—"

"Butt out, chiphead," Han growled. He turned to R2-D2. "What are you waiting for? You heard the man."

Luke barely noticed as his grimtassh hopped over to Han's ghhhk and took its place on the board. From what he could feel in the Force, Mara and Leia were fairly close to the Utegetu Nebula, but Mara had dropped into a deep Force-hibernation, and Leia seemed frustrated and impatient. Clearly, the *Falcon* had been delayed on her return trip, and Luke's patience with his "detention" had come to an end. If Juun and Tarfang did not show up soon, he was going to break out and go hunting for them.

Han sent a k'lor'slug over to assault the savrip Luke had neglected to move out of harm's way, then scowled at R2-D2 when the attack failed.

"What are you doing?" he demanded. "That was from behind! It's automatic."

"There *are* no automatic victories in dejarik," C-3PO said helpfully. "Even rear attacks have a one in ten thousand probability of failure."

"And Artoo expects me to believe he just *happened* to generate a failure when Luke makes a vac-headed move like that?"

R2-D2 emitted a defensive whistle.

"He says that Master Luke is distracted," C-3PO said. "He needs a handicap."

"I'm not *that* distracted," Luke said. "Do it over, Artoo—and use standard probabilities."

R2-D2 let out an annoyed whistle, then Luke's savrip vanished and was replaced by Han's k'lor'slug.

"That's more like it," Han said. "Now pay attention, Skywalker. The game is about to get interesting."

Luke barely watched as Han's k'lor'slug slinked over to attack his monnok. He was trying to connect the *Falcon*'s delay to Alema's attempts to make him doubt Mara. Clearly, the Dark Nest was trying to drive a wedge between him and his wife, probably to punish her for killing Daxar Ies. But he was beginning to suspect that there was another reason—that the attacks were also directed against him in some subtle way he had yet to understand.

"Luke?" Han said. "It's your move."

Luke looked up to find Han smirking at him across the hologram. Han had succeeded in taking control of the center of the board and now had Luke's ghhhk encircled, with no hope of escape.

"Artoo, have my strider retreat to the edge of the board."

"Retreat?" Han scowled. "You're sacrificing the ghhhk?"

R2-D2 whistled gleefully and did as Luke instructed, leaving Han's pieces almost alone in the middle of the board. Once Han took the ghhhk, he would be stuck with all his pieces facing center and no surprise-kill attacks available to change orientation. Luke, meanwhile, was scattered around the edge of the board, able to attack any of Han's pieces from behind.

Han took one look and kicked the hologram. Of course, all that happened was that his boot came down in the middle of the game.

"You sandbagged me again!" Han accused. "You were paying attention the whole time."

Luke shrugged. "Dejarik is an old Jedi game." As he spoke, Luke finally sensed the familiar presences of Juun and Tarfang streaking across Saras nest toward their prison. "Are we going to play it out?"

Han must have sensed Luke's rising excitement, because when Luke looked up, there was a glint in Han's eye that could not possibly have come from the belief that he could win.

"You bet," Han said. "I've still got a three-piece . . ."

Han let his sentence trail off as the guard suddenly stepped away from Luke and began to drum its thorax.

"Saras is ordering us to move away from the wall," C-3PO reported. "She seems to believe we're trying to—"

Luke sprang from his stool, already bringing his foot around in a crescent kick that sent the Killik stumbling into the wall. Han was on the insect before it could catch its balance, slamming his stool down across the back of its head with chitin-cracking force.

"—escape," C-3PO finished. He studied the unconscious Killik with a cocked head for a moment, then turned to Luke. "Pardon me, Master Skywalker, but *are* we making our escape attempt now?"

"No," Han growled. "We just thought we'd have some fun beating up our guards."

"Oh." C-3PO straightened his head. "In that case, you're going to have quite an exciting time. Saras was trying to tell you that there is a whole company of reinforcements coming up the ramp."

Luke and Han exchanged glances, then Han said, "I'll take 'em." He hefted his stool, then went into his own room and turned toward the hatch. "You just get that wall open."

Luke followed Han and went to the wall where he had been having R2-D2 scratch x's. He used his finger to connect four sets of x's together, tracing an imaginary asterisk on the wall.

By this time, the Saras reinforcements had arrived outside the cell. Luke could hear them snipping and ripping away the outer seal of the hatch, and he could see their silhouettes through the translucent wall, backlit by green shine-balls. They appeared to be holding Verpine shatter guns and electrobolt assault rifles.

"I've got it under control, Skywalker," Han said, sensing Luke's concern without having to turn around. "Just get that hole open."

The wall in Luke's room brightened with the blue glow of an exterior spotlight.

"Master Skywalker," C-3PO began. "I believe Captain Juun has arrived, and he seems to be signaling—"

"The wrong room, I know." Luke placed his palm in the center of the asterisk he had traced in Han's room, then began to pulse rapidly outward with the Force, setting up a kinetic vibration that would weaken the spinglass. "You and Artoo stand behind me."

"Behind you?" C-3PO asked. "I don't see what good that will do."

"Threepio!" There was a dull thump as Han smashed the stool into the head of the first Killik attempting to push through the hatch. "Just do it!"

"There's no need to shout, Captain Solo." C-3PO gestured to R2-D2, then went to stand where Luke had instructed. "I was merely going to point out that Captain Juun won't be extending the boarding ramp in the proper place."

"That's okay." Luke assumed a formal punching stance

in front of the asterisk he had scratched. "We'll improvise."

He summoned as much Force energy as he could into himself, then drew his arm back and slammed a palm-heel into the center of the asterisk. His hand drove through the spinglass almost effortlessly, shattering it along the stress lines R2-D2 had etched into the wall.

Outside was the blocky, carbon-scored hull of Juun's *Ronto*-class transport, hovering twenty meters off the ground, with a boarding ramp butted against the wall outside Luke's room. A dark Ewok head peered out of the ship's hatch and began to jabber at Luke.

"Of all the audacity!" C-3PO said, peering around the side of the hole. "Tarfang says we made our hole in the wrong place. The *DR-Nine-one-nine-a* isn't going to move!"

A flurry of sharp plinking sounds broke out behind them as the Saras guards began to fire through the hatch wall with their shatter guns.

"Go!" Han turned away from the hatch and crossed the tiny room in two bounds. "Go nowwwww!"

Luke barely caught hold of Han's belt as he flew past. He pushed off the side of the hole, Force-leaping onto the *DR919a*'s boarding ramp. As they balanced there, shatter gun pellets began to thunk into the hull beside them, creating a circle of fist-sized dents just three meters away.

"Blast!" Han turned to look back toward their prison. "That was too close—"

Han's exclamation came to a startled end as the *DR919a* began to bank away, the boarding ramp retracting with them still on it. He whirled toward the hatch and began to curse out Tarfang, but Luke did not hear what he said. C-3PO had appeared in the hole, pulling R2-D2 along by the astromech's grasper arm.

"Master Skywalker! Wait! Please don't—"

The droid's upper body abruptly flew forward, and he tumbled out of the hole, pulling R2-D2 along behind him.

"—ussss beeehinnnn—"

Luke extended a hand and caught the two droids in the Force, then nearly fell himself when the end of the ramp retracted into its stowage slot.

"Whoa!" Han grabbed Luke's arm and pulled him through the hatch. "You okay?"

"Of course not!" This from C-3PO, who was floating along with R2-D2 a couple of meters below the hatch. "I've been badly wounded! My systems might deactivate at any moment!"

Han guided Luke's free hand over to a grab bar inside the hatch, then knelt down to help the droids as Luke pulled them up with the Force. Once everyone was safely inside the *DR919a*, Han closed the hatch.

Juun's voice immediately came over the intercom. "Secure yourselves back there! I'm pushing the throttles to seventy percent!"

Han took a deep breath and looked genuinely scared. "May the Force be with us!"

A moment later, the *DR919a* shuddered and began to accelerate sluggishly. Han put his ear to the hull and listened for a moment, then sighed in relief and turned to inspect C-3PO's damage.

"Relax, Goldenrod," Han said. "It's an arm hit. You've got a few shorts and you've spilled a lot of hydraulic fluid, but you're not going to deactivate anytime soon."

C-3PO turned to Luke. "I'd feel much better if you would check me over, Master Skywalker. You know how Captain Solo always underestimates these things."

Han rolled his eyes but stood aside so Luke could have a look. There was a fist-sized hole in the back of the droid's arm, and dozens of internal wires had been cut, along with both hydraulic tubes. But none of that was going to be a problem—there weren't any critical systems in the limb.

"Han's right," Luke reported. "Just disable all functions in your right arm, and you'll be fine."

"What a relief!" C-3PO said. "After all I've been through, I thought I was headed for the scrap heap for certain."

R2-D2 whistled a gentle reproach.

"I'm hardly exaggerating," C-3PO said. "You have no idea what it's like to be wounded."

R2-D2 tweeted a contradiction.

"You do?" Luke gasped. He knelt beside the droid. "Where?"

R2-D2 spun his dome around, revealing a puncture the size of three fingers. When Luke peered into the hole, he saw Han's eye looking at him from the other side.

"That can't be good," Han said.

R2-D2 trilled a long reply.

"What do you mean it's not too bad?" C-3PO demanded. "Being unable to see is *very* bad!"

Tarfang threw a sympathetic arm around R2-D2's casing and started to guide the droid forward, keeping up a reassuring jabber as they moved.

"Thank you, Tarfang, but a visit to the Squibs really won't be necessary," C-3PO said, following along. "I assure you, Master Skywalker can afford to buy the finest *new* replacement parts."

They came to the *DR919a*'s flight deck. Extremely basic, it was little more than the forward end of the main deck with a couple of Sullustan-sized swivel chairs bolted in front of an instrument console. The viewport was barely large enough to justify the name, with the blue curtain of the Utegetu Nebula stretched across the micropitted transparisteel and the cragged peak of one of Woteba's high mountains protruding up in the foreground.

"Welcome aboard." Juun did not look away from his instruments as he spoke. "I'm sorry we were late, but the Saras are evacuating their nest, and the Squibs wanted us to pick up a load from the replica factory."

"*Evacuating* their nest?" Luke gasped.

"Yes, it's half empty already," Juun said. "They're surrendering it all to the Fizz."

"I don't like the sound of that," Luke said.

"Me either!" Han agreed. "I think they were going to leave us!"

"*We* wouldn't have left you, Captain Solo," Juun assured him. "We just had to avoid drawing suspicion. Now please take your seats and buckle in. Saras is sending a swarm of dartships after us."

Luke ignored the instructions and peered over the Sullustan's shoulder at the navigation display. It was filled with static, but a swirling mass of tiny dark dashes did seem to be rising from an amorphous blob of lights that might have been Saras nest.

"Can you outrun them?"

Tarfang barked something indignant, then waved a furry hand toward the passengers' seats at the rear of the deck.

"Of course—they're only rockets," C-3PO translated. "And the copilot reminds you to take your seats as Captain Juun instructed."

"In a second," Han said. He was squatting next to the copilot's seat, studying the navicomputer. "Hey, Jae, how come we're not jumping to the Murgo Choke?"

"There's a blockade," Juun answered. "We'll have to use the Mott's Nostril."

"The Mott's's Nostril?" Han objected. "That dumps us—"

"Hold on, Han."

Luke stood upright, then clasped his hands behind his back and thought for a moment, trying again to connect the *Falcon*'s delay to Alema's attempts to make him doubt his wife. Maybe the Dark Nest had just been trying to buy time, to keep him busy thinking about her instead of what was happening in the Utegetu Nebula.

Finally, Luke said, "I want to hear more about this blockade."

"Now?" Juun asked. "I'd be happy to tell you about it *after* we're safely away from the dartships."

Han frowned. "Tarfang said we could outrun them."

"Because we have a good head start," Juun said. "But if we don't jump soon, they'll catch us."

"Then please don't waste any more time arguing," Luke said. "Tell me about the blockade. This is important."

Juun let out a long breath, flapping his cheek folds in dismay. "The Galactic Alliance has blockaded the Utegetu Nebula. They're trying to prove that they're on the Chiss's side," he said quickly. "Okay? Can we jump now?"

Han ignored the question. "Don't tell me," he said. "The Colony is already expanding into the frontier again."

Tarfang chattered a few lines.

"Tarfang doesn't see why we're surprised," C-3PO reported. "What did the Jedi expect to happen when they cheated the Colony?"

"Who, exactly, is blockading the nebula?" Luke asked Juun. "The Fifth Fleet?"

Juun's jaw dropped. "How did you know?"

"Lucky guess," Han said. "And this would be the same Fifth Fleet you delivered that cargo of spinglass to?"

Juun nodded—slowly. "I guess so."

Han and Luke looked at each other slowly, then Han dropped to his knees beside the navicomputer.

"I'll set a course for the Choke."

"No." Luke shook his head. "So far, the Dark Nest has been playing us all like a bunch of Kloo horns, and the only way we're going to change that is find them and figure out what they wanted with all that reactor fuel and hyperdrive coolant."

Han sighed. "I was afraid you were going to say that."

"As was I," C-3PO agreed. "Perhaps it would be a good idea to drop off the wounded before you continue. Surely, R2-D2 and I won't be of much use to you in our condition, and we might slow you down."

"You'll be fine," Luke said. "You won't even have to get off the ship."

Han looked from the navicomputer to Juun. "Any idea where we should look?"

Tarfang chittered off a sharp string of syllables.

"I'm sorry, Tarfang," Luke said, taking a guess at what the cranky Ewok was saying. "But if you want us to get you out of trouble for delivering that spinglass to the Fifth Fleet—"

Tarfang barked a short reply, then pulled Han away from the navicomputer and began to program it himself.

"Pardon me, Master Luke," C-3PO said. "But Tarfang wasn't objecting. He was suggesting that we set a course for the Tusken's Eye."

"Why?" Han demanded.

Tarfang jabbered an explanation, but Juun beat C-3PO to the translation.

"Because that's where we've been taking all that Tibanna we've been running for the Squibs," he said. "And those pirates are hiding *something*."

SIXTEEN

Orbiting above a swirling atmosphere of yellow sulfuric clouds, Supply Depot Thrago was classically Chiss—austere, utilitarian, and bristling with defenses. In addition to the floating fuel tanks that Jacen and his team would soon be destroying, the tiny moon base was equipped with turbo-laser platforms, a shield array, cannon turrets, hidden bunkers, and a clawcraft hangar with two entrances. The weapons platforms were arranged with overlapping fields of fire, and the bunkers and hangar had been concealed with typical Chiss cunning. Even for Jedi in StealthXs, this was going to be a difficult run—especially if they wanted to minimize their target's casualties.

It had to be done. The attack on Jacen's daughter had been only a single move in the Dark Nest's plan—a plan that would ultimately lead to the eternal war Jacen had seen in his vision. Probably, that was even what the Dark Nest intended, since its larvae fed on live captives.

Jacen was not foolish enough to believe he could stop the war. The Gorog had been waging it for months already, even if no one realized it. But he *could* prevent it from becoming the eternal war of his vision. All he needed to do was rouse the Chiss, to prod them into action before the Dark Nest completed its preparations.

Of course, once the Chiss went to war, they would not

stop with one nest. They would destroy the entire species, wipe out every Killik nest they could find, and that was Jacen's plan. As long as there was a Colony, there would be a Dark Nest, and as long as there was a Dark Nest, his daughter's life would be in danger. He had sensed that much from Ta'a Chume. Gorog had promised to kill Tenel Ka's child, and she had believed the insects would make good on their word. So the insects had to go.

Unfortunately, Jacen could not say as much to Jaina and Zekk and Tesar and the others. They would argue that only the Dark Nest needed to be destroyed, that a whole species should not be condemned to protect one child.

They did not understand the Killiks the way Jacen did. The Colony had been harmless once, but Raynar and Welk and Lomi Plo had changed the insects. They had brought the knowledge of good and evil to an innocent species, had created a hidden aspect of the Colony's collective mind that would forever be obsessed with vengeance, hatred, and conquest. The Killiks had become an aberration, and they had to be destroyed. It was the only way to stop the eternal war.

It was the only way to save his daughter.

Jacen reached out to his companions in the Force, letting them know that the time had come to act. A big fuel tanker was gliding toward the supply depot, decelerating as it approached the gate, and it was a good opportunity for the strike team to slip through the shields.

As they opened the combat-meld, Jacen felt a sense of uncertainty from his sister and Zekk, and to a lesser extent from Tesar and Lowbacca. During the mission briefing that morning, they had all expressed reservations about launching a preemptive strike on the Chiss. The Ascendancy had laws against attacking first, so Jaina and Zekk had found it difficult to believe that the Chiss really intended to launch the surprise attack Jacen claimed he had foreseen.

It had been Tahiri who had pointed out that the Colony was technically in violation of the Qoribu Truce. The Killiks had moved colonists into the buffer zone, so the Ascendancy was free to attack anytime it wanted. And everything the strike team had seen over the last few days of reconnoitering suggested the Chiss *were* mobilizing for a major attack. They were moving assets forward, stockpiling fuel, ammunition, food, and spare parts, and running fleet maneuvers with live gunnery.

Of course, those were the same preparations the Chiss would make as a contingency plan. The strike team had seen nothing that pointed exclusively to a surprise attack, and even now, as they waited to move their StealthXs into position, Jacen could sense that Jaina and Zekk remained somewhat skeptical.

Jacen concentrated on the place within him that had always belonged to his sister, filling it with his own sense of certainty, hoping Jaina would interpret his confidence to mean he was sure about the surprise attack. He felt bad about using the twin bond to mislead his sister—but not as bad as he would feel if his vision became reality.

Jaina and Zekk's hesitancy began to subside, and Tesar and Lowbacca grew almost enthusiastic. Giving his companions no further chance to hesitate, Jacen activated his sublight drive and led the way down to the freighter. Though their StealthXs were almost as invisible to the naked eye as they were to sensors, the pilots took the precaution of approaching from directly behind, where there would be no viewing ports.

Once they had slipped up on the ship, they clustered together beneath the stern, tucked into the dark recess between the giant sphere of the vessel's number three cargo tank and the immense flare of its engine housings.

For several minutes, the Jedi had to float along in the shadows, able to see nothing but the swell of the cargo tank's gray skin, the colored glow of a handful of running lights, and, out the sides of their canopies, the star-flecked velvet of deep space. Then Jacen's astromech droid reported that a hole had opened in the shields, and the blue glow of an inspection light began to brighten space around the tanker.

Jacen flipped his StealthX upside down so that he could keep watch as they approached the supply depot. Since he could no longer see anything of the freighter except the round bellies of its four big fuel tanks, he had to trust Jaina to keep him in position by urging him to speed up or fall back.

It took only a few seconds before the supply depot's gate-platforms came into view. Floating vertically, they were basically crescent-shaped weapons platforms with shield generators instead of turbolasers. The inner edges were lined with cannon turrets, missile launchers, and plasma guns—all designed to defend against just the sort of infiltration the six Jedi were attempting. Shining out from behind the weapons were two semicircular banks of inspection lamps, arranged so that they would illuminate the entire girth of the freighter as it passed through the gates.

Jacen focused his attention on the vessel's port side and watched patiently as the inspection lamps lit up the exterior of the number two cargo tank. When the forward end of the number three tank slid under the light, he visually followed one of the beams back to its source, then reached out in the Force and pulled the cathode out of its mounting.

The lamp erupted into a brilliant spray of sparks, and a

ten-meter section of the cargo tank was plunged into darkness. Jacen reached out to the team, then pushed his throttles forward and led the way through the gap. A backup lamp came online no more than five seconds later, but by then the Jedi and their StealthXs were safely inside the depot's shields, tucked in a dark cranny between the freighter's bow and its number one cargo tank.

The Chiss swept their inspection lights back and forth over the number three tank a few times, but there was no question of a reinspection. Kilometer-long freighters did not simply stop and back up. Even at the vessel's current low velocity, it would have taken the braking thrusters a full half kilometer to stop the vessel, and by then any infiltrators would be well inside the shields anyway.

But Jacen knew the Chiss well enough to realize what would come next. Although lamp cathodes did sometimes blow spontaneously, the Chiss were cautious. They would almost certainly make a flyby inspection. He kept the strike team in hiding only until the freighter had cleared the shields, then dropped out of the cranny and slowly began to move away, careful to keep the huge cargo tanks between the StealthXs and the well-armed gate-platforms.

A few moments later, half a dozen shuttles appeared around the freighter, carefully working their way forward and shining their spotlights into every nook and cranny on the vessel's exterior. Jacen let out a deep breath of relaxation, then led the strike team down through a zone of floating repair docks—mostly empty at the moment—and around a line of frigates and blastboat escorts beam-anchored to the tiny moon that served as the heart of the base.

The battle-meld suddenly filled with Jaina and Zekk's doubt, and Jacen sensed them worrying about the frigates. He reached out to the vessels in Force and did not feel anyone aboard. His IR sensors suggested that internal temperatures were well below freezing, and he knew that would make Jaina question whether the Chiss were really planning a massive surprise attack.

Jacen could think of a dozen reasons the frigates might be in cold storage. Perhaps they were being held in reserve, or maybe their crews had not yet arrived . . . he tried to reassure his sister that there were many possible explanations.

Jaina and Zekk only seemed to have more doubts about his vision, and Jacen was well aware that the empty vessels just did not support his claim that the Chiss were about to launch an assault. It would take a week to bring a cold frigate online. The reactor cores would have to be lit, the vessel's temperature raised slowly to avoid stressing the hull or superstructure. Several kilometers of mechanical lines would have to be bled and filled with the proper fluids. Provisions would have to be brought aboard and properly stowed. These vessels showed no indication of any of that.

Jacen projected an air of thoughtfulness into the meld, pretending to consider his sister's feelings while he watched the tiny moon grow larger and brighter. It was little more than a hubba-shaped lump of rock, barely ten kilometers from end to end and so blanketed in dust that its thousands of craters had a soft, almost featureless look to them.

The fighter hangar, their first target, was located inside a ridge between two particularly deep craters, with one entrance opening out of a crater slope on each side. The surrounding terrain was flecked with cannon turrets, indistinguishable from boulders except for the tired sentries Jacen could feel standing watch inside a handful of them.

Jaina and Zekk projected their hesitation into the meld more forcefully.

Jacen could sense where their line of thought was

going—and he did not like it. Being careful not to let anyone else sense what he was doing, he reached out in the Force and touched the nearest sentry, urging the fellow to look up and pay attention.

Jaina and Zekk began to urge the team to pull up—

Too late. Jacen felt the sentry targeting him, then began to juke and jink as a flight of cannon bolts came streaming up from the side of the nearest crater.

Jaina and Zekk were furious, and all thought of calling off the mission vanished from the meld. Unless the strike team wanted to find itself in a very bad dogfight—while trapped inside the supply depot's shields—they had to proceed as planned.

Tesar, Lowbacca, and Tahiri barrel-rolled away and swung around to attack the hangar entrance in the far crater, while Jaina and Zekk fell in behind Jacen and banked around to make their attack run barely three meters above the floor of the near one. Cannon bolts and plasma bursts began to stab out from the sides of more boulders, but it was practically impossible for gunners to target what their sensors could not see, so most shots went wildly astray.

Jacen armed his glop bomb and ran the last hundred meters to the hangar mouth straight in, and bursts of cannon fire finally began to blossom on his forward shields. His astromech screeched a warning that the shields were about to go, and Jaina tried to move up and take the front position in the shielding trio. Jacen cut her off, then released his glop bomb and took two more forward hits as he stayed on course to guide it in.

Jaina's anger at his heroics scalded the combat-meld, then Jacen pulled up, climbing the crater wall slope so closely that his astromech began to screech about the belly shields. Jaina released her glop bomb behind him, then

Zekk's feeling of triumph confirmed that he had seen at least one of the bombs detonate and fill the hangar mouth with its quick-hardening foam.

Jacen cleared the crater rim and felt Tesar rising exactly opposite him from the other crater. He spun his cockpit around and found himself flying almost wingtip-to-wingtip with the madly grinning Barabel. They held that position and corkscrewed away from the moon's surface, the rest of the team close on their tails and the Chiss gunners lighting space around them with bright blossoms of fire.

As soon as they were out of the gunners' range, Tesar led Lowbacca and Tahiri back through the frigates toward the tank fields near the upper reaches of the shields. Jacen took Jaina and Zekk and wheeled back toward the moon. The area around the fighter hangar was so clouded in dust that the craters were no longer visible. The gunners, unable to see anything, had finally given up firing.

Seeing that his front shields had fallen to zero, Jacen commanded, "Transfer half the available power to the forward shields."

His astromech bleeped a sharp reply, then displayed a message explaining that there *were* no forward shields. The generator had been blown off when Jacen ignored the droid's warning that they were about to fail.

Jaina moved into the lead position, with Zekk behind her, leaving Jacen to bring up the rear. He could feel his sister's irritation in the meld and knew that once the team returned to the Colony, Jaina and Zekk were going to have a long talk with him about flying as a team. Until then, he would have to hide behind *them*.

The darkness above turned a flashing, brilliant orange as Tesar and his squad attacked the floating fuel tanks. Jacen knew from their planning session that the trio would bypass any tank near which they sensed a living presence, but

there was no question that most of the base's fuel supply
would be destroyed. During their reconnaissance, they had
counted more than five hundred tanks, each half a kilometer in diameter, and the only time any Chiss had been near
one was when it was being dropped off by a transport.

Jaina led Jacen and Zekk a quarter of the way around
the moon's surface toward a dust-covered hill that was the
depot's primary ammunition dump. Instead of dropping
close to the surface, this time they attacked from more than
a kilometer above, each firing a two-stage bunker-buster
torpedo.

The propellant trails had barely flashed to life before
dozens of "boulders" on the hill suddenly came alive and
began to pour fire up toward the attacking StealthXs. Jacen
slipped in close behind Zekk, then turned his hand over to
the Force and began to weave and dodge through the crimson blooms.

Then the bunker busters hit, raising a curtain of dust as
their focused thermal detonators burned a meter-wide hole
down through the roof of the dump. Half a second later
the torpedoes' main warheads—simple proton bombs—
descended through the same hole into the bunker interior.
Normally, such bombs would explode instantly, but the
strike team's were less deadly; they would spark and hiss
for five minutes to give personnel time to evacuate the vi-
cinity.

Once the dust cloud had risen high enough to obscure
the gunners' aim, Jaina pulled up. She turned toward the
second bunker, located about two kilometers away on the
horizon of the little moon, and the trio instantly fired their
second set of bunker busters. Again, as soon as the propellant trails flared to life, the Chiss laced the darkness with
defensive fire. Jacen saw one torpedo flash out of existence

as a laser cannon scored, but then the telltale curtain of dust rose from the bunker.

Jaina turned away, dropping around the edge of the moon toward the third and final dump. But she did not fire her last torpedo. It took Jacen a couple of seconds to see the problem. A small but bustling repair hangar had been built into the wall of a shallow crater below the ammunition dump. When the dump exploded, it would almost certainly bury the hangar beneath it.

Jaina and Zekk started to pull up without firing, but Jacen continued on course. Jaina and Zekk filled the meld with alarm and confusion. There were a hundred Chiss in that hangar who would not realize what was happening until it was too late.

Jacen adjusted his course toward the hangar. He would chase out the personnel; then Jaina and Zekk could take out the ammunition dump. The Chiss had to see that the Jedi were serious about stopping them, or they would simply continue with their plans.

But Jaina and Zekk did not seem to understand what he was planning—or perhaps they simply thought it was too risky. They continued to angle away from the attack.

Jacen adjusted his course back toward the ammunition dump, leaving Jaina and Zekk with two choices: chase the personnel out of the repair hangar—or leave them there to perish. It did not matter to Jacen which option they chose; the Chiss would get the message either way.

The Chiss gunners opened fire, turning space ahead into a wall of flashing cannon bolts. Jacen yielded his stick hand to the Force and weaved his way through the barrage for another two seconds, then heard his astromech squeal as it took a hit. He locked on to the ammunition dump manually and fired his last bunker buster. An instant later he saw the telltale curtain of dust rise ahead and knew the torpedo had penetrated the ammunition dump.

Jaina and Zekk poured disbelief and outrage into the meld, but Jacen felt them roll in behind him then drop into the crater. Suddenly a tempest of Chiss panic filled the Force, and Jacen knew that a bunker-buster torpedo had landed outside the repair hangar and begun to sputter its warning.

Tesar began to pour triumph and relief into the Force, and Jacen looked up to see that the flames from the fuel fires were now boiling away into space. Tesar and his squad had brought the base shields down and were already streaking toward the rendezvous point. All that remained for Jacen and his squad was to escape the moon's defenses and follow.

Abruptly Jacen felt Jaina pouring her anger into their twin bond, punching at that empty place inside him that used to be hers. Never again, she was telling him, never again would she fly with him.

But Jacen had known that before the mission began. He pulled his stick back and climbed for the fiery sky.

SEVENTEEN

As the silver whorl of the Tusken's Eye swelled steadily in the forward viewport, Luke began to feel a cold ache in the pit of his stomach, a growing sense that he was being studied. He glanced casually around the *DR919a*'s flight deck and found his companions intent on their work, Juun holding the control yoke firmly in both hands, Tarfang taking sensor readings and calculating hazard locations, Han studying the vessel's main power-supply grid and muttering to himself in disgust. Whoever was watching him, it wasn't any of his companions.

"Captain Juun, what did you do with those replicas you had before you came for Han and me?" Luke was sitting cross-legged on the floor, assembling his spare lightsaber from components he kept hidden inside R2-D2. "Are they still aboard?"

Juun shook his head. "I thought the assassin bugs might interfere with your escape." He kept his eyes fixed forward as he spoke. "So I had Tarfang drop the entire cargo in the marsh."

"I was afraid of that," Luke said.

"I could have kept them?" Juun gasped.

"No way," Han said, looking up from his work on the power grid. "Dumping those bug houses is the first smart thing you've done in this mess."

Tarfang jabbered at Han.

"How unusual!" C-3PO said. "Tarfang agrees with you. He says their first mistake was helping us escape the rehab house. They would have been much better off leaving you and Master Skywalker to be Fizzed."

Tarfang chuttered an addendum.

"Oh dear—he says you also owe the Squibs a million credits," C-3PO said. "Captain Juun incurred the nondelivery penalty on your behalf."

"Fine. Tell 'em to put it on my account," Han said. He turned back to Luke. "So what's wrong with dumping the cargo?"

"Nothing. It just means the replicas aren't what I'm feeling." Luke still had the cold knot in his stomach, an ache that did not quite rise to the level of danger sense. "Someone's watching us."

Tarfang jabbered in Luke's direction.

"Of course someone is watching," C-3PO translated. "We're in pirate space."

"Not *that* kind of watching," Han said. "I think he means through the Force."

Juun's face fell. "The Dark Nest?"

"That's my bet," Han answered.

"They know we're coming?" Juun's alarm began to fill the Force. "The *DR-Nine-one-nine-a* isn't equipped for combat. Maybe we should turn around."

"Not yet." Luke looked out the forward viewport, where the silver whorl of the Tusken's Eye was shining so brightly that it really was beginning to look like the goggled eye of a Tusken Raider. "The Dark Nest may know we're here, but we still haven't found *them*."

Tarfang barked a sharp reply.

"Tarfang says if anything happens to the *DR-Nine-one-nine-a*, you're paying for repairs," C-3PO said.

"Not a problem," Luke said.

"If there's anything left to repair," Han muttered, turning back to the main power-supply grid. "These shields couldn't stop a micrometeor."

"I'll see if I can improve our chances," Luke said.

He reached out in the Force and immediately felt the crew of a sizable spacecraft closing fast from somewhere ahead. The *DR919a* was just entering the inner wall of the nebula shell, where a miasma of glowing gas and dark dust limited visibility to almost nothing. There was little hope of getting a visual fix on the craft, or even of picking it up on the transport's rudimentary sensors. But the presences aboard the vessel were too clear in the Force to be from the Dark Nest, too distinctly individual to be Killiks, and too savage to be Alliance military personnel.

Luke glanced over at Han and mouthed the word *pirates*. Han's brow went up, and he nodded toward the entrance to the *DR919a*'s belly turret. Luke shook his head, motioning for Han to continue rerouting more power to the shields, then began to quiet his mind, shutting out the gentle beeping of R2-D2 running diagnostics on the ship's power grid, the steady chitter of Tarfang apprising Juun of navigation hazards, even the gentle whisper of his own breath.

Soon Luke was focused entirely on the Force, and he began to sense its ripples lapping over him, coming from the direction of his companions and the pirates—and from another place where he did not feel any presences at all, only a profound uneasiness in the Force. He turned toward the empty place and found himself staring into a wispy red corona that had appeared around the rim of the Tusken's Eye.

Luke reached into the corona with the Force, searching not for the Dark Nest, but for the hosts he knew it needed to grow its larvae. For a moment, he sensed only the same void as before—an absence too perfect in its emptiness to be genuine, a silence too pure in its stillness even for deep space. Then, gradually, the terror began to wash over him, the despair and suffering of thousands of paralyzed slaves being slowly devoured from the inside out.

Luke shuddered, shaken by his contact with their anguish, and vowed again to destroy the Dark Nest.

Then the corona blurred for a second, and a tiny silver crescent came into view, almost too faint to be seen through the crimson glow. Luke began to feel another set of presences, full of anger and savagery and selfishness—more pirates, no doubt.

No sooner had Luke spied the crescent than the ache in his stomach began to expand into the rest of his torso. The feeling was due to more than just being watched, he realized. Someone was touching him through the dark side, trying to distract—or perhaps even incapacitate—him. He took a few deep breaths, then called on the Force to fight off the growing chill.

"Luke?" Han asked. "You all right?"

Luke glanced over to see Han studying him with a concerned expression.

"I'm fine." Luke's answer was only partially truthful. "Somebody doesn't like me looking for the Dark Nest."

"Alema?"

"I don't think so," Luke said. "Too powerful to be her."

"I was afraid of that." Han did not bother to ask whether it was Lomi Plo. "Maybe we should turn back. You're not looking too great."

Luke frowned. "Han, are you starting to feel afraid?"

"Me? No way." Han looked back to his work a little too quickly. "Just worried about *you*, that's all."

"No need," Luke said. "We're just going to take a quick look at what's going on, then run for the Choke."

The wave of relief from Juun and Tarfang confirmed what Luke had already guessed: the Dark Nest was using the Force to project an aura of fear into the *DR919a*— perhaps into this entire area of space. Whatever she was doing in there, Lomi Plo did not want Luke—or anyone else—sneaking a peek.

Luke finished assembling his spare lightsaber, then went to the pilot's station and pointed over Juun's shoulder toward the silver crescent he had spotted earlier.

"Do you see that?" Luke asked.

Juun squinted out the viewport. "See what?"

Luke touched the Sullustan's mind through the Force, trying to project the image of the silver crescent he saw. "That sliver of light. It looks like a planet."

Juun gasped. "Where did that come from?" He frowned at his instruments, then peered over at Tarfang. "You need to adjust the calibration. We're not picking anything up, and I can *see* it."

Tarfang chittered something that sounded atypically like an apology, then studied the sensor controls and began to scratch the white stripe on his head.

"It's not the instruments." Luke touched the Ewok's mind, then said, "Try looking out the viewport first. That will help."

Tarfang glared over at Luke for a moment, as though he was suspicious of sorcery, then looked out the viewport and barked something that sounded a little bit like *chubba!*

Luke looked over Juun's shoulder at the sensor display. It showed that a white-clouded world lay dead ahead. The planet had more than a dozen moons, and it was orbiting around a fairly standard G-class star—the source of the silver glow that created the Tusken's Eye.

The screen also showed an old *Carrack*-class cruiser approaching from the direction of the planet, about a third of the way to the *DR919a*. It was escorted by a pair of blast-boats, and not one of the vessels was broadcasting a transponder code.

"The pirates!" Juun said. "They've seen us!"

Tarfang began to plot an evasion route.

"Don't worry about the pirates," Luke said. He knew by the deepening chill in his stomach that the Dark Nest was still watching their ship, trying to make it turn back. "I'll handle them."

"You sure about that?" Han asked. "We *know* where the Dark Nest is now. It might be better to go to the Choke and get some help."

"We don't have time for that." Luke turned to Han. "You know those shivers running up your spine? That tightness you're feeling in your throat?"

Juun spun around, his cheek folds rising. "You feel it too?"

"No—with me, it's something different," Luke said. "But I know what you're feeling, because it's not real. Lomi Plo is trying to scare you off."

Tarfang chittered a long opinion.

"Tarfang says she is doing us a favor," C-3PO said. "And I must say I agree. Our chances of surviving a battle with that pirate cruiser are approximately—"

"Stow it, Threepio." Han was scowling and looking toward the planet. "She knows we've found her?"

"I'm fairly certain," Luke said. "She and I are having a sort of a shoving match."

"We know where the Dark Nest is, and she's *still* trying to make us turn back?"

"Isn't that what it feels like to you?" Luke asked.

"As a matter of fact, yeah." Han's eye grew angry and

determined. "We'd better get close and take a good look, because whatever she's trying to hide isn't going to be there long."

Tarfang looked back and began to harangue them both.

"Tarfang remains *very* concerned about the pirates," C-3PO reported. "He points out that the laser cannons in the upper turret aren't working."

"The pirates won't get near us." Luke used the Force to fill his voice with reassurance. "Lomi Plo isn't the only one who can use Force illusions."

Luke opened himself wide to the Force, and it began to pour into him from all sides, filling him with a tempest of power until his entire body was suffused with its energy. Using the same technique he had used to save *Jade Shadow* from the Dark Nest's attack at Qoribu, he formed a mental image of the *DR919a*'s exterior and expanded it into the Force, moving it from his mind out into the cockpit.

Tarfang yapped in astonishment, then stood on his chair and poked a finger into the image.

"Does it look right?" Luke asked.

Tarfang studied it wide-eyed for few moments, then nodded and chortled his approval.

"Good. This next part is going to take a lot of concentration, so you'll have to follow Han's instructions for a while." Luke turned to Han. "You *do* remember what Mara and I did at Qoribu?"

"How could I forget?" Han answered. "Juun, we're going to need all the speed this tub can make. Open up those throttles."

"They *are* open," Juun protested. "The maintenance engineer on Moro Three said we'd be crazy to take them past seventy-five percent."

"Yeah?" Han slipped by Luke and grabbed both throttles, then shoved them past the safety stops. "Well, it's time to go crazy."

A low roar rose somewhere in the *DR919a*'s stern, and the deck began to shudder beneath their feet. Juun shrank in his seat, waiting for the ship to explode, and Tarfang launched into a torrent of angry chittering that left C-3PO at a loss to translate gracefully.

After a few seconds, the shuddering finally settled into a rhythmic rumble.

Juun seemed to relax a little. "That's enough, Tarfang," he said. "If Han Solo thinks we need to push the *Niner*'s drives twenty-two percent beyond spec, then we must take the risk."

Tarfang snarled a sharp reply, but by then Luke was too focused on his task to hear C-3PO's translation. He had extended the image of the *DR919a* into every corner of the vessel and was holding it there, taking his time and drawing into the image all the attributes that made up the transport's sensor signature. The effort wearied him a little, but he ignored his fatigue and expanded the illusion until it covered the entire ship like an imaginary skin.

The pirates hailed the *DR919a*. "Turn that kreetle barge around before we blast it out from under you!"

Han rushed to the comm station and took over from an indignant Tarfang. "Turn around? Gorog told us she wanted this load of hyperdrive coolant *yesterday*," he said. "You want us to turn around, talk to her."

"That was yesterday," a gravelly voice retorted. "You got ten seconds, then we open fire."

"Go ahead," Han said. "But I'd talk to Gorog first."

"*Talk* to Gorog?" A deep laugh came over the comm channel. "That's a good one. You got five seconds."

Luke brought to mind another image of the transport, this time with a stringy blue veneer that resembled the gas shell around them. Instead of drawing the *DR919a*'s sensor signature, however, he backed the image with a layer of cold emptiness.

Maintaining both illusions began to drain him, and he no longer had the energy to suppress the cold ache in his stomach. The chill began to seep through his body.

Lock-alarms began to sound as the pirates reached targeting range and prepared to make good on their threat.

"Uh, Luke?" Han said. "You *do* hear—"

"Shut down the drives in three, two . . ." Luke gave the outer skin a little extra push. "Now!"

Juun pulled the throttles back, then the image of the *DR919a* slid away, the counterfeit glare of its sublight drives forcing everyone on the flight deck to close their eyes. Luke angled the illusion off to port, as though the vessel were attempting to go around the pirates. Meanwhile, the *DR919a* remained cloaked by the second, camouflaging illusion. The lock-alarms fell silent, and the cold ache inside Luke slowly began to recede.

Tarfang howled in delight, then turned to Luke and began chuttering in excitement.

"I really don't think Master Luke is interested in giving up his position in the Jedi order," C-3PO interrupted.

Tarfang yapped sharply.

"Very well, I'll ask him." C-3PO turned to Luke and began to translate. "Tarfang would like to know if you're interested in joining the crew of the *Niner*. He's sure that Captain Juun would give you a full share. And with your talent, they could go back to smuggling and make a fortune."

Luke could barely spare the effort to throw a pleading look in Han's direction. The Force was pouring through him like fire, and it was all he could do to keep the two illusions intact.

"Threepio's right, Tarfang," Han said. "I've been making the same offer for years, and he just keeps talking about how much the galaxy needs him."

A flurry of streaks and flashes filled the forward viewport as the pirates opened fire on the counterfeit *DR919a*. Luke continued the illusion's gentle turn, keeping it well ahead of its attackers and drawing them farther away. His skin felt dry and papery, and waves of heat were rolling through his body as the cytoplasm inside his cells began to boil. He did not let up. During the past year, he and Jacen had been working on overload techniques, so he knew could endure the pain and fatigue almost indefinitely. His body would pay a steep price, aging a year in a matter of minutes, but he knew he would not collapse.

Finally, they could no longer see the pirate cruiser in the viewport, and the *DR919a*'s navigational display suggested the ship was well beyond turning back to intercept them. Luke continued to hide their real vessel while moving the decoy ever deeper into the miasma. There were still plenty of pirates ahead—and they were the least of the *DR919a*'s problems.

Han and R2-D2 returned to their work on the power grid, and the silver crescent ahead swelled steadily to a disk with one dark side, then to a hazy half-orb cloaked in white vapor. The cold ache in Luke's stomach had diminished to almost nothing, but had not faded completely. He hoped that was just residual, a spillover creeping into him through his connection to the illusion, but it could just as easily have been Lomi Plo trying to lure him into a false sense of security. There was no way to be certain. Luke just did not know enough about what she was doing to him.

As they drew close to the planet, the system's star assumed the form of an immense silver maelstrom sucking in vast quantities of nebular gas. The planet itself became an alabaster glow with no distinct edge, a cloud of white brightness surrounded by the dark flecks of a dozen moons.

The *DR919a*'s rudimentary sensor package could not penetrate the dense clouds in the planet's upper atmosphere, but the heavy concentration of ice crystals indicated an abundance of water below, and the world's general mass and size suggested a rocky core. The moons were easier to survey. They were all about eight kilometers long, egg-shaped, and radiating heat from a core area near their thick ends.

"Those aren't moons!" Han said, looking over Tarfang's shoulders. "They're nest ships!"

Luke immediately felt like a fool. Until that moment, he had believed the problem with the Utegetu nests was basically a misunderstanding; that Raynar and Unu had become upset over the Fizz and allowed their anger to place them temporarily under the sway of the Dark Nest. But there were fifteen nest ships here: one for each of the fourteen nests the Colony had established on the nebula worlds, plus an extra vessel for the Dark Nest. Even the Killiks could not have built such a fleet in only a couple of months. Either all of the Utegetu nests had been under the Dark Nest's influence for most of the last year, or Raynar and the rest of the Colony had been a part of the plan from the beginning. Luke felt betrayed either way.

Hoping the pirates would be fooled into believing their quarry had escaped into the nebular miasma, Luke gave the decoy a final burst of speed, then let it drop and turned to Han.

"I guess this answers . . . our question," Luke said. He still had to concentrate to speak, as he was continuing to hide the *DR919a*. "It's pretty clear why they've been so desperate to trade for reactor fuel and hyperdrive coolant."

"Yeah—but I really wish it wasn't," Han said.

"Why?" Juun asked. "In the history vids, you're always saying that it pays to know who you're fighting."

"Didn't I tell you to stop watching those things?" Without answering Juun's question, Han turned back to the power grid. "We can get by without climate control for a while. And who needs air scrubbers?"

Tarfang jumped out of his chair and scurried toward Han, jabbering in alarm.

"Tarfang is inquiring whether you've lost your mind," C-3PO said. "Without the air scrubbers, carbon dioxide concentration will rise twelve percent an hour."

"No problem," Han said. "We're not going to last an hour."

Juun's eyes grew large, and he looked over his shoulder at Luke. "I don't understand."

"We have to stop them," Luke explained. The fiery pain inside had begun to subside when he stopped overdrawing on the Force, but the cold ache of Lomi Plo's attention remained with him. "We can't let a whole fleet of nest ships loose."

"They'll eat whole sectors bare," Han said. "Worse— they'll turn the natives into Joiners."

Juun let his jaw fall and was silent for a moment, then he suddenly started chuckling.

"You fooled me!" He shook his head and looked forward again. "The history vids didn't say you liked practical jokes!"

"We're not joking, Captain Juun," Luke said. They had now reached the planet, a huge disk of swirling white that filled most of their forward viewport. He could feel the presence of a large mass of pirates beneath the clouds, somewhere near the world's equator. "We really need to stop them."

"We—" Juun's voice cracked. He stopped to wet his throat, then tried again. "We do?"

"I don't like it much, either, Juun," Han said. "But that's what happens when you start hanging out with Jedi."

Han's tone was joking, but there was a core of truth to his words. Luke was acutely aware that he was the only one aboard who had volunteered for this mission. Everyone else had gotten caught up in it simply because they happened to be nearby when it became a necessity, and none of them was very well equipped to survive the job. When he thought about what might happen if he went through with this, he wondered if he really had the right to pull them along. But when he thought about what might happen if the Killiks dispersed across the galaxy . . . he wondered if he had the right *not* to.

The first of the "moons" began to swell in the forward viewport. At eight kilometers long, it was an ungainly vessel, with a stony hull, giant control fins, and two cavernous docking bays—one of which was currently launching a battered five-hundred-meter passenger liner. Luke ignored the liner and reached out to the nest ship through the Force. It was filled with Killiks—probably the Taat nest, judging by the stoic nature of their presence.

Almost instantly the cold ache in his stomach began to expand again as Lomi Plo reacted to the contact. Luke took a few deep breaths and called on the Force to push the ache back down, but this time he merely succeeded in stopping it from expanding any further. Lomi Plo was growing stronger as he drew nearer.

"Captain Juun, how tight is the Alliance's blockade?" Luke asked. "Will it prevent the Killiks from escaping in these ships?"

"Of course," Juun replied. "As long as the Killiks use the standard routes to leave the nebula."

"What about the nonstandard routes?" Han asked.

Tarfang chuttered and shook his head.

"Tarfang points out that the pirates have never used the standard routes," C-3PO translated. "And neither have the black membrosia smugglers."

"Forget the blockade, Luke," Han said. He let the power grid cover clang shut, then latched it in place. "You want this done, we've got to do it ourselves."

Luke sighed. "You're right." He turned to Juun and Tarfang. "I'm sorry, but I really need your help stopping these nest ships."

"*Stopping* them?" Juun twisted around in his seat. "How?"

"I don't suppose you've got a bunch of baradium on board?" Han asked.

Juun's eyes went wide. "You carry *baradium* in your stores?"

"Han is joking, Captain Juun," Luke explained. "And we don't need to disable *all* of the Killiks' ships. I only have to stop the one carrying the Dark Nest. They're the key to this."

Tarfang chittered a question.

"Tarfang still wants to know *how*," C-3PO said. "The *DR-Nine-one-nine-a* doesn't even carry concussion missiles."

"It has an escape pod, doesn't it?" Han asked.

"Of course," Juun said. "The pod is quite functional."

"Good." Luke did not have to ask to know that Han was thinking the same thing he was—with one exception. "Then all you have to do is get close and drop me off."

"*Us* off," Han corrected.

Luke shook his head. "This a Jedi mission, and we don't even have much in the way of weaponry. You'll just—"

"If you say *get in the way*, I'm going to Hutt-thump

you," Han warned. "Leia would kill me if I let you die alone in there."

Luke sighed in resignation, then began searching for the Dark Nest again. Each time he made contact with one of the nest ships, the cold knot inside rose a bit higher into his chest. It wasn't long before he had to wage a constant Force battle just to keep the feeling in check.

They were just passing the third nest ship when Luke sensed a mass of pirate presences rising through the planet's clouds below.

"Be ready," he warned. "The pirates are coming up to cut us off."

Tarfang let loose with a long string of Ewokese invective.

"That's not fair," C-3PO said. "It's hardly Master Luke's fault that you haven't replaced the tail cannon."

"Don't sweat it," Han said. "If we have to open fire, we're starslag anyway."

Another nest ship appeared from behind the curve of the planet, and the anguish of the captives being devoured by the Gorog larvae grew clear and raw in the Force.

"There." Luke pointed at the vessel. "Do a flyby and we'll eject in the escape pod. Then head for the Murgo Choke and tell everything you know about this to the highest-ranking blockade officer you can find."

Tarfang began to gibber and shake his head.

"Tarfang doesn't think that is very wise," C-3PO translated. "The Defense Force is going to be looking for someone to blame about those replicas."

"And if you don't want it to be you two, then *you'd* better be the ones who sound the warning," Han said. "If you get there before anything bad happens, they might even give you a reward."

Tarfang's furry brow rose. "*Gabagaba?*"

"I'm sure it would be substantial," Luke said.

"Yeah, a thousand credits, at least," Han said. "You might be saving an entire fleet, after all."

"A reward would be nice," Juun said. "But that's not the important thing, Tarfang. It was our mistake, so it's our duty to correct it."

Tarfang groaned and let his head drop, but waved Luke and Han aft toward the escape pod.

"I'll keep the *Niner* cloaked as long as I can," Luke said, turning to go. "But once you're beyond interception range, get out fast. I need to devote—"

Luke's instructions were interrupted by the wail of *DR919a*'s proximity alarms. Juun shrieked, and Luke whirled around to see a blue streak of ion efflux lighting the forward viewport.

"Pirate ship?" he asked.

Juun could barely bring himself to nod.

"Relax—they missed," Han said. "Now that they're past—"

The proximity alarms screamed again, and this time Luke was thrown from his feet as the ship bucked. A loud boom rolled forward, then metal groaned in the stern and the sour smell of containment fluid began to fill the air.

Juun studied his console for a moment. "I can't believe it! We're not showing any damage."

"What a relief!" C-3PO said from where he had landed across the deck. "My calculations indicate that even if the impact was glancing, we were hit by something at least the size of a Corellian Engineering Corporation corvette."

"Uh, I wouldn't get too excited." Han rolled to his knees next to Luke. "I rerouted the damage control power to the shields."

Tarfang, who like Juun had been strapped into his seat, looked back and began to yap at Han angrily.

"Yeah?" Han rose and jabbed his finger in the Ewok's direction. "Well, we wouldn't even be here if I hadn't boosted that flit-field you two were calling shields."

A pirate frigate shot past between the *DR919a* and the Gorog nest ship, then wheeled around and opened fire with a small bank of turbolasers.

The bolts flashed past at least a kilometer overhead.

Luke returned to his feet and checked Juun's navigational display. He was relieved to see the rest of the pirate fleet—about thirty vessels, ranging in size from blastboats to frigates—executing much the same maneuver, all laying fire in a circle around a disabled blastboat floating several kilometers to their stern. His Force illusion was still working; the pirates had no idea where *DR919a* was and were attacking blindly in the hope of landing a lucky shot.

"I think the worst is over," Luke said. The Gorog nest ship was now directly in the center of the *DR919a*'s viewport and rapidly beginning to swell. "But you need to pull up a little. I think the collision dropped our nose."

"I *am* pulling up," Juun gasped.

Luke glanced at the yoke and saw that the Sullustan had pulled it back almost into his lap. Tarfang unstrapped and started aft, sputtering in alarm and motioning to Han.

"Hey, it's not my fault," Han said, following. "I didn't touch the attitude thrusters."

The *DR919a* passed under the pirate frigate and continued toward the Gorog nest ship.

Han's voice came over the intercom. "It's only a smashed relay box. We'll have it fixed in . . ."

The rest of the sentence was drowned out by a sudden, painful pop in Luke's ears.

R2-D2 began to whistle in alarm, and C-3PO said, "Are you sure?"

R2-D2 tweeted in irritation.

"Oh, my!" C-3PO said. "Master Luke, Artoo says the ship is losing cabin pressure."

"I know." Luke's ears popped again. "Han—"

"Did you feel that?" Han said over the intercom. "We've got a hull breach!"

"Where?" Juun demanded. His eyes were glued to his damage control console. "I'm blind!"

"It doesn't matter," Luke said. The Gorog nest ship was filling the forward viewport now. "Even if you *could* seal off the breach, there's no time."

Juun looked up at him. "What are you saying?"

"I guess I owe you a new ship," Luke said. "If we live that long."

EIGHTEEN

In Leia's mind, daybreak was forever.

She was floating on the edge of a purling river, relishing the soft brush of a warm breeze on her face, watching Alderaan's sun stand on the canyon rim. She had been watching it for hours, days perhaps, and it never moved. That was the point of the meditation, to still all: thoughts, emotions, mind.

But the water was growing rough. There was anger between Jacen and Jaina, a feeling of betrayal and . . . acceptance. Leia reached out to them in the Force, hoping that her love might help them heal the chasm that divided them. They were so far away, so deep in the Unknown Regions, where only the Killiks and the Chiss could find them. This was all she could do for them. They had to rely on each other. They needed to take care of each other . . . for Leia, if not for themselves.

The sense of acceptance—Jacen—closed itself off, and Jaina's sense of betrayal began to grow less bitter. For Leia, she would watch over her brother.

Leia relaxed again, trying to return to her meditations, but the water started to lap at her, to lift her and pull her out into the current. She did not try to stay close to shore. There was a familiar warmth in the water's grasp, an honest strength that she recognized as her brother's presence in the Force. She surrendered to the river, and the canyon walls began to rush past. The yellow sun climbed high into the sky, the breeze vanished and the air grew still and stale, and suddenly Leia was back in her detention cell, sitting cross-legged on her bunk, staring at the same empty place on the wall that she had been watching for . . . she checked her chrono . . . eighteen standard hours.

Leia started to respond to Luke, but he had already sensed her return to the realm of the temporal and was warning her that something was escaping, that things were terribly wrong inside the nebula. She could sense that he was in some kind of turmoil, and that Han was with him— but not much more. Her heart rose into her throat, and she pictured Saras nest in her mind and wondered if they were still on Woteba.

The only reply was the overwhelming impression that a threat was coming, that Leia had to sound the alarm. She reached for more, trying to find out if Han and Luke were in danger and needed help, but all she sensed was a raw fear that might have been her own—and then Luke's presence was gone.

Leia remained on her bunk, taking a moment to collect her thoughts. Han and Luke were in the middle of a bad situation, and she could not help chastising herself for letting Bwua'tu detain her and Saba. She had remained imprisoned aboard the *Admiral Ackbar* out of concern for the deteriorating relationship between the Jedi and the Galactic Alliance, and now Han and Luke might pay the price.

But Luke had not asked her for help. He had contacted her as a Jedi Knight, directing her to take action on behalf of the order. She was to sound the alarm, and soon.

Leia started by reaching out to Mara, who was still

in a Force-hibernation. Whether Leia and Saba convinced Bwua'tu of the danger or merely departed in the *Falcon*, Mara and the other StealthX pilots would need to be ready.

As soon as Leia had alerted Mara, she reached out to Saba and felt . . . nothing. Either the Barabel did not wish to be disturbed, or she was not awake. Leia hesitated to try again. Saba had once confided that when she sensed someone's presence while she was sleeping, she often awoke with a terrible urge to hunt them down.

Still sitting on her bunk with her legs folded, Leia reached out in the Force and grabbed the security cam hidden inside the ceiling light. She located the signal feed and pulled. A soft *clack* sounded from inside the fixture, and then she sensed the mild irritation of a guard stationed in the processing area at the front of the cell block.

Moving quickly now, Leia unfolded her legs and went to the door. She could not sense any living presences on the other side, but she felt sure there would be an EverAlert droid—a Justice Systems variant on Lando's highly successful YVH series—standing in the corridor between her cell and Saba's. She pressed her ear to the door, then looked up toward the side wall of her cell, fixing her attention approximately over the last cell on the block, and used the Force to project a loud *boom* into the ceiling.

A series of muffled hisses and metallic thunks sounded outside her door as a massive droid charged down the corridor to investigate the noise. Leia placed her hand over the magnetic lock she had seen when her door was open, then reached out with the Force and disengaged the internal catch. The door slid open with an all-too-audible hiss.

She stepped out and found the EverAlert swinging around to face her.

"Your cell door has malfunctioned." The droid planted

its foot and began to bring up the heavy stun blaster in its right arm. "Return to your cell and remain—"

Leia flicked her finger at the EverAlert's head and used the Force to flip its primary circuit breaker. The switch lay hidden beneath its neck armor, but that was no hindrance to a Jedi.

"—staaaationaaaar . . ."

The droid's chin slumped against its chest, and the stun bolt it had been preparing ricocheted harmlessly off the floor.

A metallic *clank* sounded behind Leia as the blast door at the front of the cell block retracted. She spun around to see a pair of astonished guards standing on the other side of the threshold, their blaster pistols still holstered.

"Stang!" the older one said. "She's—"

Leia swept her arm in their direction, using the Force to jerk both guards forward. She slammed them into the blast door, then dropped them across the threshold so the cell block could not be sealed off without crushing them.

The older man, a grizzled human sergeant, snapped the comlink out of his sleeve pocket. His companion, a Duros with smooth blue skin and red eyes bulging in alarm, made the mistake of reaching for his blaster.

Leia reached out with the Force and slammed his head into the wall, then summoned the blaster from his open holster. By the time she got the muzzle pointed in the sergeant's direction, he was raising the comlink to his lips.

"Everything's fine here," she said, touching his mind through the Force. "There's no need for alarm."

"W-whatever you say, P-princess." The sergeant was careful to keep his finger away from the comlink's activation switch. "You're the one holding the blaster."

Leia sighed. She was going to have to work on her Force-persuasion skills with someone besides Saba. Force intimidation was fine for Barabels, but humans needed something a little more subtle.

She gestured at the comlink. "Tell the watch officer— and no funny business. I'm a Jedi. I'll know if you use an alarm code."

The sergeant nodded, then activated the comlink. "Everything's fine here, Watch."

"Then how come she's holding a blaster on you?" came the tinny reply.

Leia looked up at the security dome in the ceiling. "Because Junior was dumb enough to reach for it." She pulled the power pack out of the blaster's handle, then tossed the pistol aside. "I'm not interested in harming anyone. I just need to talk to Admiral Bwua'tu. I have important information for him."

"Fine," the watch officer said. "Return to your cell and I'll ask for an audience."

"I'm not *asking*." Leia raised a hand toward the security dome, then located the power feeds in the Force. "And I'm not waiting. It's urgent."

She jerked the lines free, then stepped over to Saba's cell. Keeping one eye on the sergeant and his assistant, she placed her hand on the cold door and used the Force to disengage the internal catch.

The cell was empty, save for a couple of broken claws on the floor and a comlink lying on the bunk. A section of durasteel panel was hanging down at one end of the ceiling, leaving just enough room for a Barabel to squeeze through.

Leia summoned the comlink to her hand, then turned the volume down so that the sergeant and his assistant would not be able to hear Saba's end of the conversation.

"Master?" Leia whispered into the microphone.

There was a short pause, then Saba answered. "Blast! You scared them away."

"Scared who?" Leia asked.

"The gankerz," Saba answered. "This one is hungry."

"You couldn't have asked for a . . . never mind." The last thing Leia wanted to do was start a discussion about detention-center cuisine with a Barabel. "Can you meet me at the bridge? We need to talk to Bwua'tu."

"No." Saba touched Leia through the Force, initiating a combat-meld. "That will do no good."

"Saba, Luke reached out to me," Leia said. She opened herself to the meld, and an impression of vast openness appeared in her mind. "Something's happening in the nebula."

"Yes," Saba said. "The Killiks are leaving."

"And we must warn the fleet," Leia said. She recognized the vast openness as a hangar and realized that Saba was leaving the truth unspoken—no doubt because she feared some Alliance comm tech was eavesdropping on their conversation. "Luke was very clear about that."

"Bwua'tu won't believe you."

"We must try," Leia said.

The image of the *Falcon*, sitting on the hangar deck surrounded by a squad of Alliance troops, flashed through her mind.

"Then try," Saba said. "This one is still hungry. She is going to continue her hunt."

The slag that had once been the *DR919a* lay thirty meters in, an unrecognizable mass of blindingly bright metal glowing out from the crater it had blasted into the Gorog nest ship. A steady torrent of flotsam was pouring into the immense hole from the surrounding decks, dead Killiks and stony hunks of spitcrete and three lengths of twisted durasteel that looked suspiciously like turbolaser barrels. Gushing out of the surrounding walls were several cones of white vapor—air or water or some other vital substance shooting out of broken conduits into the cold vacuum of space.

Luke felt nothing from the crater itself, but the Force was filled with ripples from the surrounding area, all very sharp and erratic as stunned Gorog struggled to figure out what had just happened. Unfortunately, the confusion did not extend to Lomi Plo. She was still touching him through the Force, filling him with the same cold ache he had been experiencing since they entered the Tusken's Eye.

Luke stepped away from the escape pod's viewing port, then pulled up his tunic and turned his back to Han.

"Do it, Han."

"You sure about this?" Han asked. "Even on stun, at this range you're going to get burned."

"*Now*, Han!" Luke ordered. "Before Gorog starts to sort things out."

"All right," Han said. "No need to get—"

A searing pain exploded across Luke's back, and he dropped to his knees. Even calling on the Force to bolster himself, it took all of his willpower to remain conscious. He let the pain fill him, gathering it up and directing it down into the pit of his stomach where he felt Lomi Plo's chill touch.

Something released inside, like a knot coming undone, and the cold ache vanished all at once. Luke reached out to his companions, gathering their presences into a single bunch, then shut them all off from the Force.

They let out a collective gasp of surprise. Tarfang suddenly slumped down in his crash couch and began to babble in a frightened tone.

"Tarfang is convinced we died in the crash and don't know it yet," C-3PO explained. "And I must say, I feel something odd in my own circuits."

"I'm hiding us from Lomi Plo," Luke explained. He let his tunic down. His back was still racked with pain, but at least the cold weight inside had vanished. "With any luck, *she'll* think we died in the crash, too."

Tarfang eyed Luke warily, then sat up and began to jabber angrily, alternately pounding his fists and stabbing a furry finger at the air.

"I most certainly will *not* say that to Master Luke," C-3PO replied. "And I fail to see the harm if he *is* trying to make us feel better. It's certainly better than dwelling on a negative."

"We're *not* dead," Luke said between gritted teeth. He went to Juun's side and pointed out the pilot's viewport toward a section of deck hanging free just inside the rim of the crater. "Put the pod over there. We need to get out of this thing before Gorog sees it."

Juun dropped them into the crater. The temperature inside climbed rapidly as they drew closer to the molten remains of the *DR919a,* and the pod gave a noticeable jerk when it entered the nest ship's artificial gravity.

"Hoersch-Kessel gravity system," Han observed. "Boy are they going to regret that."

Tarfang chittered an indignant question.

"Tarfang would like to know what you think is wrong with—"

"Everything," Han said. "I just hope we can keep this rock from lighting its hyperdrive. I really hate what those g burps do to my joints."

Juun sat the pod down on the sagging edge of a deck section surrounded by antennas and dishes and data feeds, all of it very un-Killik-looking and all of it arranged around a half-melted relay station.

"They had help building these things," Han said, peering out the pod's viewport. "And a lot of it. That heat sensor looks Balmorran, and the signals package is definitely a Kuat Drive Yards Eavesdropper."

"Probably had help from the pirates—financed by the black membrosia trade," Luke said. "But we'll sort that out later. Right now, we need to get to those hyperdrives."

"Good idea." Han opened the pod's survival pack and sprayed Luke's back with bacta salve, then passed him a blaster and took one for himself. "Any idea how we're going to get there through a nest full of bugs?"

"We're not going to go *through* them," Luke said. He pulled the top of his vac suit over his shoulders and began to seal the closures. "We're going to go around them."

Juun frowned and stopped short of pulling his helmet visor down. "I don't understand."

"Outside the ship." Luke secured his own helmet to the collar ring. "By crawling across the hull."

"I was afraid that's what you had in mind," Han said.

Luke lowered his visor, then picked up the heavy survival pack and turned toward the hatch. Han and the others sealed their own vac suits, then they all left the escape pod and started to push it toward the still-glowing crater.

A shudder ran through the deck. They all scrambled back, afraid it was about to collapse. But the deck remained where it was. While it was sagging slightly, it was clearly in no danger of falling, even with the heavy escape pod sitting just a meter or so from its edge.

The shuddering grew stronger. The severed lines and equipment dangling on the walls began to bounce around soundlessly, then Han's voice came over the vac suit comm system.

"We'd better wait awhile." He pointed out through the crater hole, where the pirates' unnamed planet was starting to glide by ever more rapidly. "I'm not sure I want to be crawling around outside when this thing goes into hyperspace."

NINETEEN

Leia found the command deck of the *Admiral Ackbar* to be as spotless, orderly, and efficient as the rest of the Star Destroyer. The mixed-species crew was both alert and focused, glancing up as she stepped out of the lift, then quickly returning to their tasks when they saw she was escorted by a detail from bridge security. Bwua'tu himself was in the Tactical Salon—the TacSal—at the back of the command deck, surrounded by his staff and studying a holodisplay of the Murgo Choke. An opalescent bust of the great admiral sat in a niche on the back wall, keeping a solemn watch over the entire deck . . . and causing a cold tingle in the middle of Leia's back.

The security detail stopped outside the TacSal, where the admiral's aide, Wurf'al, met Leia with a disapproving sneer. He gestured curtly for her to follow, and as they approached the holodisplay, Bwua'tu ended the discussion he was having with his staff to greet Leia with a smug grin.

"Princess Leia, you wanted to see me?"

"That's right, Admiral," Leia said. "Thank you for not making it difficult."

"Why should I?" Bwua'tu asked. "I'm as concerned as you are."

This surprised Leia. "You are?"

"Of course," Bwua'tu said. "Even if your friends in the

StealthXs are carrying extra air scrubbers in their cargo compartments, they must be breathing their own fumes by now. I only hope it's not too late."

Leia's surprise changed to irritation. "My friends are fine. I came to warn you that the Killiks are about to contest your blockade."

"Truly?" Bwua'tu's expression remained smug, but Leia could tell by the way his neck fur flattened that this news troubled him. "And this knowledge came to you while you were staring at the wall of your cell?"

"More or less," Leia said. "Luke reached out to me through the Force."

"Of course . . . your Jedi sorcery." Bwua'tu considered this for a moment, then asked, "Did your brother also reveal where to expect this threat—or what form it might take?"

"Unfortunately, no," Leia said. "Communication through the Force isn't usually that precise. All I could tell was that Luke is very concerned."

"I see."

Bwua'tu's gaze slid back toward the holodisplay, where the starfighter complement from both the *Admiral Ackbar* and the *Mon Mothma*—well over a hundred craft—were deployed in a double screening formation between the two Star Destroyers. The admiral seemed to forget Leia for the moment and lose himself in thought, then he abruptly looked back to her.

"Master Sebatyne is more adept with the Force, is she not?"

"She is," Leia said. "That's one reason she's a Master."

"Then perhaps Master Sebatyne could provide me with a more thorough report," Bwua'tu said. "Inform her that I require her presence on the command deck."

"I've already been in contact with Master Sebatyne, as

I'm sure your comm officers have informed you." As Leia spoke, she was puzzling over what seemed an odd, almost desperate starfighter deployment. "She's unavailable at the moment."

"That's right," Bwua'tu said. "She's hunting gankers."

Leia shrugged. "There's no reasoning with her when she's hungry. Barabels like their meat fresh."

"As do we all," Bwua'tu said. "But there *are* no gankers aboard this ship, Princess Leia."

"Come, Admiral." Leia touched Bwua'tu through the Force and confirmed what she had already surmised: he did not believe a word she was saying. "There are *always* gankers aboard a capital ship."

"Not aboard my ship." Bwua'tu stepped closer and spoke in a low, gravelly voice. "Your plan is a good one, *Jedi* Solo, but you forget with whom you are dealing."

"My plan, Admiral?" Leia glanced back at the holodisplay and realized what she was seeing. The starfighters from the *Mon Mothma* were carefully working their way toward those from the *Admiral Ackbar,* slowly weaving back and forth in a tight search pattern. "You think I'm trying to stage a diversion!"

"It will do your friends in the StealthXs no good, of course," Bwua'tu said. "But I *am* impressed with the tactical coordination you Jedi achieve with your sorcery."

"You give us too much credit." Leia stretched her Force-awareness into the Choke and felt the familiar presence of a StealthX battle-meld. Then Kyp Durron reached out to her, assuring her that his team would soon be coming to help her and Saba. Leia seethed inwardly; she hardly needed rescuing. But the idea that someone could believe she *did* made her think it had been a mistake to sit in a cell just to avoid further straining relations with the Galactic Alliance. "Until I saw your starfighter deployment, Admiral Bwua'tu,

I didn't even know that Master Durron and his squadron were out there."

"Now you mock me, Jedi Solo." Bwua'tu sounded genuinely irritated. "The Rurgavean Sleight is obscure, but did you really think *I* would fail to recognize it?"

"Of course not." Leia racked her brain, trying to remember what the Rurgavean Sleight *was*. "But you must believe me. Luke's message is real. I'm not trying to distract you."

"For someone who is not trying, you are doing an exceptional job," Bwua'tu said. "If Master Sebatyne fails to report to the nearest officer within thirty seconds, the StealthX fuel will be destroyed. After that, we will move on to the *Falcon*'s drive nacelles."

"What will it take to prove I'm telling the truth?" Leia had to struggle to keep an even voice. "Would you believe me if I called in both teams of StealthXs?"

Bwua'tu narrowed his eyes, contemplating her offer, then tapped a bent claw in her direction. "Well done, Princess. A classic slide into the Mandalorian Surrender."

Leia sighed. "I'm trying to *help* you, Admiral—not capture the *Ackbar*."

A cold knot formed between Leia's shoulder blades as she spoke. She half turned, expecting to see Wurf'al or some other officer glaring in her direction. Instead she found herself looking into the vacant eyes of the admiral's bust.

"Admiral, I continue to sense something wrong aboard this ship." She pointed at the bust. "May I ask what kind of security scans were performed on that piece?"

"You may not," Bwua'tu said sternly. "I won't be distracted, Jedi Solo." He raised his hand and studied his chrono for a moment, then added, "And your thirty seconds have passed. Since we still have no sign of Master Sebatyne, I'll have to carry out my threat."

Wurf'al produced a comlink and passed it to the admiral. "Security Two, Admiral."

Bwua'tu kept his gaze fixed on Leia. "That would be the detail guarding your StealthX fuel."

"Go ahead," Leia said. She still had a bad feeling about the bust, but it seemed clear Bwua'tu would not listen while he thought she was trying to stage a diversion. "Perhaps it will convince you of my sincerity."

"As you wish." Bwua'tu activated the comlink. "Tibanna detail—"

The admiral stopped speaking when the comlink in Leia's sleeve pocket echoed his words.

Bwua'tu scowled and motioned Wurf'al to retrieve the device. Once Wurf'al had done so, the admiral raised his own comlink and spoke again.

"Tibanna detail, come in."

The call was repeated over the comlink in Wurf'al's hand—the same comlink that Saba had left for Leia to find on her bunk.

Bwua'tu raised his bushy brow and turned to Leia. "My compliments. It appears I am no longer in control of your StealthX fuel."

A loud sissing came over both comlinks.

Bwua'tu frowned, then spoke into his. "I wouldn't gloat, Master Sebatyne. I still control the *Falcon*."

This only drew more sissing.

Bwua'tu deactivated the comlink, then surprised her by not immediately ordering an attack on the *Falcon*'s drive nacelles. Instead he turned to his aide, Wurf'al.

"Send a detail to investigate what became of the squad guarding the StealthX fuel," he said. "And sound battle stations in the capture bay."

Before Wurf'al could acknowledge the order, the sharp

wail of a proximity alarm sounded from the flight deck speakers.

"Contact cluster exiting hyperspace," an efficient female sensor officer announced. "No transponder codes, outbound from the nebula."

Fifteen black triangles—the tactical symbols for unknown vessels—appeared at the edge of the holodisplay, coming from the direction of the Utegetu Nebula. Instead of stopping to reconnoiter or plot their next jumps, as most starship fleets would do, they streaked straight toward the heart of the Murgo Choke at a substantial percentage of lightspeed.

Leia was still trying to comprehend what she was seeing when Bwua'tu began to rattle off orders. "Wurf'al, make that general battle stations."

"Sir!"

"Grendyl, recall all starfighters . . . Jorga, assign targets to turbolaser batteries . . . Rabad, have Commodore Darklighter bring the *Mothma* forward to support us . . . Tola, start a withdrawal toward the *Mothma* . . ."

The acknowledgments came faster than Leia could track them—"Sir . . . sir . . . sir . . . sir . . ."—and the flight deck erupted into a controlled frenzy as the officers jumped to execute their orders.

"Batteries five, nine, and seventeen have acquired targets, Admiral," a Duros gunnery officer reported.

"Well done, Jorga. Open fire."

"Open fire?" Leia gasped. "You don't even know—"

Bwua'tu raised a finger, warning her to remain silent. An instant later clouds of tiny black triangles began to stream from the fifteen larger vessels.

"Contacts launching fighters," the sensor officer announced.

Leia was stunned. The Killiks were not merely attempting to run the Galactic Alliance's blockade, they were going to *attack* it. Implications and ramifications raced through her mind in a mad swirl, and she was filled with the deepening fear that she was watching the outbreak of another galactic war—one born of desperation and misunderstanding, and all the more tragic for it.

The colored glare of an outgoing turbolaser barrage flashed through the viewport and lit up the *Ackbar*'s flight deck. A couple of seconds later the tactical display showed strikes against three different targets.

"Affirmative hits," the sensor officer reported. "No shields, damage unknown."

The unknown-vessel triangles began to assume three-dimensional shapes, each with a figure ranging between 7,952 and 8,234—its length in meters—shining inside it. They looked like fifteen egg-shaped rocks, all trailing stubby tails of ion efflux. The fighters were just clouds of tiny slivers, but an inset in one of the swarms displayed the image of what was basically a dartship mounted on an oversized ion engine.

"Interesting." Bwua'tu seemed to be speaking to himself. "The Killiks have some new toys. I wonder what other surprises they may have brought us?"

Leia's thoughts went instantly to all the busts of Admiral Bwua'tu she had seen aboard the *Ackbar*. They resembled spinglass too much to be anything else. She turned toward the one watching over the TacSal and did not even need to reach out in the Force to know she was right. A bolt of danger sense shot down her spine, so cold and crisp that she broke into goose bumps.

Leia turned to Wurf'al. "Excuse me, Captain, where is the nearest disposal chute?"

"Disposal chute?" Wurf'al frowned as though he was going to question her need for one. Then the rest of the

Ackbar's batteries cut loose, filling the command deck viewport with a multihued glare and causing the overhead lighting to flicker and dim. He pointed absentmindedly toward a spotless cover-flap on the far wall. "There."

"Thank you."

Leia used the Force to slide the bust, which was about forty centimeters high, free of its mounting. A Mon Calamari lieutenant commander let out a startled cry as it drifted out of the niche, then stepped in front of Bwua'tu to shield him.

"Sorry to alarm you," Leia said. She floated the bust over to disposal chute and began to push it through the flap. "But this thing *has* to go."

"The admiral!" Wurf'al cried. He dived after the piece, jamming his arms into the chute up to his shoulders. "It's okay. I have him!"

Leia felt the barrels of several blasters swing her way. The petty officer in charge of her security escort warned, "Don't even think about moving, Princess."

She kept her hands in plain sight but did not otherwise acknowledge the threat.

Bwua'tu peered over the shoulder of the lieutenant commander in front of him, scowling first at Leia, then at Wurf'al.

"Captain, what the blazes are you doing with your arms down in a disposal chute?"

"Holding on to your bust, sir." A muffled clink sounded inside the chute. "Bloah!"

Bwua'tu frowned. "Captain?"

"Sorry, sir, but something—rodder!" Wurf'al suddenly straightened and pulled his arms out of the chute. His hands and wrists were covered in dozens of blue, thumb-sized insects. "They're biting!"

"They're Gorog!" Leia reached out in the Force and pulled the chute cover closed. "Dark Nest Killiks!"

Wurf'al dropped to his knees, screaming and trying to shake the insects off. Those that came free buzzed up to his head and alighted on his eyes. His screams grew primal, but the TacSal seemed frozen in its confusion, and even Leia was at a loss as to how to help the aide. After a couple of seconds he threw his head back and collapsed, a raspy gurgle coming from his throat.

The assassin bugs exploded into the air, spreading their wings and droning off in every direction.

"Commando raid!" Bwua'tu yelled.

He pulled his sidearm and blasted a Killik from the air. Half a dozen bolts sizzled past Leia's shoulder, taking out another insect. Then the rest of Bwua'tu's staff began to react, drawing their own blasters and lacing the air with fire.

They were not entirely effective. A Duros lieutenant commander slapped at his throat, then fell to the floor and began to convulse, and perhaps two dozen of the insects escaped out onto the command deck.

Once the shock of the initial assault wore off, Bwua'tu stepped over to the disposal chute and slapped the VOID button to suck the contents down into the *Ackbar*'s waste tanks.

"Well done, Princess." He slapped the button again. "What alerted you?"

Leia used the Force to flick an assassin bug away from his ear, then splattered it against the wall. "Jedi sorcery."

"Marvelous stuff." Bwua'tu eyed the blue-and-yellow smear, then looked past Leia to the petty officer in charge of her security escort. "You, take your detail and secure this deck."

"Sir. And the prisoner?"

"Prisoner?" Bwua'tu snorted. "She was *never* your prisoner, son. She was just being polite."

"Thank you, Admiral," Leia said. "I don't know what the Killiks are up to, but I hope you understand that the Jedi aren't—"

"Say no more." Bwua'tu raised a hand to stop her. "The Jedi may be idealistic fools, but they are not traitors—as you have already proven."

"I'm glad we understand each other." Leia tried not to bristle at being called a fool; under the circumstances, she was glad just to have earned Bwua'tu's trust. "If I might make a suggestion, Killik nests share a collective mind—"

"Of course." Bwua'tu turned to the intercom and opened a shipwide channel. "Infiltration alert. Seal all hatches, blast anything with six limbs, and dump all statuary down the nearest disposal chute. This is not a drill."

Bwua'tu paused a moment to look out at the chaos on the *Ackbar*'s command deck—at least a dozen stations were empty while the crew fought the remaining assassin bugs—then returned to his place at the holodisplay.

"All right, people, we've got a battle to win," he said to the TacSal staff. "Back to your stations."

Leia stepped to the holodisplay with his officers. Most of the Killik fleet was headed straight for *Mon Mothma* and the heart of the Choke, and clouds of insect starfighters were already boiling past the thin screen of Alliance defenders. But a small task force—five ships and several thousand dartships—was veering toward the *Ackbar*, preparing to intercept it and prevent it from reaching the *Mothma*.

Knowing how valuable any intelligence about one's foes could be in a battle, Leia oriented herself to the fighting, then turned toward the Killik ships and, one by one, began to reach out to them in the Force. She sensed the presence of a single Killik nest aboard each of the large ships, often accompanied by dozens or even hundreds of Joiners, and she even recognized the stoicism of the Taat and the artistic sensibilities of the Saras among the vessels headed for the *Mothma*. But when she came to the last ship of the group moving to intercept the *Ackbar*, she felt no presences at all, only an empty place in the Force.

"Something you wish to share, Jedi Solo?" Bwua'tu asked.

Leia looked up to find the Bothan studying her. She pointed at the image of the "empty" vessel in the holodisplay.

"I think that is the Dark Nest's ship," she said. "Of course, we don't know how the Killik fleet is organized, but that will be as close to a flagship as they have."

"I really shouldn't be surprised by what you Jedi can tell, but I am." Bwua'tu thought for a moment, then turned to the Mon Calamari captain who had tried to shield him earlier. "We won't show our hand *yet*, Tola."

"Very good, sir."

"But when that ship enters effective range, let's be ready to give it everything we have," Bwua'tu said. "Maybe we can surprise *them* for a change."

"Yes, sir," Tola said. "I'll have all batteries lock it in as a secondary target now."

"Good. Designate it Bug One." Bwua'tu turned back to the holodisplay, but said, "And one more thing. Have the capture bay stand down. All Jedi craft are free to come and go as they require."

Tola acknowledged the order, then turned to pass on the admiral's commands.

Leia smiled. "Thank you, Admiral," she said. "But if I can be of some service *here*—"

"I was thinking of your StealthXs, Princess," Bwua'tu

interrupted. "They're going to need a place to refuel and rearm."

"They are?" Leia asked. "I mean, if the Jedi can be of any help—"

"They *will* be." Bwua'tu began to pace, but his gaze remained glued to the holodisplay. "Inform them that they're now under my command."

"Uh—"

"Is there a problem with that?" Bwua'tu demanded.

"No, sir," Leia answered. "Just thinking about the best way to let them know."

"The way that makes it clear. These are bugs with a plan, Princess." Bwua'tu stopped pacing and scowled along his snout at her. "We need to stop them here, or we won't stop them at all."

Leia swallowed. "I know that, Admiral. I'll do my best."

She closed her eyes, then stretched her Force-awareness out into the Choke. She found Mara and her team first, very calm and focused. A bright circle of ion glow, surrounded by the stern of a large rocky vessel, appeared in Leia's mind; they were sneaking up on a Killik ship. She filled her thoughts with good feelings about Admiral Bwua'tu and silently repeated the word *respect*.

Mara and the others seemed puzzled, but willing.

Leia reached out to Kyp's squadron next and was immediately engulfed in a conflagration of fear and exhilaration and anger, all blasting her at once. She allowed herself to sink into the emotional turmoil and began to glimpse flashes of exploding dartships and fiery white propellant trails.

Kyp's presence touched Leia, assuring her that he was on his way. She replied as she had with Mara, by filling her mind with good thoughts about Bwua'tu and silently urging Kyp to respect him.

Kyp poured indignation into the Force. Leia repeated the

sentiment more strongly, trying to impress on him that the problem was the Killiks, not the Fifth Fleet. Kyp grew frustrated, but his stubbornness slowly gave way to willingness.

Leia opened her eyes in time to see Tola, the Mon Calamari, drop to his knees, gasping for breath and clawing at his throat. Bwua'tu glanced over and calmly smashed the butt of his blaster into the back of Tola's skull. There was the sound of crunching chitin, then the lieutenant commander pitched forward, a string of insect gore momentarily connecting his head to the admiral's blaster handle.

"Stay alert, people!" Bwua'tu ordered. "I can't have my staff dropping dead around me."

A pair of security guards stepped into the TacSal to carry the convulsing Mon Calamari away. Leia pushed aside the sorrow she felt for him, then caught Bwua'tu's eye.

"The StealthX crews have agreed." She pointed into the holodisplay, indicating the five Killik ships moving to intercept the *Ackbar*. "Mara's team—half a squadron—is somewhere behind this group, moving up on one of the ships."

Bwua'tu frowned. "What's her status? Mara's team can't be combat-ready after so long in space."

"They can make one attack run, but dogfighting is out of the question until they refuel," Leia said. "Other than that, they're good."

Bwua'tu looked doubtful.

"Trust me, Admiral." Leia smiled. "It's Jedi sorcery."

Bwua'tu snorted. "If you say so."

Leia pointed at a cluster of dartships that seemed to be gathered between the two groups of Killik ships for no apparent reason. "I think Master Durron's squadron is engaged here."

"On their way to free you and Master Sebatyne,"

Bwua'tu surmised. "We don't need them here. Have them withdraw toward the *Mothma*."

"It might be more precise if you spoke to our teams yourself." Leia went to the comm station and opened a channel to the StealthXs. "They can't acknowledge, but they'll hear your orders."

"Very well."

Bwua'tu stepped away from the holodisplay and told the StealthXs what he wanted. Leia felt acknowledgments from everyone except Mara, who seemed firmly opposed to abandoning the target she had already selected. When Leia allowed her bewilderment to rise to the surface of her mind, Mara flooded the meld with concern for Luke and Han.

"Everyone except Mara is a go," Leia reported. "Mara is going to stay with her current target. It has something to do with Luke and Han."

Bwua'tu cocked his thick brow. "*Something* is a rather imprecise term, Princess."

"I'm sorry, Admiral." Leia reached out into the Force, searching for her brother's presence, and felt nothing. "That's all I know."

Bwua'tu frowned, clearly unaccustomed to having his commands modified in this manner. "That will . . ."

He let the sentence trail off as the leading elements of the Killik fleet filled the holodisplay with flashes of light. *Mon Mothma*'s image changed to yellow, indicating that its shields were absorbing more energy than they could rapidly disperse. The *Ackbar*'s image remained blue.

"Enemy weapons are identified as turbolasers," the sensor officer reported. "Unknown manufacturer, but clearly Alliance technology."

"At least we know who the Tibanna tappers have been supplying," Bwua'tu observed. He turned to Leia. "Have

Master Sebatyne prep the *Falcon* for launch. The StealthXs may need a mobile refueling platform."

Leia retrieved the comlink Saba had left on her bunk. "Master Sebatyne, would you prep the *Falcon* for launch? Admiral Bwua'tu may need it to refuel the StealthXs."

"It *is* prepped," Saba retorted. A muffled *phew-phew* sounded in the background. "But this one does not know how long we can keep it that way."

Leia frowned. "Is that the *Falcon*'s blaster cannon I hear?"

"Of course!" Saba replied. "Those little Gorog are everywhere!"

Leia started to report to Bwua'tu, but he was already at a wall display, punching codes into the control panel. He paused, then punched more codes and cursed. The screen never showed anything but static.

"These bugs are good," he growled. "They've been cutting our status feeds."

Leia activated the comlink again. "We're blind up here, Master. What can you tell me about the situation?"

"It'z bad!" Saba said. "If this one had not already disabled the capture bay batteriez, you wouldn't be talking to her now. The crew is down, and bugz are everywhere."

"Okay," Leia said. "Maybe you'd better launch now."

"Without *you*?" A rhythmic hissing came out of the comlink. "You are alwayz joking, Jedi Solo."

Saba closed the channel.

Leia looked up to find Bwua'tu speaking to a young Sullustan ensign wearing the double-lightning bars of the engineering staff.

"—didn't Captain Urbok inform me the *Ackbar*'s situation was this bad? Damage assessment is her responsibility."

"B-because she's dead, s-sir?" the lieutenant stammered.

"What about Lieutenant Commander Reo?"

"Also dead, sir."

Leia could sense Bwua'tu's anger building, but he maintained a civil tone. "And Lieutenant Aramb?"

"Paralyzed and unable to speak, sir," the ensign reported. "Apparently, the Killik venom isn't as effective against Gotals."

"Well, then, who *is* running engineering?" Bwua'tu demanded.

The Sullustan looked back toward the decimated command deck, then asked, "You?"

"Wrong, *Captain* Yuul." Bwua'tu pointed to the ship engineer's chair. "Now get to your station, get on the comm, and find out the condition of this ship!"

"Sir!"

As the Sullustan turned to obey, Bwua'tu looked to Leia and shook his head. "These Killiks are beginning to worry me, Princess. What other surprises do they have tucked under their chitin?"

Without awaiting a reply, he returned his attention to the holodisplay. The *Mon Mothma* was concentrating its fire on the lead ship, blowing off so many pieces that the thing looked more like an asteroid field than a capital vessel. But the Killik dartship swarms had already overwhelmed the Alliance fighter screens, and for every turbolaser strike the *Mothma* delivered, it took ten.

The *Ackbar* was faring better, at least outside the hull. Although space beyond the viewport was bright with turbolaser blossoms, the Killik gunners seemed to be having trouble accounting for the gravitational effects of the binary stars behind the Star Destroyer. Most strikes fell short or passed harmlessly below the *Ackbar*'s belly, and the few that landed were not powerful enough to seriously challenge its shields.

The *Mothma*'s likeness suddenly changed to red, indicating that it had suffered a shield breach. Bwua'tu sighed audibly, then turned to a female human who had been sticking close to his side.

"Grendyl, tell Commodore Darklighter to withdraw. Have all surviving Fifth Fleet starfighters disengage and meet him at Rendezvous Alpha."

Grendyl's eyes grew round. "Even *our* fighters, Admiral?"

"That's what I said, blast it!" Bwua'tu barked. "Is something wrong with those little pink flaps you call ears?"

An astonished silence settled over the surviving members of Bwua'tu's staff, and all eyes went to the holodisplay.

Bwua'tu took a breath, then said, "I apologize, Grendyl. That was uncalled for. Our unfortunate situation has put me rather on edge, I'm afraid."

"It's quite all right, sir." Her voice was about to crack. "I'll send the message at once."

"Thank you," Bwua'tu said. "And make it a direct order, to both Commodore Darklighter and the starfighter squadrons. I won't have them wasting valuable Alliance resources on pointless displays of bravery. The *Ackbar* is lost."

Grendyl brought her hand up in a smart salute. "Sir."

The rest of Bwua'tu's staff remained silent, staring into the holodisplay and contemplating the admiral's grim conclusion. The *Ackbar* was trapped with its back against a binary star, with five Killik capital ships and a swarm of several thousand fighters coming at it with nothing in the way except a few atoms of hydrogen. The situation was hopeless, and Bwua'tu was both astute enough to see that early on and sensible enough not to deceive himself or anyone else about their chances of escaping the trap.

Leia felt Saba urging her to return to the *Falcon*, but she remained where she was. Something did not feel right. The

Ackbar's turbolasers were hammering all five enemy ships coming toward it, but its own shields were barely flickering.

After a few moments, Bwua'tu said, "I think the time has come for our surprise." He went to the comm and opened a channel to the turbolaser batteries. "All batteries, switch targeting to Bug One. Acknowledge when ready."

The *Ackbar*'s turbolaser batteries fell silent for a moment, then the acknowledgments rolled in so fast that Leia could not keep track of them.

When the comm fell silent again, Bwua'tu said, "Fire on my mark . . . three . . . two . . . mark!"

Space beyond the command deck viewport grew brilliant with turbolaser fire, and the deck shuddered with kinetic discharge. They waited, breathless, during the instant it took the barrage to cross the vast distance and land. Bug One's symbol turned yellow on the holodisplay.

"Affirmative hits," the sensor officer reported. "Estimate ten percent loss of mass."

An enthusiastic cheer rose from the survivors in the Tac-Sal and on the command deck.

Bwua'tu spoke into the comm. "Well done, gunnery! Odd-number batteries maintain fire—"

Leia did not hear the rest of what Bwua'tu said, for Mara was suddenly reaching out to her, full of alarm and worry for Luke and Han. Leia frowned, confused, and the image of a Killik ship appeared in her mind. There were several tiny figures on it, creeping across its broken surface, noticeable only because of the pinpoints of light coming from their helmet lamps. Then turbolaser fire began to rain down on it like a Nkllonian meteor storm, blowing huge, ragged holes into the ship's hull, hurling fountains of stone into space, and hiding the tiny figures behind a curtain of dust.

And then, suddenly, Leia felt Luke's presence, somewhere near Mara and even more alarmed.

Leia sprang to Bwua'tu's side. "Stop! Luke and Han are on that ship!"

Bwua'tu lowered his furry brow, as confused as Leia had been a moment ago. "What?"

"Luke and Han are on Bug One!" Leia explained. "That's why Mara wouldn't retarget earlier. She saw them!"

Bwua'tu's eyes widened. "You're sure?"

"I am," Leia said. "I just felt Luke in the Force—he must have been hiding before."

Bwua'tu narrowed his eyes. "I see." He thought for a moment, then returned to the comm. "Batteries ending in five or zero maintain fire on Bug One. All others return to normal targeting."

Leia frowned. "That's still ten batteries!"

"If your brother and husband are aboard that ship, they're either prisoners or stowaways," Bwua'tu said. "If they're prisoners, their best chance of escape lies in disabling the ship. If they're stowaways—"

"—we might draw attention to them by stopping the attack," Leia finished.

Bwua'tu nodded. "We'll make a fleet admiral of you yet, Princess."

They returned to the holodisplay. The tiny triangle of an unidentified vessel was just separating from Bug One and starting to accelerate toward the *Ackbar*.

"Sensors, give me a reading on that right *now*," Bwua'tu demanded. "What is it? A missile?"

There was a short pause, then the image changed to the triangular cylinder of an old Kuat Drive Yards frigate.

"New contact is confirmed as a *Lancer*-class frigate," the sensor officer reported. "Affiliation unknown."

Bwua'tu frowned, then looked toward Leia. "Can your sorcery be of any help, Princess?"

Hoping to sense Luke and Han aboard the frigate, she reached out to the vessel in the Force . . . and found Raynar Thul instead. She immediately tried to break contact, but as she withdrew, he followed, and an enormous, murky presence rose inside her mind. Her vision grew dark around the edges, and a dark weight began to press down on her, so heavy and cold and draining that her knees grew weak and buckled.

"Princess Leia?" Bwua'tu and Grendyl stepped to her side, their blaster pistols cocked to smash the first crawling thing they saw. "Where did it get you?"

"I'm . . ." Leia tried to rise and failed. "Not bugs . . . frigate . . ."

Bwua'tu frowned. "The frigate?" He pulled her up. "What about it?"

Leia wanted to answer, to tell him who was coming, but the dark weight inside was too much. She could not bring the words to mind, could not have spoken them even if they had come.

"I see," Bwua'tu said. "Grendyl, designate that vessel hostile . . . and make it a high-priority target."

A few moments later a turbolaser barrage streaked toward the frigate. A deep pang of sorrow washed over Leia as she awaited the coming explosion. Whatever Raynar had become among the Killiks, he had once been a Jedi and a close friend of her children, and she knew that his loss would leave her feeling empty and dismal.

Then, as the strike neared Raynar's vessel, the dark weight inside vanished, and Leia's strength surged back. Still gasping, she was about to report who was aboard, but the turbolaser barrage suddenly veered away and blossomed in empty space.

Grendyl cried out in astonishment, a murmur of disbelief rose from the survivors on the command deck, and Leia finally understood why the Killik gunners were such bad shots.

They weren't *trying* to hit the *Ackbar*.

When the second volley of turbolaser fire also veered away at the last instant, Bwua'tu narrowed his eyes and turned to Leia.

"What is it?" he asked. "Some sort of new shield?"

Leia shook her head. "It's Raynar Thul," she said. "And I think he's coming to take your ship."

TWENTY

The exterior of the nest ship was knobby and shadowed, a broken vista of narrow trenches zigzagging between giant blocks of spitcrete. Han knew that the blocks were almost certainly primitive heat sinks, necessary to keep the hull from cracking open in the extreme temperature swings of space. But that didn't make navigating around them any easier. The vessel's surface was like an immense spitcrete maze, stretching ahead almost endlessly, then suddenly vanishing against the blue brilliance of a massive crescent of ion efflux. Han felt as though he were walking into a sun—an impression supported by the droplets of sweat stinging his eyes and rolling down his cheeks. With the four real suns of the Murgo Choke blasting him in the side and shoulders, the *DR919a*'s cheap escape pod vac suits were not up to the task of cooling their occupants. He was afraid they would start melting soon.

Han stopped at the base of a heat sink—a spitcrete monolith two meters high—that Luke had scaled to study the terrain ahead, then tipped his helmet back so he could look up. There was another nest ship a hundred kilometers or so above, and a constant stream of tiny colored dashes came and went as it traded fire with an Alliance Star Destroyer somewhere inside the Murgo Choke.

Han activated his suit comm. "Are we there yet?"

"Almost, Han." Luke continued to study the horizon, one glove shading his helmet visor. "There's a square shadow at eleven that might be a thermal vent."

"Do you see any heat distortion above it?"

"No."

"Then we're not there." Han tried to keep his disappointment out of his voice—he did not want to encourage any more jabbering over the suit comm from Tarfang. "A hyperdrive for a ship this big is going to release heat for hours. When we get near a vent, we'll know it."

"I suppose." Luke turned to climb down, then suddenly tipped his helmet back to look over their heads. "Incoming! Get—"

Space turned white, and Luke's voice dissolved into the telltale static that meant a turbolaser strike was all too precisely targeted. Han tried to drop behind cover, but that was next to impossible in a stiff escape pod vac suit. He made it as far as bending his knees; then the nest ship hull slammed up under him, hurling him into the side of the heat sink. He tumbled down the surface and came to a rest at its base, the inside of his faceplate so smeared with perspiration that he could not tell whether he was lying facedown or face up.

The hull continued to buck and shudder, bouncing Han's nose against his faceplate, and the strike static grew deafening. He chinned his suit comm off so he could listen for the hiss that would mean his vac suit had been compromised, then slowly brought up his arms and determined that he was lying on his belly.

Han rolled to his back, then wished he hadn't. Space above was one huge, blurry sheet of turbolaser energy—most of it incoming—and filled with roiling spitcrete dust and tumbling chunks of heat sink . . . and something that looked like a half-sized vac suit, spinning out of control and waving its spread-eagled limbs.

Han activated his suit comm again and heard even more static. Some Alliance Star Destroyer was hitting them with everything it had. He stood and nearly got bounced free of the ship's artificial gravity himself, then came down hard beside C-3PO.

The droid turned his head and looked as though he was speaking. Fortunately, Han could not hear a word.

Trying to keep one eye on whoever it was floating off up there, Han rolled to a knee and, through the thickening haze of barrage vapor, found Luke about five meters away. Han scrambled over, then touched helmets so they could speak without the comm unit.

"Someone got bounced!" Han pointed toward the slowly shrinking figure. "We're losing him!"

Luke looked in the direction Han was indicating. "It's Tarfang."

"How can you tell?"

Luke pointed at a pair of shadows tucked behind a heat sink. "Juun and Artoo are over there."

He lifted his hand and used the Force to draw Tarfang's spinning form back down. The ship's artificial gravity caught hold of the Ewok about two meters above the surface. He landed hard, then bounced to his feet shaking his fist and jabbering behind his faceplate. When another close strike launched him off the hull again, Han had to think twice before he reached up and caught the Ewok by the ankle.

Tarfang noticed the hesitation. He glared vibrodaggers as he was pulled back down, but that did not prevent him from grabbing Han's utility belt and holding tight. Han tried again to activate his suit comm, but with space flashing like a Bespinese thunderstorm, all that came over the helmet speakers was strike static.

Luke did not need the comm. He simply stood and looked toward Han, and Han understood. They had to keep moving. Luke had used the Force, and now Lomi Plo could feel them coming.

They gathered Juun and the droids and started forward, following the spitcrete troughs between the heat sinks, zigzagging their way through the barrage with giant columns of shattered spitcrete and vapor shooting up all around. Within a few minutes, the turbolaser storm faded to a fraction of its former fury, but it remained fierce enough to make them fear for their lives. Several strikes landed so close that everyone was bounced off their feet, and twice Luke had to use the Force to pull someone back down into the nest ship's artificial gravity. The barrage haze grew steadily thicker, obscuring visibility to the point that Han came within a step of leading Tarfang and C-3PO off the edge of a cavernous blast hole.

Perhaps half a kilometer later, Luke stopped short and pointed toward a billowing column of dust and shattered spitcrete about fifty meters ahead. It was roiling with convection currents and rising at a steady rate.

"We're there, Han." Luke's voice was scratchy but understandable; under the lighter barrage, the electromagnetic static had diminished and no longer jammed their suit comms completely. "But be ready. I think we have a reception committee."

Tarfang stopped and planted his feet. *"Wobba jobabu!"*

"Don't worry," Luke said. "We'll have backup."

"Backup?" Han turned to look, peering through the barrage haze. "Out here?"

"Mara is keeping an eye on us from a StealthX," Luke explained. "I think she spotted our helmet lamps when she was sneaking up to attack the nest ship."

"She's in a StealthX?" Han asked. "And you still want to do this the hard way? Why don't we let *her* drop a shadow bomb down that thermal vent and jump this rock? We can trigger our rescue beacons and wait for a ride."

"That's not a bad idea, Han," Luke said. Something that sounded like chattering teeth came over the suit comm, and he turned toward the thermal vent. "I'd like you to take the others and do exactly that. It will make things easier for me."

"Easier *how*?" Han asked suspiciously. "I thought all we needed to do was blow the nest ship's hyperdrive, and Mara can do that a lot easier with a shadow bomb than we can with a lightsaber and two crummy blaster pistols."

"There's a complication," Luke said. "One we can't hit with a shadow bomb."

"A complication?" Han put his faceplate close to Luke's and saw that the Jedi Master was shivering uncontrollably. "You mean Lomi Plo?"

Luke turned to Han and nodded. "I should f-finish her off while I have the chance."

"I don't know who you think you're fooling, but it isn't me," Han said. "She's got ahold of you again, hasn't she?"

Luke sighed. "That doesn't mean you should stay."

"You come with us, and I won't," Han said.

"And m-make us all targets?" Luke shook his head. "I'm going to stay here and see this thing through."

"That makes two of us," Han said. He turned to Tarfang and Juun. "How about you two?"

Tarfang launched into tirade of angry jabbering, then renewed his grasp on Han's utility belt and shook his head. Juun merely stood there, blinking at them out of his helmet.

"Well?" Han asked.

When Juun's expression did not change, Han tapped the side of the Sullustan's helmet. Juun frowned and shook his head.

"I guess it's unanimous," Han said. "Juun can't risk jumping off this rock with a faulty comm. If his beacon fails, too, he'll be a goner out there."

"I wish you'd reconsider, Han."

"Yeah, and I wish we had a satchel full of thermal detonators and a few kilos of baradium," Han said. "But that's not going to happen. Let's go."

They started to move again. But instead of traveling straight toward the thermal vent, Luke carefully circled it. Every few meters, he would stop and remain motionless for five or ten seconds, then adjust his course and creep ahead even more slowly.

Finally, he motioned for a stop, then sneaked forward to peer around the side of a heat sink. Han followed and saw several dozen hazy, bug-shaped figures wearing the bulky carapaces that Killiks used as pressure suits. They were all crouching in ambush, still facing the direction he and Luke had been approaching from a few minutes earlier.

"Everybody be ready," Luke unhooked his lightsaber, then took the blaster pistol out of his utility belt and passed it to Tarfang. "Mara's making her run."

"Then what?" Han asked.

"Then Lomi Plo will have to show herself," Luke answered. "After we finish with her, we trip our rescue beacons."

"I'm holding you to that," Han said. He motioned Juun

to stay with the droids and keep down—without a comm or a blaster, the Sullustan would be no good in the fight anyway—then twisted around to look up into space. "What's taking so—"

Luke jumped up and ignited his lightsaber, pointing the tip toward the hiding Gorog. In the same instant, the dark shape of a Jedi StealthX appeared behind the insects and began to stitch the nest ship's hull with fire from its four laser cannons. A curtain of spitcrete dust, hull chips, and bug parts boiled spaceward, and then the StealthX was gone, vanished against the star-flecked void.

A moment later a small line of pressure-suited Gorog came charging forward between the heat sinks, spraying electrobolts and shatter gun pellets ahead of them. Han returned fire, cursing in frustration as most of his bolts bounced harmlessly off the insects' carapace pressure suits. Luke simply made a sweeping motion with his hand, and one end of the Gorog line went tumbling into space.

Then brilliant spears of cannon fire began to stab down from space again, churning what remained of the insect line into an amalgam of chitin and gore. Han continued to fire, more to make sure Mara knew where he was than because he thought he was going to kill anything. In a moment the StealthX's dark shape swept past only a few meters from their hiding place, so close that Han could see Mara's head swinging back and forth as she selected her targets.

Han was still watching her when something tinked the back of his helmet. He spun around, half expecting to feel that painful final pop as a shatter gun pellet tore through his head, but there was nobody behind him except Juun and the droids.

The Sullustan pointed toward something on the other side of Luke. Han glanced over and found nothing but the usual barrage haze. Luke was standing just as he had a moment before, his lightsaber blazing and his attention fixed on the few would-be ambushers that had survived Mara's strafing runs so far.

Juun began to gesture violently, this time a little closer to Luke. Han looked again, saw nothing but dust, then spread his hands in a gesture of helplessness.

Juun beat his fists against his helmet, then leapt to his feet and raced in the direction he had been pointing.

"Look out, Luke!" Han warned over the comm. "You've got a crazy Sullustan—"

Luke whirled, bringing his lightsaber around in a high guard—then stopping cold in a flicker of sparks.

Han scowled. "What the—"

Luke suddenly doubled over in the middle, as though he had been kicked hard in the stomach. Then Juun slammed to a stop about a meter in front of Luke, his arms wrapping around something Han could not see.

Luke brought his blade up and hit nothing but air, then flipped the tip over his shoulder in a back-guard maneuver that resulted in another flurry of sparks. He followed this by dropping into a spinning leg sweep that caught whatever Juun was clinging to. The Sullustan's arms came loose, and he went rolling across the spitcrete into the side of a heat sink.

Han opened fire on the general area, and a flurry of blaster bolts flashed past his shoulder as Tarfang did the same. Most of their attacks did nothing more harmful than burn divots into the hull of the nest ship. But a couple of times, the shots were mysteriously deflected, and once Han thought he saw the flash of a scarred face, so haggard and misshapen that he could not be sure whether it was human or insect.

Luke danced back into the combat, slashing high and low with his lightsaber, missing more often than not, but spinning directly into the next attack, his blade sparking and flashing as it blocked and deflected the unseen strikes coming his way. Han and Tarfang scrambled after the fight, firing more or less where the Jedi was attacking, drawing just enough attention so that Luke could continue to drive the unseen enemy back.

They continued to press the attack for perhaps five or ten seconds; then a row of six-limbed figures wearing bulky Killik pressure suits emerged from the heat sinks. Han's heart rose into his throat—he wondered if that was what Jedi danger sense felt like—and he stopped advancing.

"Uh, guys?" He glanced to each flank and saw that there were more bugs to each side. "Get down!"

There was a flurry of motion as the insects brought up their weapons. Han was already dropping to the hull. He landed on his side and kicked behind a heat sink; silver flashes began to dance across his faceplate while flying chips of spitcrete beat an irregular cadence on his helmet. He curled into a fetal ball and counted himself lucky.

A moment later Luke's voice came over the suit comm. "Cover!"

"What do you think I'm—"

Han's comm gave a sharp pop, then a series of sharp concussions reverberated through the hull. The sound of the chips striking his helmet was replaced at first by a dozen seconds of static, then by utter silence. He uncurled and carefully raised his head.

The barrage dust had thickened to a murky gray cloud, but it was not too thick to prevent him from seeing the brilliant streaks of Mara's laser cannons chasing off the Gorog survivors. Han rolled to his knees and turned in the other direction. The hull ended about three meters from where he was kneeling, opening into a deep, dark crater filled with flotsam, floating corpses, and shooting streams of vapor.

"Han?" Luke's voice came over the suit comm. "Are you okay?"

"That depends." Han stood and turned in a slow circle, then finally saw Luke coming toward him from about ten meters away. "Did you get Lomi?"

Luke shook his head. "I can still feel her."

"Then I'm about as un-okay as you can get." Han began a slow rotation, his blaster held ready to fire. "I *hate* being crept up on by stuff I can't see. Let's get back to where we left Juun."

"Why do you want Juun?" Luke asked.

"Because he can see her," Han said.

Luke stopped three paces from Han. "You're sure?"

"Didn't you see the way he tried to tackle her? Of course I'm sure." Han did not like the surprise in Luke's voice. "Does that mean something?"

"Yes," Luke said. "It means I'm wrong about Lomi Plo."

"Great," Han growled. He would have liked to suggest again that they leave the ship and activate their rescue beacons, but he did not want Luke telling him to go ahead on his own. He was afraid the temptation might be too much for him. "Wrong how?"

"I thought she was using some sort of Force blur to hide herself," Luke said. "But if Juun can see her, and *I* can't . . ."

When Luke let the sentence trail off, Han said, "Yeah, that scares me, too." He turned back the way they had come. "Maybe Juun can explain it."

"Wait a minute," Luke said. "What about Tarfang?"

"Tarfang?" Han took a quick look around, then

tipped his helmet back. "Don't tell me he got bounced again!"

Luke was silent for a moment, then said, "He didn't. Tarfang is below us, inside the nest ship." He turned and looked toward one of the holes Mara's shadow bombs had knocked in the hull. "I think Lomi Plo has him."

TWENTY-ONE

With a cloud of assassin bugs droning behind them and elite Unu soldiers zipping shatter gun pellets down every side corridor they passed, Leia knew her small company was in trouble. They would never hold off the Killiks long enough to initiate the *Ackbar*'s self-destruct sequence.

What Leia did *not* know was how to break the news to Bwua'tu. They had been forced to abandon the command deck after a swarm of assassin bugs had erupted from the ventilation ducts. Since then, activating the self-destruct cycle had been the admiral's only concern, but the Killiks had foreseen the move. Every primary access terminal Leia and the others passed was damaged beyond all hope of a quick repair—usually by an electrobolt blast to the keypad.

Leia came to another intersection, and Bwua'tu's voice barked out from the middle of the group behind her. "Right!"

With the assassin bugs buzzing up the corridor behind them, there was no question of pausing to reconnoiter. Leia simply ignited her lightsaber—which Bwua'tu had retrieved from his wardroom vault as they fled the bridge—and led the charge around the corner.

Not surprisingly, there was a squad of Unu soldiers coming the other way. They were as large as Wookiees, with golden thoraxes and big purple eyes and scarlet carapaces covering their backs, and in their four pincer-hands they carried both shatter guns for ranged combat and short tridents for close fighting. They opened fire as soon as Leia rounded the corner, and the corridor broke into a cacophony of zipping and pinging.

Though lightsabers weren't much good at deflecting shatter gun attacks, Leia began to spin and whirl forward, slipping and dodging past the flying pellets with no conscious thought, surrendering herself to the Force and trusting it to guide her steps.

Her companions—a ragtag band of ship's crew whom she and Bwua'tu had been picking up along the way—raced into the corridor a step behind her and poured fire at the Killiks. No one hesitated to shoot past their shipmates or Leia. Twice, she had to deflect friendly blaster bolts, and once she nearly stepped in front of a shatter gun pellet to avoid being hit from behind. She did not blame her fellows for being reckless. There was just no time to be careful.

Leia reached the Unu soldiers and Force-shoved the nearest one into the Killik beside it. She lashed out with her lightsaber and separated the insect's head from its golden thorax, then whipped the blade back and opened another across the middle.

A pair of huge mandibles clamped down on Leia from the side, and then she saw a set of trident tines rising toward her chest. She used the Force to shove the weapon away, then deactivated her lightsaber, flipped the handle around, and reignited the blade as she pressed the emitter nozzle to her captor's thorax.

An ear-piercing shriek sounded in Leia's ear. She brought her foot up and kicked aside a shatter gun another Unu soldier was raising toward her, then flipped her lightsaber downward, slashing her captor open and bringing the blade up between the legs of her would-be attacker. Both insects collapsed with their lives flooding out of them.

Then Leia's companions reached the melee, and the battle erupted into a savage gun-and-pincer fight. Badly outmatched in size and strength, the *Ackbar*'s crew poured blaster bolts into the Killiks at point-blank range. The Killiks used one set of hand-pincers to fire their shatter guns and the other to slash and thrust with their tridents, sometimes using their mandibles to grab an attacker, sometimes whipping their mandibles around to knock someone off his feet.

Leia glanced back to check on Bwua'tu and found the admiral on her heels, as covered in insect gore as she was and firing a blaster pistol with each hand. His aide Grendyl was behind him, tossing a thermal grenade back into the approaching cloud of assassin bugs.

"Go!" Bwua'tu pushed Leia up the corridor. "There should be an access terminal ahead, outside the hatch!"

Leia spun and cut her way through a soldier-insect that had been winning a grapple-and-shoot fight with two Alliance ensigns. An orange light flashed behind them as Grendyl's grenade detonated, rumbling off the walls and filling the corridor with acrid fumes, then Leia stepped out of the fray into empty corridor.

Ten meters away, a cluster of much smaller Gorog soldiers—lacking carapaces and only about shoulder height—were rushing out of a side corridor to block a security hatch marked CAPTURE BAY ACCESS. With them was a slender Twi'lek female armored in blue chitin so closely formfitted that it looked like a body stocking. One arm was hanging limp beneath a sagging, misshapen shoulder—a result of her fight against Luke a year earlier at Qoribu—and as soon as she saw Leia, her full lips twisted into a contemptuous sneer.

"Alema Rar!" Leia said. "I've been looking forward to this."

Leia reached back and caught one of the last standing Unu soldiers in a Force grasp, then brought her arm forward and hurled the insect sideways down the corridor. She followed a few steps behind, using its body as a shield, listening to shatter gun pellets drum into its carapace.

A couple of moments later, she heard the *snap-hiss* of an igniting lightsaber, then a blade so blue it was almost black sliced the insect in half. Leia pressed the attack, leaping between the body halves as they dropped away, hitting Alema with a Force shove and bringing her own blade around in an overhand power strike.

Alema barely got her guard up in time, and sparks filled the air as the two blades met. Leia brought her foot up in a driving stomp kick that rocked the Twi'lek back on her heels, then rolled her lightsaber into a horizontal slash at Alema's limp arm.

Alema had no choice except to pivot away and bring her weapon around in a desperate block that left her sideways and out of position. Leia swung her foot around in a powerful roundhouse kick that caught the Twi'lek behind the knees and swept both legs.

Alema landed flat on her back, her mouth gaping and her green eyes wide with alarm. Leia allowed herself a small smirk of satisfaction—recalling how lopsided the combat had been in Alema's favor the last time they fought—then blocked a desperate slash at her ankles and slipped into a counter, angling the tip of her blade toward the Twi'lek's heart.

Before Leia could drive the thrust home, a thrumming mass of blue chitin hit her in the chest and bowled her over backward. She tried to bring her lightsaber up and found her arms pinned to her chest, then her attacker pressed the muzzle of a shatter gun to her ribs. She used the Force to push the weapon away, but then the insect's mandibles were clamped around her head, its needle-sharp proboscis darting toward her eye.

Leia shot her free hand up between its mandibles, catching the proboscis between two fingers and continuing to shove until it snapped. The Gorog let out a distressed whistle and bore down with its mandibles, and the edge of her face exploded into pain. But by then she was shoving at the insect with the Force, opening enough of a gap so she could bring her lightsaber up and slice her attacker in two.

Leia started to spring up—until a storm of blaster bolts streamed past overhead, tearing into a trio of Gorog at her feet. Half a dozen crew members rushed past and crashed into the wall of insects in a deafening cacophony of blows and small-arms fire, then Bwua'tu appeared at her side, reaching down to help her up.

"Princess! Are you—"

"Fine!" Leia brought her feet under her, automatically raising her lightsaber in a high block. "Get ba—"

Alema charged out of the melee, her lightsaber already descending for the kill. Leia caught the attack on her blade, then delivered a Force-enhanced punch to the Twi'lek's chitin-armored midsection.

It was like hitting a wall. She felt a bone snap in her hand, and she did not even drive Alema far enough away to buy space to stand. The Twi'lek brought her knee up under Leia's chin, snapping her head back with such force that her vision went black for a moment.

Leia lashed out with her free arm, hooking it around the knee that had just struck her, then launched herself into a back roll. Alema had to sprang in the opposite direction, executing a backflip, and they both came up on their feet facing each other. Leia's hand throbbed, but not so badly that it prevented her from grasping her lightsaber handle with both hands.

Bwua'tu and the rest of the crew members were behind Alema, pressing the attack on the Gorog and driving them back toward the capture bay. On the other side of the hatch, Leia sensed Saba and the Noghri, struggling to override the security system so they could join the battle. Coming down the corridor behind her, working their way through the smoke left by the Grendyl's grenade, Leia heard the distant drone of the surviving assassin bugs.

Alema studied Leia with narrowed eyes. "You've been practicing."

Leia shrugged. "A little."

"It won't matter," Alema sneered. "You're too old to start being a real Jedi now."

Leia raised her brow. "I think I need to teach you some manners."

Leia sprang forward, once again attacking the side with Alema's crippled arm. This time, the Twi'lek did not make the mistake of underestimating her opponent. She gave ground quickly, pivoting around so that her crippled side was protected.

Their blades clashed time and again, each Jedi augmenting their lightsaber strikes with Force shoves and telekinesis attacks, each trying to take advantage of the other's weakness. Leia's face had become so swollen that she could barely see out of one eye, and Alema kept circling to find a blind spot. As Alema tried to protect her weak side, Leia kept slipping toward it, forcing the Twi'lek to retreat toward the security hatch. All the time, the drone of the assassin bugs drew nearer.

Then Bwua'tu and the *Ackbar*'s crew began to overwhelm Alema's company of insect-soldiers, forcing them past her toward the access terminal. Though the Twi'lek's back was now to the main fight, as the admiral and his followers drew closer to the terminal, the knowledge came to her through Gorog's collective mind. Her eyes flashed with alarm, then she sprang back, locked her blade on, and hurled her lightsaber at Leia's legs.

Leia had no choice but to block low and pivot away, and in that second Alema pointed at Bwua'tu's spine and let loose a crackling stream of Force lightning. Leia started to grab the admiral in the Force, intending to jerk him out of the way, but his aide Grendyl was already leaping to protect him.

The lightning caught the woman full in the chest, hurling her back into Bwua'tu and knocking him to the deck.

Leia leapt at Alema, striking for the shoulders. The Twi'lek spun away . . . and launched Leia into a wall with a whirling back kick to the ribs.

The blunt clang of skull against durasteel sounded inside Leia's head. Her mind turned to gauze and she thought for a moment that the bloodcurdling howl assaulting her ears was her own. Then she noticed the meter-long segment of amputated lekku flopping around on the deck like a baagalmog out of water.

Leia looked up and found Alema trembling and screaming in pain, the cauterized stump of one nerve-packed head-tail ending just above her shoulder. But the Twi'lek's pain did not prevent her from releasing another stream of Force lightning—this time into the access terminal itself.

The unit exploded into a spray of sparks, pieces, and fumes. The security hatch gave the telltale hiss of a breaking seal, and Bwua'tu cried out in frustration.

Leia sprang to her feet and started toward Alema.

The Twi'lek was already stretching her arm up the corridor, calling her lightsaber back to hand. Leia heard the sizzle of the blade growing louder behind her and dropped into a deep squat as the weapon spun past overhead, then stabbed for Alema's heart.

The Twi'lek brought her blade down and blocked easily, then brought her foot up in a side-snap kick that caught Leia in the base of the throat. The blow was more painful than harmful, but Leia dropped to her seat, coughing and choking and trying to make it sound as though her larynx had been crushed. She could hear the drone of the assassin bugs only a few meters behind her and knew the time had come to end this fight—and she could see by the unreasoning fury in Alema's eyes that the wounded Twi'lek was primed for a mistake.

Leia rolled her eyes back in her head and let herself collapse to the floor. She heard Alema slide forward, then felt a knot of anticipation form in her stomach as the time approached to bring her blade slashing up through the Twi'lek's abdomen—and that was when Leia felt a surge of relief from Saba and the Noghri. A loud grating sounded from the security hatch, and she knew her Master and bodyguards had finally forced it open.

The pulsing whine of Meewalh's T-21 repeating blaster echoed down the corridor, then Alema's blade began to hiss and sizzle as it batted blaster bolts away. Leia opened her eyes to find the Twi'lek dancing along one wall of the corridor, just beyond reach and retreating into the droning cloud of assassin bugs.

When their eyes met, Alema's brow shot up in surprise. She flicked her lightsaber up in a brief salute, then gave Leia a spiteful sneer and fled out of sight.

Leia locked her blade on and spun around to throw her lightsaber, but the Twi'lek was nowhere to be seen.

Leia felt herself sliding across the deck, then realized Saba was using the Force to draw her away from the approaching cloud of assassin bugs. Cakhmaim and Meewalh appeared at her sides, spraying the corridor with blasterfire.

"Jedi Solo," Saba said. "Why are you lying on the floor at a time like this?"

Leia deactivated her lightsaber and stood with as much dignity as she could manage, considering how much her hand was beginning to hurt and how swollen her face was.

"I was laying a trap."

"Laying a trap?" Saba shook her head and began to siss hysterically. "You are beginning to sound just like Han."

TWENTY-TWO

The shadow bomb had opened a velker-sized hole in the hull of the nest ship, but the blast had penetrated only as deep as the second deck, where Luke now stood amid a tangle of devastation. The Force was too filled with ripples to tell where Lomi Plo had gone, but he knew by the cold knot in his stomach and the ache in his limbs that she was somewhere nearby, watching and waiting for the right moment to attack again.

Luke could sense Tarfang about thirty meters ahead, slowly moving away. Hearing the Ewok was even easier. Tarfang was chattering angrily into his suit comm, though it was anyone's guess whether he was cursing his captors, or Luke and Han.

Then Han's voice came over the comm as well. "All set here, Luke."

Luke looked up and saw Han and Juun two stories above, dimly silhouetted against the star-flecked void of space. C-3PO and R2-D2 were nowhere in sight; Han had left the damaged droids on the exterior of the ship, where they would be easy to retrieve on the way out.

Luke grasped Han and Juun in the Force and lowered them through the hole, being careful to keep them well away from any jagged edges or sharp protrusions. *DR919a*'s escape pod vac suits were about as flimsy as space suits came; one tear would be the end of the person inside. Once they were down, Mara's StealthX appeared in the breach and descended on its repulsorlifts, slowly spinning in a circle.

Luke kneeled at Juun's side and touched helmets so they could converse. "Did you see Lomi Plo up there, when she tried to sneak up on me?"

"I aw *omeding*," Juun said. Sound waves never carried well through helmets, and his nasal accent made the situation worse. "I did na know it wah *her* until you had the lisaber fight."

"Good enough," Luke said. He stood and turned toward Mara's StealthX, now settling onto the deck next to them, and activated his comm unit. "We're a little short on weapons."

Mara nodded inside the cockpit. A moment later the canopy opened, and she passed Luke the E-11 blaster rifle from the survival kit attached to her ejection module.

"What about destroying the hyperdrive?" she asked over her suit comm. "We can't let this nest ship leave the Choke."

"I know," Luke answered. "But we have to get Tarfang back first. I dragged him into this, and now I have to drag him out."

This drew an affirmative Ewok yap over the suit comm.

"We don't have much time," Mara warned. "And we're only going to have one chance to hit that thermal vent you and Han found. I'm down to my last shadow bomb, and the *Falcon* can't do this."

Luke nodded. He had felt Leia's relief as she and Saba escaped the *Ackbar*'s captors aboard the *Falcon*, and now they were on their way to the Gorog nest ship to retrieve him, Han, and the others. But the *Falcon*'s concussion missiles would not be accurate enough to reach the nest ship's hyperdrive—or powerful enough to destroy it even if they did.

"What about Kyp and all the other Jedi I sense out here?" Luke asked. "Maybe I should call them over to help."

"You could," Mara said. "But you'd have to countermand Admiral Bwua'tu's orders. He has them targeting the hyperdrives of the other nest ships. This one is my responsibility."

Luke raised his brow. "*Kyp* has been helping with this blockade?"

"Hardly," Mara scoffed. "It's complicated, but it all started when Leia and Saba were captured by the *Ackbar* on our way back to Woteba."

"An Alliance vessel arrested *Jedi*?"

"It gets worse," Mara said. "From what I've been able to pick up eavesdropping on comm traffic between the *Ackbar* and the *Mothma,* the Chiss have been holding the Jedi and the Galactic Alliance responsible for the Killiks' return to their border. Chief Omas tried to appease them by blockading the Utegetu nests, and to keep the Jedi from interfering, he placed Corran Horn in charge of the order."

Luke frowned. "Chief Omas doesn't choose Jedi leaders."

"That's what Kyp and his team thought," Mara said. "So they commandeered a squadron of StealthXs to free you and Han from the Killiks, and Leia and Saba from the *Ackbar*. It's a mess."

"That's an understatement." Luke shook his head in frustration. He had always taught that Jedi should act in accordance with their consciences, trusting that the Force would lead them to do what was best for the order, the Alliance, and the galaxy. Clearly, his faith had been misplaced somewhere along the line. "Then why is Kyp—and everyone else—following Bwua'tu's orders now?"

"Because Leia urged us to," Mara said. "Nobody wants Killiks loose in the galaxy with these nest ships."

"At least everyone agrees on that much."

Luke had a terrible, hollow feeling in his stomach. In his efforts to build an order of self-directing Jedi, he had left the order itself adrift. No one had made a selfish or wrong decision—not even Chief Omas—but there had been no one to make them work together, no one to channel their energy in a single direction.

In short, there had been no leadership.

"Don't be too hard on yourself, Skywalker," Mara said. "You were stuck on Woteba."

"I remember," Luke answered. "But it shouldn't have mattered—not if I had prepared the other Masters properly."

Mara shook her head. "This is on Kyp and Corran and the rest of them. You can't be there every minute."

"No, but I *can* provide direction . . . and vision," Luke said. "If I had been doing that, the Masters would never have let Omas split them."

Han came over to stand beside the StealthX. "Maybe you two can talk command theory later," he said. "If we don't reach Tarfang before the bug queen drags him into a pressurized area, we'll never get him back."

"Sorry." Luke reached up and rested his glove on the sleeve of Mara's vac suit. "We've got to do this. I can't leave him."

Mara sighed. "I know—and so does Lomi Plo. She's trying to draw us in."

Luke smiled. "Her mistake."

"It better be," Mara said. "I'm not going to raise Ben alone."

"You won't have to." Luke patted her arm, then stepped away from the cockpit. "I promise."

Han started to follow Luke away from the StealthX, but Mara motioned him back toward the cockpit.

"Take this." She passed her lightsaber to Han. "If things get close, it will do you more good than a blaster."

Han's faceplate remained turned toward the weapon for a moment, then he nodded. "Thanks. I'll try not to cut up anything I shouldn't."

Mara smiled inside her helmet, but her eyes betrayed her concern. "After you three get Tarfang, jump on my wings," she said. "I'll lift you out of here fast, then go drop a shadow bomb down that thermal vent."

"Sure," Han said. "It'll be just like my swoop-riding days."

Once Han had stepped back, Mara closed the canopy and lifted the StealthX off the deck again. She turned in the general direction of Tarfang's presence, then activated the external floodlamps and began to creep forward.

Luke waved Juun to his side, then leaned down and touched helmets. "Stick close to me." He gave the blaster rifle from Mara's survival module to the Sullustan. "And when you see Lomi Plo, don't hesitate. Start blasting."

Juun's eyes widened inside his faceplate. "Me?"

"You want to save Tarfang, don't you?"

"Of course." Juun flipped the safety off. "I'd wo any-wing."

"Good," Luke said. "Just remember: stick close."

He motioned Han to the StealthX's other flank, then started to follow the starfighter forward on his own side. The deck seemed to have been little more than a storage level. There were a few Gorog bodies, their eyes burst from sudden decompression, but most of the debris looked like broken waxes of black membrosia.

"These bugs are really starting to scare me," Han said

over the comm. "This ship design is sturdy . . . really sturdy."

"Even with no shields?" Luke asked.

"Doesn't need 'em," Han said. "Every deck is a shield layer itself. Blast through one, and there's another just like it right below. Given the size of these bug haulers, you might have to go down a hundred decks before you hit anything important."

Luke had a sinking feeling. "What about Bwua'tu's plan?"

"Oh, that'll work," Han said. "All ships are weak in the stern—even these monsters. But those shadow bombs better go right down the thrust channels. If they hit a wall and detonate before they reach the hyperdrive itself, all they'll do is throw the bugs off course when they jump."

"I was afraid you'd say that."

Luke opened himself to the combat-meld, trying to impress on Kyp and the other pilots how important it was to be accurate when they targeted the other nest ships. He perceived a variety of emotions in response, from joy at sensing his presence, to gratitude for the advice, to frustration that the warning had come so late. The StealthXs were in the middle of their runs; some had already launched their bombs and were turning back to join the *Falcon* in coming after Luke and Han.

Luke poured reassurance into the meld; then the light from Mara's floodlamps fell on a section of spitcrete wall. A band of about twenty pressure-suited Gorog were nearing one of the leathery membranes Killiks used as air locks. They were holding—*struggling* to hold—a small, kicking figure in a vac suit.

Mara touched Luke through the Force, wondering if she should take a shot.

He gave her a mental nod, then warned Han, "Watch your eyes! Cannons!"

Luke averted his own gaze and reached down to cover Juun's faceplate, then Mara fired the StealthX's laser cannons. The flash was so bright that Luke's eyes hurt even looking at the floor.

When the light faded an instant later, he raised his gaze and found that the blast had destroyed not only the membrane, but much of the wall around it as well. Dozens of Gorog were spilling out through the gap, their limbs and bristly antennae flailing as they suffered swift but painful decompression deaths.

Many of the bodies tumbled into Tarfang's captors, knocking some off their feet and turning the band into a tangled knot. One of the Ewok's arms came free, and he began to thrash about so violently that the tangle became a snarl of whirling carapaces and flailing limbs.

Han rushed forward, firing half a dozen times before he traded the blaster pistol for Mara's lightsaber. When he ignited the blade, the gyroscopic effect of the arc wave caught him off guard, and he spun in a complete circle before bringing the weapon under control and slashing through a Gorog's midsection.

By the time Luke and Juun arrived, the Gorog had recovered from the initial shock of Han's attack and were turning to fight, their shatter guns rising to fire. Luke used the Force to sweep the barrels aside, then ignited his own lightsaber and opened four pressure suits in a single slash. Juun clung to his back, firing point-blank into any insect that made the mistake of trying to close from the sides.

With their mandibles and pincer-hands enclosed inside their carapace-like pressure suits, the Killiks were reduced to simple blows or using their shatter guns. Luke concentrated on the weapons, defending himself, Juun, and Han with his lightsaber and the Force, lopping off gun hands and deflecting aims.

That left Luke and his companions vulnerable to hand-to-hand attacks, and several times Luke was almost knocked off his feet when a carapace slammed into him or a flailing limb smashed into his legs. But Mara was watching their backs from the StealthX, using the Force to seize any bug wielding anything that looked sharp enough to tear their flimsy vac suits, then sending it crashing into a jagged stub of broken wall.

When they had carved the band down to the last half a dozen insects, Mara's lightsaber began to trace a frenzied, twirling, rolling pattern through the middle of the fight. Luke thought Han must have locked the blade on by accident and dropped the weapon. But then he caught a glimpse of orange vac suit behind the handle, and the lightsaber began to slice through Gorog pressure suits, dropping four insects in half as many seconds.

"Han?"

"Not me," Han answered over the suit comm. He appeared a couple of meters away from the lightsaber, picking himself up off the floor. "I got knocked over."

The lightsaber dropped another Gorog, then Luke cut the legs out from under the last insect as it spun around to fire its shatter gun.

Clinging to the lightsaber handle with both hands, being tossed around like a rag in sandstorm, was Tarfang. He was chattering in mad delight, swinging his legs around like a rudder, vainly attempting to counterbalance the weapon's gyroscopic effects.

Luke stepped in and blocked, bringing the wild ride to a sudden halt and allowing Tarfang's feet to drop back to the deck. He used the Force to deactivate the blade, then summoned the weapon out of the Ewok's trembling hands.

Tarfang stood wobbling for a moment, then drew his shoulders back, chittered something grateful sounding over the suit comm, and held his hand out for the lightsaber.

"Sorry," Luke said. "You'd better take the blaster."

Tarfang placed his gloves on his hips and snarled.

Then the StealthX's floodlamps began to dim, and Luke felt Mara's confusion through their Force-bond. Tossing the lightsaber to Han, he whirled toward the StealthX and saw nothing but the fading glow of the floodlamps.

Han stepped to Luke's side. "What is it?"

"Trouble!" Luke said. He gave Mara's lightsaber back to Han. "Lomi Plo is draining the energy from Mara's flood—"

He stopped in midsentence as Juun opened fire with the blaster rifle, aiming for a dark area just behind the StealthX's cockpit. A trio of bolts passed only a meter above Mara's canopy, then abruptly reversed course and came streaking back toward Juun.

The chill ache in Luke's joints was slowing his reflexes, so he would have never have been quick enough to save Juun had he not known that Lomi Plo would deflect the attack. But when she did, his lightsaber was already dropping into position, and one after the other he intercepted the bolts, batting them back toward their original target.

The first bolt was deflected toward the ceiling. The other two simply passed over the StealthX and vanished into the darkness beyond.

Mara twisted around in her seat, trying to see what they had been attacking, but the StealthX's floodlamps were already returning to their normal brightness. Lomi Plo had been forced to retreat.

"It's okay," Luke commed. "We're coming!"

He grabbed Juun by the shoulder and started toward the

StealthX, but the Sullustan suddenly stopped and dropped to a knee, trying to look under the craft.

Luke knelt beside him and touched helmets. "Where is she?"

"Behind de strut." Juun's voice was muffled. "Don't you see her leg?"

"No," Luke said. "I *can't* see her."

"*You* can't see her, Madter Skywalker?"

"No, Jae," Luke answered. "*You're* the only one who can see her."

"But when you foughd her, you blocked her addacks."

"The Force was guiding my hand," Luke explained.

Juun was quiet for a moment, then asked, "And when she dent my shots back at me?"

"The Force was guiding my hand," Luke repeated.

Juun remained silent a moment longer, then exclaimed, "Madter Skywalker, you set me up!"

"I knew she would deflect your attacks," Luke admitted. "But I did block her attacks . . . and you said you'd do anything to save Tarfang."

"I suppose I did." Juun sounded disappointed in himself. "All wight. What now?"

"Start shooting again. We need to chase her away from the StealthX before she does any more damage."

Juun shouldered the blaster rifle, but did not open fire.

"What's wrong?" Luke asked.

"I can't dee her, either."

Luke's heart rose into his throat. "What do you mean? Did she move?"

Juun shrugged. "I don't know. Her leg just dort of disappeared—right in front of my eyes."

Han and Tarfang came and knelt beside them.

"Let's climb on that StealthX and get out of here!" Han urged over the suit comm. "If Lomi Plo darkened those lamps, it's because she doesn't want us to see the reinforcements coming up behind us."

"You're right." Luke rose and started to lead the way forward, circling out of the StealthX's line of fire. "But we need to be careful. She's still up there, and now Juun can't see her, either."

"Why not?" Han demanded.

"I don't know," Luke said. "When he realized *we* couldn't see her, he stopped . . ."

He let the explanation trail off, for he suddenly understood why Juun had lost sight of Lomi Plo.

"Doubt!" Luke turned to Han. "*Cloud your vision, doubt will.* Blast it! How many times did I hear that from Yoda?"

"Probably about as many times as I've heard that from you," Han said, sighing.

Luke ignored the barb. "That's how she's doing it, Han. She's using our doubts against us!"

"Only one problem with that theory," Han said. "I believe in her, and I can't see her, either."

Tarfang added a positive yap.

"It doesn't have to be doubt in *her,*" Luke said. They drew adjacent to the StealthX, and Mara began to back the starfighter toward the opening on its repulsor drive. "If Lomi Plo can sense any doubt in a mind at all, she can hide behind it."

Han fell quiet for a moment, then said, "That might explain why Alema was trying so hard to make you doubt Mara."

"I'm sure it does," Luke said. "And now that I know what she was trying to do, I know that it's without basis."

He glanced in the StealthX's direction and saw . . . nothing.

When Luke remained silent, Han seemed to sense his disappointment.

"It won't be that easy, kid," Han said. "Nobody knows how to twist up a guy inside better than a Twi'lek dancer. And Alema's got the Force to help."

Although Mara could hear their discussion over her own suit comm, she limited her response to the sharp sense of curiosity—it was almost suspicion—that Luke felt through their Force-bond. The idea of anyone, especially Alema Rar, sowing doubts about her in Luke's mind angered Mara, but she was trying not to be hurt—at least until they reached someplace where Luke could explain himself in private.

One of the StealthX's floodlamps suddenly exploded in a brilliant burst of light, then sparks began to flash off the starfighter's dark armor. A dozen forks of lightning lanced down from under the fuselage, and the repulsorlift drive began to emit a steady shower of sparks. The StealthX started to wobble

Luke glanced back to see a line of pressure-suited Gorog swarming after them, pouring shatter gun fire into Mara's craft.

Mara opened fire with her laser cannons, filling the chamber with flashing light. The shatter gun fire dwindled off as the Gorog pursuers dived for cover or were blasted apart. Deciding the time had come to chance a meeting with Lomi Plo, Luke grabbed Juun by the shoulder and started toward the StealthX.

Then the cannon fire began to dim and grow erratic, and he knew that Lomi Plo had returned to the starfighter. She was somewhere on the StealthX, draining its power again—or worse.

Luke pushed Juun toward the hole through which they had entered the nest ship, then said, "Han, run for the breach!"

He activated his lightsaber and Force-leapt onto the upper wing of the wobbling StealthX. He advanced behind his whirling blade, trying to force an attack from his unseen foe.

The tactic succeeded almost too well. As he reached the engine next to the fuselage, Luke felt the Force moving his lightsaber down to block a knee strike. Then a loud *thunk* sounded in his helmet as a kick or elbow or *something* sent him cartwheeling off the nose of the craft.

He reached out and caught hold of the engine cowling, then swung down in front of the lower wing.

To his astonishment, Han was crawling onto the lower wing with Juun and Tarfang.

"What are you doing?" Luke demanded. "I said *run*."

"*You* run," Han said. "I'll take the cover."

A series of shatter gun pellets punctuated Han's point by sparking off the engine mount next to Luke's head. He glanced back and saw that the Gorog swarm had renewed its charge. With the StealthX's laser cannons out of commission, the Killiks were firing blindly around the starfighter, hitting whatever they could.

Mara shut down her last functioning floodlamp and accelerated backward toward the hull breach, the StealthX wobbling wildly and nearly dragging its overloaded wing on the deck. Tarfang filled the suit comm with howls of fear—or maybe it was excitement. Juun simply stared wideeyed at Luke, his legs flapping off the wingtip like a pair of orange streamers until Han pulled him the rest of the way up.

Luke used the Force to do a twisting flip up onto the top of Mara's canopy, then began to advance behind his whirling lightsaber again. It took only an instant before his blade intercepted Lomi Plo's in another flurry of sparks. He pirouetted into a spinning hook kick that may as well have connected with pillar of durasteel. His foot stopped cold.

Something hard smashed into his inner knee and sent pain lancing up his leg.

Still unseen, Lomi started to push Luke off the other side of the canopy. Then Luke saw Han's helmet and shoulders pop up behind her, and Mara's lightsaber came sweeping across the fuselage at ankle height.

Lomi stopped pushing. Sparks flashed as she blocked Han's attack and sent Mara's lightsaber skittering off the tail of the StealthX.

Luke sprang forward, slashing for the place where Lomi's midsection was sure to be, knowing that this was the death strike—then suddenly the StealthX was bucking and shuddering beneath him, and it was all he could do to Force-stick himself to the starfighter's fuselage.

"Hang on!" Luke yelled over the suit comm. "We're going up!"

The edge of a ruptured deck flashed past, followed by the breach in the vessel's hull, and suddenly the StealthX was out in space, wobbling and listing a dozen meters above the nest ship.

Han was still clinging to the wing with both hands, his legs floating free now that they had escaped the artificial gravity. Tarfang was clasping the barrel of a laser cannon with both hands, yowling wildly and fluttering his legs as though he were swimming.

But Juun was spinning off into space, his arms grasping at the void, his feet kicking at nothing. Luke caught the Sullustan in the Force and began to pull him back toward the wobbling StealthX.

Then his lightsaber began to flicker and fade, and a cold knot of danger sense formed between his shoulder blades. Luke did not even take the time to turn around. He simply stepped into a powerful back-stomp kick that caught his invisible attacker square in the chest.

Even with the Force reinforcing it, the kick was not powerful enough to launch Lomi off the StealthX—but it did save Luke's life. Her blade scraped across the equipment pod on the back of his vac suit, and he pivoted into the attack, bringing his arms around in a double block that first slammed, then trapped both of Lomi's arms.

Juun was still five meters from the StealthX, reaching for Tarfang's fluttering boots.

"Tarfang, hold still!" Luke ordered, using the Force to pull the Sullustan the rest of the way back to the wing. "My hands are full, and Juun needs . . . help!"

Tarfang continued to kick, but Juun caught hold of a boot anyway. The Ewok glanced back, saw his captain hanging on to his boot, and finally obeyed.

Something sharp and powerful smashed into the pit of Luke's stomach, taking him by surprise, since he still had both of Lomi Plo's arms trapped.

Mara wheeled the StealthX around, going for the thermal vent, and Luke almost lost his balance. C-3PO and R2-D2 flashed by below. They were still standing where Han had left them, C-3PO's photoreceptors following the StealthX as it passed overhead. One of Tarfang's hands came loose, and for a moment the Ewok and Juun were hanging from the cannon barrel by one hand.

Again, something sharp and powerful smashed Luke in the stomach—could it be a third elbow?—and this time it drove the air from his lungs. He kicked one of Lomi's legs, twisting the two arms he *did* have under control, trying to wrest her lightsaber free.

The third elbow slammed Luke another time. When he tried to fill his lungs again, it felt as if he were trying to suck down a chestful of gauze.

Luke was out of air.

He glanced at the status display inside his helmet and

found only darkness. The slash across his equipment pod might have killed him after all. He tried one more time to wrench the lightsaber from Lomi Plo's hands, but he was losing his strength.

Then the gentle *clunk* of a launching shadow bomb pulsed through the fuselage. The StealthX bucked as they shot through the heat plume above the thermal vent. Lomi Plo immediately released her lightsaber and slammed Luke with a powerful Force shove, trying to rid herself of his grip so she could divert the bomb.

Luke almost came free . . . until he hooked a leg around one of Lomi's and slammed down on top of Mara's astromech. He used the Force to stick himself in place, then saw Han across from him, holding on with one hand and aiming Tarfang's blaster with the other. His lips seemed to be moving inside his helmet, but whatever he was saying remained unheard. Lomi's slash had disabled Luke's comm unit as well as his air recycler—or perhaps he was just slipping into unconsciousness.

A brilliant flash lit space behind them, then Mara banked the StealthX around and Luke saw Tarfang and Juun, still hanging onto the cannon barrel, silhouetted against a huge column of flame. It died down for a moment, then suddenly shot up again as a secondary explosion shot out of the thermal vent. Had there been any air left in Luke's lungs, he would have cried out in joy. At least they had disabled the Dark Nest's hyperdrive.

Mara stretched out to him through the Force, ordering him to hold on just a little longer. Luke was already doing just that. He could feel Leia and Kyp and the rest of the Jedi pilots touching him through the battle-meld, assuring him that help was close by. He began to calm his mind and his body, to slow his heartbeat and other natural processes in preparation for entering a Force-hibernation.

Then an unseen weight settled astride his chest and invisible fingers began to scratch at his helmet, attempting to open the faceplate or break a seal. Luke lashed out as best he could, but he was starting to grow dizzy, and his reactions were slow and weak. He heard an ominous *click* behind his ear, near the faceplate hinge, and reached out with the Force, trying to shove his attacker off.

Lomi shoved back, slamming his helmet into the top of Mara's canopy. Energy bolts streamed past his head as Han opened fire with the blaster, and finally Lomi turned her attention to deflecting the attack.

Mara urged Luke to hold on tight, and Han suddenly stopped firing. The StealthX flipped upside down, and Luke found himself looking down at the knobby hull of the nest ship, less than three meters away. He used the Force to pull himself even tighter to the fuselage, then glimpsed the blocky shape of a heat sink swelling in front of him. He tried not to waste his last breath on a scream.

Whether Lomi Plo jumped or was scraped off as they passed, Luke could not say. But in the instant beforehand, he saw two bulbous green bug eyes staring down at him through the transparent face panel of a Killik pressure suit. They were set in a melted female face with no nose and a pair of stubby mandibles where there should have been lower jaws. Luke would have sworn that when the mandibles opened, he could see a smiling row of human teeth . . . or maybe his oxygen-starved mind was merely beginning to hallucinate.

Then the weight vanished from inside his chest, too, and he was suddenly free of Lomi Plo, still using the Force to pin himself against the StealthX. He turned his head and saw Han wedged between the fuselage and the engine cowling, clinging to the shield generator mount with both hands, screaming something inside his helmet that Luke was just as glad he could not hear.

Mara suddenly flipped the StealthX right-side up again. A flight of dartships went streaming past overhead, then wheeled back around to attack. A dozen propellant trails streaked from their bellies. Mara ducked behind a boulder, and an instant later a series of orange flashes lit the heavens on the other side.

Luke's vision began to darken around the edges. He glimpsed the *Falcon* streaking past above, her repulsor beam already stabbing out to send the dartships tumbling on their way, then felt Leia and Saba touch him through the Force, urging him to hold on just a little longer, telling him that the *Falcon* was coming right behind him. Finally, Luke's vision went completely black.

But he did not fall unconscious. He reached out to Mara and Leia and Kyp and all of the other Jedi, even to Han and Juun and Tarfang, and their strength held him out of the abyss.

EPILOGUE

Outside the viewport hung eleven distant nest ships, a string of dark dots silhouetted against the sapphire curtain of the Utegetu Nebula. They were blocking the Murgo Choke, as though the Killiks believed that the small task force of cruisers and frigates with which the battered *Mon Mothma* had returned actually intended to launch an assault. Han fancied that he could even see a dark blur where the screen of dartfighters was deployed in front of the bug fleet. Their caution was somewhat reassuring, suggesting as it did a certain military naïveté. No commander in his right mind would attack the bugs' fleet with anything less than a three-to-one Star Destroyer advantage, and it would be weeks before the Alliance could assemble a battle group of that size.

Han only hoped that some genius on the general staff did not get the bright idea of trying to hold the bugs off with a couple of StealthX squadrons. So far, there was no indication that either Jaina or Jacen was anywhere near this mess—and that was just fine with him. They had both faced more death and treachery in their young lives than any ten Jedi should ever have to.

The door to the briefing room whispered open, and Han turned to see Gavin Darklighter emerging, his dress whites slightly rumpled after the long session inside. He paused long enough to run a hand through his dark hair, then he let out a deep breath and came to stand with Han.

When he didn't say anything, Han asked, "Any word?"

"Bwua'tu is still asking questions," Darklighter said. "He's fair for a Bothan, and your statement did a lot to exonerate them both. But I couldn't get a read on how he's going to handle having the *Ackbar* commandeered. Juun and Tarfang are a pretty convenient-looking pair of scapegoats."

Han nodded. "I figured that, but I was asking if you had heard anything about Luke." He gestured toward the guards at the lift station. "They won't let me leave the deck until I'm dismissed by Bwua'tu, and medbay is too busy—"

The lift doors started to open, and Luke's voice said, "We're fine, Han." He stepped into the corridor with Mara at his side. He looked as pale as a shaved wampa, but seemed alert enough and steady on his feet. "I told you that aboard the *Falcon*."

"No, what you said was '*ooormmgg fffff*,' " Han said, flashing a crooked smile. "Then you passed out."

"Did I?" Luke asked half seriously. "I don't remember."

"Yeah, you did," Han said. "I don't suppose the EmDee droids let you see Leia before you came up here?"

"Better than that," Mara said. She stepped aside, and Leia and Saba emerged from the rear of the lift. "They told us they needed the bed."

After the fight with Alema and her bugs, Leia's face was still swollen and so swaddled in bacta wrap that she looked like a Tusken bride. But the sight of her lifted Han's heart as it had not been lifted since the births of Anakin and the twins, and he went to her and took her hands—at least the one that wasn't in a cast—in his.

"Hello, beautiful."

Leia smiled—then winced. "You need to get your eyes checked, flyboy."

"Nope." Han kissed her on the lips . . . very, very gently. "I'm seeing better than ever."

Saba slapped her tail against the deck, then rolled her eyes and walked away sissing.

"Yes, well, we're glad to see both of you well again," Darklighter said. He motioned Leia toward a couch near the viewport, then turned to the guards stationed in front of the briefing room. "Inform Admiral Bwua'tu that Master Skywalker is available to make a statement."

The guard acknowledged the order with a salute, then disappeared through the sliding door.

"Thank you, Gavin," Luke said. "Juun and Tarfang risked their lives trying to warn the fleet about what was in those statues. I owe it to them to make certain Admiral Bwua'tu understands that."

"Han has already made a report," Darklighter said. "But hearing your account will certainly add weight to it."

Luke nodded, then went to the viewport and looked out at the string of nest ships. "How bad is it?"

"Not as bad as it could have been," Darklighter said. "The Killiks got out with four nest ships and the *Ackbar*, but the Dark Nest's ship is still here—along with ten others. I'll do what I can to make sure that the Jedi receive the credit they deserve in the official report to Chief Omas."

"Thank you," Luke said. "That will go a long way toward rebuilding the trust between us. We're going to need that, if we're going to prevent this from erupting into a full-scale war."

Darklighter looked uncomfortable. "I'm afraid we're running out of time for that, Master Skywalker."

"Chief Omas has already decided to go to war?" Leia asked.

"Not Omas," Darklighter said. "A courier arrived for Admiral Bwua'tu a short while ago. The Chiss are claiming that a group of Jedi launched a preemptive strike against one of their supply depots."

"That's impossible," Luke said quickly. "Jedi don't launch preemptive strikes!"

"Then a handful of Jedi loaned their StealthXs to some Killiks," Darklighter said. "The Chiss sent along a security holo from one of the ammunition dumps that was taken out. It shows a pair of StealthXs pretty clearly. And Jagged Fel seems convinced that one of the pilots was Jaina. He claims he recognizes her flying style."

"Jaina?" Han slapped his forehead. "Why would she do something like that?"

"That's what the Chiss would like to know," Darklighter replied. "Nobody was killed—and that convinces *me* that it was Jedi—so the Chiss aren't treating the attack as an act of war. But they *are* taking it as proof that they need to handle the Killiks themselves. They've declared the Qoribu Truce violated and are preparing to launch an assault to push the Colony back."

Han shook his head. "Jaina knows the Chiss better than anyone," he said. "She'd *know* how they would respond to a preemptive strike. Something stinks about that report."

"Actually, the preemptive strike can be a very sound tactic," a gravelly Bothan voice said. "Especially if you are trying to *provoke* a response."

Han looked over to see Bwua'tu stepping out of the briefing room. Juun and Tarfang followed a pace behind, their chests puffed out and smug grins on their faces.

"That's what I mean," Han said. "Jaina and Zekk are practically bugs themselves! She'd never do anything to make the Chiss launch a major attack against the Colony."

"I'd like to take your word for it, Captain Solo,"

Bwua'tu said, going to the viewport. "After all, you know your daughter better than I."

The admiral stared out at the nest ships in contemplative silence, then spoke without looking away from the viewport.

"Commodore Darklighter, have the task force launch all fighter squadrons and deploy in attack formation."

Darklighter's jaw dropped even farther than Han's. "*Attack* formation, sir?"

"You may choose which one, Commodore," Bwua'tu said. "I don't believe it will matter."

Darklighter made no move to obey. "May I remind the admiral that we barely have a ten-ship advantage over the Killiks, and that most of our vessels are significantly outclassed?"

"You just did." Bwua'tu turned to glare at Darklighter. "After the *Ackbar*'s capture, I may not be in command of the Fifth Fleet much longer. But until I am relieved, you *will* obey my orders. Is that clear, Commodore?"

Darklighter jerked to attention. "Sir!"

"Carry on," Bwua'tu said. "Report back when you are finished."

Darklighter pulled a comlink and stepped away to carry out the admiral's orders. Han, Luke, and the rest of their group exchanged nervous glances, clearly wondering what the Bothan could be thinking. Only Leia did not seem convinced that he had lost his mind; her expression was one more of curiosity than apprehension.

Either oblivious to their expressions or pretending not to notice, Bwua'tu turned to Luke.

"Captain Solo gave a glowing account of Juun's and Tarfang's actions once they learned the true nature of the statuary they delivered to my fleet. Would you concur?"

"I would," Luke said. "They aided our escape from the

Saras rehabilitation house, lost their own vessel while investigating the Killik plans, and fought valiantly on the Gorog nest ship. It's unfortunate that my Artoo unit was damaged, or we would be able to provide documentation."

"That's quite unnecessary," Bwua'tu said. "The word of a Jedi Master is documentation enough."

An uncomfortable silence followed while the admiral continued to stare out the viewport—and while Han, Luke, and the others silently considered what they might be able to do to stop the attack on the nest ships and prevent the loss of yet more Alliance lives.

Finally, Darklighter returned and reported that the admiral's orders had been issued.

"Very good," Bwua'tu said. "I was very impressed with Captain Juun's and Tarfang's knowledge of our enemy. Sign them on as intelligence affiliates and see to it that they're assigned a scout skiff. Make certain it's stealth-equipped. I imagine they'll be doing a lot of work behind the lines."

Han and Luke exchanged surprised glances, then Luke asked, "Admiral, are you sure that's a good idea?"

Tarfang stepped over to Luke and let loose a long, angry string of jabbering—to which Bwua'tu replied in kind. After a short exchange, the admiral looked back to Luke with a scowl.

"Tarfang doesn't understand why you're trying to undermine him and Captain Juun," Bwua'tu said. "And frankly, Master Skywalker, neither do I. You seemed quite impressed with them a few moments ago."

"Captain Juun and Tarfang are very earnest," Luke responded. "But that doesn't mean they would make good intelligence agents. They can be, uh, rather naïve. I worry about their chances of survival."

Tarfang started to yap an objection, but Bwua'tu silenced him with a soft chitter, then turned back to Luke.

"So do I, Master Skywalker." Bwua'tu looked back out the viewport, where the task force frigates were beginning to move out toward the flanks. "I worry about us all."

Luke frowned, clearly at a loss as to what he could say to make Bwua'tu change his mind. Han caught Leia's eye, then nodded toward the admiral and raised his brow, silently asking if he was crazy. She flashed a reassuring smile, then gave a slight shake of her head.

"Trust me, Captain Solo," Bwua'tu said, speaking to Han's reflection in the viewport. "Your friends are capable of more than you think. They usually are."

"Uh, actually, I was worried about your attack orders," Han said. "You don't think that seems a little crazy?"

"I do," Bwua'tu said. "But right now, these bugs are unsure of themselves. More importantly, they are unsure of *us*."

"And we need to keep them that way," Mara said, approvingly.

"Precisely," Bwua'tu replied. "You Jedi tossed a hydrospanner into the Killiks' plan. They'll be wondering what else you can do, and I intend to use that doubt to make them believe they *lost* this battle."

Luke's brow went up. "And force a negotiation!"

Bwua'tu shot Luke a impatient frown. "Not at all, Master Skywalker. I expect them to retreat."

"And if they don't?" Luke asked.

"Then I will have miscalculated . . . again." Bwua'tu turned to Han. "I've been thinking about your daughter's preemptive strike. By all accounts, she's a sound tactician. What do you think she would do if she *knew* the Chiss were preparing a major attack?"

Han's stomach sank. "How could she know something like that?"

Bwua'tu shrugged. "I have no idea. But if she *did,* a pre-emptive strike would be a stroke of genius. It would force the Chiss to attack before they were ready—or risk having their preparations disrupted completely. It might well be the Colony's only hope of survival."

"*Survival?*" Leia asked. "Didn't the Chiss message say they were only going to push the Killiks away from the frontier?"

"Yes, and their previous message said that they were going to let the Jedi handle the problem," Bwua'tu replied. "That's the trouble with Chiss messages, isn't it? You never know when they are telling the truth."

"Wait a minute," Han said. He couldn't believe what he was hearing—didn't want to, anyway. How many times would he face his children flying off to war? How many times *could* he? "You think this war is already *starting*?"

Bwua'tu nodded. "Of course. It started before their messenger left Ascendancy space." His gaze remained fixed on the viewport, where the task force cruisers were moving out in front of the formation. "The irony of it is, I believe the Chiss are worried that we'll side with the Killiks. Their message may be just a ruse to reassure us, to keep the Alliance from taking action until it's too late to save the Colony."

"This is just nuts!" Han said.

"Not nuts—scary," Mara said, her face falling. "What are the Chiss going to think when the *Admiral Ackbar* shows up on the Colony's side? It'll only confirm their suspicions. They'll think the Alliance *gave* it to the Killiks."

"Exactly," Bwua'tu said. "If I am right, this is going to be a very interesting war."

Leia closed her eyes for a moment, then reached out and

squeezed Han's hand. "I'm afraid you are right, Admiral," she said. "Jaina and Jacen are in the middle of something bad. I can feel it."

Han's heart sank. *Not again, not so soon.*

Bwua'tu sighed. "I'm sorry to hear that, Princess." He turned to Darklighter again, then said, "Commodore . . . have all batteries open fire."

The room was compactly furnished, containing a three-tier bunk bed against one wall and a fold-down table and bench seats on the other. Beside the bunk bed were three large drawers built into the wall, while to the right was a door leading into what seemed to be a compact refresher station.

"What do you think he's going to do with us?" Maris murmured, looking around.

"He'll let us go," Qennto assured her, glancing into the refresher station and then sitting down on the lowest bed, hunching forward to keep from bumping his head on the one above it. "The real question is whether we'll be taking the firegems with us."

Car'das cleared his throat. "Uh . . . should we be talking about this?" he asked, looking significantly around the room.

"Oh, relax," Qennto growled. "They don't speak a word of Basic." His eyes narrowed. "And as long as we're on the subject of speaking, why the frizz did you tell him we knew Progga?"

"There was something in his eyes and voice just then," Car'das said. "Something that said he already knew all about it, and that we'd better not get caught lying to him."

Qennto snorted. "That's ridiculous."

"Unless there were survivors from Progga's crew," Maris pointed out.

"Not a chance," Qennto said firmly. "You saw what the ship looked like. The thing'd been peeled open like a ration bar."

"I don't know how he knew," Car'das insisted. "All I know is that he *did* know."

"And you shouldn't lie to an honorable man anyway," Maris murmured.

"Who, Mitth'raw'nuruodo?" Qennto scoffed. "Honorable? Don't you believe it. Military men are all alike. And in my experience, the smooth ones are the worst of the lot."

"*I've* known quite a few honorable soldiers," Maris said stiffly. "Besides, I've always had a good feel for people. I think this Mitth'raw—whatever. I think he can be trusted." She lifted her eyebrows. "I don't think trying to con him will be a good idea, either."

"It's only a bad idea if you get caught," Qennto said. "You get what you bargain for in this universe, Maris. Nothing more, nothing less."

She shook her head. "Your problem is that you don't have enough faith in people, Rak."

"I got all the faith I need, kiddo," Qennto said calmly. "I just happen to know a little more about human nature than you do. Human *and* nonhuman nature."

"I still think we need to play completely straight with him."

Qennto snorted. "Playing straight is the last thing you want to do. Ever. It gives the other guy all the advantages." He nodded toward the closed door. "And this guy in particular sounds like the sort who'll ask questions until we die of old age if we let him."

"Still, it might not be a bad idea to hang around here for at least a little while," Car'das suggested. "Progga's people are going to be pretty mad when he doesn't come back."

Qennto shook his head. "They'll never pin it on us. Not a chance."

"Yes, but—"

"Look, kid, let me do the thinking, okay?" Qennto said, cutting him off. Swiveling his legs up onto the bunk, he lay back with his arms folded behind his head. "Now everyone be quiet for a while. I've got to figure out how to play this."

Maris caught Car'das's eye, gave a little shrug, then turned and climbed up onto the bunk above Qennto. Stretching out, she folded her arms across her chest and gazed meditatively at the underside of the bunk above her.

Crossing to the other side of the room, Car'das folded down the table and one of the bench seats and sat down, wedging himself more or less comfortably between the table and wall. Putting his elbow on the table and propping his head up on his hand, he closed his eyes and tried to relax.

He didn't realize he'd dozed off until a sudden buzz startled him awake. He jumped up as the door opened to reveal a single black-clad Chiss. "Commander Mitth'raw'nuruodo's respects," the alien said, the Sy Bisti words coming out thickly accented. "He requests your presence in Forward Visual One."

"Wonderful," Qennto said, swinging his legs onto the floor and standing up. His tone and expression were the false cheerfulness Car'das had heard him use time and again in bargaining sessions.

"Not you," the Chiss said. He gestured to Car'das. "This one only."

Qennto came to an abrupt halt. "What?"

"A refreshment is being prepared," the Chiss said. "Until it is ready, this one only will come."

"Now, wait a second," Qennto said, taking a step forward. "We stick together or—"

"It's okay," Car'das interrupted. The Chiss standing in the doorway had made no move, but he'd caught a subtle shift in lighting and shadow outside that indicated there were others outside the humans' line of sight. "I'll be fine."

"Car'das—"

"It's okay," Car'das repeated, stepping to the doorway. The Chiss moved back, and he walked out into the corridor.

There were indeed more Chiss waiting by the door, two of them on either side. "Follow," the messenger said as the door closed.

They trooped down the curved corridor, passing three cross corridors and several other doorways along the way. Two of the doors were open, and Car'das couldn't resist a furtive glance inside each as they passed. All he could see, though, was unrecognizable equipment and more black-clad Chiss.

He had expected Forward Visual to be just another

crowded high-tech room. To his surprise, the door opened into something that looked like a compact version of a starliner's observation gallery. A long, curved couch sat in front of a convex floor-to-ceiling viewport currently giving a spectacular view of the glowing hyperspace sky as it flowed past the ship. The room's own lights were dimmed, making the display that much more impressive.

"Welcome, Jorj Car'das."

Car'das looked around. Mitth'raw'nuruodo was seated alone at the far end of the couch, silhouetted against the hyperspace sky. "Commander Mitth'raw'nuruodo," he greeted the other, glancing a question at his guide. The other nodded, stepping back and closing the door on himself and the rest of the escort. Feeling more than a little uneasy, Car'das stepped around the near end of the couch and made his way across the curve.

"Beautiful, isn't it?" Mitth'raw'nuruodo commented as Car'das arrived at his side. "Please, be seated."

"Thank you," Car'das said, easing himself onto the couch a cautious meter away from the other. "May I ask why I'm here?"

"To share this view with me, of course," Mitth'raw'nuruodo said dryly. "And to answer a few questions."

Car'das felt his stomach tighten. So it was to be an interrogation. Down deep he'd known it would be, but had hoped against hope that Maris's naïvely idealistic assessment of their captor might actually be right. "A very nice view it is, too," he commented, not knowing what else to say. "I'm a little surprised to find such a room aboard a warship."

"Oh, it's quite functional," Mitth'raw'nuruodo assured him. "Its full name is Forward Visual Triangulation Site Number One. We place spotters here during combat to track enemy vessels and other possible threats, and to coordinate some of our line-of-sight weaponry."

"Don't you have sensors to handle that?" Car'das asked, frowning.

"Of course," Mitth'raw'nuruodo said. "And usually they're quite adequate. But I'm sure you know there are ways of misleading or blinding electronic eyes. Sometimes the eyes of a Chiss are more reliable."

"I suppose," Car'das said, gazing at his host's own glowing eyes. In the dim light, they were even more intimidating. "Isn't it hard to get the information to the gunners fast enough?"

"There are ways," Mitth'raw'nuruodo said. "What exactly is your business, Jorj Car'das?"

"Captain Qennto's already told you that," Car'das said, feeling sweat breaking out on his forehead. "We're merchants and traders."

Mitth'raw'nuruodo shook his head. "Unfortunately for your captain's assertions, I'm familiar with the economics of star travel. Your vessel is far too small for any standard cargo to cover even normal operating expenses, let alone emergency repair work. I therefore conclude that you have a sideline occupation. You haven't the weaponry to be pirates or privateers, so you must be smugglers."

Car'das hesitated. What exactly was he supposed to say? "I don't suppose it would do any good to point out that our economics and yours might not scale the same?" he said, stalling.

"*Is* that what you claim?"

Car'das hesitated, but Mitth'raw'nuruodo had that knowing look about him again. "No," he conceded. "We *are* mostly just traders, as Captain Qennto said. But we do sometimes do a little smuggling on the side."

"I see," Mitth'raw'nuruodo said. "I appreciate your honesty, Jorj Car'das."

"You can just call me Car'das," Car'das said. "In our culture, the first name is reserved for use by friends."

Mitth'raw'nuruodo lifted his eyebrows. "You don't consider me a friend?"

"Do you consider *me* one?" Car'das countered.

The instant the words were out of his mouth he wished he could call them back. Sarcasm was never the option of choice in a confrontation like this. Particularly not when the other side held the power of life and death.

But Mitth'raw'nuruodo lifted an eyebrow. "Not yet," he agreed calmly. "Perhaps someday. You intrigue me, Car'das. Here you sit, captured by unfamiliar beings a long way from home. Yet instead of wrapping yourself within a blanket of fear or anger, you instead stretch outside yourself with curiosity."

Car'das frowned. "Curiosity?"

"You studied my warriors as you were brought aboard," Mitth'raw'nuruodo said. "I could see it in your eyes and face as you observed and thought and evaluated. You did the same as you were taken to your quarters, and again as you were brought here just now."

"I was just looking around," Car'das assured him, feeling his heart beating a little faster. Did spies rank above or below smugglers on Mitth'raw'nuruodo's list? "I didn't mean anything by it."

"Calm yourself," Mitth'raw'nuruodo said, a distinct touch of amusement in his voice. "I'm not accusing you of spying. I, too, have the gift of curiosity, and therefore prize it in others. Tell me, who is to receive the hidden gemstones?"

Car'das jerked. "You found—? I mean . . . in that case, why did you ask me about it?"

"As I said, I appreciate honesty," Mitth'raw'nuruodo said. "Who is the intended recipient?"

"A group of Hutts operating out of the Comra system," Car'das told him, giving up. "Rivals to the ones you—the ones who were attacking us." He hesitated. "You *did* know they weren't just random pirates, didn't you? That they were hunting us specifically?"

"We monitored your transmissions before we were in position to intervene," Mitth'raw'nuruodo said. "Though the conversation was of course unintelligible to us, I remembered hearing the phonemes *Dubrak Qennto* in the Hutt's speech when Captain Qennto later identified himself to me. The conclusion was obvious."

A shiver ran up Car'das's back. A conversation in an alien language, and yet Mitth'raw'nuruodo had been able to memorize enough of it to extract Qennto's name from the gibberish. What kind of creatures *were* these Chiss, anyway?

"Is the possession of these gems illegal, then?"

"No, but the customs fees are ridiculously high,"

Car'das said, forcing his mind back to the interrogation. "Smugglers are often used to avoid having to pay them." He hesitated. "Actually, considering the people we got this batch from, they may also have been stolen. But don't tell Maris that."

"Oh?"

Car'das winced. There he was again, talking without thinking. If Mitth'raw'nuruodo didn't kill him before this was over, Qennto probably would. "Maris is something of an idealist," he said reluctantly. "She thinks this whole smuggling thing is just a way of making a statement against the greedy and stupid Republic bureaucracy."

"Captain Qennto hasn't seen fit to enlighten her?"

"Captain Qennto likes her company," Car'das said. "I doubt she'd stay with him if she knew the whole truth."

"He claims to care about her, yet lies to her?"

"I don't know what he claims," Car'das said. "Though I suppose you could say that idealists like Maris do a lot of lying to themselves. The truth is there in front of her if she wanted to see it." He took another look at those glowing red eyes. "Though of course that doesn't excuse our part in it," he added.

"No, it doesn't," Mitth'raw'nuruodo said. "What would be the consequences if you didn't deliver the gemstones?"

Car'das felt his throat tighten. So much for the honorable Commander Mitth'raw'nuruodo. Firegems must be valuable out here, too. "They'd kill us," he said. "Probably in some hugely entertaining way, like watching us get eaten by some combination of large animals."

"And if the delivery was merely late?"

Car'das frowned, trying to read the other's expression in the flickering hyperspace glow. "What exactly do you want from me, Commander Mitth'raw'nuruodo?"

"Nothing too burdensome," Mitth'raw'nuruodo said. "I merely wish your company for a time."

"Why?"

"Partly to learn about your people," Mitth'raw'nuruodo said. "But primarily so that you may teach me your language."

Car'das blinked. "Our *language*? You mean Basic?"

"That *is* the chief language of your Republic, is it not?"

"Yes, but . . ." Car'das hesitated, wondering if there was a delicate way to ask a question like this.

Mitth'raw'nuruodo might have been reading his mind. Or, more likely, his eyes and face. "I don't plan an invasion, if that's what concerns you," he said, smiling faintly. "Chiss don't invade the territories of others. We don't even make war against potential enemies unless we're attacked first."

"Well, you certainly don't have to worry about any attacks from *us*," Car'das said quickly. "We've got enough internal troubles of our own right now."

"Then we have nothing to fear from each other," Mitth'raw'nuruodo said. "It would be merely an indulgence of my curiosity."

"I see," Car'das said cautiously. Qennto, he knew, would be into full-bore bargaining mode at this point, pushing and prodding and squeezing to get everything he could out of the deal. Maybe that was why Mitth'raw'nuruodo was making this pitch to the clearly less experienced Car'das instead.

Still, he could try. "And what would we get out of it?" he asked.

"For you, there would be an equal satisfaction of your own curiosity." Mitth'raw'nuruodo lifted his eyebrows. "You *do* wish to know more about my people, don't you?"

"Very much," Car'das said. "But I can't see that appealing very much to Captain Qennto."

"Perhaps a few extra gemstones added to his collection, then," Mitth'raw'nuruodo suggested. "That might also help mollify your clients."

"Yes, they'll definitely need some mollifying," Car'das agreed grimly. "A little extra loot would go a long ways toward that."

"Then it's agreed," Mitth'raw'nuruodo said, standing up.

"One more thing," Car'das said, scrambling to his feet. "I'll be happy to teach you Basic, but I'd also like some language lessons myself. Would you be willing in turn to teach me the Chiss language, or to have one of your people do so?"

"I can teach you to understand Cheunh," Mitth'raw'nuruodo said, his eyes narrowing thoughtfully. "But I doubt you'll ever be able to properly speak it. I've noticed you don't even pronounce my name very well."

Car'das felt his face warm. "I'm sorry."

"No apology needed," Mitth'raw'nuruodo assured him. "Your vocal mechanism is close to ours, but there are clearly some differences. However, I believe I *could* teach you to speak Minnisiat. It's a trade language widely used in the border regions around our space."

"That would be wonderful," Car'das said, nodding. "Thank you, Commander Mitth—uh . . . Commander."

"Yes," Mitth'raw'nuruodo said dryly. "And as long as we're going to be spending time together, perhaps I can make it easier on you and the others. You may call me by my core name, Thrawn."

Star Wars: New Jedi Order: Star By Star

Troy Denning

Written by *New York Times* bestselling author Troy Denning, *Star By Star* is the thrilling heart of darkness of the *New Jedi Order*. This is a must-read for every fan of *Star Wars* fiction and the *New Jedi Order* series in particular!

It is a dark time for the New Republic. The Yuuzhan Vong, despite some recent losses, continue to advance into the Core, and continue their relentless hunt for the Jedi. Now, in a desperate act of courage, Anakin Solo leads a Jedi strike force into the heart of Yuuzhan Vong territory, where he hopes to destroy a major Vong anti-Jedi weapon. There, with his brother and sister at his side, he will come face to face with his destiny – as the New Republic, still fighting the good fight, will come face to face with theirs . . .

arrow books

Star Wars: New Jedi Order: Dark Journey

Elaine Cunnigham

The dazzling Star Wars space adventure continues in this latest instalment from *The New Jedi Order* series.

Following intense personal loss, Jaina Solo descends to the dark sode, determined to take her revenge on the Yuuzhan Vong. In the process, she learns something new about how to fight the alien invaders, but she must also remember that revenge is not the way of the Jedi – even when it seems the only way to fight the enemy.

arrow books

Star Wars: New Jedi Order: Dark Tide Onslaught

Michael Stackpole

Twenty-one years after the destruction of Darth Vader and the Emperor, the Star Wars galaxy has been hit by a threat more deadly than anything that has gone before.

Now, in a climate of mistrust – especially of the Jedi – Leia cannot convince the New Republic that the threat may not be over, even as the next wave of alien warships are entering the galaxy . . . It is up to Leia, Luke and the Solo kids – Jedi Knights all – to defend the Outer Rim planets from invasion!

arrow books

Star Wars: New Jedi Order: Rogue Planet

Greg Bear

Rogue Planet is an unforgettable journey stretching from the farthest reaches of known space to the battlefield of a young boy's heart, where a secret struggle is being waged that will decide the fate of billions. That boy is twelve-year-old Anakin Skywalker. The Force is strong in Anakin, so strong that the Jedi Council, despite misgivings, entrusted the young Jedi Knight Obi-Wan Kenobi with the mission of training him to become a Jedi Knight. Obi-Wan – like his slain master Qui-Gon – believes Anakin may be the chosen one, the Jedi destined to bring balance to the Force. But first Obi-Wan must help his undisciplined, idealistic apprentice, who still bears the scars of slavery, find his own balance.

Dispatched to the mysterious planet Zonama Sekot, source of the fastest ships in the galaxy, Obi-Wan and Anakin are swept up in a swirl of deadly intrigue and betrayal. For there are others who covet the power such superfast ships could bring. Raith Siener, a brilliant but unscrupulous weapons and ship designer, has the brains to decipher the Zonama Sekot ship design. Commander Wilhuff Tarkin has at his disposal the forces of the mighty Trader Federation with which to extract the secret. Together, they make a formidable foe – one a small and undeveloped planet can hardly hope to stand against . . .

arrow books

Star Wars: New Jedi Order: Traitor

Matthew Wooding Stover

The New York Times bestselling series, *Star Wars: The New Jedi Order*, continues with an intense, character-driven tale of Jedi teaching, life and death, and heroism behind enemy lines.

Deep in the bowels of the captured planet of Coruscant, a hunted Jedi is hidden with an unexpected mentor who teaches him new ways to understand the Force – and what it means to be a Jedi.

arrow books

Star Wars: New Jedi Order: Shatterpoint

Matthew Stover

A must-read for everyone who saw *Star Wars: Attack of the Clones* and *Star Wars: Revenge of the Sith*! A special treat for fans of the Mace Windu character from the movie and for fans of Jedi action in general.

In the midst of the Clone Wars, Master Mace Windu returns from his separatist-occupied homeworld, where his former Padawan, Depa Billaba, has been working as an undercover agent. But Depa hasn't been reporting in lately, and Republic intelligence has been gathering disturbing hints of bloody ambushes and terror-strikes in the deep outback. Mace trained Depa – he knows that no-one but he can hope to even reach her, let alone save her from the darkness . . .

arrow books

Star Wars: New Jedi Order: Rebel Stand

Aaron Alston

The bestselling series, *Star Wars: The New Jedi Order*, continues with the second book in the *Enemy Lines* duology of military and political action-adventure.

Luke Skywalker's daring mission to halt the Yuuzhan Vong's nefarious plot to overthrow the New Republic is struggling on all fronts. And time is slipping away for Han and Leia Organa Solo, trapped on a small planet whose rulers are about to yield to Yuuzhan Vong pressure to give up the Jedi rebels.

On Coruscant, Luke and Mara Jade Skywalker have made a shocking discovery that is preventing the Yuuzhan Vong from exerting complete control. But when the enemy tracks them down, Luke and Mara are thrust into a fierce battle for their lives. Suddenly, the chances of escaping appear nearly impossible. And in space, another battle rages, one that holds ominous consequences for the New Republic – and for the Jedi themselves.

arrow books